Deal With The Devil

AN ENEMIES TO LOVERS BILLIONAIRE ROMANCE

VIVIAN WOOD

Author's Copyright

As always, thank you to my team — to Patricia, Angela, and Honey. You folks turned my rough uncut stone into a dazzling gem!

I want to thank my beta team too — Priscilla, Rachael, Amanda. Without you, my book would be full of weird anachronistic bits and I would never remember what color anybody's eyes are supposed to be.

Dare and Talia's romance really shines bright because of y'all.

Playlist

Doja Cat — Vegas
Glass Animals — Heat Waves
Run The Jewels — No Save Point
Fleetwood Mac — Gold Dust Woman
Garbage — Only Happy When It Rains
Sufjan Stevens — Chicago
Taylor Swift w/Lana del Ray — Snow On The Beach
Ariana Grande — Positions
The Rapture — House of Jealous Lovers
Lizzo — About Damn Time
Phoebe Bridgers — Georgia
Bruno Mars w/Cardi B — Finesse
Yeah Yeah Yeahs — Gold Lion
Boygenius — Bite The Hand
Neutral Milk Hotel — Holland, 1945
Peaches — Fuck The Pain Away
Chris Isaak — Baby Did A Bad Bad Thing
Pixies — Here Comes Your Man
The New Pornographers — The Bleeding Heart Show

SZA — Kill Bill
Crystal Castles — Crimewave
Sam Smith w/Kim Petras — Unholy
Bad Bunny — Tití Me Preguntó

Catch it on Spotify!

Chapter One

TALIA

Money is the root of all evil. There is no way for most people to know that, though.

It's the type of knowledge that comes with firsthand knowledge of just what it's like to be poor. Counting all your quarters and dimes to afford public transit, eating peanut butter straight from the jar because you can't afford bread this week, choosing between going to the dentist and being able to pay rent kind of poor.

I fidget with my necklace, the only piece of jewelry I have that my mother gave me as a child, and try not to grimace as I stand in the tiny bit of shelter provided by the building I'm huddled in front of. The street is dark and the night rain-slicked. I blow on my aching fingers to keep them from freezing as I wait. Each minute seems to drag by, with me pulling my flip phone out of my pocket regularly to check the time.

No texts.

I pull a battered copy of Alice's Adventures in Wonderland from my pocket and try to get lost in the story, but it's just too damned cold for me to focus.

Across the street, I watch as a party of drunk people climb the stairs of The Raven's Head Club, talking loudly and laughing.

These are the exact kinds of people I'm talking about. The men are in dark overcoats, their expensive watches and designer suits showing as they reach for the door. The women are huddled under umbrellas. Their expensive red-soled high heels clack against the stone pavers underfoot. There is no doubt that beneath their wool coats are expensive dresses in showy colors, golds and silvers, and bright pink satin.

I detest these people. And to drive it home for me, as a group they are too involved with themselves to even notice me glaring at them, waiting in the chilly rain for my friend to show up.

Ugh, I am only waiting for five more minutes at the very latest.

Glancing at my watch, I shiver. Olivia is late, as is her wont. It's basically her only flaw in a lifetime of wonderful friendship, so I let it slide.

But I'm still stuck waiting for her here, having stepped off the bus into the rainy early winter evening. Now I'm waiting for her to appear, as instructed, unsure about why I'm looking at The Raven's Head Club. I've never seen the place before in my life, not that there is much to see.

Just a set of stairs, a large black door, and a little plaque telling the world that the club is by invitation only.

I hear a voice calling out and turn, hopeful that it is Olivia. But no, it's a group of girls whispering and cackling amongst themselves.

"Shhh," one of them says to the rest. "Hurry, we don't want to be late. Burn was very specific about us being on time."

There is an explosion of giggles.

"Burn is so hot!" one of the women whispers in response. "It's unbelievable that someone so rich can be such a hunk."

Another round of giggles, coupled with a couple of soft agreements.

"He's dreamy," another girl says wistfully. "They both are."

"I like Dare. He's so angry and brooding. It makes me think that he's an absolute dragon in the bedroom."

Their names mean next to nothing to me, but the whispered comment does make me wonder. Who are the girls talking about? Obviously, the sort of men that inspire this kind of gossip in this group of well-to-do girls are something to be seen.

Then again, judging solely from the vacuous giggles and the long, expensive-to-maintain hairstyles of the group, the guys might just be the usual bland men in skinny black ties, designer black suits, and so much cologne that it makes you want to barf. Yeah, on second thought, I probably don't want to meet any guys that this crowd of women talks about. Hard pass.

I turn and scan the street, trying to see who they might be talking about. But it's impossible to know. There are no men in sight, just brilliantly beautiful and flamboyantly dressed girls. Their faces are all young and excited, all exuberantly beautiful.

The girls don't even look my way as they hurry across the rain-slicked street. It's unlikely they even know I am here and I make no move to change the status quo. If they did spot me, what would they see?

Just a pale girl drowning in an oversized, shabby coat. A flash of coppery hair and a pair of bargain-bin ballet flats— the nicest shoes I have. A vintage boho bag, large and functional, with worn leather that is a dull brown.

Olivia spoke in the strictest tone when she called earlier and told me to meet her here... and to dress nicely. I knew from her tone that she meant something other than the bulky brown sweater and knee length black skirt I usually wear.

I am totally out of my depth tonight.

Across the street, I notice that the girls have paused at the entrance to the disreputable-looking gray building that towers over the street corner. It must have been a very nice church when it was built. But time and weather have done their work on the building's outside, with water leaving dark streaks down the side of the building and the windows mostly boarded up.

The girls seem to make a decision, falling into a vee formation as they climb the broad stone steps of the gray stone building. The girl at the front tucks her long blonde hair behind her ear and steps forward, all but disappearing in the church's Gothic-styled hooded cupola.

As I look on, I cannot help but to count the extravagant, showy signs of great wealth that the girls have proudly chosen to wear. One of the girls is wearing expensive, red-soled high heels. I see a glint of diamond earrings nestled in the earlobes of another. One girl clutches a tiny black Prada bag. I cannot see what they are wearing beneath their black wool coats, but I am sure it is short, tight, and expensive.

For a moment, I wonder what it would be like to be one of those girls. What would my life be like?

I admit to myself that it is not at all like it actually is. These girls don't have to worry about whether or not their next paycheck will be able to buy them groceries and pay the rent. It must be nice...

"Talia!"

I turn my head to see Olivia hurrying down the dark street. She holds a newspaper over her head to shield her from the rain, but it isn't working. As she rushes toward me, a halo of droplets shines in her dark hair, and her cheeks are bright pink.

Try as I might, I can't help but smile at my best friend. She's usually late and a little frazzled.

"Olive!" I greet her. "How are you?"

She tosses the newspaper onto an overflowing trash bin, making a face and dusting off her dark jacket. Then she grabs me by the arm and pulls me along toward the church's front door.

"Hold on a minute, Lia." She calls out to the girls that have only just begun to disappear through the door. "Stacey? Wait! We're here!"

The group ripples, stopping before the door in a graceful pack. A girl turns and looks impatiently behind her. I realize it's the girl with the bright red-soled heels.

My pulse speeds up. I clench Olivia's hand. She's too busy to do more than give my hand a pat in response.

"Oh." She stares down imperiously as Olivia rushes to pull me up the stairs to join them. "You made it after all. I thought you might bail."

"Sorry for the lateness," Olivia starts.

But Stacey has already dismissed her, ushering the other girls ahead of her into the gaping doorway. To the right of the doorway is the small bronze plaque that reads, *The Raven's Head Club, By Invitation Only.*

My stomach does flip-flops. We're in the seediest part of Harwicke right now, with the docks on one side and the run-down warehouse district on the other. The few blocks surrounding the church seem desolate. And yet, here is a plaque admonishing trespassers.

It's all quite odd.

My eyes dart over the large, curved doorway, seeing only

a black morass within. Aside from the pervasive rap music, there is not even a hint of what is inside.

"Olive," I say. There is a bad feeling in my gut that demands that I absolutely should not go inside.

She clutches my arm tighter, hissing her reminder. "Talia, you're the one who got all emotional and told me that you're worried that something is wrong with you because you still haven't lost your v-card."

My entire face floods with heat. "Shh! Are you crazy? Don't announce that to the world."

"I'm not trying to shame you, Lia." She squeezes my arm and tilts her head. "My intentions are just to get you out of the rut you have been in. To meet some new people and let loose just once. I've known you for almost twenty years, and yet I can't remember you ever just having a good time." She cocks a brow. "And this place? It's apparently crazy inside. It might call itself a bar, but I hear that it's really a sex club."

She drops her voice, whispering the last two words. My cheeks flush and I shake my head. "We aren't the sort of girls that go to a sex club. You're a frigging PhD student, I'm a retail employee."

She cups my face, using her thumb and forefinger to squeeze my cheek. "Loosen up. If you want to shed your v-card so bad, there will be plenty of guys inside just lining up to claim it."

I scrunch up my face, considering her words. She's right about the fact that I cried on her shoulder about being an uptight virgin just last week. Could this party be a gateway into a more relaxed, happier life for me? I know it's a sex club, but… I don't want to die a virgin, do I?

"I know what I said," I acknowledge. "I just hoped that you had forgotten about the whole thing."

She sighs and pulls me closer. "You promised me that you would come to this party. Give it a chance, at least."

I swallow the retort on the tip of my tongue and try not to make a face. "I know. I'm keeping an open mind."

But I'm not. As we step through the doorway, a gust of cool air swirls around my ankles. Smoke trickles down from the darkness above. Rap music blares around me, vibrating the worn leather of my purse.

Ahead of me, I see a doorway open, showering us in pale pink light.

"What the heck is this place?" I mutter to myself.

It only takes a few moments for me to find out. I move forward through the doorway and into the Raven's Head.

With Olivia practically yanking me along, I stumble forward as I look around the room. It's luxurious to the point of being ostentatious. Black booths line the whole room, with matching brown wooden tables clustered against the walls. There are ostrich feather displays on each table, the feathers gold and black.

In the middle of the room, a low-lit black bar dominates the space. But that's not the part that intimidates me.

No, that would be the people. The bar patrons look exactly like the girls that we came into the room with. Young, white, wealthy, and having a good time. Almost everybody clutches a tumbler or wineglass. At the table to my left, champagne is being poured, and the young man in charge of the bottle is grinning as he fills the glasses of several giggling girls. There are people openly making out in every corner of the room.

In the far back, I see a blonde standing on a table, her black dress unzipped in the middle to show her bare chest, her breasts perky and looking quite rosy. A circle of admirers surround her and she laughs, sounding more than a little tipsy.

A dark haired girl in a tight red dress sprays whipped cream on her tits.

The blonde gasps as the woman moves to lick the whipped cream from the tip of her breast. When a dark haired young man vaults himself onto the table and quickly licks the other nipple clean, the blonde leans down and French kisses him with a lot of deep tongue.

I guess I'm not in Kansas anymore.

"Whoa," I breathe out, my eyes widening. I turn to point the girl out to Olivia but Olivia is already five steps ahead of me.

All around me is complete chaos. The barely controlled party is mayhem. This is the complete opposite of my usual Friday nights at Hope House, the local emergency shelter for children. I can't even imagine what the kids would think of me in a bar like the Raven's Head Club. They would probably ask me why.

It's a fair question. Why am I here, exactly?

I hurry along beside Olivia, my eyes taking in every raucous laugh and good natured scream. I have a suspicion that most of the entertainment here is powered by champagne.

My stomach churns at this. Is this what my town's wealthy elite have been doing all this time? I have been so busy with work and volunteering at Hope House that I have barely had time to sleep. But these people seem comfortable in this space, as if it's a regular haunt for them.

My mouth twists with a sour expression.

Olivia drags me forward a few steps to a large group of people. I can see the young woman with the red heels greeting a suited young man. He offers her a glass of wine, a knowing smirk on his face. I am rather tempted to step forward and smack the wineglass out of her hands. But in the next second, Olivia pulls me forward again and we become officially part of the group.

Several men are seated on the bench seats against the wall. All around them are groups of smiling, giggling girls. Every one of them is dressed to kill, pulling off dark coats to reveal short dresses in dark hues. I feel severely underdressed and am loath to take my coat off when Olivia does. But she gives me a look, arching an eyebrow.

So I slide my coat off, exposing my body. I'm wearing one of Olivia's dresses that she got from a thrift store. It is pink and sparkly, and at least it covers my arms and chest. But it is very short, with the hem hitting mid-thigh. Olivia approaches me, gently squeezing my arm.

"Just relax. I promise you a good time. You promised me that you would let me plan a night out. Give it a chance."

My cheeks flushed a little. "I will. I swear."

"Seriously, it's just one night. After this, you can go back to your regularly scheduled volunteering at Hope House. No one is trying to tear you away from it. I'm just showing you how the other half lives." She gestures around us, her hands sweeping wide. My gaze follows her hand, taking in the bar. I swallow.

I can't believe that this place is real. It seems so over-the-top.

In the next moment, my thoughts are interrupted by a waiter who comes around with a tray full of drinks. He hands out the glasses of wine without asking if I want any or not. I accept it because that's what everybody else seems to be doing. I look at the purplish liquid in my wine glass, flushing it around a little. A note of coconut rises to my nose, and I sniff the wine.

"What is this?" I ask. I'm guessing this is wine.

A tall, good-looking man turns around and looks at me and Olivia. There is a little smirk on his face.

"I'm Burn", he says. "Are you here with Hannah?"

Olivia smiles at him and nods emphatically. "We are. It's our first time here. We were talking about the drinks we've been handed."

I examine Burn silently as they talk. Aside from his height, his slicked back dark hair and blue green eyes sparkle like a lake on a sunny day. His eyes are only bolstered by his gorgeous smile. I'm not sure why he's even talking to the two of us, although I suspect that Olivia is more of a draw than I am. She tosses her hair and gives him a flirty look.

Burn purses his lips.

"It's called elixir. Try it; you'll see why."

Olivia flashes a smile at him and does as he suggests. She smacks her lips and looks at the glass in her hand, surprised. "Oh! It's good." She elbows me. "Try it, Talia."

I flush under his inspection and take the tiniest sip possible. Although the drink is as dark as wine, it is light and fruity in flavor. I look at my cup with some surprise. "Is there even alcohol in this?" I ask.

The man chuckles. "There is, so be careful." But... His eyebrows lift a little. "Not too careful, if you know what I mean."

I take another sip and try to suss out the alcohol flavor. Usually, alcohol tastes very strong to me. But my second sip confirms that there is absolutely no alcoholic undertone.

I don't know if I should be more or less worried about that.

"So what are you doing here?" Burn asks. "Are you from out of town or something?"

I take another sip of the elixir while Olivia answers for us both. She shakes her head. "Nope. We are from Harwicke, born and raised. We're just not usually out socializing with this set of people." She looks around her, taking it all in. "I guess we're normal."

I snort, and she looks at me, elbowing my ribs. I hide my reaction to it by taking another long drink of elixir. When I look up, I find Burn staring at me with a mischievous smile.

His piercing blue eyes skewer me, seeming to be able to see to the bottom of who I am and how much I am worth. I glance away, but the feeling that I am being judged doesn't fade.

I hate to think what I am worth in Burn's estimation. If I had to guess, I would say not much at all. But in the next second, he surprises me.

"Has anyone ever told you that you have very pretty eyes?"

"My eyes?" I croak, suspicious. "What do you mean?"

"Yeah. They are sort of a deep blue that you don't see every day. They're sexy."

He thinks I am sexy? The idea is unfathomable.

My cheeks turn the color of a beet. I open my mouth to respond. But Burn just shakes his head and laughs.

"Don't argue with me. I can tell that you want to. You just need to relax and enjoy yourself at this party. You're so freaking uptight."

I glance at Olivia, my brow furrowing. But Olivia is talking to another young man, her body turned a quarter of a turn away from mine. She is entirely absorbed by the conversation and seems to be having a good time.

I swallow. Is Burn right? Do I just need to stop imagining that everyone at this party is out to get me?

Burn's big hand comes down on the back of my shoulder like a burning brand. I tried to brush it off and wiggle out from under his grasp, but he just grips me harder. "I know what we need."

The words are spoken in a loud whisper, and his face is suddenly very close to mine. Close enough that I can smell his aftershave, the delicious bergamot scent winding around me. I close my eyes for just a moment, inhaling the scent, and a shudder runs through me.

Is this normal? Do other girls go to parties just like this one to have handsome men like Burn complement their eyes and touch their shoulders? Because if so, I can suddenly see why these parties keep happening.

It feels deliciously good to have someone as gorgeous as Burn paying attention to me.

"You know what you need?" he asks.

My eyes flicker open and my lips part. I look up into his aquiline gaze and think about how it would feel for him to kiss me. Would it feel nice? When I find being kissed by this handsome rich boy very thrilling?

I lick my lips, feeling a vague want.

I am very aware of Burn's sudden movements, of where his hands are, of every expression that crosses his face. I think… I think I might be tipsy. I've only had a little bit of the elixir, which I am still clutching, but I am having an out-of-body experience somehow.

Burn tilts his head towards the back of the room. "Have you ever been to the VIP area?"

I frown, shaking my head. "This is our first time here," I say by way of explanation. As if that were the only reason that I hadn't been invited before.

"You should come to the back area with me. Your friend as well. We should all do a shot. And then we can play a game."

"A game?" With a snort, I ask the question, "What kind of game?"

I'm uneasy with the amount of attention Burn is paying me. Why is this rich guy with his carved cheekbones and his beautiful blue eyes interested in me?

He shrugs a shoulder, his gaze leaving mine and wandering down to my shoulder. He sweeps away the bit of copper-colored hair that he finds there, pushing it back with his fingers. His skin brushes against mine ever so slightly, but it causes a shock wave to run through my bloodstream.

When Burn speaks, I'm entranced. "Whatever you feel like. Spin the bottle, strip poker, naughty truth or dare. Whichever one gets you naked the soonest sounds like a winner to me."

My lips part and I lean my head back, a smile pulling at my lips. Burn smirks and slides his arm around my waist. He towers over me, pulling me close.

This guy, this handsome Greek God that I am staring at, is definitely hitting on me. I can't even believe it. When I thought of coming here and socializing, I never considered that I would be doing any more than standing on the edge of the party and familiarizing myself with pretending to be cool. But the idea that I would walk into this party and immediately hit it off with the very first guy I talk to...

It's almost unthinkable. I lick my lips and look away. Burn must sense my hesitation because he smirks and looks down at me. He snakes his hand down to my hip and squeezes me close.

He lowers his head to my ear, tickling it as he murmurs sweet words into it.

"You're not afraid, are you? I won't bite. If I do, I promise that you'll love it."

I flush and put my hands on his arm, ready to push him away. But he licks his lips and quirks his eyebrows, his expression amused. For some reason, my will to protest disappears.

Burn grins. "I'll take that as a yes." He lets me go for just a second to grab Olivia's wrist and give it a tug. She turns with a frown on her face. But once she takes him in, she blushes and awkwardly smiles.

"Hi." The single word is so flirtatious that I'm shocked. Olivia doesn't flirt with men so openly, especially not men I am interested in. Maybe this is a new Olivia that I haven't met before, a special sex club Olivia.

His lips twitch. "You were wrapped up in talking to Byron. I didn't want to draw attention away from a friend. But your friend and I are going to head into the VIP section. Are you coming?"

Olivia's eyebrows fly up. She looks at me, her gaze startled. "You are? I mean... Of course. I just didn't expect..."

The warmth of Burn's body returns as he puts his arm around my shoulder once more. He jerks his head toward the back of the room. "Come on then. We'll go together. Apparently your friend will not go anywhere without you, so..."

Olivia looks like a deer in the headlights as he escorts us toward the back of the room and into the VIP area. People move out of his way almost unconsciously. He is quite tall, but lean. I gawk as they clear a path for us.

Olivia does manage to grab my hand for a moment as Burn lets go of me to open the door. She swallows and looks at Burn, ducking her lips down close to my ear.

"Be careful with him," she says. "He looks like trouble."

But before she can say anything more, Burn picks me up and throws me over his shoulder. I yell and Burn claps me on the ass with a firm hand. His hand leaves a definite print on my butt, five burning fingers that sting. My face flushes, and my pulse grows erratic.

Is this what I have agreed to?

I get a glimpse of the VIP area as he carries me. The lights are very dim, and the music is slower and more sultry. A lot of black leather couches and people in various stages of undress are piled on top of them. Several waiters make the rounds in the VIP area, and Burn barks at one of them as he passes.

"You! Come with me. Bring that tray of shots you are carrying."

Burn steps into a private room of sorts, just a few couches pushed together with a tall floor-to-ceiling chrome stripper pole in one corner. He puts me down and sends the current occupants of the room away.

"Out," he growls.

To my surprise, a half-dressed guy and the two girls with him immediately get up off the couch and just hurry out of the way. "Of course, Burn." I hear the man grumble as our group slides in and takes their place on the couch.

Burn sits down and pats the spot next to him. His look is playful. "Come here, kitten. Sit with me and have a shot."

Olive plucks at my hand, trying to pull me away. But I'm already staring at Burn, drawn in by his intense, probing gaze. Again, I wonder exactly what it would be like to kiss him. Before I know it, I am already moving toward him, with Olivia right behind me. I take the seat he picked out for me, and he smiles as I sit down. Olivia sits right next to me, her gaze watchful.

Burn pulls the silver tray out of the server's hands and passes me a shot glass with a pale yellow liquid. Olivia takes one of her own, and on the other side, the guy she was chatting up takes one too. Burn smirks as he raises the shot glass.

"To us. Let's get in trouble."

He taps his shot glass against mine and winks at me. "Bottoms up."

Looking at him, I swallow and then toss back the shot. I was expecting that the liquid in it would burn or be unpleasant. But in fact, it is the opposite. It's warm and smooth and tastes like pineapple juice. It isn't very much like alcohol at all.

"Wow," I say, looking at my empty shot glass. "That was actually really tasty."

Burn laughs and orders another round from the server. It's only then that I look over at Olivia, who is eyeing Burn rather intently. I notice that she has only taken the tiniest sip from her shot glass, and I just scrunch up my face.

"You don't like it?"

"It tastes fine. I just want one of us to be somewhat sober in case something happens. I thought that it would be you... But don't let me stop you from having fun."

I lean back. Burn drapes his arm around my shoulders again, and he whispers in my ear.

"You hear that? She wants you to have a good time. Do you want me to show you how I have a good time?"

I swallow and look up at him, all dark hair and high cheekbones, faded blue green eyes, and pouty lips. Darting my tongue out to lick my lips, I slowly nod.

"I really do," I whisper.

He grunts and stands up, offering me his hand. "Come with me. I'll show you how it's done."

I don't check in with Olivia this time. I don't check with anyone. I just put my hand in his and let him pull me along into a new experience.

Chapter Two

TALIA

Burn's face is bathed in the devilish red glow of the stop light.

He could be the devil. I'd believe it.

I suspect he's not a nice guy.

The fact that I'm even riding in his fancy ass car is not because I *like* him — not as a person, I mean. On paper, he's probably a catch, of course.

Tall.

Dark.

Handsome.

Probably born into a good family.

Filthy fucking rich, obviously.

As evidenced by this insane car we're riding in. As soon as I comment on it, he's frothing at the mouth to brag about it.

"It's a Maserati, obviously."

Obviously. I suppress the urge to roll my eyes.

"A Cielo MC20. They're only making fourteen hundred a year. And they're not even out yet. I pulled some strings and got mine before they were officially released. It cost twice as much to make that happen, but whatever. It's only money," he smirks, so full of himself.

If he was anyone else, such blatant arrogance dripping from his tongue might make him less attractive, but when one is born with classical sex-god genes like Burn's, there isn't much he can do to turn them off.

He probably wouldn't even think to try to be humble, because only a nice guy would do that, out of consideration for people less wealthy.

But like I said, I'm not here because Burn's nice.

I'm here because Burn intrigued me with his offer. And I said yes, without thinking. Because at the moment, the idea of being in the company of someone so completely opposite of what I was used to was extremely appealing to me.

When the light flashes to green, the Maserati shoots forward so quickly it slams me back into my seat.

Burn's about as foreign as I can get with his obscene display of wealth and good looks. And, I'd be lying if I said that sitting in this car while he speeds down the road isn't thrilling as fuck. It's fucking undeniably sexy, is what it really is.

And sexy is the one thing I need more of in my life.

Being a virgin at this age is getting real old, real fast. In fact, it had been real old for a really long time, which is why Olivia dragged me to that club in the first place.

I was done. Put a fucking fork in me.

Well, maybe not a fork…

To say I'm ready to discard my virginity in a fiery ritual of self-sacrifice and a long-overdue farewell celebration is an understatement.

My eyes linger on Burn's face, the amber glow of the street lights flashing over his chiseled features as he speeds past them. Even though I know hardly anything at all about this man — other than he's obscenely wealthy and is so handsome he could have been on the cover of GQ — I consider him a strong possible candidate for getting the job done.

I'd considered many candidates before but I've never quite found the right situation.

Now, I'd been waiting for so long I've almost forgotten why I'm waiting or what I'm looking for in the first place.

Sure, in the beginning, I had those girlish fantasies of Prince Charming sweeping me off my feet and expertly taking me in a breathy romantic dream under a fucking blossoming magnolia tree or some equally fragrant floral situation, followed by an enthusiastically recited promise of everlasting love and devotion by my new mate.

But I'm a grown ass woman now — and I know the best I can really hope for is a good fucking story to tell when I'm an old woman, sipping tea on my wrap-around porch, with a bunch of my also ancient girlfriends, as we try to out-do each other with stories about our lives.

I figure a hot rich dude in a limited edition Maserati might just make a good enough story.

Burn catches me watching him, the corners of his mouth tugging up into a crooked grin that damn near makes me swoon. That's a good start, I figure. I reach over and let my hand rest on his thigh, watching his face for any sign of disapproval.

He doesn't flinch. He just deepens the smirk, like this happens to him all the time.

I leave my hand there and he shifts gears, revving the engine as he picks up the pace and we race out of town.

We'd left the club without discussing our next destination. I hadn't even told Olivia where I was going, which was completely irresponsible, but I'd make it up to her later.

As Burn merges onto the freeway heading to the outskirts

of town, the realization that I have absolutely no idea where we're headed hits me.

If I was being reasonable, I'd be worried.

Hell, I'd at least ask a few questions.

But I'm not reasonable right now — and going off into the night with a stranger like Burn without knowing a damned thing about him — that wasn't reasonable either.

Instead, I sink back into the butter soft seat and let my hand slide further up his thigh, hoping I'm being brazen enough for him to get the message. When he reaches over and slides his hand up my thigh in one swift, confident movement, a slow smile stretches across my face as I slowly spread my legs, allowing him as much as access as he dares.

And dare he does.

When he sees my knees part, his mouth opens just a little and he slides his warm palm along my inner thigh, his wealthy man's hands as soft as velvet from probably never having seen a rough day of work in his life.

But his warm soft skin on my tender flesh is a welcome sensation and I lean back in my seat, jutting my hips out just barely, just enough to let him know I want him to keep going.

But he doesn't.

Instead — he removes his hand, leaving a shock of a cold in the absence of his palm.

He reaches his hand forward to the dash, hitting a button that changes everything around us. The entire car begins to shift — the middle of the roof seems to magically cut itself in half, the small trunk of the car opening at the same time, and the entire roof disappearing into it in about six and a half seconds of unexpected wizardry — and then we're racing down the freeway topless, the wind whipping at our hair, the cold air hitting our faces in an exhilarating change from the sultry slide of Burn's warm hand up my thigh just seconds earlier.

If it wasn't for the thrill of it all, I might have been disappointed.

Instead, I'm on fire for him now. I push away the tendency to reject the cliché of the filthy rich sexy guy showing off his car and my panties melting off me in response, and just go with it.

Fuck it, I tell myself. You only live once.

And I'm ready to fucking live. The entire time, my hand stays right where it is, firmly and intentionally planted on Burn's mid-to-upper thigh in my uncharacteristically brazen attempt at letting him know I was interested. But now, I graduate from interested to a firm 'down-to-fuck'.

I lift my hand and put it right on his cock, the warmth of my hand quickly warming the thick fabric confining it.

To my pleasant surprise, he's firmly hard. When it throbs and twitches under my hand, my breath catches in my throat.

Burn slyly looks over at me, his dark eyes crashing into mine.

He lifts a brow, and I take it as a dare. My fingers wrap around his shaft, gripping him as tightly as I can through his pants, his heat seeping through the fabric to mingle with the heat of my palm.

"I knew it," he scoffs, raking his gaze over my lips and landing on my tits before sliding back up to my eyes, filled with scorching hot confidence.

"You knew what?" I ask, my voice laced with a boldness I don't recognize. I squeeze again and he closes his eyes, slowly shaking his head. He turns his eyes back to the road for the briefest instant before looking back at me. His hand lands on my thigh again, sliding up as he smiles at me.

His smile isn't happy, though. It isn't joyous. It isn't light and sexy.

It's fucking dark as night. It's *knowing*. Like he recognizes something inside of myself that I've never known was there. Until now.

"You're fucking hot, Talia. I can tell you aren't fucking around, and I like that."

His words fuel my fire. He isn't perfect. He isn't kind. He probably won't be gentle.

He definitely isn't someone I'm going to introduce to my family.

But he's perfect for what I need him for.

One night. One act.

"You're right," I close the short distance between us, whispering hotly in his ear, "I'm not fucking around. Is there somewhere we can go?"

His eyes widen slightly as his cock twitches under my fingers.

"My penthouse," he nods.

"No. Outside. In your car."

His head snaps over to look at me, his eyes dilating in surprise. "It's like that, is it?"

"Yeah," I hiss, squeezing his cock again as my lips land on his neck. He draws in a gasp as my tongue darts out, tasting his skin. "It's like that."

"I know a place," he growls, reaching over and cupping my pussy. A gasp escapes my lips as his thumb slips into the side of my panties, scraping over my clit quickly.

"Damn, woman," he says, reluctantly pulling his hand away. "I need to drive. You're so fucking distracting."

I can't help but smile at his words. "Is it far away?"

"Talia baby, in this car, *nothing* is far away," he quips, hitting the gas again hard, the force of the car's speed pushing me further back into my seat again. I can't help but laugh with glee at the sense of danger that rushes through my veins.

Being in this car with Burn is like being on the scariest roller coaster in the amusement park. I know the hard part is coming up but it's the anticipation of it all that's getting me so worked up. I squeeze his cock again, pulsing with excitement as I imagine how it might feel inside of me.

Within minutes, Burn has exited the freeway and turned off onto a rural road with a few farmhouses scattered in the distance. Seconds later, he turns onto a dirt road, the fat tires of his car throwing up dust behind us.

"My family owns this land," he says. "Nobody uses it."

The dirt road winds through a patch of trees, then opens up to reveal a big red farmhouse that sits in the middle of a huge meadow. The golden glow of the moon bathes the entire scene in an eerie light that leaves me breathless. When Burn pulls up next to it and turns off the engine, the silence washes over us like a wave.

"There's nobody here?" I ask, taking it all in.

It's fucking perfect.

Burn. The moon. The farmhouse. This fucking car.

That cock…

"Just us," he says, turning to me with a slow smile, his eyes slowly drinking me in.

"It's perfect," I say.

"Perfect for what, Talia?"

The fire inside of me blazes, sending flames of desire tearing through me with the solid knowledge that my moment has finally fucking come. I'm so ready to get it over with that I have to remind myself to slow down.

Burn's full of confidence. But he has no idea what I've kept leashed all these years. He has no idea what is about to explode out of my body, like a juiced up racehorse just waiting for her chance to sprint out of the gate at long last.

"For this," I hiss.

In a flash, I'm straddling him, the steering wheel digging into my back and the gearshift fighting for space with my knee. For a split second, I think it might be impossible in such a confined space, but I'm determined and there is nothing that is going to keep me from accomplishing my goal tonight.

Our mouths crash together, our lips and tongues colliding with hungry passion. His cock presses up into my pussy, hot and throbbing and hard.

Maybe I should tell him I've never done it before.

Maybe I should stop to ask if he's okay with being my first.

Maybe I should wait for Prince Charming's safe fairytale dick.

But I don't do anything like that.

I kiss him like a hungry harlot, embracing my inner bad bitch, and take him like I know I'll remember every detail for the rest of my life and I want to be proud of myself.

My hips roll, my pussy grinding against his hardness, as I kiss him deeply as my dress rides up over my hips. His hands grab my tits, pinching my nipples hard through my pink dress. But I want those hands on my skin, so I break my lips away from his, and grab the hem of my dress and pull it over my head, revealing my bare breasts to his waiting lips.

"Fuck," he growls, his eyes dilating as he takes me in.

He captures my nipple with his mouth eagerly, groaning as I sink my fingers in his hair, arching my back as I revel in the feel of his wet mouth.

"Fuck," I groan, rolling my hips again, grinding my pussy hard into his throbbing heat.

He pulls his lips from my nipples and stares up at me with his black as night eyes.

"Goddammit, you're fucking hot, Talia, you sexy bitch!" He grabs a handful of my hair at the nap of my neck, pulling it back as his lips land on my neck, sucking hard and nibbling, my flesh stinging under his heat. "I'm going to fuck you so damned hard."

His words leave my thighs shuddering, my pussy spasming with anticipation against his hardness. He twitches and bucks his hips up toward me impatiently.

"I can't fucking wait," he growls, his eyes peering into mine — savage and demanding. He reaches down between us, his hands delving into my panties as he slides his fingertip over my clit again, then slides down to feel the slickness of my desire. He groans, shaking his head. "Christ, you're fucking wet."

Bringing his fingers to his mouth, he holds my gaze as he tastes me.

"Fucking delicious," he says, shaking his head. "Are you going to let me fuck you, Talia?"

Speechless, I nod slowly.

"Good girl," he growls, his lips brushing against my ear, sending shocks of pleasure straight to my clit. "I have an idea, though."

He reaches behind me and hits another button on the dash and the car doors swoosh skyward. I'm still straddling him, and he grabs my hips, his long, thick fingers digging into my flesh as he carries me out of the car and sits me down on the hood. I smile up at him as he puts his hand on my chest, and gently pushes me back until I'm lying down, the curve of the car mimicking the arch of my back.

Burn stands between my thighs and begins undressing

under the moonlight, slowly removing his clothes in a clear effort to tease me.

It works.

When he pulls his black t-shirt over his head, exposing the ripped muscles that stretch under his skin, my mouth waters. When he reaches down to unbutton his jeans and step out of them, I can't tear my eyes away. And when his massive cock twitches and throbs freely between his legs as he stands up, I begin to question every moment that's led up to this.

He's huge. Long and thick and so raw and ready that I have the sudden urge to flee.

My eyes dart behind Burn, wondering how far I'll have to run to get home.

Before I can sit up, Burn sinks to his knees in front of me, his fingers grabbing my panties and sliding them down my thighs quickly, before delving down, his mouth landing squarely on my pussy, his lips engulfing my clit with his hot wet mouth. I gasp in surprise, my voice carrying up into the trees.

He moans with pleasure and I lean back, all thoughts of escape completely gone.

His mouth sucks and nibbles at my clit, leaving me writhing in pleasure beneath him. His own moans seem to add to the intensity, knowing he's enjoying what he's doing turns me on even more. I open my thighs, welcoming him in as he pulls every ounce of pleasure out of my body.

"Burn, fuck," I moan, my fingers sinking into his hair, my hips grinding up into his mouth. He sucks my clit into his mouth, his fingers diving into my pussy and leaving me shuddering as the pressure builds to a raging force.

Just before I explode, he eases away and murmurs in my ear. "God, I need to be inside you. Right fucking now."

He leans down, his lips crashing into mine again.

And then, he does what I've been waiting for for way too long.

He doesn't ask. He doesn't go slow.

He doesn't hesitate for a fucking second.

He knows I'm ready.

Before I can even take another breath, he slides the head of his cock inside of me.

When he stops, he looks up at me quizzically, his dark eyes cutting right through me.

"Talia?"

"Do it. Fucking do it. Please, Burn, fuck me."

Slowly, he shakes his head. For a hot second, I think he might refuse.

"Unfuckingbelievable, Talia," he mutters, before pushing his hips forward.

My eyes widen with surprise at the pain and I yelp.

He leans down, kissing me again, his mouth swallowing up my whimper, his tongue twirling hotly with mine.

He wraps his arm around my waist, holding me tightly, and thrusts forward, breaking through completely and sliding into me entirely.

I cry out but he only kisses me harder, his mouth grinding into mine as he holds me in place, the scorching heat of the pain seeming to rip through my body.

He growls, his hot throbbing cock twitching against the walls of my pussy.

He breaks the kiss and stares down at me with a storm of desire swirling in his eyes.

"Shh, you got this," he whispered, shifting his hips. "Just relax."

I nod, taking a deep breath. And then another. When he senses me relaxing, he begins to slowly move again.

The burn of the pain envelopes me with a hot, stinging

heat that I'm sure will take every ounce of consciousness from my body, but just as I think I'm about to crash over the edge, Burn reaches down and begins to gently, but firmly, massage my clit.

"Ah!" I cry out.

"There you go, good girl," he growls. The combined assault of his cock inside of me for the first time, the burning of the sudden stretching and fullness, the intense shocks of pleasure and pain rocking through me from his touch, send my body exploding in hot waves of intensity that leaves me shuddering in his lap.

"Your pussy is so fucking tight, Talia," he growls. "I had no idea you'd feel this good! Just relax, baby, you feel so fucking good."

He grunts, carefully watching me, his dark eyes seeming to clock my every movement as he expertly rubs my clit.

"You like that don't you, you little slut? You like getting fucked like this? Your little clit is so swollen, look at you," he sneers.

"God, yes," I say, my pussy opening up, the burning subsiding and being replaced with the most exquisite cocktail of pain and pleasure that I've ever felt. My hips begin moving on their own now, rolling up and down his cock, exploring every angle of this new deliciousness.

"Look at you, baby, your pussy loves my cock, that's it, ride me, Talia, fuck me," he grunts, pushing up inside of me as he stands still, watching me writhe on the hood of his car. "You're so fucking hot, Talia."

He lifts his hand from my hip and reaches up towards my neck, his fingers gently closing around it, his thumb pressing down on my pulse. His eyes flash with the darkest desire, that evil smirk that hooked me in the beginning stretching across his face.

I know he's dangerous.

I know he can wreck me in a second.

But somehow, that makes me want him more.

I want his hand on my neck. I want his cock slamming into me with wild abandonment. I want the recklessness of fucking this near-stranger in the middle of nowhere, with nothing but the moon to witness whatever he decides to do to me.

He could do anything at all.

And that's what thrilled me most of all.

Fuck the pain.

I reach up, putting my hand over his as he tightens his grip on my neck. My eyes meet his and I smile back into his darkness, meeting it with my own, as I slowly but steadily pick up the pace of my hips, fucking him harder and faster, slamming up into his cock.

Recklessly.

Dangerously.

Addictively.

His breath catches just as I feel his cock swell inside me.

"Talia," he warns, his gaze hot and intense. "Your fucking pussy is sending me over the goddamned edge."

I meet his gaze boldly, lifting my chin, his fingers still wrapped around my neck.

"Come," I say. "Come inside me, Burn. Fill up my pussy, do it," I demand.

"You little slut," he says, releasing my neck and grabbing my hair again, pulling it back and claiming my mouth once more as he takes over now, fucking into me harder, our hips flailing against each other as our bodies search out the release we both so desperately need. His mouth breaks away again as he grabs my hands now, holding them over my head as he pins me down on the hood with his body. He slams into me

— harder and faster and deeper, with an urgency that seems to possess his entire body.

Just before I climax, he stiffens and grits his teeth.

With a roaring growl, he throws his head back, his cock swelling hotly inside of me, the first splashes of his thick release hitting my walls. Burn cries out in ecstasy, the sound echoing up through the trees in a ribbon of musical pleasure.

I'm left unfulfilled, but I'm too nervous to say anything else as we both suck in harsh breaths of the late night air.

Chapter Three

DARE

I stand near the window in my grandfather's study, my brows drawn low. I should be scowling, but I keep my face as blank as I can so that my brother can't read what I am feeling.

That's the longstanding game between us. We have been playing poker for our entire fucking lives.

Burn looks at me, a tiny smirk on his lips, his tall frame perched almost jauntily on the corner of our grandfather's desk. He arches a brow, his expression practically screaming in my face.

You're wrong. I'm right. It's the same story as always.

If I flinch, if I so much as let a sneer rise to my upper lip, he wins. We've been playing this game since we were born; he was born only twelve minutes after me. And lately, I've been on a losing streak.

My fists bunch at my sides, and I cross my arms to hide my anger. My losing streak can't go on for much longer.

Not with so much at stake.

"Just hold on a second here." My grandfather, Remy Morgan, grouses. He flips through a couple of sheets of paper that are spread out on the desk before him. "What page are we on?"

I run a hand down my crisp white button up and dark silk tie, pursing my lips. Remy controls the room without a thought, pulling his reading glasses out. Everyone waits for him because he said so. He's the big swinging dick around here and he won't hesitate to use it to publicly fucking humiliate anyone who steps out of line.

Remy's navy sweater and blue button up are rumpled, his shock of white hair is finger combed back, his skin sallow and papery. He narrows his eyes at the papers before him, his mouth puckering in concentration. Eighty-eight years' worth of wrinkles begin at his temples and pour down his face like sluggish water, culminating at his lips.

"This is fucking gibberish," he mutters. He slices his gaze at me, skewering me. "Did you put this packet together, Dare?"

My neck heats, and I straighten. I can feel my twin brother grinning at me, but I don't give him the satisfaction of my attention. I gesture toward Dr. Phadreet, a tiny man who seems to be doing his best to blend in with the navy wallpaper.

"I brought a scientist to walk us all through exactly what I have planned for the drilling project."

Dr. Phadreet steps forward, raising his hand as though he needed to be allowed to speak. But Remy waves him away before he utters a word.

"Bahhhh," my grandfather growls. "I'd rather hear what the accountant has to say first. At least he works for Morgan Oil. He wants what's best for all of us. Don't you?"

The accountant clears his throat. "Ah, yes, sir."

Remy looks up at all of us—his two grandsons, his two sons, Dr. Phadreet, and the accountant. We all wait for him to speak, like he's doing us a favor by letting us be here. Like we don't all work for him because he is the owner and CEO of our billion dollar company.

A bitter feeling sweeps through me, proving very hard to stifle.

"Well?" Remy asks the accountant. "Let's hear it. What has Dare been working on for half a year? Why would buying mineral rights off the coast of Maine be such a fucking fantastic idea?"

The way he tosses it off tells me everything I could ever want to know about how Remy feels about the project. I try to guard my expression and not give away my anger and frustration as I prepare myself to listen to the accountant tell the group of men gathered what a bad investment deep sea drilling off the Maine coast would be.

The accountant stands before the members of my family, looking rather nervous as he gestures to the large map on the easel in front of him. He has a funny way of clearing his throat before he speaks that makes me want to punch him in the mouth.

"You see in this area," he says, pointing to a sliver of blue water just off the green land. He clears his throat, making me tense up. "This area is where the most valuable resources would be for us. Studies have been done with ground-penetrating radar and sonar—"

"For God's sake, man. Hurry up. Time is money!" Burn snaps.

Remy purses his lips and then inclines his head. "He has a point. Get to the good stuff."

The accountant flushes. "There is a lot of oil down here, along with natural gas and probably even other more traditional minerals. Tanzanite, lucite, and even titanium, maybe." He flips over a page on the easel, revealing two big columns, one on the left in black and one on the right in red. The cost of the drilling versus putting the hypothetical money into another already profitable project. He turns, a frown on his face. "It would take us seven to ten years to turn a profit, considering the immense cost of the drilling. We don't even have the technology to extract everything that's down there yet. And I don't think I have to tell you that research and development can be quite a money pit."

"So you're recommending against the project," Burn announces, a barely checked glee in his voice. "That's the gist of it, right?"

The accountant looks at his figures and nods. "Yes."

Burn smirks and crosses his arms, disguising a victorious fist pump. "I knew it."

"You're being very shortsighted," I snap. "In twenty-five years, when we have tapped nearly all of the gas and oil deposits here on earth, deep sea drilling will be our only recourse. Then you'll be wailing about how we should have been developing this exact project for years. I'm trying to anticipate our next move as a company."

Remy's head swivels, and he looks at me with a contemptuous expression. "And what would you know about looking out for a company's long-term profits? You barely made it through your fancy namby-pamby college. And I am telling you right now that, as long as I am alive and I am still in charge, you will not get a dollar to put towards this fucking deep sea drilling project. It's better that you just come to terms with that right now."

Embarrassment floods my system. I grit my teeth and look at Remy. He isn't even looking at me anymore, though.

He looks at Burn instead, rolling his eyes. "So, what are you grinnin' about? I don't see you trying to move the company forward at all."

Burn's eyebrows raised slightly. "I'm just being realistic. We're making a killing off of the oil rigs and natural gas rights that we currently have. Now, we are about to venture into strip mining in Columbia. We are the country's richest company outside of the tech world. What more is there to do?"

Remy looks disgruntled.

"Get out of my office," he says, jabbing his finger at the door. "All of you. At least Dare is willing to dream big. Even if that means falling flat on his fucking face."

He shoves himself away from his desk, standing up with an accusatory gaze that sweeps the room. Everyone shuffles their feet until Remy snarls and chucks a book from his desk at the wall.

Apparently that gets us all to move.

Turning on my heel, I gesture at Dr. Phadreet, flicking two fingers to indicate that we are leaving. Burn is right on my tail, squeezing through the carefully studied doorway just as I step through it. I grimace and brush off my sleeve, as though he's dirtied it somehow.

"Pussy," he whispers as he moves past me.

My whole body tenses, but Burn just keeps moving with a grin on his face. His immaturity always blows my mind.

That, in a nutshell, is why he can't take the reins of Morgan Oil when Remy kicks the bucket.

We step out into the wide hallway, all lined with dark paneling. Portraits hang all along the hallway. A portrait of my great-grandmother's father looks down at me from the wall, looking right at me with his insane person's hair and his massive jowls. My distant relative has massive, florid cheeks and judging from his expression, he terrorized everyone in his path back in his day. I avoid his glare as I look around for Clive, the mansion's butler.

Burn lies in wait and then falls in step with me, jostling me with an elbow. It takes everything in me not to snarl at him. But that would be losing the little game we play. Instead, I just look at him.

"Don't you have somewhere to be?" I ask, gesturing to the front door of the mansion. "I thought for sure you would be out trolling for your next hookup. Or is that not of interest to you anymore?"

He sticks his tongue out at me, making a wickedly taunting face. "I have other things to worry about, brother. Like Daisy, for instance."

I come to a halt, my gaze narrowing on him. "Don't tell me that she already figured out that you're useless and is ready to break up with you?"

His lips twitch. "Not a chance. It'll be a cold day in hell before I let her slip away. I'm not about to repeat the mistakes that you made."

Resentment, bitterness, and no little portion of anger slide through my gut. I'm riled by his words, but I can't let him win.

Not ever, not after he stole Daisy from me.

I shrug a shoulder. "I'm just waiting for you to fuck up and step over the line. You will eventually. And then we'll see who Daisy comes running to."

Burn rolls his eyes and turns away toward the front door. "Yeah, we'll see. You have to catch me first, don't you?"

Before I can respond, he whirls and merges toward the front of the house. I watch him go, my face contorting. It's so strange to see my own reflection acting completely differently than I ever would. Even though I've been alive for almost thirty four years, watching Burn move around the world with such ease, such daring, still makes me uneasy.

I'm so caught up in staring at the empty room where Burn

just was that I almost don't hear anyone approaching until Clive and my Uncle Felix are almost on top of me. I flinch when my uncle reaches out, grasping my shoulder with a steel grip.

"Hey," he says.

He and Clive circle around me. Clive is dressed in a black tux with tails, my uncle in a green leather jacket and dark slacks. At age sixty, he still dresses like a much younger man. His age is written on his face in the creases bracketing his mouth and shadowed hollows under his eyes. I look at the two men, scowling to cover my reaction to their sudden presence.

"Ah. There you are," I say, feeling stupid. "I didn't hear you coming down the hall."

Clive just bows his head, as close and silent as always. He's been with my family since before I was born. He is tall, thin as a whip, always seems resolute, and his face remains as unlined as I remember it being as a boy. Everything about him is tightly wound and well-polished. He's old school as far as butlers go, and I appreciate that about him.

Felix, on the other hand, is downright chatty. He claps me on the back of the shoulder and smiles grimly. "This old manor plays tricks on your perception. At least, it does to me. It always has, ever since I was a little boy."

I glance at Felix, taking in his silvery hair and his gaunt face. He has the same probing blue green eyes that mark him as a Morgan, the same blue green eyes that I share with Remy, Burn, and my father.

I suck in a breath and release it. "Yeah, well. When I take over the family business, I'll move the Morgan Oil headquarters away from this damn town. We should be doing all our business in New York City. When Remy finally passes away, I will take Clive here and move the whole operation to fancier digs." I pause, looking around the house dubiously. "Good riddance to bad garbage, if you ask me."

Clive's expression tenses for a moment. I gesture to him. "No offense. You keep this house perfectly well maintained. But I want to see you tackle a new challenge, perhaps a penthouse with a view of Manhattan. Doesn't that sound exciting?"

Felix licks one of his canine teeth, glancing at Clive. "The kid's got a point of view. At least we can give him that, huh?"

Clive frowns. "Indeed," he says.

He bows his head and spins, crisply tapping his heels to gather before he starts down the hallway. I can never tell if I've just offended Clive or if he is just busy running this sprawling household. Felix notices me watching Clive and gives me a knowing look.

"Don't worry about Clive. He is on our side. He knows that one day soon, Remy will finally kick the bucket, and he also knows where his bread will be best buttered. I've talked to Clive at length about our plans to expand. He is definitely amenable."

I jerk my head toward the front of the house, a small sigh on my lips. "Speaking of our plans, we should talk."

"I'm guessing that the presentation for Remy didn't go well?" Felix asked.

I shake my head and press my lips together. "No, it did not go well. Basically, everything bad that could happen did happen. Remy asked that spineless accountant for his recommendation on the project. And as we anticipated, the accountant shut down the idea of deep sea drilling."

"That is not surprising." Felix reaches the front door and pulls it open, stepping back to hold the door for me. I step through it and suddenly wish for a coat. A sea breeze blows straight through my clothes, but I repress the shudder that follows.

I continue the conversation where we left off.

"He's shortsighted. The whole damn family is downright myopic. And when the oil and gas run out in twenty years, everyone is going to be asking themselves why they didn't start drilling in the ocean before. It's a sad reality."

As he walks across the driveway and into the grass, Felix nods, crosses his arms, and coughs. The entire property is fenced in and his gaze roves around the grass, his lips pursing.

"My father is many things," he says. "First among his most awful qualities is that he's a miserable, money loving old fool. He drove my mother and three other wives to their graves. He has been through a slew of advisors and accountants. But he's almost eighty-eight years old. He is definitely on his way out of this world, one way or another. Billionaire or not, nobody lives forever. So when it comes to thinking of the future for our company, for our whole freaking country that is so dependent on gas and oil, we can't be looking to Remy for advice on what to do. He is not looking to the future."

I nod slowly. Sneaking a glance at Felix, I purse my lips. "Remy has made some mistakes."

A snort bursts from Felix's nose. "Mistakes? Ha!" He shakes his head, a dark chuckle emerging from his throat. "That old fucker cut me off without so much as a warning. I'm lucky to be getting my allowance of one hundred thousand dollars per year. We all know that Remy is loaded. And yet, he refuses to share his wealth with his own son."

His expression is intense and bitter. I glance off into the distance, my footsteps wandering toward the edge of the cliff overlooking the town of Harwicke. It is true that Remy did cut Felix off from his one time inheritance. Felix is older than my father and the rightful heir—or he would be if he were not an inveterate gambler.

Though I wasn't around when he was cut off, I always want to keep in mind the fact that Felix is the opposite of risk-averse. Not the best thing to have in a business partner. But that's for another time, perhaps.

Do I actually care for my uncle in the way that family should? No, I definitely do not. In fact, I find him generally distasteful. But I need him, until this whole deep sea drilling mess has been sorted.

I stifle any retorts for now.

Instead, I stare out at Harwicke, watching the town from afar. From this distance, I can just make out the landmark buildings as the land slopes down to meet the sea. I see several boats at the busy harbor and a few cars on a long stretch of highway approaching the town. The people of Harwicke are busy, and they have no idea that I am standing here, plotting to shape their futures.

After all, when I move the company's headquarters from this little know-nothing town, it will likely die. The Morgan family supports all the sports teams, gives to the local hospital, and generally has a hand in every piece of charity pie that goes on around here. Without the family, the town will inevitably fall into decay and die a slow, suffocating death.

Too bad that Harwicke became so reliant on the Morgan billions.

"Dare!" Felix prompts me.

Drawn out of my thoughts, I turn to him.

"You know our deal," I say to Felix. "You are going to help me get the deep sea drilling deal off the ground. And in return, I will personally guarantee the return of your share of the inheritance when I take the reins of the company."

"Yes, yes." Felix flicks his hands out, waving away the discussion. "We've talked about it so many times now that I can't be bothered with another discussion. We both know exactly what we have to do."

I give him a sidelong glance. "Very true. I expect you to continue with the plan to get the mineral rights for the coast of Maine. We're going to need them. Morgan Oil may not be ready, but the future is coming faster than we realize. If we have to, I will execute a hostile takeover and drive Remy out of the company. We will be in the deep sea drilling business, whether Morgan Oil knows that or not."

Felix nods in agreement. "I'll talk to the people and see what we need to do to keep moving forward with the deal."

"You do that." I walk away from him, sauntering again toward the overlook, my thoughts drifting as I imagine how different this scene will look ten years in the future.

Chapter Four

TALIA

I carry a patchwork quilt in my arms as I descend Hope House's narrow stairs. It's cold here in the ancient house, as it is every winter, being that we are so close to the shore. The house is precariously close to being eaten up by the warehouse district. It stands amongst the last remaining row of ramshackle homes, once proud, now gone to seed. Everything else has been boarded up and torn down, but the children's shelter and the few houses around it have somehow survived.

I step off the stairs into immediate chaos in the downstairs living room. Olivia is very patiently sitting in the middle of the circle of girls who are putting makeup on her. To my left is a row of couches that another group of children are currently trampling over, playing a rowdy game of tag. I walk over to put the quilt down on a pile of blankets and start picking up toys to return to the toy box in the corner.

Olivia turns, her bright smile growing as she sees me, and looks at her watch. "It's almost three o'clock. Time for their nap."

I give her a watery smile. What she really means is that

she will send the kids upstairs to nap soon, and we will both slip out unnoticed. At least, that's what we have planned. Leaving here is always really hard for me and slipping away is the only way I can do it and not be an overwhelmed mess for at least an hour afterward.

"That sounds good." I say, though I don't mean it. I feel wrung out and paper thin after spending the morning here. I know it's good for the soul, but that doesn't stop me from feeling emotionally drained after spending so much time with the kids.

One very small girl with reddish blonde hair tugs on my sleeve. She looks between me and Olivia, sinking her hands into the pockets of her secondhand, oversized overalls and sticking out her bottom lip.

"Are you coming upstairs to nap with us?" she asks.

I look at Olivia, my breath catching. This little girl looks exactly like me twenty years ago. She even ended up here at Hope House, just like I did early in my life.

Olivia sees my distress and rushes over to the little girl, trying to explain to her in the gentlest tone possible. "We have to go home, Maddie. That's where we keep our toothbrushes, our nap blankets, and our extra clothes. But we will be back before you know it. I promise."

Maddie glances at me, her lower lip starting to quiver. "You're going, too?"

She looks between me and Olivia, her eyes wide, her chin wobbling.

"Don't leave," she asked. "Miss Olivia, Miss Talia, I want you to stay with me."

She appears to be on the verge of tears. "Olivia and I have to head home. We have to go to sleep and go to work. But we will be back very soon." I cross the room, kneeling near her feet. This is the hardest part of volunteering at a children's shelter. Telling the kids that you have to leave in order to sleep or work or really do anything but hang out with them is incredibly hard.

"Olivia and I have to go home. But Bert and Miss Alina are just coming in to get you ready for your nap. Don't you want to see Bert? He brought his puppy with him."

Maddie tilts her head back, inconsolable. Usually the puppy is a great way to draw a kid's attention to something positive. But not today. She flings her arms around my shoulders and starts sobbing. "You can't leave! Everybody leaves all the time, and it isn't fair! I don't want you to go!"

Everything in my body seizes up. I raise a trembling hand to the back of her head, putting her wild curls into a gesture that is supposed to be soothing. I glance at Olivia, my eyes welling up.

She knows exactly what I'm struggling with and how much I want the little girl in my arms to be able to rely on me. The only problem is that after Maddie is long gone, I need to stay here at Hope House, ready to open my arms to dozens of other kids without anywhere to go.

Olivia comes over to us, kneeling beside Maddie. She puts her hand on Maddie's shoulder, rubbing it reassuringly.

"I know. I know that it doesn't seem fair. You're allowed to have big feelings about it. That's totally valid. But I'm going to tell you right now, if you don't go upstairs for your nap, Miss Alina is going to miss you. You don't want that, do you?"

Maddie pulls back, her head turning to consider Olivia. Her crying slows, and she wipes a hand across her snotty nose.

"Miss Alina will miss me?" she asks.

"And Bert too. It's their turn to put you to bed and tuck you in. We can't take that away from them. That wouldn't be fair." I stroke Maddie's hair one more time and then gently separate our bodies. She seems pretty fragile, but another older child comes over and grabs her hand.

"I heard that we get pudding cups for snack. Come on, let's go see."

Maddie allows herself to be pulled away from me, her gaze shifting toward the stairs. I give the older girl a sincere thank you glance, but see that her desire for pudding was genuine. Olivia stands up, offering me her hand. I take it and get to my feet. Olivia gestures toward the stairs, calling the kids.

"Come on, everyone. Ms. Alina is waiting for you. Let's go."

The sound of tiny feet clattering up the stairs soon drowns out my anguish. I take a deep breath and look at Olivia, shaking my head. She just jerks her head toward the door, heading over to put on her heavy coat and gloves. "Come on. It's hard to be here, I know."

Bundling myself up, I sigh. "It's necessary, though. If we didn't volunteer, who would take our place? Somebody has to be here for the kids."

Olivia gives me a quiet smile and opens the door for me.

As soon as we step out on an icy, windy day, I want to shrink down into my coat. The cold weather will not leave me any room for emotion. Any tears on my face or any bit of water sniffling from my nose will become frozen soon enough.

Olivia looks out at the cobblestone street, her gaze going straight down to the frenzied gray-green sea. You almost can't see the dark shoreline today because the wind is making the waves so wild.

She shivers and pulls me close, turning away and toward the center of town. We walk along the sidewalk, the houses getting progressively nicer until we reach the commercial district, where the buildings become three and four story tall brick structures.

The town here is admittedly quite charming, with everything looking like it came out of a retro, post-war movie.

All the brownstone houses are well maintained, and the plate glass windows of the businesses are often decorated this time of year with Christmas and Hanukkah lights. As we take a right, we pass by our favorite bakery and cafe; its broad display window is all decorated with tiny snowflakes. It's a magical winter wonderland, white and red cakes and pies nestled in a white silk centerpiece. I force myself to walk past it, but I definitely notice that there is a big cherry pie sitting next to a red velvet cake with a piece cut out of it right in the front of the display.

I rarely spend money on luxuries like dessert and coffee, especially when someone else makes them. But my stomach rumbles; it's long past lunchtime, and I am getting quite hungry. My footsteps slow.

"Do you want to stop?" Olivia asks.

I blush and shake my head. She always notices my moods —one of her best and worst qualities.

"No, it's fine. I have some leftovers at the bookshop."

Olivia shrugs her shoulders and doesn't press the issue.

At least now that we are closer to the heart of our town, we are farther away from the sea and a little bit warmer.

"Should we talk a little bit about the plans we have for the future of Hope House, of getting a newer house in a better part of our town?"

Olivia is not too interested in the conversation after a moment, so I let it go.

I see that Olivia has a tear in the back of her dark coat. I stop, catching the ends briefly with my fingertips. "You have a tear." Olivia looks back and grimaces. "I know. I just got it last night. I tried to climb over my neighbor's fence to grab my cat, and I heard it rip. Does it look terrible?"

I shrug and start walking again. "Not terrible. But you should let me sew it. There is no need to go around looking tattered and frayed."

"I was just thinking of getting a new coat," she says. "This one is four years old. It has lived a good life."

"You're going to give up a coat that has served you so well without so much as a fight?" I roll my eyes. "Let me take a crack at it. Then you can decide when it's fixed whether you want to spend your precious dollars on a new coat or something more important."

Olivia frowns a little. "Maybe I want a new coat. Maybe I want a different style. I know that you won't approve, but I don't have to patch every hole and mend every ripped seam. I am not as handy as you are."

I shove my hands into my pockets and give her a long look. "You don't have to be. That's what I'm saying. I'm offering to fix your coat for you."

Her mouth bunches up the way it often does when she wants to say something but bites her tongue. I know that look exactly. After all, we've been best friends for almost our entire lives.

"What?" I ask.

"We should talk about something else. Have you got plans for the rest of the week?"

I reply, feeling like I didn't really get my point across about her coat. "Not exactly. I work at the bookstore every day. I'm thinking of cooking a lasagna tonight because I have these coupons that go bad pretty soon that are for ground meat, noodles, and cheese. All totaled, I won't have to spend more than fifteen dollars to make the whole pan of lasagna. And I know that Minnie likes it when I cook, so..."

"Fifteen dollars?" Olivia looks at me, surprised. "That's really cheap."

I slide her a sly smile. "I know. I've gotten to be an expert at extreme couponing."

She smiles and shakes her head. "Of course you are."

"What, I am!" I say in protest.

Her face splits into a smile. As we round a corner and go by a dollar store, she mock bows to me. "All hail the queen of penny pinching, Lady Talia."

I grin. "I'll take that praise. When you have to take on the mantle of household finances at age ten, you develop a keen sense of how money can be spent or saved."

Olivia looks thoughtful. "Yeah, I can see it. Minnie seems like a lovely person, but I don't imagine that she is particularly spectacular with money."

I snort. "Spectacularly bad, maybe. Or rather, it isn't that she is even bad with it. It's more like she gives it away when she doesn't even have anything to give. It's a little frustrating." I scrunch up my face. "Not that I am complaining about her being charitable, I guess. She did adopt me."

Olivia frowns and puts her hand out, shielding me from walking into the street. We stop, and a police officer runs by, clearing the street I was about to step into. He steps closer to me, looking to his right. Glancing down the street, I am able to get a glimpse of the beginnings of a large black hearse. The cop runs ahead to the next intersection, and the procession of vehicles approaches.

I can see from here that all the vehicles following the hearse are limousines, each one long and black, with their windows tinted so that I can't make heads or tails of who is inside.

My mouth pulls to the side, as I am temporarily distracted.

I can tell by the niceness of the hearse that the funeral procession is heading up toward the nicer cemetery, up by the Morgan estate that looks down on the town. Everybody else has to be buried in the same place, about five miles south of our little town, but not the rich people. My mouth puckers, and I feel a wash of resentment for someone that I don't even know.

Olivia isn't distracted and continues our conversation, though.

"She's your aunt, Talia. Not a random stranger. I love Minnie as much as anyone else, but you make it sound as though she adopted some child she didn't even know." I can feel the words of protest filling up my chest. I peer down the road, not sure what we are stopped for.

This is an old argument between Olivia and I, nothing new. We are not about to cover any new ground right now if we bicker.

"Hey, can I ask you to change the subject again?"

Olivia looks surprised, but she just shrugs. "Sure. What do you want to talk about?" Then she gets a mischievous smile on her face. "Maybe about going back to the Raven's Head Club?"

My entire face turns bright pink. I look at her and wish that I hadn't ever been so loose with my emotions and with my body. That's one way to say it, at least.

"I think I still have a hangover from drinking all that alcohol. Can you have a hangover for a month?"

She grands. "Maybe. Or maybe you're experiencing withdrawals from the really wild sex that you had that night."

"Olivia! I didn't tell you any of the details because I didn't want you to get any ideas about having another night out like that one."

"No, but you did say that you lost your v-card. When I found you the next morning, you were still wearing your same clothes. I asked what you had been doing, and you went bright pink and couldn't meet my eyes. We've been friends for long enough that I know exactly what that means."

In order to appear as prim as possible, I fold my hands just below my waist. "For your information, I think I was more drunk than I should've been. And you didn't say anything when I left the place with Burn."

"Should I have?" Olivia frowns and sticks her hands in her pockets.

"No, I mean not exactly. I certainly had fun. And he was... very attractive. But it's not a chapter of my life that I am particularly proud of, nor one I care to repeat."

Olivia bleats out a laugh. "Sorry. It's just, if you'd asked me what I thought you felt about that night, I would have repeated that exact line. She had fun, but she doesn't care to revisit the experience."

I sigh, thinking of Burn's blue-green gaze. It was mesmerizing, almost more intoxicating than the alcohol. And I really let it all hang out when I was with him, as they say. It was very unlike me.

I straighten my coat, feeling rather embarrassed over the whole thing.

Olivia puts her arm around me, hugging me. "Come on. You had fun. No harm was done. Condoms were used. Everyone got what they wanted out of the night."

"Condoms?" I give her a look.

"Yeah. Condoms. Burn seems like the kind of guy that gets around and doesn't worry about protection too much."

She pauses, a question in the air between us. "Please tell me that you were safe."

My cheeks couldn't be more red. "Well, no. I honestly didn't even think about it. Do you think I have anything to worry about?"

Olivia comes to my rescue fairly quickly. "Surely not. I'm just saying, you know, for the future, make sure you use condoms. You don't want to end up carrying some stranger's baby or anything."

"Can you imagine?" I say with a laugh. "I mean, how would I even go about finding a random guy that I got super drunk with and did the nasty with? It's laughable."

"I don't even know. You have always been such a good girl in comparison with literally everyone else. It would be surprising, to say the least."

I blow out a breath.

"Well, it's the first and the last time that we ever have to go down that specific road. After all, you only lose your virginity once. It's more than okay for you to have gone out and gotten your jollies, but I think the Ravens Head is not exactly the scene you want to hang out at."

"Definitely not. It was thrilling for one night. But I don't think it will be an everyday thing for me. Even if I didn't pay for a single drink all night."

Olivia grins. "Yeah well." She comes to a street corner and then pauses, looking both ways. "I have to go to the public library. They have a book on hold for me. Should I come by the store later?"

"Yeah. I just found a DVD player at the dollar store and I have a pile of old Fawlty Towers DVDs. So that's what I'll be doing all night tonight."

"Sounds thrilling. Tell Minnie I said hi, will you?"

She gives me a tiny hug and then heads off. I turn and

walk the remaining two blocks, stopping just outside the book shop.

I slow to a stop, realizing that Aunt Minnie has started changing the display. Currently, there are red, green, silver, and navy gift boxes sketched onto the glass with erasable glass markers. Gold marker urges people to buy their holiday gifts inside the store, the beautifully decorated font swirling off to blend in with the ribbons decorating the packages, the contrasting colors looking very neat.

Aunt Minnie spent hours on the design, carefully blending and smudging her drawings until they looked practically lifelike.

Now, she's added a new element to the design. Behind the glass window, there are many gift-wrapped packages on our table, enticing customers to enter the store. Next to it is a stack of all sizes of books, each carefully wrapped in brown paper. The large hand lettered sign next to the stack encourages customers to buy a mystery date with books they don't yet know.

I smile. Aunt Minnie isn't here, yet her touch is undeniable.

I hold the door open to the shop, and immediately I'm engulfed by the smell of old and new books. It's cold in the store—barely warmer than outside—but I start smiling the second I enter anyway. Bookcases line the walls of this room and the one beyond, floor to ceiling, stuffed with books. There are books absolutely everywhere, overflowing the aisles, stacked in cascading piles placed precariously everywhere you can see.

It's a barely contained world of chaos and a good representation of what's in Minnie's brain. I like to imagine that I am inside her thoughts when I dust a high corner or gently reorganize a pile of books. I can't seem to figure out what system Aunt Minnie uses when putting them together.

This is Minnie's world. This is all her doing.

I carefully make my way to the cash register at the front of the store. Aunt Minnie pops up from behind the counter, her gray hair looking more disheveled and completely uncombed than usual. Her dark purple velvet muumuu is obviously in the way because she picks it up from the floor and shows off her thin, sharp knees as she kicks free of whatever is entrapping her feet. She mouths something as I come up behind her.

"Damn drapes."

Sure enough, there is a huge pile of black velvet drapes sitting on the floor behind the counter. I unintentionally startle her as I try to suss out what the situation is.

"Doing all right there, Aunt Minnie?"

She practically jumps out of her skin. She turns her head to face me, clutching her heart. "Oh! Oh, Talia. I didn't see you there. I was just trying to straighten out these drapes that I found. Would you believe that the elementary school is just giving them away?"

My lips twitch. "Do you have something in mind for them?"

She puts her hands on her hips, dragging a hand through her long gray hair. "Not yet. But I'll think of something."

Of that, I have no doubt. I slide past her and look at the stack of boxes immediately in front of the cash register. "What are those?"

She bends down and bungles the heavy cloth in her arms, picking them up with a groan. "Oh, those are the books that the Morgan family ordered. Apparently, they made a mistake and ordered them twice, so they won't be needing those twelve hundred copies of "The Night Before Christmas.""

I squint at her. "Where else could they have ordered them from? We are Harwicke's sole bookstore." A little frown tugs at my lips. Minnie waves a hand. "You know what that means. They got them at a better rate because they bought them on some discount website or something."

I pick up the stack of invoices from beside the cash register and shuffle them, peering at the books. "They have to take them. We special ordered them."

Aunt Minnie shrugs. "We can send them back, can't we?"

"No. I was very clear with the guys from the Morgan Foundation who I spoke with on the phone. The books are not returnable. And we are not taking them back. They have to be picked up and signed for by someone from the Morgan family."

"I will call them, okay?" Minnie's lips twitch. "Those damn Morgans. It isn't enough that they're so rich that they have more money than God himself. They are the wealthiest family in town, and they're the main source of charitable donations for the local hospitals and sports teams. They have all those ridiculous gala events at their fancy house that over-looks the town. It's outrageous, really."

I set the stack of papers down and look at her quite seri-ously. "They have to pick up the books. I know that they are trying to use their charitable foundation to organize some kind of Christmas giveaway. We have heard about it at Hope House. But they cannot just expect us to eat the cost of those children's books. They were expensive!"

Aunt Minnie drops the drapes, leaning on the counter. She looks out of breath suddenly, which is a little weird. "This is the fourth year that something has gone wrong with their order around this time of year. And it is never something on our end. It's always something on their end, like they don't have the right book or they don't have enough. Remember last year when they said that they ordered twice as many copies of *Thomas The Tank Engine* than they actually did?"

I grit my teeth. "Boy, do I. Every single time this has happened, they have backed out and left us holding the bag. It's not right, and it's not fair."

Minnie spreads her hands. "I know, the prospect of the Morgan family buying a thousand or more dollars' worth of books has always been too tempting for us to pass up."

I draw myself up, glaring at the tall stack of boxes. "This is the last time," I declare. "This is the absolute last time this is going to happen to us. I'm going to do something about it."

"Like what?" Minnie says, giving me a skeptical look. "What are you going to do, go confront the Morgan family? It's better to just eat the cost ourselves."

"With what money?" I ask, my words coming off a little more venomous than I really meant them to be.

Aunt Minnie goes quiet, something painful passing through her expression. I give her a little smile. I tilt my head.

"What?" I ask.

She shrugs one shoulder, her hands nervously gripping the front of her dress. "We can talk about it after the holidays. I don't want to stress you out right now."

My pulse picks up, and I grow tense. I cross my arms and furrow my brow. "Well, now you have to tell me. What are you talking about?"

Minnie can't meet my gaze. She looks down at the floor, pawing it with her heavy shoe. "Well... I didn't want to loop you in on this or anything. But the store is in some debt."

I reach up, placing my hand around my own throat. "Since when?"

She struggles again. "A few months ago, Hope House needed money for roof repairs. So, I offered to pay for it. But then it turned into foundation problems and issues with zoning. Blah, blah, blah. They were having issues getting financing, so I loaned them some."

"How much?" I narrowed my eyes on her face. "Where did you get the money?"

"A friend of a friend. He provides loans for people in need."

"What does that even mean? Is he a bank?"

"No. He is more of a businessperson. He manages a ton of these small loans," she says.

"Small loans? I do not understand. If he is not related to a bank, then that means that he is a private financier. And that means he can charge you a ton of interest. Is that what you don't want me to be mad about?"

Aunt Minnie drops her gaze to the floor again. "Well, I was planning on paying him back when I got the money from a busy Christmas season."

My breath catches. "How much money are we talking about? And how did you even get it?" Minnie looks straight at me, her brown eyes worried. "At first, it was just ten thousand. But that quickly became twenty, then forty, then..." She trails off. "I lent the administrator at Hope House almost one hundred thousand dollars."

For a brief moment, my mind is filled with static and crackling. I blink and try to wrap my head around that figure. "One hundred thousand dollars? Where did you even get that? The last time that you tried to lend Hope House money, the bank wouldn't give you a second mortgage on your house. So where did you go to get that kind of money?"

Aunt Minnie licks her lips and looks at me, holding a hand out to forestall my protest. "You can't be mad. After all, it's for a good cause. If I didn't lend them the money they needed, the people at the shelter were looking at having to rebuild all the walls. On top of that, they needed a mold inspection and..."

"Aunt Minnie. Be serious. Did you get the money from a loan shark?"

Her expression pinches and she looks away. "Some people might call him that, yes."

For several seconds, I can't speak. "And what did you put up as collateral?"

Her mouth twists. "The bungalow. It's the only thing they would accept."

My pulse pounds. I swallow hard, anger rising like a tidal wave in my chest.

"So now you have to pay some crook back a hundred thousand dollars plus some crazy amount of interest or he takes our house? Is that the sum of things?"

Aunt Minnie winces. "I have to start paying him back in a couple of months. That's plenty of time for me to figure it out."

"Figure it out?!" My exclamation bursts from my lips. "Aunt Minnie, we don't have that kind of money! In fact, we are already in the hole for those stupid books that the Morgans don't want! How can you think that we are going to figure it out?"

Minnie licks her lips and runs a hand over her hair. "Someone will come through. You'll see. Just have a little faith."

My hands bunch into fists and I drop them to my sides, feeling another pulse of anger throb through me. I want to yell. I want to call her names. To demand to know why she has put us both in such an impossible situation. But the way she is looking at me right now, her eyes pleading with me not to be angry, keeps me from unleashing my voice.

This is not the first time that I have been extremely let

down in my life, nor will it be the last. Smoothing my hands down the front of my coat, I collect myself. I clear my throat, trying to school my expression.

"Okay. We should talk about this again sometime when I am less emotional."

Minnie reaches out and grabs my forearm, her gaze searching my face. "You aren't mad, are you Talia?"

I force myself to shake my head. "Nope. Not mad."

The lie feels oily leaving my lips but Minnie brightens.

"Oh, that's a relief. I thought you would be angry with me."

I bow my head, my face contorting. "Nope."

Minnie pats my cheek and gives me a quick hug. Then she scoops up a stack of books, hustling into the hallway, and disappears.

I look at the mess she's left by the cash register, little scraps of paper, the glass markers strewn about, a tattered book of poems left open with a page ripped out and left disconnected.

Unable to control myself, I reach down and sweep everything off the desk, sending it all flying in every direction. It is a satisfying feeling for a whole of three seconds... until I see the mess has now expanded, taken over the floor where it has landed.

With a heavy sigh, I step around the desk and begin picking up the rubble.

Chapter Five

DARE

Another day, another horribly lavish party at the Morgan estate. I stand in the mansion's huge living room, leaning against the wall, and watch as one hundred people that I have never seen before, dressed in their absolute best suits and gowns, float around me. The guests are all smiling, pleased that they were able to wrangle an invitation to Remy Morgan's house. It's all very gauche, in my opinion.

I throw back the last ounce of scotch that's in my tumbler and push myself off the wall. Beside me, my Uncle Felix contemplates the crowd as well.

"Freaking yuppies," he mumbles. "Every single person that's in this room relies on our family for their fortunes. It's sick that Remy calls, and they all come running to celebrate whatever he feels like celebrating. I doubt that most of these idiots even know what Twelfth Night is."

Inclining my head, I flash the whole room a frown. "It's a joke. A sycophantic joke. It's disgusting, but what else are toadies for if not to kiss the King's ring?"

His lips twist sourly. "What a bunch of assholes. Do you know what I plan on doing with my cut of the inheritance?"

He unbuttons the top button of his tuxedo shirt, undoing his bow tie. We've been here for two hours now, and a glance out the window tells me that it's almost dark outside. It's nearly time for my uncle to get properly soused.

I spot a waiter and motion him over, ordering another scotch. My uncle does not seem to notice whether or not I am actually paying any attention. He carries on his monologue, his tone and the volume of his voice rising steadily into a rant.

"I'm going to take my money, catch a flight to Eastern Europe, and never look back. I can set myself up there for life with enough money to live like a king. I'll have women, I'll have land, and I will never think about the family business again. I promise you that."

My lips twitch. Felix certainly looks as though he means every word of it. But whether it will come to fruition is dubious. Felix doesn't seem to be able to stay away, not when it comes to the Morgan family. At least, that's what I have seen him do time and time again. He grows angry and resentful, he makes a huge scene before leaving the family forever, and then a few months later he comes back with his tail between his legs.

But I don't say any of this to my uncle. It's not worth starting a fight over something so meaningless right now. Instead, I just clap him on the shoulder.

"When we take over the family business, everything will be different."

He shrugs and looks away. "Maybe. It does seem that no matter what I do, I always get pulled back into the dealings of this family."

I accept a fresh tumbler of scotch and raise my glass to

my uncle. "Here's to not being caught in the cycle again. If this goes right and I take the business from my brother, we will both go out of our way to establish new patterns and set new trends."

"Yeah, we will!" He pulls his bow tie off and crumples it in one hand. "I am going to head into town. I am over whatever's happening here."

I don't say anything as my uncle leaves me. He is soon lost in the sea of black suits and glittering multicolored dresses. I take a last sip of the scotch and then leave the tumbler behind on a side table and start navigating my way around the party. I step out of the living room and dart into the cool darkness of the servant's corridor.

Closing the door, I head down the dimly lit passage. This is the only place in the entire house where cobwebs build up. I flick my hand out as I pass one. These servants' passages run all around the house, running between many of the rooms and culminating at the kitchen. As kids, Burn and I would always run through them, giggling and looking through the various peepholes into the rooms on the main floor. Now, I rarely use them, as I am rarely back here on the estate. It is even rarer that I should happen to be alone on one of my visits.

I walk past the billiard room and the solarium, then pass Remy's office. I make a sharp right turn at the large library and come to a set of steel doors. Pushing my way through them, I let myself into the kitchen, where a fragrant tomato sauce bubbles away on the stove just to my right.

In front of me, there is a vast kitchen island and a large open pantry on the wall just behind it. To my left, there is an old woman who has her head buried in the oversized double refrigerator. As I make my way around the large kitchen island toward the stove, she pulls her head out of the refrigerator.

When she sees me, her entire face lights up, and she pushes back a few strands of her gray hair that have escaped from her bun. She's dressed in all white. Her white apron around her thick waist is covered in red stains, presumably from whatever vegetables she had to chop up and put in the tomato sauce.

"It smells good, Magda."

"Dare!" She says. "Oh, it's so good to see you! I was wondering when you would come and visit old Magda."

She hustles over and gives me a hug, mindful of the stains on her apron. I don't mind her touching me in the least. Honestly, at some points in my childhood, Magda was the only person who would give me hugs and worry over me in the way that you would expect from a parent.

Not my parents, of course. But some other, more stable parents, perhaps.

I squeeze her gently and then turn her loose. She starts to push me toward the seat at the massive kitchen island. "Sit, sit! I will make you a plate of my special cake. And a glass of milk, yes?"

I smile and take a seat at the island, feeling as though I were a boy again.

"If you're not too busy. That would be nice."

"I'm never too busy for you, Dare. You know, your brother was just in the hall. If you want me to, I could…"

Before I can even say no, the door slams open, and I hear footsteps. I don't even have to look to know that it is my twin brother. No one else in the family has enough courage to intrude here, in Magda's fortress. The kitchen has long since been her domain, it was already this way before I was even born.

My lips curl and I move my gaze to the open door. Burn appears, one hand in his slacks pocket, a smirk on his face.

He greets me. "Hello, brother. You're looking particularly wretched this evening."

My smile drops away. I fix him with a glare, wishing like anything that I had the kitchen and Magda to myself.

"Burn," I say as a greeting. "Don't you have homes to wreck? Villages to pillage? Peasants to burn?"

Magda looks back and forth between us, her hands going to her hips and a frown kneading her brow. "Boys, please don't fight. You know I love you both. Burn, come sit down. Have some cake."

She waves him over and heads to the refrigerator once more. I press my lips into a thin line as I watch him come closer, smirking all the while. He settles himself on the stool next to mine and looks me up and down.

"So? What's new?"

I can't help but want to smack his teeth down his throat when I see his handsome face. "Quit smiling at me, you bastard."

I whisper it low so that Magda doesn't hear it. But she has ears like a dog, and she intercedes before he can even say anything.

"Dare!" she says. "Come on now."

She brings a cake stand and two plates with a cake server over to us. Burn looks like he has something to gloat about as she uncovers the beautiful chocolate cake and carefully cuts us each a slice. The cake looks amazing and delicious, with no less than five full layers of death by chocolate. Though I am very angry right now, my mouth automatically starts watering at the sight of Magda's cake. It's been too long since I sat at this exact table and let Magda mother me.

With my mother dying at a young age and my father busy

drinking himself to death, I received all of my attention as a child from Magda.

Magda cuts two thick slices of cake and plates them, pushing them across the island to us. Burn looks at me with a smirk and picks up his fork, toying with the cake slice. I know that he'll do what he always does, eat the cake from the inner edge to the top corner, where the frosting is smooth across the top and the sides. He was always one for delayed gratification like that.

I look at him and gather a forkful of the best part of the cake, right at the joint of the two frosting sides. I smile at him thinly as I put the fork to my lips. The sweet bitterness of the chocolate cake bursts across my tongue. But it's not as sweet as I imagined. Nothing is, not since my brother stole from me.

Magda leans her thick forearms against the stainless steel top of the kitchen island and leans forward, looking between us. "Well? Are you going to make me ask?"

Burn plays it cool. "About what?"

I still have another forkful of cake and shove it in my mouth, chewing and swallowing angrily.

"Why has Dare been so distant for the last six months?" she asks.

I can feel her watery eyes trained on me. I look down at the cake and frown. "It does taste as sweet and wonderful as I remembered, but suddenly I've lost my appetite altogether." I put my fork down.

Burn laughs a little. "You'll have to ask Dare about that. I don't know exactly why he does the things he does. Eh, brother?"

I push my plate away and glare at him. "You know very well why I don't come around anymore." I dart a glance at

Magda and then smooth the front of my tuxedo. "I've been busy working on a new project."

"Yeah, a new project that Remy hates. He already told you exactly what he thinks about your project." He laughs to himself. "Deep sea drilling. What a fucking crazy idea."

I hurriedly stand up, my fists bunching. But Magda settles the fight, as she has been doing for our entire lives.

"Boys, boys. You two are brothers. I do not know why you sit around and pick at one another like two chickens eating bird feed. Why can't you just be nice?"

She comes around to where I am standing and puts her hand on my shoulder, pressing down to get me to sit. She is short, probably no more than five feet tall. Having her gentle hands on me makes me give in, though with anyone else I would fight the touch. She smiles and pats me on the shoulder, then rubs the back of my hand the way she has always done.

It's not chicken soup for the soul, but I do relax a little bit. Burn is somewhat chastised, and he looks at the two of us with an expression of longing. Magda sweeps a hand across his back as she heads to the stove. She picks up a wooden spoon and stirs the tomato sauce.

"Now what's this all about, really?" She asked. "Surely it's about something serious, no?"

I grit my teeth. "It's nothing, Magda."

Burn is quick to rat me out, just like when we were kids. "It's not nothing. He is mad because his fiancée dumped him, and then I started dating her after they were totally done."

I glare at him. "Yeah, five minutes after. As far as I know, you and Daisy were cheating on me while we were still together."

He rolls his eyes. "And I am telling you, we did nothing wrong. After it came to light that things weren't working out between you and Daisy, she decided to leave you for the better version of you. That is not my fault."

I snarl at him. "You told her a bunch of lies in order to get her to break up with me. There's nothing about that that is confusing. I wasn't angry that Daisy broke up with me; I am angry because I thought that you and I were closer than any two people on the planet. But I guess I was wrong."

He arches a brow at me. "I guess you were. When it comes to matters of the heart, Daisy and I were meant to be together, and you were meant to do... I'm not sure, something else. Go find another girl. There are plenty of fish in the sea."

"That's rich, coming from the guy who stole his twin's fiancée."

"It's not my fault that Daisy and I are drawn to each other. Find somebody else to be your wife and have your babies, you weirdo."

"That's not the issue," I grit out. "And I don't want to even have kids. After what we went through as children, with our dysfunctional parents and our grandfather pretty much raising us, I'm not even interested in having children at any point."

Burn shrugs at me. "So, what's the issue?"

"What's the issue?" I ask, as if he is truly dense.

A red light over the door switches on. Burn and I both look at it, knowing what it means. Magda pulls off her apron, looking at both of us sternly.

She points at us both. "No arguing until I get back from finding out what your grandfather needs. Do you hear me? And Dare, please don't leave without at least saying goodbye this time. I have barely seen you these last few months."

Glaring at my brother, I nod stiffly. "Of course, Magda."

Burn nods but does not respond. We wait in silence as she fusses with her hair and then disappears out of the room into the servant's passage. Burn plays with his cake, looking at me as he spears chunks of it and destroys it messily.

What a child he is.

"So? Are you still planning on this whole deep sea drilling business?"

"I think you know that I am," I say. I lean back in my seat and tilt my head.

"That will never work."

I fan my hand out, gesturing uselessly. "So you say. We'll see who's right."

He leans forward on his elbows, dropping his fork. "Remy will never allow you to take charge of the company. He knows what your little plan is. You want to move everything to the coast and shut down the headquarters here in Harwicke."

I scoff. "That just goes to show that you have no idea what you're talking about. I do plan to move the operation to the shore, and I do plan on shutting down the headquarters here. But I want to maintain an office in New York City. It's a pain in the ass to drive all the way out here to Vermont from Manhattan. You have no idea, I assume."

"So what? It's only a forty five-minute helicopter ride from Harwicke to Manhattan. Not that it even matters, because I'm going to take over the business and run it just like Remy would have."

"We'll see about that."

"Yeah, I guess we will."

I push myself to my feet, practically radiating with angry energy. I turn to head out of the main door, but Burn's voice stops me cold.

"You'll never get her back. Daisy? You know that she made her choice when she chose me over you."

My fists gather into bunches. My entire body tenses. I

don't turn to look at him, but I do stop before I head out of the room.

"Enjoy Daisy. While you have her, that is. Because Daisy has one hard and fast rule. She wants to be the only one to whom you give all your attention. And while I did not find that challenging, I know for a fact that you have always cheated on every girlfriend you've ever had. I have no doubt that you have done the same to Daisy. And I am going to find proof and rub it in her face. I'm going to destroy your relationship just for the sake of destruction. Then, and only then, will I be happy."

I push open the swinging doors and stride into the hall without another word. If Burn has a reaction to my words, I don't hear it.

Grabbing my coat, I quickly head for an exit. The door I choose puts me out in the back of the house, between the hedge maze and the beautiful sculpted gardens, brought in to remind my grandmother of the Palace of Versailles. Pulling on my coat, I see that there are a number of guests out here, stepping on the immaculately cut grass and trampling the trailing roses.

It disgusts me, the symbol of what our family once was or could have been if all these greedy gold diggers hadn't destroyed it. Remy loves them, loves entertaining these sycophantic strangers. Meanwhile, his own family can hardly bear to look at each other; the only goodwill toward him stems from the possibility of inheritance.

I am the only one of my family that is left with any kind of common sense or basic fucking decency. According to Daisy, I am emotionally closed off and pathologically unable to listen or compromise. She told me so right before she wrenched the promise ring off her finger, called me cheap, and left me for my twin brother.

Now I'm just walking around with a massive hole in my chest, hoping that my common sense and ability to look fucking forward will see me through the rest of this year.

I look toward the driveway, which is just out of view around the front of the house. If I can just get out of here, past the sea of Morgan wannabes, I can make it to my car and get the hell out of here. Even if it means taking a late-night flight, I need to get out of this house, this town, and this whole fucking state.

Squaring my shoulders, I use my height and my musculature to my advantage. It's often useful in crowds like this, where people turn and scoot out of my way as soon as they see me coming. I'm sure that my scowl doesn't seem inviting to them either.

Out of my eyes, a few people ahead, I can make out the outline of a young woman in a dark gray wool coat that is obviously a dozen seasons old. Owing mainly to the way that it has worn the patches at the elbows and on the bottom. I cock my head as I walk, thinking that even from this distance I can see that her coppery hair is piled up in quite a disheveled looking bun. Her shoes are honest to God army boots that hover just below a plain brown skirt.

What on earth is someone who is dressed worse than the help doing out here?

As I push past the last person in front of her, I can hear her arguing with one of our suited security guards, whose head is shaved bald and whose colored shirt has an earpiece sticking out of its ear.

"Miss?" the man says. "Miss, are you an invited guest? If not, you need to go."

The redhead turns, a panicked expression on her bright blue eyes. She is young, probably just out of school or college, maybe. And beneath that disheveled hairstyle, she has a proud nose and high cheekbones, she's quite beautiful. Like a diamond that has yet to be polished, I suppose. She heads full speed towards me, barely looking where she is going.

I have about three seconds to process that she is on a collision course with me before she comes crashing into my arms, the glass of red wine that she is clutching dashing against my white shirt and spreading like a blood stain. Her mouth opens in a silent scream.

She looks up at me, blinking. There is a moment of recognition, before she curls her lip out of some sort of distaste.

She thinks I'm Burn.

It's not the first time that I've been mistaken for my twin brother, to say the least. Not even the first time that she has been somewhat repulsed and wanted nothing to do with me or Burn.

She looks up at me, her slight frame rests against mine. "What are you doing here?"

A fleeting thought comes over me. If this woman knows my brother as I think that she does, it could be useful to me. She could be the key to embarrassing Burn and crushing his relationship to dust.

Smiling down at the woman, I slip my arm around her waist and pull her closer. "Don't you know? This is my house. And now you have come to me, haven't you, darling girl?"

The disgust in her bright blue eyes gives me hope that I am going to hear exactly what I want to hear from her lips.

Chapter Six

L ooking around the gala at the Morgan estate, I am immediately certain that I don't fit in. My clothes are too shabby. My hair is quite tousled. My smile hasn't been straightened by orthodontics, as I am sure that the smiles of everyone here in their gowns and tuxedos certainly have. I feel downright dowdy, up until the point when the security guard calls out to me.

I turn, clutching my glass of red wine, my heartbeat soaring. All my attention is on the guard behind me, and as I begin to run, I barely look at the people before me. They are surely too elegant and refined to even deal with an intruder like me.

My run is short lived, because I soon crash into a wall of a man. I peer up at him as I spill red wine across his tuxedo shirt, my eyes widening as I take him in. He is very tall, with dark, slicked back hair and insanely carved cheekbones. An aristocratic nose and a set of lips seemingly made for the sneering expression they currently wear which complete his visage.

I crumple into him and look up into his piercing blue-green eyes. He is none other than Burn, whom I never thought to see again. Especially not here, when I am sneaking into a party. I brush my messy hair out of my face and look up at him with wide eyes.

"Oh. It's you." The comment slips from my mouth before I have a chance to think about it.

Burn's eyes narrow on my face, and I have the strangest feeling that I am suddenly in a much more dangerous situation than just running from the security guards. He looks down at the wine dripping down his shirt and scowls at me.

"So it is," he says. His expression is as dark as a thunderclap.

I raise my hands to his chest, uncertain. The visions are dancing before my eyes, memories of the last time I saw him. Quiet sighs, the feel of his burning hot lips, the exquisite way he tastes, the way he touched me, the sounds of our exultation.

A flush creeps across my cheeks. Because we both know each other rather intimately, I expect that he will look at me with surprise or possibly even happiness. But instead, he is looking at me with this cold, calculating glare.

Does he not remember that we spent a night together?

I start to open my mouth to ask him that question, but the security guard catches up with us, drawing a sleek black weapon out of his coat pocket.

Burn looks up at the security guard, and I see a flash of fury on his face. He pushes me roughly and moves to stand in front of me. And he raises an arm, pointing a finger at the security guard.

"Fuck off," he commands. "She's with me."

My heart warms just a tiny bit. My stomach is still flip-flopping, as I feel unsettled. But Burn doesn't ask me anything about what I am feeling at this moment.

Instead, he grabs the top of my arms just below the shoulders and marches me toward the front of the house and away from the sea of people at this party. I feel the weight of a thousand gazes on my small frame, but Burn is the one in charge right now. He's made a decision, and I can only barely keep up with his long strides.

Burn continues our roughneck pace, pushing and pulling me in turns down the length of the back of the huge house.

We take a right turn into a less crowded garden; this one is a pretty ornamental affair, with pairs of people holding hands and whispering to each other as they wander through it. There is an elaborate set of sculpted hedges at the far end, and nearer to me is one of many broad, shallow pools with water features that gently ripple. There are roses everywhere, growing on trellises and in bushes. Burn pushes me forward and points toward the far edge of the garden.

I try to look at his face to get an idea of what he is feeling. I remember him being as open as a book and laughing a lot when we met before, but now he is closed off and his expression is set in a grimace.

I start to wonder, looking at his fancy tuxedo and the ease with which he wears it, who is this man? I only know him from our one meeting at the Raven's Head Club. Now I am wondering what else I should know about him. I am starting to feel more than a little intimidated by his attitude toward me.

"Burn!" I begin. There is no plan for my words, exactly. But my words seem to cause him some kind of torment, because he curls his lips.

"Not here," he growls. He pushes me down a pebble lined path, as neatly manicured as everything I have seen tonight. When he clamps my arm and takes a sharp right into the hedge maze, I start to think that maybe he knows this garden a little too well.

I blame my panicky brain for the ideas it's producing. Because it's not as if Burn is one of the Morgan family or anything. Believe me, I would know if I had fucked one of the members of the ultra-elite. *Yuck.*

I shiver to myself and force my attention back to the present moment.

Burn surprises me by clamping his fingers around my arm and pulling me into the hedge maze. On the other side, there is a large pond with an explosion of multicolored tulips framing it. A gorgeous Grecian statue stands sentinel in the corner, flanked by two white marble benches. He calls me over to the statue, ignoring my struggle. Then he abruptly turns me loose, rounding on me with a snarl.

"Do you even know who I am?" He demands to know. His face is furious for some reason.

I swallow and step backward, feeling the brush of leaves from the hedge at my back. I look up, licking my lips. He has no right to look as attractive as he is, with the spots of vivid pink color in his cheeks and his haughty expression as he peers down at me. I draw my arms across my body, hugging myself and frown.

"I know your first name. Burn. I was under the impression that you didn't think that knowing each other's names was necessary. Actually, I think you said that it wasn't very sexy when I asked you for your last name."

"Then why in the hell are you here, then?"

He prowls around me, first one way, then the other. I swallow and try to figure out just what is going on.

"I'm here to confront Remy Morgan. He owes my book-store a lot of money. Plus, I am pretty sure he's our landlord, so he's the person to talk to about forgoing some of these crippling mortgage payments, too. I came to talk to him and try to get him to cough up what he owes us. It's not like he'll even notice the cost. Have you seen this place?" I snort and stand back, motioning to the whole Morgan estate. "Talk about decadence."

His jaw tenses. "You came to talk to Remy Morgan? Really?"

I draw myself up, dropping my hands to the side, and lifting my chin. "Yes. I came to collect the debt that is owed. It may only be a few thousand dollars, but it's a lot to me."

Burn looks at me speculatively, poking his cheek out with the tip of his tongue. "You don't just talk to my grandfather like that. You have to have an appointment. You have to know people. He is a fucking billionaire, not a busybody philanthropist."

My eyes widen. "Wait, your grandfather? So... You're..."

He narrows his eyes and crosses his arms. "That's right. I'm a Morgan. Now who the fuck are you?"

My cheeks stain with blood. "I... I'm Talia Chance. Don't you remember? We met at the Raven's Head Club not that long ago."

"Oh? When was it? What day?"

I scrunch my brow in confusion at his questions. Tilting my head, I find myself at a loss. "What do you mean? You were there just like I was."

I definitely remember him. His intensity, the grace with which he moved, and his astoundingly good looks. When I laid eyes on him tonight, I remembered his name. *I'm not the crazy one*, I try to remind myself.

Burn gives me a smirk, stopping dead in front of me. He looks me over, assessing me. I don't think I come up as very highly valued, but I'm still trying to put Burn together with this whole lavish estate. The two don't seem to intrinsically fit.

He makes the gesture, flicking his hand. "Fine. You got me. I was very drunk when we met. I was on a lot of mushrooms, too. So I don't remember ever meeting you, although you are telling me that we know each other. I'm assuming that we fucked, though?"

I swallow, my eyes going wide. Hearing him say that is somehow dirtier than the vivid imagery that runs through my mind.

"Well… I had a lot to drink too."

Burn zooms in, lurching toward me, and grabs my arm hard. I struggle against him, trying to buck his touch. But it's no use.

He snarls through his teeth. "You're going to tell me right now if we fucked or not. So did we?"

He insists with a little shake of my arm, causing me to wonder whether or not I should just wait for a moment when his back is turned and then run. He gets his face close to mine, practically oozing anger at me that I don't understand.

Why would he be angry at me?

"Yes!" I practically shout at him. "Now let me go, please! You're scaring me."

With another snarl, he lets go of me. I start to move, perhaps indicating that I am about to flee. But he throws up his hands, holding them wide.

"Hold on. Don't run away from me."

I don't look at him. Instead I keep my eyes trained on the gap between the hedges, licking my lips.

"Talia," he says, his tone quieter. "That's your name, right?"

The sound of my name on his lips is more appealing than I thought it could be. Pausing, I dart a glance at his face.

I toss my hair and jut my chin out. "Yeah?"

"I can listen to your complaints and pass them on to Remy himself. My grandfather doesn't meet many strangers. But for me, he'll listen." He pauses, his eyes narrowing. "But you would have to tell me exactly what happened the night we fucked. And I mean that I want details. I want to know where it happened, when it happened, and exactly what I said."

A sick feeling washes through me. There's something wrong here, I can tell. Something is definitely not right. But I'll be damned if I know what it is.

"So you'll plead my case for me? You'll tell your grandfather that he owes me for the books he already ordered and make him cut me a break on the mortgage?"

Burn seems as though he is barely listening. I feel like I'm a ghost somehow, here, in front of him. I reach out and grab his arm, giving him a tiny shake. "Burn?"

He pushes me off, stepping backward. He still looks angry, but when he speaks, his tone of voice is very blasé. "Listen, I know that you're only talking to me because you need something from me. I get it, okay? What I need to know is that you will give me the details. Preferably right now."

My mouth pulls to the side. "There's something off about you and your requests. I can't figure out what is bothering me about it so much."

"Do we have a deal, though?"

I size him up, indecisive. "Maybe. You just need to know the details, I can probably tell you that, although I have to say that it's very weird being asked for this kind of thing."

He sneers at me. Before he can say anything, I hold up a hand.

"I'll do it for you if you can get me an audience with Remy Morgan."

Burn actually laughs in surprise. "No. No way. There is absolutely no way in hell that he will agree to meet you."

I cross my arms and give him a tiny glare. "I thought that you had a good relationship with him."

"You inferred that incorrectly. Remy Morgan has a good relationship with his money. That's about the end of that story right there."

My lips bunch up.

He waves a hand in the air, silencing me before I say a word. "When it comes down to making a decision, I have to ask, what's in it for me? So if I tell Remy your tale of woe, what's in it for me?"

Before he can get out another word, a woman screams a word across the gardens.

"Dare? Dare, where are you?"

He goes rigid at the sound of her voice. Whipping his body around, he looks toward the back of the house, where the voice came from.

"Shit. Just… Just give me a minute. I have to deal with this. Don't move."

He doesn't actually look back at me, though. I have the feeling that I am once again like a ghost to him, an idea more than a person. As Burn hurries out of the enclosure and ducks through the hedges, I already know what I have to do.

Leaving is the only reasonable solution. Especially since I doubt Burn intends to reveal anything to his grandfather. If I am not going to meet him, there is no way to know whether Burn will live up to his promise.

Ducking through the gap in the hedge, I flee toward the front of the house. I find my friend Olivia in her beat up blue Honda, parked along the driveway not very far from the large front turnabout. Glancing back at the mansion, I have the feeling that I am leaving behind centuries of criminality and angst. It has the semblance of a mobster's mansion, for sure.

When Olivia finally looks up, I am already pulling open the door to her car. "Let's go!"

She pales and starts the engine hurriedly, looking at me with wide eyes. "Well? Did you find Remy Morgan?"

I give a little laugh, shaking my head. "Definitely not. I have no idea what is going on with that family, but my best bet is to retreat and try some other tactic."

Olivia pulls out of the driveway, heading down the sloped driveway toward Harwicke. She glances at me, barely able to contain her curiosity. I wave her off though; I'm not ready to talk about it just yet. There is so much that I am still trying to come to terms with.

"Just take me back to the bookstore. Then I can tell you what happened."

"You got it." Olivia puts her foot on the gas.

I lower the visor on my side, looking at the receding house behind me. I glimpse a lone silhouette standing and waving an arm, trying to catch my attention. But I press my lips together and flip the advisor back up, not saying another word.

Chapter Seven

DARE

I clench my teeth and stare out the window of the Windsor hotel, irritated by the phone cradled to my ear. "Yes, hello? This is the third time I've tried to call down to the concierge."

I listen for a minute, nonplussed by the answer. I'm annoyed, and not just by this hotel's lack of service.

"When I say that I want an omelet with something green in it and a kale and apple juice smoothie, I don't understand why you have sent the wrong items for two days now. And besides that, my wake-up call for 6 AM this morning didn't ever come through. What are you doing? Don't you know who I am? I could put you out of a job!"

I pace in front of the window of the bedroom, my movements tense. Behind me, the bed is unmade. And out the window, there is a beautiful view of downtown Harwicke, mountains sprouting up in the far distance.

After a few more seconds of assurances from the concierge, I hang up my phone with a snarl. "Idiot."

I stride out into the living room, tossing it onto the bed. I, of course, have the best room that the Monteleone has to offer. The room is large and airy; it has a dining room and sitting area and a huge office in addition to my bedroom. But honestly, it is not anywhere near living up to my standards.

I open my laptop, the web browser still pulled up for Talia Chance. Another failure, coupled with the woman's disappearance last night and the annoyances at the hotel this morning. I rub the bridge of my nose, annoyed beyond reason.

There is a knock at the door. I look up, and the door opens unceremoniously, against my expressed wishes. Climbing to my feet, I am all ready to vent my frustration at the cleaning lady for being foolish enough to ignore my Do Not Disturb sign. But in the next second, my friend Tristen pops his blonde head in, his easy-going grin readily available.

"Knock, knock," he says. He straightens up and enters my room, and I am very glad to see him.

I throw my arms wide. "I didn't know you were going to be in town," I declare. "If I had known, I would have reached out to you sooner. I thought you were going to Australia with your fancy law firm."

Tristen's eyes roll back in his head, and he just shakes his head. "I thought so too. But I guess I was wrong. But hey, now I am here in town when you're here, so what's up?"

He steps in the room and closes the door, spinning back to me with a smile on his face. He looks good, wearing yet another of his many three-piece suits, this time in a navy and dusty brown combination of colors. I look him up and down and grin.

"Have you seen any of our other high school classmates?"

Tristan makes his way over to me and collapses into a light-colored armchair. "Nah. This is all very last-minute. I just flew in from Boston for the sole purpose of seeing you. Well, you and my mom. You know how she is. She would not be very happy with me if I came into town and didn't at least take her out to a nice dinner."

The image of Mrs. Bond floats into my consciousness— blonde and smiling and extremely chic. In many ways, she and her son are basically the same person. That is, if she had a job in corporate finance, taking apart businesses with a ruthless passion that is belied by an easy-going nature.

"Well, I'm glad to see you. I'm afraid that you'll have to bear with me for a little while, though. I'm trying to track down a woman that I saw at the gala event that Remy hosted last night. I think that she holds the key to taking down my brother."

I sit down, paging through the laptop that's open before me. Tristen sits up, his eyebrows rising.

"Oh?" He says. "When you call him that name, I often get confused. It's not like you have any other brothers to distinguish Burn from."

Shooting him a look, I shrug. "You know him as well as anyone. After all, you went to high school with my brother too."

He grimaces. "Everybody that's from a good family in the Tri-County area went to St. Mary's. We were raised with blue blood in our veins." His lips twitch. "Some of us more so than others."

"Are you perhaps referring to my brother?"

Tristan stands up, moving toward the window. "Not him specifically. But yes. He seems to have taken who your grandfather is more to heart than anyone I know. Like your grandfather being a billionaire is something that Burn himself personally accomplished. It's a little..."

He breaks off, perhaps searching for a word. I wave him off. "There's no need to be nice for my sake. I know just what Burn is. He's a snake and a toad, at best a boot licker." I push up my sleeve. "It's hard to realize that I've grown apart from him sometimes. But we could not be more different."

"I would agree with that. Now what exactly is your plan with this random girl that you think your brother knows?"

Pushing my laptop away, I lean forward. "Right. So I think that Burn fucked her."

He turns to me with a frown on his face. "And? Your brother being a cheating scoundrel should not be any great surprise. It certainly isn't to me. I played Monopoly and Connect Four with him as a kid. He was a cheater then, and he's a cheater now. What's the surprise there?"

I purse my lips. "No surprise, really. But I still want him to pay for stealing away my fiancée."

"Not this again. Daisy isn't that great, man. Don't you realize that you can date and marry any woman on the planet?"

"Not *any* woman. Daisy left me. She told me that my brother is a better version of me."

"So what? She is crazy, obviously. I don't understand why you are willing to go to such lengths to get her back."

I sit back in my seat, affronted. "I'm not planning on getting her back. I am planning on showing her that she made the wrong choice. She jumped ship to become engaged to my brother, and I for one want her to realize that it was the biggest mistake of her whole life."

Tristen schools his expression, pushing back his hair with a hand. "And this girl is going to help you do that?"

"Yes. Talia. But the very first step is to figure out who she actually is. Make sure that she's legit."

Tristan pulls out his phone and looks down at it, mumbling halfheartedly. "What'd you say her last name is?"

"Chance. Talia Chance. At least, that's the name she gave me."

He screws up his face as he searches for something on his phone.

"Ah." He moves closer to me, his brow furrowing. "I got her. Talia Chance, a two thousand eighteen Harwicke High School graduate." He turns his phone toward me. "Is this her?"

There she is, her coppery hair braided over her shoulder, her expression reserved and muted. She is standing with a cluster of girls, holding a patchwork quilt, and looking as though she would prefer not to be in the photo at all. I cock a brow, wondering if she might be more attractive if she just dressed differently and did something with her hair. She has creamy, flawless skin and vivid blue eyes. In certain lights, I suppose she could be considered attractive.

"That's her," I say. "She ran away from me last night while I was trying to find out what Daisy wanted."

Tristen sends me a short look, choosing not to comment on that. Instead, he pulls his cell phone back and looks through the page, trying to gain insight from it. "Well, it says that she works at a local bookstore. And there are a number of posts here about being *'thrifty'*. Patching jeans, resoling her shoes, mending a coat. A disgusting amount of posts about getting money from recycling. So... It's likely that she doesn't come from money."

I picture her, remembering the little details about her from last night. Her obviously worn coat, her frumpy skirt, her army boots. My lips twitch.

"No, that much is obvious. She doesn't seem to have two nickels to rub together. It's funny that a woman like that should even know my brother. I wonder how they came into contact?"

He squints down at his phone and shrugs. "It's weird, most of the pictures on her Instagram are about books or places here in town. There are no flashy cars, no pictures of her partying, and no new vacations. So I would say that either she met Burn when she was a fish out of water, or vice versa."

"That much is crystal clear."

He presses his lips and tilts his head. "You know, in another life, with a better haircut and a stylist, Talia would be quite a beauty. Her hair is really something else."

I scowl at him. "Do me a favor? Stop trying to make Burn's bad decisions seem like okay ones. The girl is frumpy and poor, just like Burn's decision-making process."

Tristen rolls his eyes. "You're the boss. I'm just here on vacation."

Closing the lid of my laptop, I rise and stretch. "Is it too early for a drink at the Raven's Head Club?"

Tristen checks his watch and frowns. "Yeah, I think they are still closed. But we can go to that other place I like… What's it called again?"

I scrunch up my face. "I think you mean Herbsaint."

"That's the place that all the cute, lower class girls work at?"

I smile ruefully at him. "The very same. Come on, if we hurry, we can be there in time for happy hour. They serve this whiskey punch in the afternoon that I really adore."

"All right. Let's go."

After I don a suit jacket and slick back my hair, we head down to the lobby, talking about Tristen's recent surfing trip to Australia. He is just describing to me how it feels to look down and see what he thinks is a great white shark, when we step out of the hotel and practically run into Daisy.

Petite, dark-haired, and wearing a short white dress that shows off her miles of legs under a dark wool cape, Daisy is unmistakable. She has a beautiful face, a glossy dark mane of hair that falls to her waist, an upturned nose, and a wide, aristocratic forehead. Add a perfect, plump pout and a pair of flashing hazel eyes, and you have Daisy to a T.

"Watch where you're going!" she says angrily. Then she realizes that she just ran into Tristan and me. Her expression quickly changes from scowl to sly smile. "Oh, it's you."

It's funny, that's the second time in twenty four hours that I have heard those words from a woman's lips. Steeling myself for the inevitable argument that is to come, I smile thinly and hold my ground. Daisy steps back after a long second, and Tristen jumps in.

"Hey Daisy," he greets her. "How's it going?"

She looks at him, her expression as sour as if she were sucking on a lemon.

"I'm doing well. How are you, Tristen? I figured that you would have moved to the city for good."

He arches his brow curiously. "I did move to the city. That was years ago, by the by."

"Was it?" she asks. "You've always dressed like an old man, so perhaps that is why I get so confused when I look at you."

His face tightens. He looks at me for support. My lips curl, and I smirk a little bit.

"You are kind of an old man," I tell Tristen. "Hell, even I am going to be thirty-three this year. It does seem like it was a long time ago, though."

Daisy straightens, pulling her dark cape more snugly around herself. "Time does fly, no matter how old you are. Is that not right?"

Tristen runs his tongue over his teeth. "You act like you aren't the same age as we are. But we all went to college together. You just entered Princeton as we were leaving, a freshman to our senior class."

She puts her hands in her pockets and tilts her head, talking to him as if talking to a child. "I remember. I was there. Now, are you back in town or are you living in New York City?"

"No, I'm definitely not back. I am just visiting for a day or two."

"Well, that's a pity. Harwicke could really use someone of your lineage. From what I can see, the whole town is going to the dogs. Everyone that I meet seems to be absolutely classless. It's reprehensible, really."

Tristan purses his lips. "Then why do you still live here? You have the ability to live anywhere. If I remember correctly, you come from money just like I do."

"Yes, well." Her answer is not really an answer. "As you know, I've accepted Burn's ring. So I'll be staying here as long as he's here. That's what people who are married do for each other."

"Oh, is that all?" Tristen mutters.

Daisy rolls her eyes, dismissing Tristen so easily. She turns to me, her head tilting, her expression growing worried. "How are you, Dare? I saw you last night, but I didn't think to ask. Are you back in town for a while?"

"I'm not. Not really."

Her gaze is drawn to my face. "Are you still upset with me? It's been almost a year now."

I push out my cheek with the tip of my tongue, aggravated.

"No, Daisy. Honestly, I usually don't even remember that you are alive."

She smiles with a flash of teeth. "Ouch, Dare. Well, it's good to see that you have moved on. I feel like that's the least I can hope for you, since I fit so well with your brother. Being engaged with Burn is like breathing. Just totally natural and effortless. And I was thinking that maybe you would meet someone new who would feel the same way. You know, I think that Sarah Harding is unattached at the moment. I could set something up for you if you want."

I watch her closely, seeing the pleasure in her eyes at my discomfort. I push it down, blinking. Just like with my brother, to show her exactly how I'm feeling is to let her win.

"Well, we have to be off. We have an important meeting to attend. I'll see you around, Daisy."

To this, she smirks. "Not if I see you first, Dare."

With a wink, she strides off, heading toward the hotel lobby. I watch her retreating figure for a moment, resentment boiling up in my body.

"What a total bitch," I spit out through gritted teeth.

Tristen glances at the door that she just disappeared through, and he reaches out and pulls me by the arm. "Come on," he says. "The more space that's between us and Daisy, the better. I forgot that she was so unpleasant."

I look at him a little skeptically. "What do you mean? You used to like Daisy."

He rolls his eyes. "I was putting on an act for the good of our friendship. I never liked her. She was always bitter to me."

We walk down the street, and I think about the fact that Tristen never got along with Daisy. "It's news to me, though I admit that it's not unwelcome to me now. You were just putting up with her because I was dating her?"

He shrugs his shoulders casually. "I know the type of girl she is. She's a lot like my sister—spoiled and shallow. I knew that my sister often drove the friends of her boyfriend away if she decided that she didn't like them. So, you know... It was easier to keep up appearances than to say anything."

"I wonder if that is how Daisy came to be this way, with

such an entitled personality. It always amazes me that no one ever checked her or put her in her place."

"Yeah, well. Maybe you will be the first one to change that. Isn't that what the entire point of rubbing Burn's infidelity in her face is?"

I wrinkle my nose. "That is one of the possible outcomes. The other one is that she digs her heels in and becomes more entitled than before. Which one she will choose is unknowable as of yet."

Tristen lets go of my arm and cuts me a look. "I think I have an idea."

"Oh yeah?" I say, still engrossed in my doom and gloom.

"You should start dating this Talia girl. See how Burn likes it. Rub it in his face. And then, if you feel like it, eventually you can tell Daisy that Burn has been unfaithful."

A bark of laughter leaves my lips. "What?"

"Seriously, think about it. It's beyond time for you to find another girl. Someone who is actually loyal. Why not this girl?"

"Women are only interested in me for my money and my name. I'm not like my brother. I am not charming or Machiavellian. I'm not a drunk like my father or a gambler like my uncle. I am the reasonable one, the one who usually compromises with other loud personalities in my family so that we can come together to accomplish even the most basic tasks. No one actually wants me for my personality. Trust me."

"Maybe you're just not looking in the right places. I mean, there are tons of women out there in the world that are great matches for you, I'm sure. My point is, why not get the ball rolling with a girl that could actually be useful for you? She could be attractive with a little polish. And Burn would look at her and realize that you have turned the tables on him."

I turn a corner, exhaling a deep breath. Ignoring the terrible advice that Tristen is currently giving me, I resume my train of thought, pretending that he didn't even suggest it to me.

"I treated Daisy like a queen. You know that? I would never have cheated on her. I would never have been unfaithful. And for what? It seems like she left scars where my heart used to be. How will I ever trust anyone again after Daisy left me for my own brother?"

Tristen gives me a sympathetic glance. He claps me on the back of the shoulder. "I know. I know that was pretty harsh for you. Honestly though? It was what was best. If you guys hadn't broken up, I was looking at having her in my life forever. Selfishly, I am beyond glad that it happened."

I frown. "I know. It just makes all of this Morgan Oil company business even harder. I feel like I've already been passed over, even outright rejected. If Remy looks at me the way that Daisy does, I have no chance of taking over the company. I have no chance of getting the inheritance I deserve. It makes my blood boil."

He looks thoughtful. "We should have that drink that we talked about. But we should also hatch a plan. There is a way to persuade your lovely young Talia to tell you stories about Burn. So Daisy will get her comeuppance, I'm almost certain of it."

My lips lift at the corners. I pull out my cell phone and dictate a text to my personal assistant, asking him to extend my stay at the hotel. When I'm done, I look at Tristen with a grim smile.

I'm right where I need to be right now. I'm here in Harwicke, at Remy's house, close at hand in case my grandfather has any need for me. I will stay as long as Burn does. I will win this battle, come hell or high water.

Chapter Eight

Walking briskly along the sidewalk, I hug my coat closer as I try not to freeze. "Brr!"

Beside me, Olivia looks up at the steel gray sky. "It's three in the afternoon, but it might as well be midnight from the look of things." An icy wind whips past as she shivers dramatically.

"It's definitely going to snow tonight."

"It was your idea to go to this bar instead of doing what I suggested," I remind her.

She gives me the side eye. "You wanted to stay at home and make soup. That's not really a relaxing, social atmosphere."

I huff out a laugh. "Relaxing and socializing usually aren't one and the same for me. I generally find those to be total opposites."

Olivia's lips pressed together. She gives me a long look. "I think it might be less of an introvert issue and more of a personal issue. I know we were both total nerds in college and spent most nights at the library. But it won't kill you to try something new, will it?"

"I did try something new!" I protest. "The last time that I decided to unwind by drinking a lot, I ended up with Burn, getting hot and heavy in his car." I pause, putting my hand up to silence her arguments. "Listen, I am going to this bar with you. But please, do me a favor and stop me when I've had two drinks. Drag me out by the hair, if you have to."

Olivia's face crinkles with a smile. "They have a whole section of mocktails on their menu. You don't have to drink alcohol at all."

"Now you're talking," I say.

We get to the bar, Herbsaint. This place is the opposite of the stuffy, dark, and snobbish Raven's Head Club. Here the walls are a crisp white, with light oak furnishings and clusters of white linen covered tables. It's like a breath of fresh air, and I look around at the bar patrons, a tiny smile curving my lips upward. Everyone seems to lean into their conversations. The sound of muffled speech, and the distant clink of china and glass makes this bar much more approachable than the Raven's Head Club.

After a polite young hostess waves us on to the bar area, we slide into our seats. I glance around and notice the wait-staff that flits from table to table like a trained team of hummingbirds.

"Wow, this is so different from the other bar," I observe. Looking down at the menu in front of me, I run my fingers over it. And the menu looks so good. "I think I would like to come here for dinner."

In the next moment, I glance at the prices, and I blanch. "Gosh, it is so expensive! I take it back, I could never spend this much money on one dinner. In fact, I don't see how we are sitting here just for drinks."

Olivia grabs my hand, giving it a squeeze. "First of all,

you deserve something nice every once in a while. Second of all, I'm not letting you weasel out of this one. I am paying for our drinks. Plus, we might get hungry. I'll pay for that too. I just got a raise at the biology lab, and now I am looking to celebrate."

My brow furrows. "I know I can't tell you how to celebrate. But I can't in good conscience drink a cocktail that costs this much. Hope House has a roof that leaks and walls that are crumbling. Every penny that I spend on anything that isn't a necessity seems like wasted money in light of that."

"But I just explained to you that I am paying for everything today. So, no more feeling guilty about how much money is spent. Okay?"

I run my tongue over my teeth and give her a sour look. "One drink. A mocktail. That's it."

She picks up her menu and wiggles her eyebrows. "Come on, if you're just going to have one drink, it better be something spectacular. And then, once you've picked it out, you can tell me all about how Hope House needs a new roof."

"It does need a new roof!" I say.

"You should order a drink so that you can tell me about it." She gives me a little side eye, and then the bartender takes our drink orders. We both end up with sparkling cocktails, hers is a Cure Royale and mine is a mocktail with tropical flavors. After we toast to her promotion, I go right back to my concerns about Hope House.

"We need a newer, bigger house that can accommodate more beds. One that doesn't have the structural problems that our current house has."

"It would help if it were in a better neighborhood and not in a neighborhood that looks like it's about to break off from the town and float away to drown in the sea."

I scrunch up my face.

"Being so close to the water has indeed taken a toll on the building," I say with a slow nod. "You know, I found out that Remy Morgan owns the whole neighborhood? I saw the mortgage check in the office yesterday, and it goes straight to Morgan Investment Company, not an actual bank. That's the Morgan family, isn't it?"

"I think the Morgans do own a bank." Olivia's eyes narrow, and she looks off speculatively. "I know that they own most of the land that the hospital is on and that whole surrounding neighborhood too."

"Ugh, like they need to own another thing. The Morgans are the main charitable source in this town. But they are also the biggest contributors to our problems as a society. This capitalist stuff completely sucks."

A trace of a smile passes over Olivia's lips as she takes a sip of her drink. "It's hard to thrive when you weren't born into money. There are people living among us that want to drain our life savings away a little bit at a time. It's obscene, really."

I pull a face. "I bet Remy Morgan and his heirs don't have to worry about anything at all. They just live up there at their huge estate, being smarmy, throwing galas, drinking expensive cocktails, and laughing as they crush commoners with their feet."

"That's a bit much. But yes, I bet the Morgans do live a different lifestyle than I am accustomed to."

"Getting an audience with Remy Morgan is practically impossible. He has teams of publicists and bodyguards and other people to act as a barrier between himself and the hoi polloi."

"Have you tried visiting his house again?"

I give a cold little laugh. "Not since the other night. It

turns out that when the Morgans are hosting a lavish gala, it's impossible to get past the doorman and armed security guards to see the man himself. I even tried to show up at a ribbon-cutting ceremony that he had yesterday. I'm pretty sure that I'm on a list of would-be stalkers now."

"What about Burn? You said that he made you an offer of some kind."

My lips twist. "He did make me an offer. But it definitely sucked for me. In exchange for reminding him of just what happened the night we hooked up, I get an audience with Remy. But that doesn't even promise me anything. Remy could take one look at me and send me away. There is just no guarantee. It has been a pretty frustrating experience all around."

"What's your next plan of attack? Should you take Burn up on his weird offer? Or do you have another strategy up your sleeve?"

I shake my head. "I don't know exactly. I just know that Minnie says that unless we pay a lot of money to some very bad people, those people are going to come looking for the money. She said that Hope House could potentially be affected too. So I'm not sure what to do. The only thing I know for sure is that I have to help Minnie, I have to save Hope House, and Remy Morgan could be the answer to all my problems. If, and it's a big if, he is feeling charitable and generous."

"You know, Minnie is your aunt. She's not one of the kids at Hope House. She is completely capable of making her own decisions and taking care of herself."

"Is she, though? I'm not sure. Apparently she went to a bunch of sketchy loan sharks and asked them for money to save Hope House. She put up our house as collateral. She's gotten herself into a situation that looks bleak. I am wondering now if she should've been asked a lot more questions before these people just gave her money."

Olivia reaches out, putting her fingers gently on my arm. She looks me dead in the eye. "You are not responsible for her. She is responsible for you. You're her kid."

"Well…" I look away, steeling myself before continuing. "Technically, I'm not her kid. I'm her niece. And she did me a huge favor by taking me in when my mom dumped me off at Hope House and vanished. I've been trying to be as quiet and small and helpful as humanly possible ever since I was old enough to be a person. I've tried to model myself after Aunt Minnie, to be as helpful, giving, and generous as her."

She squeezes my arm again. "I know, Talia. I think you have done a good job of that, given the circumstances."

I exhale a long, shaky breath. "You know, we might have scrimped and saved and counted every single penny when I was growing up. And yes, sometimes we went through really lean times because Aunt Minnie pledged more than we had to give away. But I'll always owe her. I mean, how do I repay someone who basically gave up her life for me?"

Olivia sets her glass down and looks at me sharply. "I know that Aunt Minnie does not feel that way. You live your whole life trying to be small and to blend in with the wallpaper. I've watched it happen time and again. But I think that right now is the perfect time for you to step out of the shadows and form a new, more confident identity. I think that your Aunt Minnie would want you to do so."

I roll my eyes and wave her off. "Olivia, quit being nice. You have to sugarcoat the truth for my sake."

"I am not," she says. "I'm telling you the truth."

I stare at her for several long seconds, trying to figure out what her angle is. But when she doesn't waver, I relent, sighing. "Sorry, Olivia. I'm probably bad company right now. Maybe I should go."

She points a finger at me, putting me in place with her gaze. "Don't you dare. You've hardly even touched your drink."

I shrug and stay in my place, but I don't pick up the drink. I'm about to open my mouth to tell her that I don't think I am in the mood. I twist in my seat, my mouth bunching up, when, out of the corner of my eye, I see the last person I would expect to frequent this place.

Tall, dark, and dressed in a big black overcoat, he's still as handsome as ever. Burn Morgan.

He follows the host toward the back of the bar, heading away from me. With him is a tall, refined looking blonde man in a navy three-piece suit and a brown suede overcoat.

I suck in a breath and, with my head down, bring up a hand to shield my face. Seeing the man who I hooked up with, whose hands I can still easily imagine on my hips and thighs, makes the blood rush to my cheeks. I feel as if I might faint.

"Talia," Olivia says, giving me a little shake. "What is it?"

I lick my suddenly dry lips and dart a glance over at Burn. He is settling into a booth just now, his expression a cool little smirk as he looks around the room. I resist the urge to make a scared noise, and I slide out of my seat.

"It's Burn! He is here."

Olivia immediately turns her head, surveying the room. She spots him and turns back to me, nodding slowly. "Is that Burn? Or is that Dare?"

I scowl, not understanding her question. "What do you mean? Of course that's Burn."

She turns her head again, a look of concentration crossing her pretty face. "Is it?" She asked again. "I'd be hard-pressed to pick the twins out of the lineup and tell you which one is which."

My pulse thunders, my breathing stutters. I look at her, my eyebrows rising. "What did you say about twins?"

Olivia gives me a bit of a puzzled look. "They're twins. Identical twins. Did you not know that?"

I swallow, feeling like I am full of bile. I shake my head slowly.

"How do you know?"

She snorts. "The question is more like, how do you not know? Everyone knows them."

"I feel like I am crazy, but I have literally lived in this town for as long as anybody else, and I've never even heard of Burn or Dare Morgan until this moment."

"Ha. Well, they are an established entity, you could say. I remember quite clearly how half the girls in our grade had their pictures pasted on the front of their notebooks. Our very own billionaire bad boys have come to life. If I remember correctly, it was kind of fun to think about one or the other boy asking us out."

I pick up a cocktail napkin and twist it, ripping it into pieces. "How could I not know? I mean, it makes way more sense that the hot guy I met the other night claimed not to remember the details of our hookup. If he was actually Dare, he would have no way of knowing what happened between me and Burn." I feel the blood slide from my face. "Or maybe it was Dare instead of Burn at the Raven's Head Club that night, and now Burn is trying to find out what happened. God, that is all kinds of fucked up."

"I'm sorry, I thought you knew. You were hanging all over Burn's arm by the time I even realized that you two had even met. I knew that they were twins, but I figured that he was who he said he was. Why would he lie?"

I school my expression and look at her sternly. "Why would he have asked me for the details of his brother's sexual adventures? There is definitely something foul going on here, though I can't tell what exactly it is. All I know is that it gives me a bad feeling."

Olivia takes a final swig of her fancy cocktail and digs in her purse for a wad of cash. Dropping it on the bar, she stands up. "Let's go then. Come on, you are not going to drink that mocktail anyway. I know you too well."

Grateful for her, I reach forward and give her a quick hug. "Thank you."

Her lips twitch. "Come on, let's head outside. I think if we sneak by the wall over here, we can head out the back with no one being the wiser."

Pushing out of my chair, I take Olivia's hand. I try to look as inconspicuous as possible while I look away from the main bar. I try to keep it casual, covering my face with my hair and moving quickly. Unfortunately, I don't really get a glimpse of Burn before I leave. I hesitate, then glance over my shoulder. The spot where I expected him to be is empty.

"Oh God." I squeeze Olivia's hand and rush toward the back door, hoping that no one notices our quick exit. Olivia quickly leads me, heading down a dark back hallway toward a glowing exit sign. It is not until she pushes on the door, opening it into the back alley, that I start to feel as though I might have made it.

Olivia steps back and ushers me through the door first. I step out into the dimly lit back alleyway, hugging my coat around myself. But as soon as I do, a familiar voice calls out from the wall just beside me.

"And here I was, searching high and low for you."

Jerking my head to my right, I see the outline of a tall

man, blue green eyes glittering from the shadows. He pushes off the wall and starts to move toward me.

My heart pounds, and I tense up, preparing to run.

.

Chapter Nine

DARE

Pretty little Talia with her coppery red hair is looking at me the way one would look at a venomous snake. Her eyes are wide and innocent, her cheeks flushed, and her throat working as she regards me. She looks as though she is trying to decide between fight or flight.

I smirk and move forward, my hand grabbing her forearm and my lips drawing away from my teeth.

"Where do you think you're going, Talia?"

Her lips part in a sneer. She pins me with her gaze and yanks at her arm, but I am so much bigger than her that it is an almost comical attempt to free herself. I squeeze her arm, pulling her closer. She doesn't come easily; her expression is a combination of fear and hatred. When I see the loathing in her eyes, I am a little taken aback. It's not like I am used to strangers having such a profound distaste for me.

"Let me go," she hisses.

She yanks her arm from my grip, but just as quickly, I manage to grab her by the shoulders. She looks so incredibly pretty right now, her head thrown back and her eyes glittering. I realize that she must be an absolute firecracker in bed.

Rile her up enough, and you would certainly get a show. I can just imagine her in the middle of an orgasm, her head thrown back, a moan escaping her lips, calling my name into the air as she begs me to make her cum. Feeling her feeble struggles and seeing her fight against me, her hands scrabbling at my coat, I can't help my reaction. In an instant, I feel my cock harden.

"I know about you," she says through clenched teeth. "I know about your little deception. I know that you have a twin. So which one are you? Burn or Dare?"

Fuck, I really thought that I had an advantage there. No matter; it was bound to come out sooner or later.

I let out a menacing chuckle and pull her closer, enjoying the panic written all over her face. "If you must know, little girl, I am Dare. Not that that's going to help you any. In fact, I don't think anyone can help you."

Her cheeks flush a deeper shade of red, and she looks angry. "You're horrible. Let me go. You can't just grab women in back alleys."

I want nothing more than to draw her in and make her behave like a good little girl. But in the next second, her friend is standing next to me, her hands raised like she is going to hit me.

Would it hurt if she hit me? Probably not. She's a tiny thing, and she has no visible weapon that I can see. But I let Talia go for a second, taking a quarter of a step back and raising my hands as a gesture of goodwill.

I turn to the other girl and try to give her a pacifying glance. "Easy. Your friend knows me."

The girl scoffs. "I've heard stories about you, Dare."

"I need you to fuck off now. I have to talk to Talia alone, and you are butting into the middle of our business." I flash her an icy smile.

Talia backs up a little, but I grab her shoulder, pinning her in place. The friend looks terrified but stands her ground, "No way. I'm not leaving her here."

Talia struggles again, and before I can even focus on her, she hauls off and pops me right in the jaw. I am so stunned for a moment that I let go of her shoulder and put my hand to my face.

My eyes connect with Talia's. When I speak, my words are dripping with venomous sarcasm.

"Well aren't you a darling girl?"

The friend pulls out a cell phone and starts dialing. "I'm calling the police, just so you know. You need to get away from us right now."

I narrow my eyes on her face and then look at Talia. I know what she wants. I know what everyone wants from me, especially pretty young girls.

More than anything else, they want money.

If I throw money at the situation, the problem will magically resolve itself. I've seen it time and time again. Running my tongue over my teeth, I pull out a wad of cash from my money clip. Holding it up, I tilt my head to the side.

"Will this change your mind, Talia? If you talk to me right here and now, you get the cash."

Talia's eyes widen. She looks nervous, and a flush creeps from her face down her neck. But her eyes are glued on the money.

Of course they fucking are. She's just the same as every other fucking girl in the world. It's the only thing that women ever want from me.

I hold out the money toward her. I can see the dollar signs in her eyes, the calculation she has to do. I have no doubt that the money will win out over any worries she might have about talking to me here in the dark.

Talia's friend grabs Talia's wrist and pulls her away from me. I let Talia go because I have already baited the hook. After I flashed a little bit of money, I knew that I would get what I wanted. The question is whether she will force me to listen to her friend's nonsense for another couple of minutes.

I cross my arms and ready myself, pressing my lips into a thin line. Talia glances at me and hooks her hair behind her ears.

"Just tell her already," I say. "Tell her to leave you here."

The friend pulls at her sleeve again. Talia grasps her arm and looks her in the eye. "It's fine, Olivia. He says that he just wants to talk to me."

Her friend looks at me with skeptical eyes. "You sure?"

Talia nods and very gently removes her friend's hand from her wrists. "I am absolutely sure. I'll text you on my way home so that you don't worry about me. Okay?"

Her friends' eyes tighten on my face. For a moment, I think that she will keep putting up a fight. But eventually she lets out a long sigh. "Okay. If you are sure, I'll go."

Talia reaches out and touches her shoulder. "Thanks Olivia. I mean it."

Giving me a final glare, Talia's friend heads out of the alley. I watch her go, pushing my cheek out with my tongue. When Talia looks back at me, nervously fidgeting and compulsively swallowing, I jerk my head toward the other end of the alley.

"Follow me. Let's go to my car. I want to be able to speak freely without anyone listening in on our conversation."

As she follows me down the alley, Talia gives me a puzzled glance. "Do you think that anyone actually cares what I have to say?"

I shrug, exiting the alley and pointing towards my sleek black Porsche two-seater. "Better safe than sorry."

I head around to the passenger side first, opening the door and impatiently motioning for Talia to get in. She hesitates for just a moment, her eyes meeting mine, as if she could tell just by looking at me whether my intentions were pure. When she climbs in, I smirk and shut the door. Then I hustle around to the other side, climbing into the driver's side seat.

Once I am settled, I turn to her. This close, I notice her small stature; her figure is much more petite than what I am used to. I live in a world of glamorous supermodels and Instagram influencers, all of them at least five foot ten inches. My dating pool is exclusively made up of beautiful women with dazzling smiles and deep tans. Women who generally know what their best angles are when anyone brings out a camera.

Talia couldn't be more different if she tried.

She looks up at me, her expression guarded. I have serious doubts that she has ever been the sort of girl who is noticed for anything, much less her looks. Not that she is not pretty, just that she lacks the charisma and self-assurance I usually find in the women I sleep with.

Taking a deep breath, I inhale a lungful of her flowery scent. There is something about her, something untouchable and pure. Something possibly refreshing.

"Are you going to ask me questions or what?" she queries.

Pushing away thoughts of whether or not I find her attractive, I tilt my head to the side. "I want to know about my brother's exploits. In fact, I want to tape-record them. If you are willing to spill your guts on camera, there will be five thousand dollars in it for you. How does that sound?"

Talia scrunches her face up. "I don't know. You want me to admit to sleeping around with your brother on film? Why would you even ask me for that?"

I purse my lips. "What does it matter to you? It's five thousand dollars. You should be happy with that money."

A flare of disgust burst over her face. "You Morgans always seem to throw money at every problem, don't you? It's disgusting."

I arch a brow. "I dare you to act like you don't want this money. Like you don't need it. Everybody needs my money. Everyone thinks that they have a right to it."

She looks away, a muscle working in her jaw. "You don't know anything about me, okay?"

"That's okay. I've got your number. You're just like every other girl. For the right price, you're for sale. Maybe when this is all over, I can entice you to perform for me. I wouldn't have sex with you, of course, but I would like to watch you squirm. Watch you at my mercy. I bet you will do anything for the right price. All women do at some point."

She lets out a humorless laugh. "Maybe all the women that you are used to. In my world, people have integrity."

"Integrity? That's what poor people worry about."

She flashes a bloodless smile at me. "It's good to know that's how you think."

"I'm right. You know I'm right. Can we get on with things now?"

Her lips twitch. "How about this? If I can meet Remy and you give me the five thousand dollars, then I will spill the secrets that you're looking for."

My eyes tightened on her face. "I don't know."

She gives me a pointed look. "I haven't known you for all that long. But I think you know that this is a good deal for you. I am not interested in being videotaped unless I get to meet Remy."

I look at her, wondering if she thinks that meeting Remy will somehow lighten the load placed on her shoulders. I'm pretty sure that Remy is going to laugh her out of his office, assuming that he even agrees to see her. But hey, that's not really my problem, is it?

Nodding slowly, I finally agree to Talia's terms. "Okay. The five thousand dollars, and you can meet Remy at some point."

She comes right back with, "When? When is some point? Because I am not going to record anything until I've already talked to him."

My brow furrows. "And I'm just supposed to trust you?"

Talia looks offended. "Remember how we were just talking about integrity being for poor people? I have integrity in spades. And I will expect you to have it, too, even though I already think you're kind of scummy."

"Scummy?" I reply.

"Yes. It's scummy to ask for a filmed confession of your brother's sex life. It's scummy to hit on me while you try to work this out. You might be a rich man, but I'm starting to think that you might be completely lacking a moral compass."

The way she is looking at me just now, her head turned back and her eyes glinting with accusation, is so confident that I am a little startled by it. My eyes are on her face, scanning her one last time for any trace of deception. But from what I can tell, she seems completely genuine. So, what the hell... Why not just fulfill her one demand right now?

I reach over to the dash of the car, pressing the ignition button. The car roars to life, and I lift my eyebrows in question.

"You said you wanted to meet Remy. Why don't we go right now?"

She pales, her whole-body tensing. "Now?"

"Right now. Unless you have something better to do?"

I watch her as she takes a deep breath, looking all kinds of nervous. "No, I'm not busy."

I throw the Porsche into drive and speed off without another word while she scrambles to pull her seatbelt around her body. I grin to myself, gunning the Porsche's engine and racing off into the night.

Chapter Ten

TALIA

Dare is all grins as we pull up the long, sloping driveway of the Morgan estate. I look behind me and watch as the town of Harwicke falls away, just as the sprawling Gothic revival breaks from the landscape and juts out boldly. I can feel Dare's eyes on me as we pull up the gravel drive, our tires crunching as we come to a stop. Dare jumps out of the car, looking like he can't wait for me to meet Remy. I have a sour feeling in my stomach as I get out of the Porsche and run my fingers through my hair.

I can't look anywhere but at the mansion itself, which stands alone on the top of this bluff like it owns the very air around it, like it was always destined to be here. Without the crowds of people and the cars cluttering the driveway, the mansion itself seems to loom over everything, standing alone and separate from the rest of the town of Harwicke.

"Well?" Dare grips my arm and motions to the huge oak doorway. "Come on then, darling girl. It's your time to shine."

For some reason, his words set my teeth on edge. I make a sour expression and pull from his grip, but he redoubles the contact, gripping my arm harder, forcing me to take his hand. He swings open the massive front door without a word, and I step through, my eyes scanning the massive foyer.

It's all marble and slate floor tiles here. Beyond the foyer is a massive, long hallway clad in dark wood and bright red carpet.

From what I can see right now, the foyer and the hallway beyond could fit my whole tiny two-bedroom bungalow three or maybe four times. To say that I am in awe would probably be an understatement. I'm trying to rapidly calculate how much it must have cost to build and maintain this structure for so long, as the house itself does appear to be quite old.

Dare takes one look at me, rolls his eyes, and reaches out to close my gaping mouth. "Don't act like you've never been anywhere nice before," he hisses.

I clench my jaw and fire a sharp look his way, but he is already looking in another direction. He drags me down the hallway, and I can't help but notice the expensive velvet chairs, long side tables, and priceless art that lines the hallway as soon as we get into it.

I wasn't sure what to expect when I thought of visiting the Morgan estate for the very first time. But this certainly exceeds all my expectations. It may be a desolate old mansion on the highest bluff in town, but its design is quite exceptional, not to mention its vast size.

A man in a full tuxedo with tails appears to our left, coming out of seemingly thin air. His burnished brown skin and close-cut dark hair, graying just at the temples, make him seem distinguished. But when he speaks, it is his English accent that completely throws me for a loop. With a bow, he greets Dare.

"Mr. Morgan," he says. "Welcome back. May I take your coats?"

"Thank you, Clive," Dare says. He claps the man on the shoulder, which seems to give the man a jolt. "That will not be necessary. We're just here to talk to my grandfather."

"Good," Clive says. He bows again. "Mr. Morgan is currently meeting with someone, if you don't mind waiting."

"Really? Who?"

Clive looks at me as if he were deciding whether or not I am trustworthy. His lips press into a thin line, and then he puts his hands behind his back, his face smoothing out into a pleasant expression.

"He is with Charles Adams, Sir. The chief financial officer of Morgan Oil. Mr. Adams is also one of Mr. Morgan's oldest friends, if I were to read between the lines of their business partnership."

The two men interact as though I no longer exist. I peer at the magnificent painting on the wall just behind me, a reproduction of one of Monet's *Water Lilies*, if I am not mistaken. It's enormous in scale and flanked by two overstuffed velvet chaises in delicate gold and amber hues.

I tilt my head, lost in thought, as I try to calculate the cost of just the painting and the chairs. Five thousand? Ten thousand? Yet these two don't even glance at it, despite the painting looming quite largely over everything in this hallway. They have become used to the luxury, I suppose.

"Yes, I know Charles Adams. He has been by Remy's side for ages. He is definitely an esteemed figure." Dare bobs his head, seeming a bit perplexed. "Any idea why he would be meeting with the head accountant of Morgan Oil?"

Clive shakes his head. "That I am afraid I do not know, sir. If you would like, I can take your coats. You can wait by the fire that I have laid in the living room."

"All right, all right." Dare shrugs out of his coat and hands it over.

I freeze, looking at Clive with some bewilderment. I need my coat as a kind of armor against the Morgans. Besides, my fists are balled inside my pockets. If I took the coat off, I would have to figure out what to do with my hands.

My lips twist. "I'll keep my coat, thank you."

Clive lifts a brow but does not respond. He bows again and heads off, disappearing behind a door made of the same wood paneling in which the interior of the long hallway is clad.

Dare walks a little way down the hall, opening a door on the left. He strides through it, expecting me to follow. I frown and hurry after him into the living room. The name of the room made me think of something closed off and cozy.

But the room is vast and has a distinctly masculine energy. There are huge, overstuffed leather couches lining the walls, wood paneling on almost every surface, and the mounted heads of deer, goats, and even a lion. In one corner of the room stands a full-size stuffed bear, fangs and claws outstretched. There are a few bookcases here and there, but most of the floor is taken up by plexiglass displays of smaller creatures that have been stuffed and are posed in the most menacing fashion imaginable.

Dare saunters over to a brown leather couch near the fire-place and sinks down onto it, a pout on his face. He watches me closely as I cross the room and take the seat furthest away from him on the same couch. Our gazes clash, and he raises an eyebrow.

"Would you like a drink?"

"A drink?" I shake my head. "No thanks. I'm here to do business, not have fun."

"Very well," he says. He gives me a little smirk and sits back, pursing his lips. His eyes glitter blue-green with menace.

"You know, in all my hurry to get you to agree to talk about my brother on tape, I haven't asked you a very important question."

I cross my legs and tilt my head. I'm busy looking around, trying to guess how much the trophies that I see displayed in the room actually cost. Were they secondhand, perhaps? Or could I factor in a vacation and a hunting trip for every single one?

It would easily be in the hundreds of thousands of dollars.

"What question is that?" I ask.

"How was the sex?" He grins at me. "I have to say, Burn doesn't seem like the kind of man who makes a satisfying lover. But I have been wrong before. So how was it?

I sputter, shocked. "What?"

"I've always wanted to know what women like about Burn. I mean, he is charming. But how does he even get women into bed? It cannot be very pleasant to someone so self-involved. He is verging on narcissistic, and I think it's very telling."

"You can't be serious. That's very personal." Turning red as a beet, I scowl at him.

Inside, I am really beating myself up because I allowed myself to be put in this situation. Though I can't see how I could've avoided it, I feel stupid.

Dare, on the other hand, seems to be thoroughly enjoying this moment. "I'm just testing the waters. You know you have to be quite explicit when I take your statement. You can't just say that you had sex. I won't be satisfied with that."

I put a hand to my cheek, feeling like I might burst into flames from the embarrassment he is clearly causing on purpose. The knowing look in his eye makes it even worse.

Standing up, I start to pace the floor. "You know, that gives rise to another question. Why do you want to hear about your brother's dirty laundry so badly? You don't seem to me as though you particularly enjoy spending time with me. So, there must be a reason behind your insistence on getting everything on videotape."

He puffs out his cheeks and shoots me a tiny glare. Then he shrugs, clearly irritated by the question. "What business is it of yours?"

Is it strange to say that I get a little pleasure from finding something that is so off-putting to him? I turn on my heel, trying out a smirk on him. It seems to make him fidget, his long fingers drumming rapidly on the brown leather of the couch.

Good. Turnabout is fair play, after all.

"So? Are you going to tell me? Or is it a secret?"

He snarls, jumping up off the couch with surprising speed and grace. He moves towards me, opening his mouth to respond to the question. But just then, I hear a distant voice. The voice is feminine, and it ends with a distinctive, tinkling laugh. I turn my head and realize that Dare has frozen in place, his expression turning black like a thundercloud.

He gives himself a shake, and then he's on me, grabbing me by the arms and hissing a direction at me. "Let's go. Come with me."

I struggle against his grip, looking up into his distracted face. He is looking over his shoulder, and I try to wrench my arms from his grip. He looks at me then, snarling, showing me a glimpse of his perfect teeth. But he doesn't yell at me. Instead, he bends down, grabs me by the waist, and throws me over his shoulder.

My mouth opens and I make a garbled sound of shock, but he smacks me on the ass, hard enough to leave a mark. My ass stings, and I release a howl of shock. But before I say or do anything else, Dare opens a doorway that blends in with the rest of the wood paneling and docks inside a dark passageway.

What the hell? Where is he taking me? That question is very much on my mind as Dare rushes down a passage, then climbs up a set of stairs, taking them two at a time.

At the top of the stairs, he turns left and then opens a door that leads out into the hallway, much like the wood-paneled hallway that I saw earlier. Dare quickly opens another door, this one leading into a navy blue and teak wood bedroom, so I don't get to see much of it. The whole room is dominated by a huge four-poster bed and smells faintly of a delicious bergamot cologne that reminds me instantly of Dare.

It's the cologne that Dare wears. I realize suddenly that this must be Dare's room. Funny, I didn't ever think about what his bedroom would look like. I hadn't even thought about anyone in the Morgan family sleeping anywhere. For all I know, they all sleep upside down, hanging from the ceiling like vampire bats.

But here is the proof. He carries me a few more steps and tosses me down on the bed. My entire body tenses awkwardly, and alarm bells are going off inside my head.

"What are we doing here?" I demand to know. "You can't mean to try to take me to bed like this. I would think that you would at least be more... beguiling, I guess."

He scoffs and backs up, staring at me blackly. "No, you wish."

"I don't want you. And I don't want to be in this bedroom with you right now. In fact, I would very much like to leave now."

Dare laughs; the sound is ugly. "Every woman wants me. Or perhaps I should say that every woman wants my name, my money, and my prestige. Admit it, you would kill to have even a little of my wealth and power."

My chin juts out in defiance. I throw my head back and look up at him.

"I admit nothing. I don't want anything to do with your family. Especially you."

"Really," he challenges. "I think that you don't even know what you want."

My lips part, and I prepare to respond with an argument. But he steps forward again, leaning down close to my face. He moves between my legs and then his big hands grip my waist and pull me against his hard body. He whispers against my lips.

"I'll prove it to you, darling girl."

Without another word of warning, he grabs me like he owns me. He slides his hand up into my hair and pulls my head back, pressing his lips against mine. His lips cover mine; his mouth is so hot that it could melt steel. His tongue snakes out, teasing me, as slippery as an eel but as enticing as ever.

This… This is being kissed.

I am so taken aback that I open my mouth to him and close my eyes. Dare is a very good kisser; his hands are in my hair, and the tip of his tongue is coaxing mine. My pulse is sky high.

In the heat of the moment, I must admit that the weight of Dare's body pressing against mine is alluring. I can admit to myself that, in this moment, I do find him physically attractive.

Not that I ever want him to know. I wouldn't be able to stop him from getting his head around ideas about sex that I have little to no interest in following through on.

So I have to take control of this situation. If I don't stop him, I don't know how far he'll take this.

I push against his chest, but he doesn't even seem to

notice. He is too busy angling my head just so and taking pleasure from my lips on his. I bite his lower lip hard, more on instinct more than anything else. But he immediately shoves me away, touching the spot that I just bit. He looks up at me with outrage in his eyes.

When he pulls his hand away, I can see blood.

"Fucking tease," he hisses.

Breathing hard, I barely have a chance to catch my breath. "You know, you shouldn't kiss people against their will. It's very last century."

Dare pulls a pocket square out of his jacket and wipes away the blood as best he can. He glares at me. "Let's get one thing straight. If I decided I wanted to seduce you, I would. Not only that, but I would make you beg me for it. Not that I would actually fuck you, because you are just a little girl with no money, no class, and no prospects. Are we clear?"

I suck in a breath, cut to my very core. I feel the threat of tears stinging at the corners of my eyes. Dare looks at me, smirking with a self-satisfied expression, blotting off his lip.

Just like I expected. A billionaire is a privileged guy who has never had to worry about anything in his whole damn life. There is a reason that I don't like the Morgan family as a whole. And he is the very personification of just that reason.

Over Dare's shoulder, a throat clears. Dare rolls around and moves out of the way, leaving enough space for me to see that Clive is standing in the doorway, his posture stiff and formal.

He bows and says, "Excuse me, but if you want to get in to see Mr. Morgan, now would be the time. He is wrapping up things with Mr. Adams now, and he has another meeting in just ten minutes."

Dare glares at me dramatically and straightens his posture. "Let's get this over with."

Dare turns and follows Clive, and I in turn follow them both down a narrow set of stairs to the first floor. We emerge just in front of a pair of pocket doors, through which I can hear the low rumbling of a voice. Then suddenly another voice, low-pitched and male, comes in, practically screaming at the other voice to get out of his office.

The pocket doors are wrenched open by an older man in a gray sweater and black slacks, dabbing at his balding forehead with a handkerchief. He looks at Dare and nods ever so briefly, hurrying past and down the long hall toward the foyer.

My eyebrows rise as I turn to see Remy Morgan himself, a squat little man with two huge white lines for eyebrows and a balding pate. He grimaces and swings his head around to take in Dare and I. He is wearing a dark pair of khaki pants and a tan golf shirt. He looks about as inviting as a skull found by the side of the road.

His face crinkles, and he steps out from behind his huge desk, waddling out to the doorway. It takes him a minute, but when he gets there, Clive slides in and hands him a polished black walking cane with an intricate gold monogrammed M carved into the handle. He thanks Clive and then waves him goodbye.

"Well? Clive says that you want to talk to me, Dare. Time is wasting."

Dare tightens his tie and steps forward, a balanced smile on his face. "Hello, grandfather. How have you been?"

Remy looks at his watch. He huffs, standing his cane against the floor. "It's been a busy day. If you could please just get on with it, I have another meeting to attend to."

Dare's lips tighten, but he keeps smiling. "Very well. Grandfather, this is Talia. And she has come to ask for clemency in a financial matter."

Remy cuts Clive a look and leans on his cane, licking his teeth. "That's very demanding of you, young lady."

My heart rate jumps up, making it hard to speak for myself. I clear my throat and stumble over myself as I try to explain my situation.

"Well, sir. You see, my Aunt Minnie has a bookstore and a bungalow, both of which belong to a real estate group owned by your family. In fact, it's our little bookshop that your family shorted when they decided to buy the children's books for the Christmas event at another place after already placing an order for the same books with us. You see, we rely on that money to keep the bookstore afloat. Without it, we are going to have serious financial difficulties. Maybe even with that money, honestly. Aunt Minnie, God bless her, is so charitable and generous that she borrowed money from some suspicious loan shark types to pay for..."

Remy starts yawning during my last sentence, and he throws a hand out, beckoning me to stop mid-sentence. "God, don't make me listen to you tell me the entire financial history of your aunt."

My heart beats so hard in my chest that the blood rushes in my ears loudly. "Sir, that is why you should forgive our debt and pay me for the books that you ordered for Christmas."

"Oh, is that all?" he asks. "For fuck's sake, Dare. I only have a limited number of hours left on the planet. And yet you bring me this?"

Dare shrugs, his smile vanishing. "I don't mean to waste your time, Remy. I brought her here because I thought that you might be inclined to hear her out. My grandmother, Shelley, was often found lost in that bookstore. I thought that maybe you would show some clemency for her favorite store in town."

Remy's eyes narrow on Dare's face. "Don't bring your grandmother into this; God rest her soul. She's got nothing to do with our real estate holdings."

"Sir, if you could just..."

Remy holds up his hand again, stopping my speech mid-sentence once more. "That's enough from you. Now get the fuck out of my office before I start to get upset. And Dare, don't bother me with this little shit ever again."

With that, he turns away, leaning heavily on his cane while he hobbles back toward his desk. Clive looks at us out of the corners of his eyes as he closes the pocket doors of the room.

The tears that threatened earlier? Now they have made good on their promise, blurring my vision. I don't want to cry in front of Dare or Clive. I never want to cry in front of anyone, really. However, having this avenue of financial culpability suddenly cut off from me is a significant blow.

Clive opens his arms and begins to shoo us away from where we are standing. I put my hands over my face, feeling my cheeks fill with blood. This is embarrassing. I've never been rejected quite like this before.

Dare's arm snakes out, and he pulls me along, turning a corner and walking back into the main hallway. "Don't make a scene," he tells me. His voice is flat and emotionless, giving nothing away.

"I'll make a scene if I want to make a scene," I say. I shake off his touch and give him a filthy look. "You don't understand anything. There are people who depend on me just to get by. Then again, how could I even think that you could understand? Just look at you. Look at this place. Look at the splendor and opulence that you grew up around. You have a freaking butler, for God's sake."

Dare frowns at me. "Clive is my grandfather's butler, for your information."

"It doesn't matter!" I shout. "None of it does. Most people don't have this kind of luxury. And it's enough to make me sick."

He looks at me, crossing his arms. He makes no move to comfort me or change my mind in any way.

"Beggars do not get to be choosers, darling girl. You wanted a chance to plead your case to Remy yourself. I gave you that opportunity. Now you give me what I want. That's how this whole thing works. Or am I suddenly the only one with integrity?"

"You know what you are? You are a bastard. A complete heartless bastard."

Turning on my heel, I rush toward the front door, my thoughts a mess.

Chapter Eleven

DARE

Standing in the middle of the echoing hallway, I watch Talia's retreating figure as she practically sprints out of the mansion. I let her go, feeling as though she will come around. Maybe Talia will be mad for a couple of days. But money motivates her. Like all the other women I've ever known, she will eventually fold and take my money.

I look to my left and find Clive standing there, hands behind his back, his eyes narrowing on the door. I jerk my head toward the entrance to the house. "Can you send one of the chauffeurs after her and offer her a ride home? Otherwise, I think she's actually stubborn enough to walk the whole way despite the weather."

Clive bows his head and wordlessly bustles off toward the driveway.

No sooner do I watch Clive disappear do I hear a low rumble of the pocket doors to Remy's study opening. "Clive! Gather all the family. Tell them all that I need to see them now. I expect that they will all be waiting in my study in an hour. I have an announcement to make that I think everyone will find important."

I feel a flutter low in my belly. It may be something like anxiety—a feeling of uncertainty that I usually don't have. I narrow my eyes and push the feeling down, pushing my shoulders back and tensing my jaw. I believe that a person is exactly whatever they want to be; if I want to be confident and ruthless in my business dealings, then by wanting that I shall be. It doesn't work for everyone, I find. But it works for me.

I make my own destiny.

A while later, I'm sitting, drumming my fingers against the dark leather of the couch when Burn arrives with Daisy on his arm. I straighten my posture and cut a glance toward them as they enter. Burn scowls at me. Daisy looks at me, her eyes brightening and a smirk forming on her beautiful lips.

She sashays over to me, her hips swinging, her long hair a dark mass that wraps around her nearly like a cape. She comes right up to me with a hand on her hip and stops to pose and toss her hair.

"Hello, Dare." Her eyes twinkle with a dark kind of mystery.

I struggle not to express my true feelings, which are anger and annoyance at her presence.

"Daisy," I say with a nod. "Don't you have lives to ruin somewhere else?"

She smiles, showing me a hint of her teeth. "Come on now, Dare." She touches my arm, which is honestly almost painful. She rejected me. Doesn't that mean that she doesn't get to pass off such friendly gestures anymore?

I study her, not giving her the satisfaction of knowing that she is having any effect on me. I tilt my head to the side and give her a once-over with a glance.

When I don't say anything, she gives me a little smile and turns, stalking back across the room to where Burn stands with my Uncle Felix, talking about something dastardly, no doubt.

The big surprise is my father showing up. He comes into the room, his suit rumpled, his graying hair sticking out oddly. He looks around the room with a watery blue-green gaze, his smile wobbly. He's drunk, as usual. But he seems like he's only just begun drinking. Usually on any given day, he starts off jovial, then a few hours later he turns morose, and for his final act, he's like a toddler that's gone too long without a nap.

He is a man that's furious with the world and is not afraid to let everyone know it.

"Burn!" he exclaims. He ambles over to his favorite child, giving Burn a rousing clap on the back.

I look away because otherwise I will sneer at this show of filial love.

Burn gives my father a bland smile and slides his arm around Daisy, using her like a shield.

"Dad," Burn says cordially. "I didn't really..."

My father's eyebrows fly up in surprise. He raises his arms, looking around the room as if puzzled. "Do I not belong? I would think you would be glad to see me."

Burn's grip tightens on Daisy's waist. He forces a smile and says, "Of course. Welcome, of course."

My dad laughs; the sound is hard and calloused. "Thank you for your approval of my being here in my own father's home, son."

He claps Burn on the back again, making Burn flinch. Before he even bothers noticing what effects he just had on his child, his gaze swings around to me. A large group of my cousins, aunts, and uncles come in, their faces lighting up as soon as they lay eyes on my twin and his perfect fiancée. I glare at Burn, wishing for a second that I were not part of this family.

My dad is looking me up and down like he is deciding whether or not to even greet me. He smiles again, the expression colder now than it was only a moment ago when he was looking at Burn. I've always been the disappointment, the one who disapproved of my father and his drinking so strongly that I was rigid, even as a child.

"Dare, I didn't realize that you would be joining us."

I arch my brow. "Joining who? I have been here for the better part of two weeks. I think that you are just now joining the family now that Remy might announce some kind of asset splitting in his will or something."

Dad looks at me with disgust. "No. That is not why I'm here. Or not the only reason, anyhow." He fusses with his tie, a dark blue piece of cloth that has seen better days and is wrinkled beyond imagination. He makes a sound, flapping his hand dismissively.

"You always were such a little brat. You know, if it were not for me, you wouldn't even be alive. Your mother wanted to abort you, and I protested her decision. If I hadn't stuck my neck out for you, you wouldn't be standing here right now."

I roll my eyes. "Tell me something I haven't heard you drunkenly rant about five thousand times, Dad. Seriously. I can smell the whiskey coming off you in waves. It's unpleasant to be around."

He shoots me a black look and wags his finger at me.

"You know what you are? You're no fun. And on top of that, you have a bad personality. I have no idea where you got it from. Must be your dead mother."

I bare my teeth at him. "You better walk away now, Dad. Besides, I purposely sat on the other side of the room from the bar cart. I figured that if you showed up, you would be too busy pounding bourbon to bother with me."

For once, the truth is laid bare between us. It feels electric at first, but the feeling quickly goes stale. My father sniffs and walks away, making a beeline for the bar cart now that I've brought his attention to it.

I stand up, and my Uncle Felix crosses the room, frowning as he watches my father pour himself a drink from a crystal decanter.

"That was quite a showdown," Felix says.

I give a tiny shake of my head. "He was asking for it."

"No doubt. That always seems to be his idea of family bonding. He probably thinks he is doing well."

A dark kind of laughter escapes me. I look at Felix, leaning closer so that my voice will not carry. "Any news on the drilling rights?"

Felix just shakes his head and puts a finger to his lips. "Later."

I run my tongue over my teeth, screwing up my face. "Any idea why we are gathered here? Remy didn't really give me any clues."

Felix shakes his head. "No. But I have a bad taste in my mouth, like I am not going to enjoy whatever Remy has to say."

"Shit, I always feel that way too. And more often than not, I am right."

My uncle laughs and looks away. I am left wondering what Remy's announcement could be about. Could he be announcing something related to Talia in some way? It seems unlike Remy to react to talking to someone of her low stature for just a few minutes. But I can't shake the fact that Remy told everyone to gather just after Talia ran out of the house.

Clive enters the living room, looking around and then

carefully dropping a bow. "Mr. Morgan is ready. He asked that only the men of the family gather in his study."

Out of the corner, I see Burn comforting Daisy, who looks rather unhappy. He grabs her hand and kisses her knuckles, smiling at her. "Darling, when you're finally a Morgan, when we have tied the knot, then you can protest all you want."

Her face twitches, and she leans in close, whispering her displeasure into his ear. He nods and kisses her knuckles again. I try not to gag as I exit the living room, following Clive and my Uncle Felix as they make their way to Remy's study. Remy is sitting behind his giant desk, his brow furrowed as he watches us all filter in.

There are maybe twenty people that enter the space, the room is no bigger than twenty by twenty. My father and uncle drop into the seats before the desk, leaving the rest of us to stand awkwardly. I take up a position near the window where I like to stand. My brother takes his usual position by Remy's desk, sitting on its corner.

The little fucker, I think.

The view out the window, which affords the best view in the entire house, just below, the ground that the house is situated on falls away, giving a glimpse of the town of Harwicke below. Remy drums his fingers and waves rather impatiently until we are all in the office, then motions for Clive to close the pocket doors. It all seems pretty ominous, and I have that feeling again, that flip-flop in my stomach that indicates some anxiety. What is he going to announce, exactly?

He coughs when he looks at us. "Family..." He gasps and he coughs again, the sound ragged. "Family is all that matters. And not this namby-pamby, neo-liberal bullshit either. I mean, your blood in your veins is identical to mine. I want you to remember what's most important when I consider who should inherit the company."

Everyone straightens at once, their eyes widening. Whenever Remy says anything remotely like inheritance, you can be damn sure that the sycophants and followers in my family are ready to listen.

Remy clears his throat. "Your grandmother would have wanted to be here to see you get married, Burn and Dare."

I narrow my eyes and tilt my head, trying to puzzle out what he's saying. My grandmother did want her grandsons to marry well. She told us so many times. But she's been dead for years now.

"So why is this suddenly so important?"

Remy holds up his hand, stealing my thoughts. "I know that everyone here is interested in controlling interest in our family company. You're all bloodthirsty bastards, so I don't have to ask what you are thinking. You're thinking of yourselves. Which...... You don't have to explain anything to me. I am as capitalist as they come." He looks around, his eyebrows rising. "I am going to give the reins of the company over to one of my grandsons. Whichever of them marries and has a child first."

"What?" my father asks, sounding horrified. "What about the rest of us?"

Remy jabbed a finger at him, halting his words. "Shut up, Tripp. You cut yourself off when you drove your wife away with your drinking. You and your brother will both get a token amount of my money and not a penny more."

With my mouth hanging wide open, I try to take in Remy's demands. My pulse thunders loudly in my ears.

Married? I never thought about getting married, not since Daisy left me. And now I'm supposed to do it just because my grandfather makes it part of an inheritance race?

Remy glances between my brother and me. My brother

appears to be the polar opposite of frozen, which is how I am feeling. He looks at me, smirking.

Nothing has to be spoken between us for me to understand just what he is thinking. He has already asked Daisy to marry him. That's the very first step. He is already light years ahead of me, and I know it, which makes my blood boil.

Remy makes a gesture, like he's being perfectly reasonable. "Look, twelve months to put a grandchild in front of me. Perhaps eighteen months, if you really have to try." He gives me and my brother a cold smile. "You shouldn't have to. When I married your grandmother, she was pregnant within a month."

"If we don't follow through with your orders?" I find myself asking. "What if we have trouble?"

He sits back in his chair, regarding the room with pursed lips. "Well, then I would have to start looking outside the family. Maybe even selling the company and giving the proceeds to charity when I die." He leans forward suddenly, almost seeming as though he is going to fall out of his chair. He stops himself on the edge of his desk, peering around the room as if issuing a challenge. "Don't make me give the money I worked so hard for away. Bring me a grandchild, both of you."

"Don't you mean a great-grandchild?" my dad asks.

"God dammit, Tripp!" My granddad wheezes. "I am skipping a generation, obviously. Now, if you don't mind, I would like you all to get the fuck out of my office. Burn and Dare have some sweet-talking to do. And the rest of you can get out of the way of men who were actually working."

I stand here, completely shell-shocked by my grandfather's demand.

A family? Kids? Marriage? My whole life, my grandfather has always been so staunchly pro-money, pro-capitalist, and anti-charity. And now this sudden threat to give away everything he worked so hard for?

My Uncle Felix stands up, pointing a finger at Remy. "You're unwell, Dad. You sound like a madman."

My grandfather smacks his lips, giving Felix a heavy dose of side eye. "You. You're the worst one in the whole family. You're a leech and a money grubber. In my will, you get one hundred thousand dollars and not a cent more. Not a cemetery plot, not a vacation house, not the deed to this mansion. You can rot for all I care."

Trembling with fury, Felix glares at his father.

"If I am fucked up, it's only because of the way that you raised me. Look at me. Look at Tripp. Is that the way that you want your own kids to be?"

"As far as I'm concerned, Burn and Dare are my only sons. You were an aberration. I love your grandmother, but she definitely raised you wrong."

"We'll sue you. Right, Tripp?" He looks at my dad, and my dad gives a weary sigh.

"I don't know. Whatever."

Remy chuckles. "If you know what's good for you, Felix, you will toe the line and pretend to be a doting son in hopes that I have a fucking change of heart. Who knows, perhaps on my deathbed I will reconsider."

Felix shakes his head, trembling with his rage. He whirls and stomps out of the room, leaving the rest of us to look after his retreating figure.

"Well? Go on then. Get the fuck out." Remy gestures, shooing us out of his office. "Except Dare and Burn. I have something to tell you."

I glance at Burn, wondering what it could possibly be. He arches his eyebrows but doesn't say anything as the men leave us.

Clive is there to close the doors to Remy's study behind us, leaving Burn, Remy, and me. Remy rocks back in his chair, his lips thinning.

"Since you two are in the running for CEO, I figured you are ready to hear all the news about Morgan Oil, the bad along with the good."

I furrow my brow, trying to figure out what good news Remy gave us. But Burn gives Remy a complacent smile, returning to his favorite perch on the corner of Remy's desk.

"We're all ears, Remy."

Remy looks at him tartly and then opens a drawer in his desk, pulling out a thick dark binder. He waves it at us and then drops it on his desk with a thud.

"You have a decision to make. Our family money is funded through... let's say less than clean sources. Namely smuggling heroin into the country from Canada."

My jaw drops. Burn's expression is one of puzzlement.

"I'm sorry, did you say *heroin*?" I clarify. Remy must mean something else and I'm struggling to understand right now.

Surely that is it.

Remy looks at both of us with a smug smile. "What, did you think that I built this whole empire on some oil fields? No. I'm handing down what my father and his father worked their whole lives to build. Our family has always done very well because we've always been able to smuggle in anything we wanted. Heroin, cocaine, girls... I've made a lot of money loan sharking, too."

I choke a little. "Girls? You mean..."

"Like prostitutes?" Burn asks, his tone accusatory. "Loan sharks? What are you talking about, Remy? Are you feeling all right?"

Remy slides his gaze between Burn and me. "We have

always smuggled in the best stuff from wherever we could source it. It's the backbone of our family business. The oil fields and fracking and all that… that part of the business is booming now. But unfortunately, while I was making that part successful, my business partner was in charge of the heroin and the girls. And he made a mistake."

I straighten, a buzzing sensation in my head. "Mr. Adams? Mr. Adams was your business partner in this… side business?"

Remy nods and flips the binder open. He pushes it across the desk, pursing his lips. "Not a side business. It was the main business when I took up the reins. Now it's mostly in the rearview, but we have a huge problem."

Stepping forward, I pull the binder close. The very first thing I see is a huge picture of the inside of a shipping container. The doors hang open and inside, there are bodies.

Twenty or so that I can see, mostly dark haired, mostly slumped on the floor of the container. All dressed casually, in jeans and lightweight jackets. One of the young women is posed, turned with her face out, her head leaning on her arm. Her complexion looks ever so slightly blue and her pupils are cloudy. There are no other signs of her being dead aside from her not moving.

Below the picture, a headline summarizes. *23 People Found Dead After Being Trafficked By Human Smuggling Ring; Police Say They Are Closing In On Perps.*

"What the fuck?" Burn murmurs. "What is this, Remy?"

"A mistake," Remy says with a shrug. "Charles Adams was here earlier, falling all over himself to explain how it happened on his watch."

I scoff. "A mistake? This is… this is murder, Remy."

Remy points a finger at me, his eyes narrowing to slits. "Do you two really want to get into the nitty gritty details of who did what? Or do you want to know why I am involving you?"

That sucks the air out of the room lightning fast. "Ideally, we'd like to know both."

Remy grips his cane and shoves to his feet with some difficulty, snarling.

"You fucking brats. I provided you with everything you ever wanted your whole goddamned lives. Now you're going to look at me like you had no idea? If that's true, then be glad." He whips the binder off the table and it flies to the wall with a *whap*, falling with a *thunk*. "Be glad that I sacrificed for you two! I didn't have to. I chose to!!"

I am speechless. Burn swallows hard and glances at me.

Remy falls back in his chair, appearing disgusted with both of us.

"This whole mess has to be put on somebody's shoulders. We are going to turn someone into the cops and they will probably go away for life. So I called you two ungrateful bastards in here because I would like you two to be a part of the decision making process. I'm leaning away from Charles, because there is a ton of shit about company business that he could tell the cops." He winces, flip flopping his hand. "There is always the possibility of killing Charles and letting the cops find his suicide note... but I think it raises more questions concerning the company than it answers about his mistake. So I'm asking... who do you think should go down for this?"

"Remy, I don't think I have an answer for you," Burn says.

Remy slams his hand on his desk. "You'd better! I'm thinking that your father or your uncle Felix would work, but there are fifteen people in the company that this fiasco can be put on."

I clear my throat. This whole situation is bizarre. Could Remy be making it all up just to fuck with us?

"Just so I'm clear, whoever we suggest would probably end up murdered as well, right? That's what we're talking about? Murder for hire?"

Remy inclines his head once, something dark flickering in his eyes. He checks his watch then shrugs.

"My next conference call is in a couple of minutes. I have to hit the head. You two can see yourselves out."

He reaches over and pushes a buzzer on his desk, using his cane to get to his feet. He lurches toward the bathroom and doesn't give us another glance.

I look at my brother, mouthing, *what the fuck?*

Burn shakes his head. In a second, Clive rolls the pocket doors open, his expression apologetic as he shoos us out of the room.

"Mr. Morgan has several more phone calls this afternoon. It is unfortunate that he cannot see anyone for the rest of the day."

Crossing my arms, I shoot him a glare. "It's nice that you care about us enough to explain anything, Clive. But we're not fools. We know exactly who Remy is."

Burn snorts but does not say anything. He just turns, looking for Daisy. She comes tripping down the hall, a greedy smile on her face. She throws herself into Burn's arms.

I feel my own arms tensing. Not that long ago, I was the recipient of Daisy's attention. Now I am just another bystander, sentenced to watch her fawn all over my twin. A sick feeling pervades my stomach, making me disgusted by everything I see.

Burn doesn't even notice that I am watching. Instead, he grabs Daisy and swings her around, making the kind of eye contact that makes the rest of the world fade away. There are only Burn and Daisy in their happy little bubble.

"So? What was the meeting about?" Daisy asks, her voice excited.

"The old man declared that whichever of his grandsons marries and has a baby first gets the entire business. Since we're already engaged, that means that I'm going to run the company." He gives her waist a squeeze. "You hear that? I'm going to run the company, baby."

She is less excited now, but still lets Burn hug her.

I notice that Burn doesn't say any of the stuff about dead prostitutes in shipping containers to Daisy. Then again, if I were in his position, I wouldn't either. I'm not even sure if Remy's story is true.

He could just be playing us against each other, seeing who would do his bidding the fastest.

Daisy makes a kissy face and Burn leans in to kiss her, seemingly already lost in Daisy charms.

"You two idiots," I snarl. They turn and look at me, their eyebrows both rising in surprise. It's like they really forgot that they were in front of an audience.

Daisy rolls her eyes delicately. "Dare…"

"You're going to lose, Burn."

Burn scowls at me, his neck heating slightly. "It sounds like you're scared, Dare."

He kisses Daisy on the lips again, looking deep into her eyes once more. "Do not listen to his lunacy. He's just a lone man, howling angrily into the wind."

She glances at me, then slides her eyes back to him. She grins and kisses his lips, smacking them passionately in a way that is overboard and disgustingly sugary. She hugs him, burying her face in his jacket. As soon as she is not looking,

Burn looks dead at me and draws a finger across his throat, imitating a knife.

I shake my head, not interested in inflicting their happiness upon myself anymore. I leave the estate, huffing all the while, more determined than ever that I will destroy their relationship. I will get Talia on tape, describing the sex with Burn. Then I will show it to Daisy and sit back as Daisy rejects Burn.

Then I'll figure out if any of this dead prostitutes business even happened and decide what to do about it from there.

I leave the house and get into my Porsche, gunning the engine and heading towards town.

Chapter Twelve

TALIA

A week later, Dare tracks me down. I've already not been feeling well all day. Hot, cold, cranky, tear-ful... I just need a day to myself. Maybe a little rest to get over this cold or flu thing. But instead, I have pulled several all-nighters at Hope House, filling in for last-minute call-outs of employees. On top of that, I have been working both my bookstore job and my side job as a hostess, trying desperately to pull in any extra money possible.

I didn't have what I considered to be an easy life before this. But ever since I found out that Aunt Minnie owes money to her loan sharks, I have been living in my own personal hell.

I step out of the bookstore with my head down, wondering what I have to do to get myself, Minnie, and Hope House out of this terrible situation that we are in. I'm not really looking where I'm going, so when I barrel straight into a wall of black wool, I look up. An apology is already on my lips.

"I'm sorry..."

Dare looks down at me, smirking, his blue-green gaze

seeming to penetrate right through me. My stomach flips over, like I might be a little bit nauseous. He reaches out and steadies me, his thick arms going around my waist. I look up at his handsome face, feeling a hum of attraction.

God, I almost forgot how handsome he is. But in the next second, he reminds me that he's still a rich prick.

"There you are, darling girl. I've been looking for you." He flashes me a knowing smirk. I have to resist the urge to slap that expression off his face.

I jerk my chin up, looking at him defiantly. "Yeah, I've been avoiding you. It's easy enough. I just have to stay clear of the Raven's Head Club."

His lips twitch. "You're confusing me with Burn. I don't frequent the Raven's Head Club very often. But nonetheless, I have been looking for you."

I struggle with him, but he only holds me closer. I look up into his face and wonder why he's so obsessed with getting my story from me. Surely I can't be the only one who has been caught up with his brother.

For some reason, though, I can't or won't bring that up with him. I think there is some little part of me that loves that this handsome billionaire is all but stalking me.

Dare brings his hand up to my face and brushes away some of my hair from my face with his fingers. It's an unusually touching gesture. But it's followed by words that soon ruin it.

"You can't possibly still be mad, can you?"

I snap out of my reverie and push his hand away, glaring at him. "Of course I am mad. This is my freaking life, not a game. I'm going to lose the bookstore. I'm going to lose the place where I live. And also, more than that, I might lose Hope House. I know that you're richer than God and have rich people problems. But I am a normal person with normal things to worry about. Real things, not silly Morgan family politics."

Dare looks away, pressing his lips into a tight white line. For a second, I watch him, my heart beginning to pound. What is he thinking?

I can't even begin to guess.

He looks back at me, his remarkable eyes spearing me. "What if I offered you ten thousand for a taped confession?"

I blink. "Ten thousand? Just like that? No other strings attached?"

Dare must have a soft underbelly if he is willing to pay me more just because I complained and cried poverty.

Ten grand. That gets my attention. Ten grand is serious money.

He shrugs. "I think we should talk about it more somewhere that isn't icy cold."

Placing my hands on his chest, I separate myself from his body. He lets me go, and I gesture back down the street toward the bookstore. "We can head back to the bookstore. It's closed right now, but it's warm, and there is an office where we can talk."

Some emotion lights his eyes—something dark and needy. He straightens his lapels on his heavy overcoat and nods to me. "Lead the way."

I turn and pull my keys from my pocket, allowing us to enter the bookstore. After he walks in, I lock the door behind him and head straight to the back, bypassing all the books. I can see him looking around, taking in the jumble that is our store. Part of me is embarrassed that I didn't impose more order on everything.

Aunt Minnie has her way of doing things, though.

I walk down a small hallway and open the last door on the right, flipping on the lights in a small, windowless office. My office is possibly the opposite of the bookstore itself. Here, I have instituted precise order over the shelves of books. On the wall, there is a large family tree with research notes in my scrawled handwriting, and below it, an array of photocopied journals and printed headshot style photos. Along the wall, in neat cardboard cartons that are indexed and full of sticky notes, there is more research about my family in particular.

I move behind a small desk, offering him the chair opposite. He doesn't take it. Instead, he walks to the wall and examines my family tree, his finger tracing the roots. "Is this your family?"

I inhale a deep breath. "Yes," I say. For some reason, my voice sounds pinched. "My family was one of the founding families of this town."

Dare glances back at me, a little surprised. "Really?"

"Yes, really."

He roughly rips a piece of paper from the wall, ignoring the thumbtack that is holding it in place and shredding the paper. He brings it closer to his face and I clear my throat, getting up and pulling the paper from his fingers. I gave him a hard stare and replaced the thumbtack, then returned to my desk.

"If you don't mind. I would like to get this over with." I wave my hand at the chair again.

He raises his hands as if I am the one overreacting. But he eventually makes his way over to the chair and sits down.

"Whose office is this?" he asks.

"It's mine. Obviously." I gesture at the wall.

"It's very... Neatly kept."

"You should see my bedroom. Tidy and neat as a pin."

He smirks, making my fingers itch to slap his smug expression off his face. "Is that an invitation?"

I heave a disgusted sigh and shake my head. "You're defi-

DEAL WITH THE DEVIL 141

nitely not coming anywhere near my bedroom, not if I have any say over the matter."

His eyes twinkle for a moment with dark amusement. "We'll see about that."

I huff at his words. "That's a ridiculous thing to say." I adjust my skirt and cross my legs, feeling prim. "Now, about the ten thousand dollars."

He leans forward in his seat, steepling his fingers and looking contemplative. "Yes. I'm thinking that I could pay you five thousand like we talked about to get the story on tape. Then for the other five thousand, I would pay you to actually come with me and confront my brother."

I pale, my heart rate rising suddenly. "What? No. I can't do that."

"Really? Because you are the one who said that you are so hard up for money."

"That's not what I meant," I say, my expression turning bitter.

Dare sits back in his chair, staring at me like he can see right through to my very soul. A long moment elapses. Finally, he flicks his hand out in a *forget about it* gesture.

"Okay. Fine. Make it twenty thousand total. Five thousand for the videotape and fifteen thousand for the bearing witness bit."

At the prospect of twenty thousand, I find myself gripping the side of my desk. "Twenty thousand?" I echo.

"That's what I said. Take it or leave it."

"I... I can't turn that money down. That could save my house. Save this store. Save Hope House from closing."

He rolls his eyes. "Yeah, so I hear. I think I am making a very generous offer."

I lick my lips, my nerves getting the best of me. I stare at him, pinning him in place with my eyes. He doesn't squirm or fidget. He just stares right back at me, unmoved.

"You know, you're a heartless bastard."

"And you are a conniving swindler who is only interested in seeing how much money you can get out of me. We both have our flaws, don't we?"

My jaw drops. "I am not a swindler. And I am not conniving either."

"Agree to disagree," he says firmly. He folds his arms and glares at me.

Before I can even think about the repercussions, words come tumbling out of my mouth. "I think I hate you," I say, a note of confusion evident in my tone.

He doesn't so much as skip a beat. "Don't be fooled, Talia. I feel the fucking same. I just want to get this shit recorded so that I never have to interact with you again."

Staring at my feet, I run my hands along my skirt. "Well, this cannot be over fast enough for me."

He waves me down. "Sit, then. We can do the first bit right now."

Dare pulls out a cell phone, presses a few buttons, and points it at me. I watch him as he does it, wondering how to go about telling him that I don't trust him to just pay me afterward.

Before I can get a word out, he holds up his free hand. "Relax. I will wire the money as soon as possible when I have this video. Okay?"

Teeth clenched, I nod. "Fine."

I look into the camera, my face feeling hot. He stares at me, making a go on gesture behind the camera. I clear my throat and straighten my back, my crossed legs clenching.

"I met Burn at the Raven's Head Club. We talked and drank together. Then we went out to his car, drove to a spot a little outside town, and had sex." I glance at Dare, feeling like I'm at a loss. "Is that good enough?"

"No." Dare looks at his phone, frowning. "Go through it again, with more detail. Especially about you two having sex."

I suck in a deep breath, reminding myself that this moment of embarrassment would not last forever. And I will get five thousand dollars out of a few shameful moments.

"Okay." I look square at the camera, trying not to fidget. "I met Burn at the Raven's Head Club. We talked. He seemed nice enough. We were both drinking. Burn poured me drinks and made sure that I was tipsy, if not drunk. I ended up on his lap. Burn asked me to take a walk with him outside. I did, because I was all flushed, so outside seemed like a refreshingly cool place to go. We ended up walking to his car. He has a fancy car, a Maserati that's bright red. I know because I asked."

I take in another breath and exhale it in a burst of air. "We started kissing. I let myself get carried away. He suggested we get into the car, and then, once inside, we started driving, he drove just a bit out of town to some property he said belonged to his family... we hooked up. It wasn't non consensual or anything. I was tipsy and laughing the whole time. He..." I press a hand to my face, feeling how hot my cheek is. "When we were having sex, he was all raw sex. There was no calling me honey and sweetie. He... he was really complimentary of my breasts. He called them amazing fucking tits."

He looks at me, a hint of fire in his eyes. "My brother wasn't wrong about that. You do have great tits."

I go from red to purple.

"You can see them in your dreams," I say, my tone clipped. "Is that enough for your recording?"

His expression is pinched, closed off and almost angry. I prompt him again. "Is it?"

"How did you get home?" he asks.

"Oh. Well, Burn drove me. It was just a few miles away, on the way to where he was headed. I didn't know where that was. I didn't ask. I didn't even know his last name."

Dare looks at me, irritation clear in his expression. "And did he make you cum?"

I drop my gaze, my cheeks beet red. "I... don't think so. Maybe I don't know."

"How could you not know?" Dare fires back.

"Well, it's not like I do this regularly!" I look up, my expression grim. "I am not usually the kind of girl that goes out, gets drunk, and has a one-night stand with a rich guy in his fancy car."

Dare arches his brow, a little surprised. "Are you saying you were a virgin?"

I clench my teeth again. Part of me wants to lie and tell him that I wasn't. But the larger part of me, the part that values integrity and honesty, won't let me.

"Yes," I hiss. "Okay? It was my first time."

Dare gives a heartless laugh and turns the camera off, putting his phone away. "Your first time was in a car with a guy you didn't know. And you didn't even cum? That's incredible."

It wasn't in the car, it was more like on it, but I keep that to myself. I give him my most profound look of disgust and cross my arms. "Are we done?"

"I don't know. You have anything more to tell me?"

I stare at him, at his perfectly coiffed hair, at his carved cheekbones, at his aristocratic nose, and at his hooded eyes. He is a rich, domineering asshole, and he makes me feel like I am something that he found on the bottom of his shoe. The lowest sort of person. The feeling of being judged and found unworthy swirls around me, misting over my eyes. I blurt out the words before I can hold them back.

"I hate you. I really do."

Dare laughs once more, his voice callous and cold. "Well, that makes two of us. Because I hate you, too. And as soon as I can, I'll be done with you. Give me your phone."

He holds out his hand, gesturing with a *give it to me* motion. I glare at him and hand my phone over. He takes one look at my flip phone and can't contain his amusement. He gives a chortle of surprise, and then he flips it open, dialing a number.

"I didn't even realize they made these anymore." He hits the call button and waits, looking at me.

"You're despicable. A phone is a phone."

His own phone buzzes, and he flips my phone closed, spinning it and handing it back to me.

"I'll be in touch soon. Then we can wrap this business up quickly and get out of each other's hair. I, for one, hope I never see you again."

"You are preaching to the choir," I hiss at him.

With that, he takes off, leaving me seething mad and deeply ashamed of my actions.

Chapter Thirteen

DARE

A week later, I stand with my hands clasped behind my back and look out into the graying mid-afternoon sky. It is cold and rainy here, with the sky indicating that it will soon grow dark. I stand under the small amount of protection that is offered at the Morgan mansion.

Staring down the long driveway, I check my watch, thinking that Talia is going to be late. Then I see a car pulling up the long driveway. It's a Lincoln Town Car, one from a service that I hired, not a Rolls-Royce or a Ford Escalade from my grandfather's fleet of cars. I didn't want anybody to ask questions about Talia, so I decided to use an outside chauffeur service.

At last, the car pulls into the turnabout and stops. I step forward, making sure that Talia is actually the passenger. But she soon emerges, dressed in her usual dowdy corduroy skirt and the same heavy wool coat with worn patches in the sleeves. Her hair is at least brushed this time, and if I am not mistaken, she wears a little rouge on her cheeks.

She does not look half bad. I rake my gaze over her as I take her arm.

She looks at me, her expression catty. "Dare," she says by way of greeting.

My lips twitch. "Talia. You are very nearly late."

"Yet I am not. Let's go. Let's get this over with. I never want anything to do with the Morgan family ever again."

Gripping her by the arm, I turn and head inside. As I step through the threshold, I lean down and whisper a warning into her ear.

"I have you for the entire day. You are bought and sold. And I will choose the right moment to tell my twin's fiancée that he is a dirty cheater. Before that, you should just keep your fucking mouth shut. Smile pretty and act like you fucking belong here."

She shoots me a murderous look, and her mouth thins into a tight white line. I give her a cool smile and continue to usher her through the foyer.

When we reach the long hallway, I pull her to the left, opening a door to the oversized coat closet. She looks at me, poking her tongue out against her cheek, and heads into the little room. I flip the lights on, and she waits until I close the door before cocking her head and motioning at the room. "What's going on?"

"Relax. There's no need to be so uptight. I brought some clothes for you to change into."

Talia's eyebrows fly up. "What?"

Heading over to the wall lined with coats, I fish out a garment bag and present it to her. She looks at me skeptically and takes the bag, pulling the zipper down to reveal a sleek silver dress.

Her mouth turns down at the corners, and her eyes tighten on me. "You didn't say that I would be required to wear a costume."

"It is not a costume. It's a very expensive Valentino dress.

I expect you to put it on and not ask any more questions about it. After all, I could just decide that fifteen thousand dollars is not worth it to me."

Her mouth balls up tight, and she huffs. "Where am I supposed to change?"

I gesture around the room. "Why do you think that we are in a closet?"

"Absolutely not. I'm not changing in front of you."

"Oh, my God." I roll my eyes. "First of all, it's not like I haven't seen everything that you have to offer before. I have seen better, honestly. Second of all, if you are really that uptight, I'll turn my back. Does that make it better?"

"Hardly."

Sucking in my breath. I turn around and peel my own overcoat off to reveal the carefully hand stitched Armani suit underneath.

"I don't hear you changing," I say.

Talia gives a dramatic huff and starts rustling around. She doesn't say anything, so I hang up my overcoat. I turn my head one fourth of the way back, and she makes a loud buzzing sound.

"Don't!" she warns.

I face forward, rolling my eyes. "I was just going to ask if you want me to throw your old clothes away."

She makes an angry sound, and I hear clothes thudding on the floor. "Obviously not, Dare."

I grin a little to myself, unable to help it. It's too easy to mess with Talia. She's so buttoned up and extremely uptight that the opportunity just can't be passed by.

She heaves another sigh and says, "All right, you can look."

I turn around and see her acting like she doesn't know what to do with her body. She is draped in a long silver chain dress that hits the floor with a dramatic flair. At the moment, she is holding the halter top and looking rather distressed. She grimaces.

"Do you mind doing the back? I can't get it on my own."

I smirk and approach, my gaze drawn to her silky smooth, pale skin at her shoulders. Before now she dressed like a freaking nun, so seeing her bare skin is titillating in a certain way. I let my eyes rove over what little there is of her exposed skin as I circle her, drawing my hands over her shoulders.

I will admit, there is something sensual about her back and her shoulder blades. I suppose I would be the same with any woman, but it's even more so with Talia, who resents having her shoulders bare.

It's naughty when I get to look at her. And when I get to skim my hands up her neck?

She shivers, and it is unquestionably sexy. I hear her shuddered inhalation and smile as I take the fabric from her hands and knot it swiftly. As soon as I am done, I smooth my hands over her shoulders once more, but she moves away, turning on me with a spiteful look.

"That's enough," she says. "I can't believe you talked me into this in the first place."

I shrug and point to a shoebox. Talia bends down to open it and finds a pair of silver high-heeled sandals. She puts her feet in them and fastens them without another word, but she glares at me, making her feelings known.

As if I had any question about that.

Giving her a careful smile, I reach for a shopping bag and unveil a long blonde wig. It's styled to perfection, and it features a champagne colored, multi-tiered look.

Talia gives me a flat look. "I think that's overkill, don't you? After all, Burn might not even recognize me."

"Well, that's what I'm counting on. But all that lovely copper hair of yours makes you pretty easy to spot."

"Is that a compliment? Do you find me memorable?" She asks.

I level a gaze at her. "Come on. Put the wig on. Weren't you the one that was just saying how much you want to just get this over with?"

She takes the wig from me, looking at me as she puts it on. After fussing with it for thirty seconds, she puts her hands on her hips and looks at me, presenting herself for final inspection.

"What do you think?" She asks. "Do I pass the test?"

I give her a small smile and nod. "You'll do. Let's go."

We step out of the coat closet, leaving the mess of her clothes behind. As we head down the hallway once more, Talia catches her reflection in a mirror and freezes. Her eyes are wide; her gaze is glued on her figure in the dress.

"What?" I ask, losing patience with her.

"I just..." She shakes her head. "I barely recognize myself. This dress is so different from what I would normally wear."

"That's the point, don't you think?"

"I... I guess."

I put my arm around her waist, pulling her away from the mirror. She totters for a few moments, struggling to walk in the high heels I gave her. But after a moment, she finds her balance.

I cast a gaze down her figure, thinking to myself that if I weren't so laser focused on rubbing my brother's misdeeds in Daisy's face, I might be able to take the time to admit that Talia isn't horrible looking. In fact, she is rather the opposite of horrible-looking.

With her borrowed clothes and long blonde wig, I find her extremely attractive.

Her ass looks like you could bounce a quarter off it in this dress and the perky mounds of her tits almost knock the breath out of me. I can see exactly why Burn picked her.

She's hot, under all that dumpy junk that she usually wears.

She feels me looking at her and eyes me sternly. "Don't get any ideas, you overgrown bully."

Arching my brow, I feign surprise. "Me? Get ideas? I would never."

She rolls her eyes. "Are you worried about Remy recognizing me? It's only been a few days since I was in front of him in his office."

I give a snort. "No way. He has definitely forgotten about you by now. He has always been forgetful, especially of younger women. No offense, but he doesn't really see you as being a full person."

Talia elbows me in the side, scowling. I raise my hand, gesturing.

"Hey, it's not my point of view. It's my grandfather's. He's never had a good memory for people, and now he has to be reminded who the wives of his nieces and nephews are."

She stops, pulling at the side of her dress. "Okay. Let's just hurry this along. This dress is really itchy, not to mention the fact that I'm afraid that one of my boobs will fall out somehow."

"I have you for the full day. So just suck it up. It's the last day that you will ever have to see the Morgan family."

We head into the living room after I adjust our poses so that Talia holds onto my arm.

"One more thing," I whisper. She looks at me, arching a brow.

"I know that you aren't very good at hiding your emotions. Keep a blank face while you're at the Morgan estate. Trust me, you'll thank me later for warning you."

I'm expecting a glare or an eye roll. But instead she looks at me passively, not reacting to what I said in any way.

A smile plays upon my lips, and I tilt my head toward the living room. "Come on. Let's go into the lion's den."

When we enter the living room, the rest of the players are already there. Uncle Felix is standing and telling an animated story to one of my cousins. My father, Tripp, is at the bar cart, his usual hangout, pouring a drink and looking around the room suspiciously. My brother Burn stands on the far side of the room, his grip on Daisy's waist reminding me of a python and its prey. In the corner near the entrance to the servants' passage, Clive stands with his hands clasped behind his back and his head bowed as he whispers something to Magda.

Other cousins lounge here and there, but those are the main family members that I need to keep an eye on. I draw a long breath and try to steel myself.

Talia glances up at me, her fingers gripping my arm tighter. I make eye contact with her and give her a tiny head shake. I walk her over to the fireplace and try to decide which family member I should tackle first. I'm thinking of my uncle Felix, being that he is the friendliest of the bunch. By friendliest, I mean he stands to gain something by kissing my ass.

But before I can do that, Magda makes a beeline for me. I glance at Burn, seeing that he has noticed my presence. Daisy is looking at me, too, her brow lowered, a frown on her perfect lips. Actually, she's looking at Talia, not me.

Do I dare hope that Daisy is displaying jealousy over my turning up here with a new toy on my arm?

"Dare!" Magda says. She stops just short of plowing into me, instead hugging me very briefly. Her smile is over the top, with dimples upon dimples. "It's good that you came for your father's birthday."

Talia scrunches her face up and looks at me critically. "It's your father's birthday?"

I nod, already weary of the subject. "Yeah. This little shindig is just a get-together to celebrate it."

Magda puts her hand out to Talia, skipping over the part of my introduction.

"I am Magda, the house chef. And you are?"

Talia steps out of my sheltering arm and shakes Magda's hand with both of hers. She looks Magda right in the face, making it clear that she is engaged with what is going on.

"Magda. So nice to meet you. I am Talia. I am just here as Dare's date for the evening."

I move forward and slide my arm around Talia again, pulling Talia's body against my own. "Maybe she could be more. We'll see."

Talia shoots me a glance but doesn't say anything in response. Magda beams at us both, practically beside herself. She looks at Talia and then motions for her to move closer. Magda whispers something in her ear, making Talia blush. Then Magda looks at me, pats my cheek, and hurries out of the room.

I watch her go, bewildered. "What was that? What did she say?"

Talia gives a gentle shrug and shakes her head. "It was nothing."

"It did not look like nothing," I say.

Just then, Daisy breaks away from Burn and plunges across the room, her hand raised for a handshake. Her gaze is fixed on Talia, and I have a sinking feeling that I know exactly what is coming.

"Dare!" Daisy crows, a strange smile on her face. "You didn't introduce me to your guest."

Daisy rushes up to Talia, grabbing her hand and squeezing her arm forcefully. The two women are thrown into contrast for a long second. Talia, in her blonde wig and her silver dress, is nervously peeking at me. In contrast, Daisy is tall and so thin she's nearly emaciated, her long hair a dark mass on her shoulders. It occurs to me just at this moment that Talia is pale next to Daisy, who is sun-kissed and confident.

I step closer to Talia, a careful smile on my lips. "Daisy. Always a pleasure to see you. This is my date, Talia."

I slip an arm around Talia and give her an encouraging hug. The embrace is performative, more for Daisy than it is for Talia. But Talia seems to lean into me in a way that I'll admit that I like.

"How do you know Dare?" Talia asks Daisy.

Daisy flashes a smirk and raises her eyebrows at me. "I don't know. How do we know each other, Dare? What do you want to tell little Talia about our relationship?"

Burn ambles over, taking up his place next to Daisy. Daisy grabs his hand and intertwines her own, her smile dry.

"Daisy and I used to date. Now she is with my brother Burn." I gesture to Burn, and he tilts his head to the side. "They are engaged, actually."

I can tell by the slight rise in Talia's brows that she is just now putting together all the information. She looks at me, clearly unable to say whatever she is thinking. I can see her throat working as she swallows.

Talia's hand finds my forearm and grips it hard. I smile as I introduce her to Burn.

"This is Burn. If you hadn't guessed, we are identical twins."

Burn is looking at Talia with a hint of puzzlement on his face. He reaches his hand out to her, and she shakily takes it, her face somber as she greets him.

"Hello."

Burn takes a deep breath. "I see you have met my fiancée, Daisy. I'm telling you now, meeting the rest of the family is pointless. When I got here, Tripp was just telling a story about how he got out of a speeding ticket by telling the sheriff that he had Morgan money and he would get the sheriff fired. So that's the kind of mojo that we are working with."

Talia arches an eyebrow, glancing at me. She smiles and bows her head ever so slightly. "Good to know," she says to Burn.

Daisy cuts in. "So how do you two know each other? Did you meet doing volunteer work or at a flea market or something?"

"No. We just met through friends," I reply smoothly.

Burn joins in on his fiancée's gentle ribbing and smirks. "Are you sure that you didn't find her at a homeless shelter or something, Dare?"

I see Talia's face fall. She looks at Burn with a profound disgust in her eyes. "Are you suggesting that I am homeless?"

Burn seems a little caught out. He holds up a hand, as if that can excuse him somehow. "I was just joking, Talia. Just teasing my brother."

"Well, it isn't funny. It is not nice to make fun of people that you don't know just to get a rise out of each other."

She turns her gaze to me, her mouth forming a hard line. I pull her closer, unsure where this passion of hers came from. I have to admit, it's not unwarranted in this situation, and I even like it. That is, when Talia is schooling my brother instead of me.

Daisy gives a huge fake smile and tries to ease the tension between us. "Burn didn't mean anything by it, honestly. He would never intentionally make anyone uncomfortable, Talia." She looks at Burn, and he looks at her. After a second, they move together and lock lips, kissing hard and making little noises of pleasure.

I roll my eyes. I glance at Talia, and I jerk my head toward my uncle. But before I can say anything, Burn and Daisy separate and lovingly smile at each other.

That sick feeling in the pit of my stomach has now returned.

It's time for me to hint at her purpose in being here. I can see that now. I shift my weight, moving my arm from around her waist to around her shoulders, and pull her a little closer.

"You know, Burn..." My lips twitch. Though I feel ill inside, outside I am cool, collected, calm, and confident. "Did you know that Talia and I have a very deep connection as well? We've been talking about everything. And I do mean everything."

Burn stares at me, his eyes narrowing on my face. Talia looks between Daisy, Burn, and me, possibly trying to figure out what exactly our deal is.

I slip my fingers around the curve of Talia's hip, smiling as I make heavy eye contact with Burn. "We've been talking about everything under the sun. Telling stories, reliving moments from our lives."

I cock my brow at him, and his gaze hardens. I am willing to bet that Burn is now racking his brain to figure out why it is that Talia looks so familiar. Or maybe not. His clear confusion is the very reason why I spent so much time and put so much effort into dressing her up. Without her dumpy outfit and with her copper hair covered under that wig, it is nearly impossible to recognize Talia.

Burn looks between me and Talia and then gives his head a shake. He leans his head over and kisses Daisy's cheek. "My love, why don't we go and talk to my father? It's his birthday, after all."

Daisy clearly does not think much of this idea. But she forces a smile onto her lips anyway and brings his hand up, kissing the back. "Of course, my love. I'll follow you anywhere."

Burn stretches his arm out and takes Daisy by the shoulders. Daisy casts her gaze back at me with a smug little smile on her lips.

God, what a manipulative woman she is! How was I ever the object of her attentions? I have no doubt that I acted just like Burn does, but seeing it now from the outside, I shudder a little.

Whatever the case, I am planning on letting my twin brother sweat for an hour before I reveal Talia's true identity. Then I will rub the fact that Burn is a cheater in her face. It is so close that I can almost taste it.

Talia wiggles out of my grip, coming around to block my view of Daisy. She puts her hands on her hips and tilts her head, pinning me in place with her cool blue stare. "Why didn't you tell me about Daisy?"

A feeling of unease creeps up my spine like an icy hand. "I don't know what you mean. What about her?"

Talia sucks in her breath. "You didn't say anything about the fact that you are desperately in love with Daisy and trying to steal her back from your brother."

I grit my teeth, a little shaken that she might have somehow picked up on some lingering emotions between me and Daisy with such quickness. I must not be hiding my feelings well.

"That is not what's happening. I assure you that it isn't

love I feel when I see Daisy. All I feel is resentment. I want to rub her nose in the fact that my brother is a cheater."

Talia crosses her arms, looking at me with a careful expression. "You shouldn't tell her anything. Honestly. It will not matter to Daisy, not like you think it will. And then you will still be left holding the bag when it comes to things between you and Burn. You two are brothers, not enemies."

I laugh half-heartedly. "That's where you're wrong. Daisy left me for my brother because we look the same. She said that she was getting an upgrade. And Burn encouraged her. So I am going to rub her face that she chose an unfaithful man. I can't wait to sit back and enjoy the look on her face when I tell her."

Her mouth opens in protest, but I put a finger to her lips, giving her a warning look. "Mind your own business. You're only here as a bit-part actress. You should keep your opinions to yourself. You're here because you have been paid to tell your story. Nothing more. Do you understand what I'm saying?"

Her eyes flash furiously at me. Her mouth thins. But she does not say a word. She just continues to look at me as though I am disappointing her somehow.

As if I could ever be a disappointment to someone like her, someone who was born into poverty and is only here because of my money. I turn, straightening the cuffs of my shirt and looking around the room. She follows my gaze, seemingly unsure about everything.

"So, what now?"

I purse my lips and shrug. "I don't know. We were waiting for a sighting of Remy, eventually. It should be some-time within the next hour or two. Until then…" I cast a glance around the room. "Everyone in here is trying to size up Burn and me. It's a little tiring."

"Size you up for what?" Talia asked.

I flick my fingers out in a gesture that says it does not really matter. "Remy is insisting on a race between my brother and me to own the majority share of the business. Essentially, my grandfather says that the first one of us that is a married man with a grandchild to present to him will then gain control of the company and billions of dollars." I straighten my tie and roll my eyes. "It's unfair, but when was anything Remy decided to be fair?"

"That's insane. He knows that's insane, right?" She looks at me, her brow furrowed.

Giving her a sideways glance, I smirk. "You know, if I didn't dislike your personality so much, you would have made a nice wife for me. Really drive the nail head home and stick it to Burn. In fact, when you were telling me the story of the night that you got drunk after Raven's Head and thought I was my brother, I was thinking how funny it was. I almost went to the Raven's Head Club that night with Burn. But we bickered, and I decided not to go. So we almost crossed paths, except that fate didn't see fit."

Talia glares at me. "The reason that it wouldn't have taken place the way that you picture it is because your brother actually charmed me. I can't imagine you seducing anyone into anything."

"Can't you, though?" I give her a wicked grin.

She huffs a little. "I really hate you."

"And I hate you. But what is a little hatred among two attractive people? We can just fuck, enjoy each other's bodies, and then part satiated. No muss, no fuss, no feelings."

Her lips part.

But at that very moment, Remy chooses to make his appearance. He strolls into the room, his gold-tipped cane in one hand, and Clive hovering nervously near him the whole time. Remy runs a hand over his bald head and flicks a dismissive hand at Clive. "All right, I'm all right. I'm in the living room now. Happy?"

"Remy!" Daisy calls out. "It's so nice to see you."

Remy screws up his face and gestures to Clive, who whispers in Remy's ear. Remy then looks at Daisy and says, "It's Mr. Morgan to you. You're not family yet."

Daisy gulps and clutches at Burn, who is quick to give her his hand. My father stumbles away from the bar cart, drunkenly jubilant.

He raises his tumbler of whiskey to Remy. "It's good to see you, Dad. Here I was, waiting all night for you to show up. Story of my life, am I right?"

My dad laughs and looks around, perhaps expecting someone to chime in. But no one does. Everyone here is supported by Remy, in some fashion. It's better not to bite the hand that feeds you, and every single person in this room knows it.

My Uncle Felix shoves his hand through his hair and moves forward, grabbing my father and holding him up. "Tripp, why don't we get some fresh air?"

"Yes, Tripp. Why don't you get some fresh air?"

Remy hobbles away from his two sons, out into the middle of the room. He beckons to Clive, and Clive hands him a glass of red wine, giving Remy a fearful look as he hands it over. Remy grips the stem and lifts the wine high in the air. As Felix helps my drunken father out of the room, Remy starts telling a story about my grandmother.

"She was wonderful. She will always be present. And she has visited me several times in my dreams. That's how I came up with the challenge to pit my two grandsons together. The inheritance race was her idea."

At the door, my dad freezes. Felix tugs on his arm, but he

turns around and blows a raspberry. "Your story sucks, Remy!"

Remy scowls at my father. "And what would you know about it, Tripp?"

"I know that it's not real. I know the difference between reality and fantasy. That's one thing that's different between me and you."

"Fuck you," Remy hisses.

Tripp straightens and takes a wobbly step towards my grandfather. "You know, my wife might as well have died. She left the whole family in the lurch. But you don't see me blubbering on about it, do you?"

Remy goes red, seething. "You drove your wife away with your drinking. You ruined your family. That is not my fault, Tripp. No matter how many times you accuse me of it, it really comes down to you and your flaws."

I feel my whole body lock up. I don't want anybody knowing this much about my family, but especially Talia. In the usual course of things, we Morgans succeed in keeping things calm and normal as far as outsiders can see.

Most people don't realize how broken and fucked up we are.

Talia looks at me, her eyes wide. But it's difficult for me to remain calm as I watch my father and grandfather go round and round at each other.

I wish I could say that this was the first time that I've seen such bad behavior between them.

My dad leans in, his face red. "It was the family that drove her away. Not me. You can say it was my drinking until the cows come home, but we all know the truth. Nobody ever wanted her here. And that's what eventually came to be."

Remy's lips curl. "You don't deserve to have your birthday celebrated. You don't even deserve to call yourself my son. That's it, you are officially cut off. You're not getting any inheritance, and I am not supporting you financially anymore either."

"I hate you!" my father says, as he lunges toward my grandfather.

His movements are hobbled by my Uncle Felix, who catches him and pushes him against the wall. Remy growls and makes moves toward my dad, but Clive neatly sidelines him by stepping in front of him and asking him a question.

"Everybody out!" Remy shouts. "I don't want to see any of you anymore. Go back to your lairs and plot against me some more, why don't you?"

I realize that Remy can't leave the room until my Dad does. So I grab Talia by the arm and steer her over to Clive, touching his arm.

When he looks at me, I tell him in a low tone, "Can you see that Talia gets home? I have to go deal with my father."

Clive bows and agrees. I tell Talia that I will see her later; I am not in any position to worry myself over her concerned gaze.

Rushing towards the door, I help Felix grab my father by the elbow. Working together, we get Tripp out of the room and down the hall, the opposite direction Remy needs to go up the stairs.

"What should we do with him?" Felix mutters, hazarding me a glance.

"I don't know. Throw him in the gutter maybe?" I joke.

Tripp raises his head and swivels his gaze toward me. "You know," he says quite drunkenly. He is tripping over his words, all the consonants and vowels sloshing together. "Your mother would not have liked who you grew up to be. She would've been ashamed of you. You're a terrible disappointment."

I give a startled laugh and tell him to shut up. Felix looks at me sympathetically, and we each take one of my dad's elbows and hold him up, maneuvering toward the front door. I feel blooms of anger and a deep, dark sadness. But I stuff it down, just like I always do when the Morgan family is involved.

Chapter Fourteen

TALIA

"No, no," my Aunt Minnie says as she looks at how I'm stacking the books in our store's display window. "These are children's books. They may just be the books that the Morgan family didn't want. But in order to capture our target audience, that being children, we have to entice them in an unexpected way."

She gestures to the books that I've just stacked in a neat pile, with one book leaning on the front to show the illustration.

"I'm not sure how you want me to stack them. You didn't provide any instructions." I give my Aunt Minnie a long look and wave at the stack to invite her to arrange them as she wants them.

"I swear, the artistic gene just skipped over you entirely." Aunt Minnie comes over and tousles the stack of books, nudging some out and arranging them in a pleasing pattern. She looks back at me, cocking her head. "See? It's important to make the display alluring."

Muffling a sigh, I give her a small smile. The whole window display is done in Minnie's aesthetic style. She's redone the entire window and now it features loud, hot pink, and lime green paper cutouts, some in snowflake patterns, some in three-dimensional origami stars. Overall, it actually looks surprisingly attractive. But it's not something that the average person would ever dream up, especially not for a window display.

"It looks great," I tell her. "I'm sure that it will help us move all the books that the Morgans didn't pay for, or, at the very least, a portion of them."

Aunt Minnie climbs up the ladder she has placed by the window and starts arranging the hanging stars. They are tacked to the ceiling and hung with lengths of sewing thread.

They look very kitschy. It is all *very* Aunt Minnie.

This is how it usually goes. Aunt Minnie dresses the window, and I help her with a smile. Today, though, that smile is missing. Or rather, it is pasted on and phony, only brought up when I am directly challenged on why it is not there.

Minnie snaps her fingers, trying to lure me out of my daydream once again. "Talia? I swear, this window display would've been done an hour ago if your head wasn't so firmly in the clouds."

"Sorry." I shake my head. "I'm not sure why I am so distracted today."

Minnie arches a brow and holds a beautiful three-dimensional star up by its long string, shaking it gently. "It wouldn't have anything to do with what I told you the other night, would it?"

My cheeks flush. Her news, which she told me the other night, that she owes some bad people a lot of money, has not been far from my mind since she uttered it to me. But that isn't really the whole reason.

I push that reason down in my mind, forcing a smile onto

my lips. "It's nothing. I promise. Just... Something Olive told me. Nothing to do with the store."

It isn't technically a lie. More like a fib. An omission of the truth. After all, Olivia did tell me to get the test, which now lies in my purse behind the register.

Aunt Minnie looks down, frowning in concentration as her fingers fly over a piece of paper. About a year ago, Aunt Minnie picked up origami as a hobby of sorts. Since then, she has gone from flooding the bungalow that we live in with paper cranes to these more elaborate three-dimensional stars that take her fifteen minutes to build.

I drift off again as she works, my mind pulled into my actual worry. *What if I am pregnant?*

The only way to find out is to take the test, obviously. But in order to do that, I need Minnie to leave me alone in the store for an hour, just to be sure that I can have loud, messy emotions without her finding out.

I gulp. Aunt Minnie straightens and pulls a paper hat on her head, lifting a funny, bright green paper mustache to the top of her lips. She strikes a pose, raising her eyebrows in question. "What do you think? I'm thinking that I'll hang a few hats like this one from the ceiling, and then I'll have a dish of these mustaches handy, making our display window a cool place for people to take selfies."

I blink and nod slowly. "Wow. I did not think you would be so forward about something involving modern technology. That's really progressive of you."

Grinning, Aunt Minnie wiggles her eyebrows. "This old dog still has new tricks up her sleeve."

I narrow my eyes on her face, trying to parse out the two idioms that she mashed together to produce that sentence. Of her many quirks, that's one of her most confusing ones. It's definitely a verbal tic, because when it was pointed out to Aunt Minnie, she claimed to not realize that she even did it.

"I think it's a great idea," I add. "Definitely forward-thinking."

Aunt Minnie pauses, still holding the hat and mustache in place. "You think so? I'm just trying to keep the young people engaged. Would you take a picture of me?"

This time, my smile is more genuine. "Of course." I pull my cell phone out and snap a couple of pictures, though my cell phone doesn't capture images very well. I figure that's fine, since I don't think that Aunt Minnie cares so much about my skill as a photographer anyway.

Minnie gets wobbly on the way down when she finally descends the ladder. I step in and put my hands under her elbows, helping her down the last couple of steps.

Aunt Minnie turns around and hugs me, burying her face in my hair. She's the same height as me, but frail and wiry, her gray hair tickling my nose as she presses her face against my shoulder.

"Thanks, kiddo."

She holds me close for several seconds. I take a deep breath, inhaling her scent of violet perfume and menthol cough drops. The scent is comforting, sinking into my bones. It occurs to me that I haven't hugged anyone in a while, and I feel like I should hug Aunt Minnie whenever I get the chance. I never know what life is going to throw my way. If I have learned anything, it's that my time with my loved ones is a precious commodity.

When Minnie pulls back, gently pushing against my shoulders, I let go. I am quick to wipe away the moistness that pools in the corners of my eyes.

Feeling silly, I clear my throat and look Minnie in the eye.

"I love you," I say. "I don't know if I told you that recently or not."

Aunt Minnie gives me a beautiful smile. "I love you, too, kiddo. I feel like maybe I don't say it enough. But your coming into my life was the best thing that ever happened to me."

She turns on her heel, heading away from me. I am left blotting the corners of my eyes; my voice has been stolen by Aunt Minnie dropping that bomb on me.

In a world that seems hard and unfeeling, I have at least one person in my corner. It is always really nice to be reminded of that.

"Talia!" Minnie calls. She is rooting around in the back hallway. I close the front door and change the sign to say *back in a minute.* Then I head into the back, finding Minnie in her small space.

Minnie's space looks like an absolute disaster, a closet straight out of an interior designer's nightmare. There are art supplies and books and odd scraps of paper with Aunt Minnie's handwriting scrawled on them, all mixed together. Aunt Minnie is pulling on her coat, which she liberated very recently from under a pile of googly eyes. She looks up at me, pulling a beret over her head, and smiling again.

"I'm off to volunteer at Hope House," she announces. "All the kids say that they miss seeing you every day."

I inhale, stinging from that revelation. "It's true; I haven't been there recently. But I thought they had a fresh batch of volunteers."

Minnie buttons her coat and gives me a look. "They do. We are beyond set up for volunteers for the next two months. That doesn't mean that the kids miss you any less, though."

I nod, my smile falling away. "I know. Things have just been crazy for the last week. I have been so busy between my shifts here and at the restaurant. Plus, I have this ongoing project that I'm working on with Olivia."

I don't mention to Aunt Minnie that *the project* is what I am calling Dare. I rush to assure my aunt. "My project will be completed pretty soon. I swear."

Minnie moves forward to give me another quick hug and pats my shoulder. "That's good, kiddo. I am just passing on a message. I'm not really concerned about it either way. I just want you to be healthy and happy."

She gently moves me out of the doorway and starts toward the front. I lick my lips, feeling terrible. Not being able to confide in Aunt Minnie is hard. But I tell myself that it will only last a little bit longer.

At least, that is the plan.

As soon as she is gone, I walk to the desk, my eyes riveted on my boho bag. I dig through the contents and quickly pull out the box that I've been thinking about all day.

I swallow, and my pulse races as I cup the pregnancy test in my hands. My hands shake as I turn it over.

In just ninety seconds, you can find out if you are pregnant.

I can feel the sweat breaking out across my brow. The bell at the door chimes, and I look up, ready to tell any customers that the bookshop is closed for lunch right now.

But then I see Olivia walk into the store, her brown hair falling around her shoulders. She has a worried expression on her face. I let out a moan, holding up the box for her to see. Her brow knits as she rushes over to me and hugs me tightly. I hold onto her for a second longer than is strictly necessary, taking comfort in her embrace.

She looks at the box in my hand and nods solemnly. "I'll

get the lock on the front door. You have got to do this right now. This is the only way to be sure."

I inhale, suddenly feeling like her words have given me a blow to my stomach. She turns and heads to the front door, and I go to the little bathroom down the hall. I nervously open the box and stare at the applicator.

My entire future has turned into a series of question marks. It's all very opaque and uncertain.

After peeing on the test strip, I can't stand to stay in the bathroom with the test. That test holds so many answers about exactly what my future will be.

I can't even look at it as I close the bathroom door behind me. I exhale when I'm on the other side of the door. As if the meager shelter is protecting me from that little test that could destroy my life.

I press my knuckles against my lips and close my eyes, trying to remember how to breathe. When Olivia's hands gently grip my arms, I jump, and my eyes pop open. She gives me a soothing look.

"Why don't we go wait in your office?"

I nod, and she herds me down the hallway and into my small, tidy space. She closes the door after me and sits me down in the chair opposite the desk. This is usually the guest chair, hardly ever used, but now it saves my shaky legs from failing me. I rest, grateful for the furniture.

"Talia," Olivia says. "Look at me."

Swallowing, I raise my eyes to her face. She kneels in front of me, her hands taking up space on my knee. She looks up at me and smiles, reaching up and tucking a strand of my copper hair behind my ear.

"It's going to be okay, no matter what the test says. Okay?"

I shake my head.

"You don't... You don't know that," I stutter.

She purses her lips and tilts her head to one side. "Talia. You are the one who has always told me that you want a family. In fact, you told me several times that you want seven kids. That's a lot, by the way."

I rub my temples, feeling like I have a headache brewing. "I do want a family. I've always wanted a chance to have a big family full of laughter and love. But this is not how a family starts. This is an accident. A mistake."

"Only if you choose to look at it that way. You don't have to. Also, there is no rule saying that you have to have a child now. Assuming that, you know, the test is positive."

The idea of having an abortion is not exactly appealing to me. I'm all for easy access to abortion and family planning. I feel strongly about it, in fact. But actually having one of my own?

I can't fathom it.

I suck in a breath. "I've always said that when I finally got the chance, I would do it right. I would find a husband who dotes on me. I would wait a year or so after we got married to ensure that we were actually meant to be together. And then I would get pregnant. Not like this. Not... with *him*."

Olivia's shrugs. "I assume that it's Burn Morgan's baby that we are talking about here, in theory."

"Yeah, unfortunately. The most unlikable asshole ever. Plus, he is definitely engaged. I have met his fiancée. She is no blooming rose, either."

Her mouth turns down at the corners. "It is unfortunate that it would be his," she admits.

I look skyward, almost pleading with the heavens. "I don't even know how I will continue to feed myself, much less another mouth. It just isn't feasible to have a baby right now. I spent my whole life going to school with brown paper bag lunches, wearing three sweaters inside the house to cut down on heating costs, and clipping coupons. I've scrimped and saved, and I've been concerned about money every waking minute of my life. I was determined never to be a burden to Aunt Minnie or anyone else." My eyes fill with tears, a sudden wall of emotion threatening to crush me.

"You are not a burden on anyone," Olivia says tartly. "I don't want to hear you talking like that ever again."

"I'm just... so disappointed in myself." I drop my face to my hands and cover my eyes. "I can't believe I went out and got drunk one time. Of course I wound up pregnant because of it. *Of course I did.*"

"You don't know that you're actually pregnant. Just to bring some sense of reality to this situation."

My eyes well up with tears, and my words are cut short by hiccups. "How could I have been so careless? I can just imagine being nine months pregnant and homeless. In what world is that okay?" My words reach a frenzied peak. "That's not even taking into consideration who the father is. I would rather run through a hail of bullets than contemplate bringing up a child in that family. I have been in the room with all the Morgans. I am telling you right now, that's a new level of dysfunction that I am not willing to inflict on a helpless child."

"Okay. Okay." Olivia pulls me into her arms, her hand caressing the back of my head. "Okay. Let it out. You're not even sure that you're pregnant. You don't even have to decide right now whether you're going to have a baby with one of the Morgans. Okay?"

I feel as if I'm being ripped limb from limb. But I try to calm my crying. I don't want to be a burden on my best friend, especially by using her as an emotional crutch. I breathe out through my mouth and try to regulate my heart-beat. At length, I raise my head, wiping my eyes. I blow out a breath and shake my head.

"I'm so sorry. I didn't mean to freak out on you. I know that you've been doing a lot of the emotional heavy lifting for the past couple of weeks."

Olivia smiles at me and tucks my hair behind my ear again, her smile gentle. "It's okay. You were there for me when Caleb and I broke up. I know that was a crappy time to be my friend. Let me repay the favor."

"Okay. Here we go. Breathe." She closes her eyes and takes a deep breath, exhaling very slowly.

I mimic her, exhaling and inhaling several times. At last, I feel calm enough to check the test.

Going into that tiny bathroom is literally one of the scariest moments that I think I've ever lived through. But once I open that door and look down at the small sink, I see my test.

My positive pregnancy test.

For a moment, I just freeze. Olivia is right behind me in the doorway. She gently pushes me forward half a step, reaching forward to drag the test closer to her with a finger-nail. Her eyebrows fly up.

"Shit!" she declares.

I can't help the bark of laughter that escapes me. "Shit is right. I... I don't even know what to say. I think I might be in shock."

I turn, and Olivia automatically steps closer, her arms going around me. My eyes well up, and I sniffle.

A small whisper escapes me. "I really want this baby. I do. Just not right now. The timing... and the circumstances... they *suck*."

Olivia pulls me close and smooths my hair back from my forehead, giving me a tight squeeze. "I know you do, boo."

"I cannot afford to be pregnant right now."

Olivia rocks me, her gentle embrace making me cry.

She whispers. "Are you going to tell Burn?"

"How can I?" As I swallow a sob, I say. "How do I even begin to find the words?"

She stops rocking me, pulls back, and looks at me very seriously. "I don't know how. But it's important that you tell him. Unless… Unless you don't keep it."

Her words are like acid in the pit of my stomach. I make a disgusted face, shaking my head. "I don't know. I don't know how. And… Shit, how am I supposed to tell Dare?"

"How about we focus on one Morgan brother at a time? Okay?"

I gulp and collapse into Olivia's hug once more, my eyes not leaving the positive pregnancy test on the counter.

What the hell am I supposed to do now?

Chapter Fifteen

DARE

I'm at Herbsaint again, sitting at the best booth in the bar. I snap my fingers at a waiter walking by, grabbing his attention. He glares at me but stops, his hands clasped behind his back.

"Can I bring you something, sir?"

I point across the table to the blonde beauty sitting across from me. She tosses her hair and flicks her hazel gaze out at the room, turning her nose up and powdering her incredibly full lower lip.

"Elsa?" I prompt my date.

"Just vodka," she replies.

Her accent is Scandinavian, perhaps Norwegian, but she speaks English fluently. She levels me with a glare. Her perky breasts look mouthwatering as she adjusts the tiny straps of her black minidress and crosses her legs.

"What is it that you businessmen like this say?" She tosses her long hair and considers me. "Time is money. I got out of bed and came all the way here from New York City just to hear whatever you have to say. I am expecting an apology for the fact that you left in the middle of the night the last time you stayed at my apartment."

She folds her arms around herself as I give her a tight smile. I look at the waiter, who is impatiently tapping his foot.

"One whiskey for me. Something expensive, served on the rocks."

He bows his head and vanishes without a word. I tilt my head to the side and consider Elsa. "I can offer you an apology, or I can also offer you five hundred thousand dollars. Does that sound more amenable to you?"

She gives me a pouty look—her signature look that she uses in all the runways and cover shoots that she is so well known for. "I'm listening."

She doesn't seem very happy about it, though. I would expect a little bit of gratitude.

Spreading my fingers across the table, figuring that, as a businesswoman herself, Elsa will appreciate it if I am just blunt with her about what I need. "I want to get married right away, maybe this month even. And then I also need to..."

The waiter interrupts, putting the two glasses down on the table a little harder than is necessary. He straightens his back and gives me a cold smile. "Anything else?"

"That will be all. We would like to be left alone now."

Without another word, he turns on his heel and walks away from our table. My eyes narrow on his back as I watch him go. Elsa reaches out and wraps her knuckles on the table, drawing my attention back to her.

"And what? You are explaining how I can earn a lot of money."

"Yes." In an effort to relax, I crack my neck, eliciting a loud popping sound. Elsa flinches, and her perfect nose wrinkles.

"I was saying that I need to have a kid right away. We would have to start trying immediately. Tonight, if possible."

Elsa picks up the glass of vodka and brings it to her lips. She takes a large swig and then tosses the remainder in my face. I blink as the vodka drips down my face, soaking my shirt.

Elsa stands up, her temper flaming. "What the fuck, Dare? How could you bring me here for this ridiculous offer? Not only do I not want to marry you, but I also wouldn't dream of having your baby. You would be a terrible husband and a terrible father. Frankly, I am surprised that you would even ask me after ghosting me for the last five months!"

She holds up a finger, grabbing my attention. "I am a supermodel, damn you. I'm not a breeding cow. I've made millions of dollars by having a perfect figure, and I will go on to make millions more. And just so you know, I have my own expectations when it comes to a romantic relationship. I want the perfect man, an elaborate wedding, and maybe, eventually, a family. But did you even ask me what I wanted?" She laughs. "No! Of course not. You're so self-involved. It's not even funny."

I roll my eyes. "Elsa, if you would just listen to the deal that I'm presenting…"

She shakes her head vehemently.

"No. No way." Her lips curl, and she turns to the door. "Goodbye, Dare. Do not contact me ever again."

She storms out, leaving me in the booth. I grab the cloth napkin nearest to me to wipe off my vodka-soaked face.

"Fuck," I mutter to myself. She's the fourth woman that I've proposed to in the last twenty four hours and the only one remaining on my list of ex-girlfriends. Well, maybe not girlfriends. Hookups that I considered cool and levelheaded enough to even listen to my offer.

My brow furrows in frustration. I don't understand why she would be so upset. I offered her half a million dollars in exchange for a quickie marriage and caring for my baby. I didn't even get to the point where I explained that I could wire her half now and half upon the successful arrival of our child.

I fish my phone out of my suit pocket and send a text.

Come inside.

Not thirty seconds later, a small, balding man with a stylish sweater and tasteful dark gray corduroy pants appears. He looks around dramatically and arches a brow at me. "Did she leave, then?"

I frown and wave my hand at where she was sitting. "Sit down, Rob. And yes, she obviously left."

My personal assistant sits down carefully, crossing his legs, and places an electronic tablet on the table in front of him. He's been waiting outside in my chauffeured SUV, right where I told him to be in case things went south with my proposal.

"I really thought that she would go for it." He looks a little perplexed. "With your money and good looks, you should be able to pull in any wife that you want. No matter what you're offering," he pauses; something obviously occurring to him. "How are you proposing the deal, exactly?"

I roll my neck again and grit my teeth. "Rob, shut up. I didn't ask you to come here to give me dating advice or tell me how I should propose marriage."

"No?" He makes a face. "What do you need, then?"

"I want you to call a matchmaker. Not just any matchmaker. Find out who the best of the best is and hire them to bring me candidates right away. Make sure that the women are told that I want certain things: I want to marry right away, and I want kids as fast as possible. Not only that, but each woman needs to be the perfect candidate."

Rob pushes his cheek out with his tongue. He gives me a long look and opens the screen of his tablet, grabbing his pen to jot down notes.

"Okay, so what makes for a good candidate, in your mind?"

I wave a hand. "Oh, you know…"

"No, I don't think I do know. What about Marilyn Jones?"

"The influencer?" I puff out my cheeks. "I don't know. She's very new age-y. And even though she looks good in photos, in real life she is very shy. Painfully so."

Rob makes a note. "So not painfully shy should be one of the requirements?"

I shrug. "I don't feel good about Marilyn. Besides, I've never met her family. Who knows what kind of genetic pool she comes from? I wouldn't want her to pop out a baby and the baby to take after Uncle Frank, who is bald and fat."

He looks at me for a long moment. "No fat babies," he adds to the list. "Okay. What about Marcia Shaw?"

My eyes squint off into the distance as I try to place the name. "Who is she again?"

Rob pulls out his phone and scrolls for half a minute. As soon as he shows me a picture, I wave the possibility off. "No. She's the girl who got drunk every time I took her anywhere. I don't want that. That's not exactly motherly material."

Rob purses his lips and gives me a funny gaze. "Never gets drunk," he murmurs. "Got it. So, can you give me a list of appropriate qualities, then?"

"That's easy," I say. Steepling my hands, I consider the question. "I want someone who is born into an upper-class lifestyle. Someone who will not stand out but is still extremely good-looking. She'll have a big family, so I know that she is fertile. I'll have to have a good picture of her mother so I know who I will be marrying in twenty or thirty years. She'll have to be willing to sign a prenup, and she'll have to want to have at least one kid. Make that two kids," I squinted.

"Right." Rob scribbles a quick list.

"What, do you have a problem with my list?"

"No. I just wonder if a girl like this exists in reality. For a girl to have literally all these qualities... It just seems like she would really have to want your money to say yes to your proposal."

I dismiss his concerns with a wave of my hand.

"I'm not asking for too much, especially not for what I would offer and return. When I gain control of the company, she will automatically become one of the wealthiest wives on the planet. That's not really anything to sneeze at."

"I just think you might be a little bit off base. If you gave up any of these characteristics, I'm sure there would be plenty of women lining up to be your wife. But this is a pretty specific list."

I give him a thin-lipped smile.

"The right woman does exist. She'll be perfect. With the right dollar amount, anyone can be bought and paid for. This is a transaction, not a real marriage. I'm not looking for flowers and romance. I'm looking for something much more tangible and within my grasp. The right girl knows exactly what she is worth, and she's out there, waiting. I'm sure of it."

Rob makes a noise that sounds like a hum of disapproval. But he just scribbles a final note and sighs.

"All right. That gives me somewhere to start with the matchmaker. Anything else right now?"

Pushing out my bottom lip, I slowly shake my head.

"No. That's all I require of my personal assistant today."

"Great!" Rob says it with a saccharine smile. He scoots out of the booth, getting to his feet.

"Don't get carried away drinking tonight. You have a call with Tokyo at three a.m."

I frown and wave my hand. "It's fine, I'm sure."

"Well, good night then. I'll talk to you two minutes before the three a.m. call."

Rob waits a second to hear my response, but he catches me mid-gulp. Rather than wait around, he turns and marches out of the bar, looking like he was stalking along a runway.

I drain the contents of my glass, hissing to myself as the alcohol slides down my throat, burning as it goes. I cast my gaze around the bar with a sigh.

The question now becomes whether I want to pick up one girl or two for the evening. The idea is appealing in a certain light. At least it would satisfy my hunger for a second.

I think of two girls, fairly close and laying on their backs, their hands between their legs, as they do every single thing I say. I tell them just how I want them to touch themselves—to play with their pussies and rub their clits. I would be in charge—the master of their orgasms. Really, it's all the hands-off dominance that I crave on a regular basis.

The only thing is, I don't actually know if I want to put the effort into finding partners to play with tonight. But something is stopping me. Something is holding me back. What could it be?

The next moment, completely unbidden, a thought comes to my head. I picture Talia and the way she looked when she was wearing that silver dress. But instead of the blonde wig, I would insist that she let her natural copper-colored hair fall all around her shoulders like the wild, wavy mess it is.

Arching an eyebrow, I squint. Is that what this is all about? Is Talia holding me back?

I already know how my next conversation with Talia will end. I'll offer her another five thousand dollars for a night in my bed. It appears to be so straightforward. I find her body attractive, but every time she opens her mouth, I want to scream at her to shut up. So, I will make our hookup clean, professional, and very transactional.

I will get to watch her make herself cum while I jerk off.

Now that I admit it to myself, the idea runs through my blood as quickly as nuclear fission. It makes me feel strange and tingly, almost effervescent.

That settles it. I should just demand that she let me use her for her body. She should respond to my offer of cash. All women do when it comes to money. That's all they want, but that makes it easy.

Then, once I have Talia out of my system, I should reward myself. I should find a new girl that I can dominate. I can take her on my boat and sail away, whatever the weather. It won't matter, because I will be too busy counting her orgasms.

I get up and leave a pile of freshly minted hundreds on the table. Pulling on my coat, I bundle up and head outside. It's a nice enough night, brisk and cold but clear. I walk aimlessly, looking at the stars.

I find myself wondering what I will do if that matchmaker doesn't come through. I realize that I need something different this time around. Someone who needs money so badly that they will never leave me. Someone that can't do better than me.

Not that there are many men who can compete with me.

Still, I will find a woman who meets almost all my criteria, perhaps sacrificing one or two points, and who desperately needs money. I run my tongue against my teeth, a little smile playing on my lips. That's the sweet spot. I should really search there.

Smiling to myself a little, I turn toward the Morgan estate, walking more swiftly toward the house on the hill.

Chapter Sixteen

TALIA

"**G**et that!"

The manager of my second job, a high-end restaurant called Tusk, points out a table where the couple has just left. His brow furrows at me as he whips his hand in a circle.

"Can you move it? I need to have you working, not gawking."

"Of course," I say. I tug on the hem of my short skirt as I hurry to clear the table. I pull off the glasses first, then stack a pile of plates. I grab the glasses and plates and turn to carry them into the dishwashing area called the dish pit. Brian stops me, hustling up to me with a large tray.

"Get everything at once. Clear the entire table. I can't believe I'm having to tell you this," he hisses. "Usually, when I train a new hostess, she is inexperienced. But I don't have to tell them things that are common sense. I'm going to need you to do better if you want to keep working here."

He says it matter-of-factly, and the table to my right notices, turning their heads and arching their eyebrows. I feel my face heat as I bite my lip, feeling a wave of shame and sadness. I don't want to cry in front of this entire room of people, but my manager is making it very hard.

Brian shoves the wide black tray at me, knocking it into my stomach so hard that I stumble backward. My breath is knocked out of me, but Brian just smirks at me, turning on his heel and threading his way through the busy, crowded dining room.

It's seven thirty at night, and Tusk is absolutely jammed with people, every single employee thrumming with energy as they move about their business.

Gulping, I clamp my lips shut, determined not to show weakness.

As I stack plates and glassware on the tray, a vague memory swims to the surface of my mind. It's the fleeting image of Dare leaning down to me and whispering that my face is too easy to read.

I thought that Dare was crazy and that he was making up rules for interacting with the Morgan family that would never apply outside of their fancy estate. But here I am, using some of the same emotional control that I have only recently discovered.

Who would have thought that Dare would be useful to me?

As I lift the tray onto my shoulder, I struggle under its weight. The thought that pregnant women aren't supposed to lift anything flits through my mind.

Is that true? I don't actually know. It's just another thing for me to worry about.

After I rush the tray to the dish pit, I head back out front and make a beeline for the hostess stand. There is another hostess working, as is the usual schedule for hosts on the weekends, or so I'm told. I'm working with Anna, a gorgeous young blonde with a short black dress and the highest heels

I've ever seen anybody successfully walk in. She spots me and gives me a disapproving look.

"Where have you been? I needed you to take over at the hostess stand so that I could go around the restaurant and ask everyone how their meal was. I can't leave the hostess stand unattended."

Bowing my head, I find myself flushing once more. "Sorry. Brian asked me to..."

"Brian doesn't know anything," she cuts in. "He thinks he does because he is the front-of-house manager, but he can't even book a reservation. He is clueless." She rolls her eyes. "Okay, can you stay here while I do a round of the room?"

"Of course," I say.

She looks at me out of the corner of her eye. "When you have a little downtime, you should put in an order with the kitchen for a meal. We don't have time to eat while we're here, but getting a boxed up meal is one of the only perks for us. We get fed, and we sometimes get a percentage of the tips. It depends."

Nodding my head, I make a note. "Okay. What are the rules for food again? We get seventy-five percent off or something."

"Actually, the hostesses get their food for free, up to one hundred dollars' worth. It's actually a really nice perk."

My eyebrows fly up. "Oh. That's really nice."

"Yeah. On some nights, when the restaurant is slammed and everyone is in the weeds, it doesn't seem like that great of an upside. It is not always enough to balance out the downsides. But you know." She flips her hair back and gives me a pasted-on smile.

"I'm only doing this as temporary work anyway. I think this is the second job of almost everybody who works as a hostess."

I nod. "I know it is for me."

Anna is already turning away, starting toward the first white linen-covered table, and asking them if there is anything they need.

One hundred dollars goes pretty far, even at Tusk. It's a huge benefit for me, although I suppose that no one else needs to realize how much it will help me out. If I don't have to feed myself, I could save whatever I normally spend on myself for groceries every week. Probably seventy-five dollars, give or take.

A couple walks by the hostess stand on their way out.

"Have a good night!" I call out for them. The woman glances back at me and gives me a cool smile. They are outside the doors before I can say anything else.

Pulling a menu out from beneath the phone and computer that sit on top of the hostess stand, I purse my lips and peruse. Steak, chicken, lobster, fish, all kinds of different salads... I'm going to eat well while I work here.

I am too busy trying to decide on what I'll order first to notice that a tall, extremely thin, dark headed woman struts through the doors, trailing a string of four children behind her. She walks straight up to the hostess stand and slaps both of her palms down onto the stand. It startles me, and I jump, looking up at her like a deer in headlights.

"Excuse me," she says. She has a thick European accent, perhaps Spanish or French. I can't exactly pinpoint it. "I need service!" she cries.

"Oh, of course. I'm sorry." Moving to the computer, I pull up the reservations screen. "Do you have a reservation?"

Her face turns angry, as if I have just challenged her somehow. "No. My family wants to eat. We are very hungry."

I swallow and look back at the packed restaurant. There isn't a single empty seat in the whole restaurant. There are actually already people sitting in chairs that were brought in by the waitstaff from a back hallway. We are over capacity, even at the long marble countertop that serves as our bar. Every single seat was reserved months ago, and it is bordering on insanity that this woman doesn't understand that.

"Ma'am," I say. "Unfortunately, we don't have..."

"No! That is not acceptable. We will eat now." The woman puts her arms out, and her children filter into her embrace. She looks at me as if she has somehow presented an argument that is undeniable.

"As you can see," I say. I turn and wave a hand to indicate the dining room. Our entire restaurant is full at the moment. "We are not taking walk-ins. There are guests with reservations all the way up until nine thirty."

She arches her brow and crosses her arms. "That is unacceptable. I know chef André. He would be extremely dissatisfied if he knew that you were turning me away right now."

Casting a sneaky glance around, I try to get Anna's attention. But she is off on the other end of the restaurant, beaming at a cluster of customers as they interact with her.

Chef André is both the chef and the owner of this establishment. But I don't know him, and I don't feel like heading back into the kitchen and asking him at this exact moment is really wise.

I steel myself and force a smile onto my lips. Looking at the woman, I bow my head. "I'm sorry. We are booked. Perhaps you would like to make a reservation for the future?"

She turns around, swinging a hand wide to indicate the empty benches in the foyer. "We can just sit there. No problem."

My brow furrows. "I don't think..."

The woman once again slams both of her hands down on

the host stand, making me jump. "You are an idiot! You are terrible at your job. They should not let you work here. I am not just going to leave here with my family. My family is hungry, and we want to eat Chef André's food!"

"I'm sorry…"

"No!" She turns and points to the bench. "Go sit down, kids. We are going to eat here. Your mom said you would eat at Tusk, so you will eat at Tusk. Don't make me do something rash."

The last part was obviously meant for me. I realize that at some point, her accent fell away and now she is talking with a normal American accent, possibly one that says she was raised in Boston.

"Ma'am, I don't know what you want me to do. I can't seat you. There is literally nowhere to sit in the restaurant. Those benches are not tables, they are a waiting area. What you are asking for is against the restaurant's policies."

"You know what you are? You're a bitch and a liar. We have seats right here." She waves her hand at the benches again. "Now get us some menus and some waters. Better yet, get us another person to deal with. Someone who doesn't shake and tremble at every little thing that is said to them."

That's the moment that Brian appears, straightening his navy suit and looking between myself and the customer skeptically. "What's going on?"

I draw in a gulp of air and try to answer, but the customer cuts me off.

"Your hostess is a moron," she says through clenched teeth. "I tried to explain to her that I am a friend of chef André's. A *close* friend. But she says that she can't seat us, even though there are plenty of chairs right behind me."

Brian tilts his head to the side. His lips purse, and he

squints at me. I am so flustered. I can feel tears pressing at the corners of my eyes, threatening to descend. My face burns.

Brian smacks his lips and arches a brow at me. "Maybe you need to go on your break. Go take ten minutes in the back." His gaze narrows on me. "Now."

The customer looks at me with a little smirk as I walk away. I turn and duck my head, weaving through the tables, trying not to knock into anyone as my tears fall.

Heading into the back hallway, I run into Chef André. He is maybe forty years old; his dark hair is starting to thin on top, and his frame is angular and athletic. Someone once said to me that you can never trust a skinny chef, but I just try to smile, pretending that I am not crying as I try to sneak past him.

He approaches from the back door, having just been outside. He takes one look at me and exhales a long sigh, smelling like he just smoked a cigarette. "What is your name?" he asks.

I stop and wipe away my tears the best I can. "Talia."

"Okay. There are a lot of rules for working in a restaurant. But one of them is that there are no tears. Or rather, maybe that should be the number one rule. In any event, I think I will send you home early."

God, how embarrassing. I shake my head, trying to wipe away my tears. "I swear, Mr. André, I don't normally cry at work."

He holds up a hand to stop my protests. "I'm too bored for you to keep talking. Also, I have to get back to the kitchen. Listen, I want you to go home, calm yourself down, and when you come back, bring a better attitude. You must do better the next time you come to work."

I look at him with wide eyes, not even sure what to say.

He looks at me, his expression intent. "I need you to say that you understand what I'm saying to you."

I gulp in a breath and nod quickly. "Of course. I understand. It's just…"

He waves a hand, dismissing me. "Okay. Don't let it happen again, Talia. One time, I let it slide. Two times and you're out. You understand?"

I nod, a little stunned. He rolls his eyes and turns on his heel, heading down the hallway toward the kitchen.

I want to scream. I don't because I'm afraid I'll lose my job. But I can feel pressure building in my throat, heated by rage. I don't normally think this about people, but that chef can go fuck himself. I take a deep breath and remind myself that I need every penny I can get at this point. That's assuming that I keep deferring my decision about my pregnancy and run out of time to make a rational choice. It's only been a few days since I found out, but it feels like it's been a thousand years.

I pull out my phone, unsure who to text. It's a short list that I have to choose from. Olivia, Aunt Minnie, a few other work contacts… or Dare, I suppose. God, if I wanted my day to get worse, I could definitely call him.

Instead, I text Olivia and ask her what she is doing. She texts back right away, asking if I'm done with work. And then before I can answer, she follows up that question with an offer to drive me home. I wipe my eyes and text her back. We plan that I will just meet her at my house.

I catch the bus home, and my stomach rumbles as I walk the few blocks to my house. I live in a fairly prosperous part of town, but my house is just on the other side of a very rich neighborhood. I walk down the street, seeing the familiar row of little bungalows. They have yet to be torn down and rebuilt, so if you just looked at my street, you might think you were in the post-World War II USA. Well, if you squinted a little and ignored the dingy, worn-down quality of the houses on my street.

Just as I trudge up my front walkway, heading to my little drab green bungalow, I see that Olivia is in fact waiting for me on the front porch steps. She looks up and raises a pizza box in the air, wiggling her eyebrows in invitation.

Running the last few steps up to her, I help her up and then hug her hard. She laughs and balances the pizza box with one arm as she embraces me. "That bad of a night, huh?"

"You have no idea. The people who eat at Tusk are so wealthy and entitled. In fact, I am pretty sure that Dare Morgan must hang out there all the time."

She smiles. "Well, that really stinks. But on the upside, I did bring you dinner. Are you hungry?"

"I am starving. I got sent home before I had a chance to order anything at the restaurant."

Unlocking the front door, I let myself in and carefully hang up my heavy overcoat by the front door.

The front door leads directly into the crowded living room. It only has a TV and the couch, as I have been cleaning and throwing away all the clutter that Aunt Minnie brings home on a regular basis.

Olivia closes the door behind her and pulls up a battered folding table, setting the pizza down. She shoos me over to the couch. "Sit down. Take a load off. I'll grab the plates."

A wave of exhaustion hits me suddenly and I nod. "Okay. But just because I have been on my feet for like twelve hours straight today between working at the bookstore and at the restaurant. That's the only reason I am going to let you feed me expensive takeout."

She rolls her eyes and shakes her head. "It's Carl's Pizza. Nothing fancy at all. I just got mushrooms and pepperoni.

And because I went to the store and picked it up, it was like fifteen bucks."

I collapse on the couch and stick my feet out, grimacing at the way they are throbbing. When Olivia returns with a stack of cloth napkins and two thrift store plates, I fix her with a solemn look. "Fifteen dollars is a lot to blow on one meal."

She hands me a plate and a napkin and sits down beside me. "First of all, no, it isn't. You're just cheap. Second of all, this pizza will probably last me at least one more meal, if not two."

She opens the pizza box, and the most amazing smell ever wafts out. She places two slices of pizza on her plate before turning the box to face me.

I try to be economical and only pull one slice out of the box. But she points to it with a stern look. "Take another slice. Really. I insist."

"You're spending your money on needless things!" I protest.

"The key word there is *my* money. Let me spend it how I want to," she chides me. "Come on, I'm being generous. Let me enjoy the moment."

I heave a sigh and lean forward, taking a second slice. Olivia already has a huge mouthful of pizza, so I give her a quiet smile. "Thank you, Olivia. This is just what I need right now."

She giggles. "It's what we all needed, deep down."

The pizza smells amazing as I bring it to my lips. I am eating with my eyes as much as I am preparing myself for such a decadent treat. Take-out pizza is not something that is usually on the menu for me, that's for sure.

But the second I put the pizza slice in my mouth, I feel my belly gurgle. I was starving literally half a second ago.

But now that my mouth is closed around the tip of the pizza, taking in a mushroom, my hunger has shifted to nausea. Before I can even take a solid bite, I retch in my throat.

I fling the pizza away from my face, spitting the chewed-up remnants into my hands. A wave of nausea hits me, and I retch again, pressing my nose into my arm.

Olivia stands up, alarmed. "What's going on? What can I do?"

I cough, shaking my head, and run to the bathroom. I barely have time to dump the chewed bits of pizza in the sink before I throw up a little bit of burning liquid. I retch for another minute and then step back, feeling perplexed.

Why did the pizza make me feel so sick, so suddenly? I have no idea. It takes me another couple of minutes to clean up after myself in the bathroom.

When I walk out of the small bathroom and emerge into the living room, I am hit by the smell of pizza once more. I gag and turn towards the kitchen, covering my nose and mouth with my hand. "The pizza... Can you..."

"Oh God, yes." Olivia is on her feet, carrying both the plates and the pizza box. She takes them outside, leaving the door open and letting the room fill with cold air. I drink in gulps of the fresh air, trying not to vomit.

Olivia sticks her head in the front door, looking at me with concerned eyes. "Are you going to be okay?"

I nod. I hold my mouth in just a certain way that seems to be keeping me from throwing up and I just ride out the wave of nausea until it passes. At last, I sit down on the couch again and sink back, looking up at the ceiling and letting my head fall back.

"Oh my God. If that's a sign of pregnancy, maybe I don't want to deal with it right now." I'm half-joking, my remark not really meaning anything. But Olivia shuts the front door, looking at me carefully as she takes her seat again.

"Does that mean you have made up your mind about it?"

I look over at her, shaking my head. "No. I was just kidding. I haven't made up my mind one way or the other."

"Well," she sighs and looks around the room, as if deciding how much to say. She has a tendency to nag and I really appreciate her clear attempt to reign it in now. "You know you are going to have to decide one way or another eventually."

She's rustling her overcoat off and throwing it over the arm of the chair. Standing up, I take her coat and hang it beside mine.

"I'm going to make myself some dry toast. You want some?"

She shrugs. "Sure. I could go for some dry toast. Why not?"

She follows me into the small kitchen. Everything in here is a shade of brown. Brown ceramic tile on the counter and floor, with light brown near the cabinets. I wrestle a loaf of bread from the pantry cabinet and place two slices in the toaster. Then I turn, leaning against the counter.

Olivia leans against the opposite counter and crosses her arms, looking me up and down. "Okay, here's the thing."

She quirks her head, curious. "I'm listening."

"So, I definitely want a family. Like I said before, I really want to have a bunch of kids. And now I am wondering... What if this is the only chance I will ever have to get pregnant? What if I never conceive again after getting an abortion?"

She purses her lips. "That is not really a common side effect or anything. In fact, it's not even a rare one. It's possible, but in the same way that it's possible that you might win the lottery without even buying a ticket. You know? Not unthinkable, but just really, *really* unlikely."

I exhale a sigh. Our toast pops up, and I offer her a piece, grabbing her the peanut butter and a knife. She spreads peanut butter on her toast and looks at me.

"It makes me nervous," I say finally.

"People go on to have really beautiful children after an abortion. Don't let a lifetime of fear mongering and incomplete information make your decision for you."

I take a tiny nibble of my toast, nodding slowly. "You're right, of course."

"I am a scientist by nature. I seek the truth."

"And I am very glad to have inner circle privileges. But... here's the thing: telling Burn Morgan that I am pregnant with his child? It seems... I don't know, unfathomable. Especially after I met his fiancée."

Olivia looks at me, her eyebrows arching. "Tell me more about that."

"Oh yeah. Burn and his fiancée Daisy were at the Morgan estate the other night. So, I realize that in sleeping with me, Burn was essentially cheating on Daisy. Actually, he was not doing anything essentially. He was just plain cheating. And now I'm supposed to show up with news that literally no one wants to hear?"

"Well, it's your decision. But if you want, I will go with you to tell Burn. Whenever you decide to do it, that is. Because if you decide to have this baby you definitely have to tell him."

"How am I supposed to show up with this news that no one wants to hear? What is Burn going to think? He is going to think that I'm a burden. He's going to think that me and my child are both an albatross—a weight around his neck pulling him down into the water. And I don't want anyone to ever feel that way about me. I don't want my child to grow up thinking that they are imposing on someone. No way. I've done that my whole life."

"You may have felt that way, but realistically, you were never a burden. You couldn't have been. Without you, who would have kept Minnie from drowning in her own mess?"

For a moment, I think that Olivia is referring to Aunt Minnie's loan from a loan shark. But that's when Olivia gestures around her, to the disaster of a house that I've spent so much time cleaning.

"I guess," I say apathetically.

"So?" Olivia asks.

I give a slow nod. "Yeah. I think that I can't stop feeling a little bubble of excitement in my heart at the thought of having a baby. I know that it will probably be chaotic. And probably not the best childhood that I could've provided if I had only waited a few more years. But..." I motion with my hand. "How can I get rid of this bundle of cells when I have such a deep yearning for a child?"

She gives me a tiny smile. "I don't know. I don't know if you can."

I push off the kitchen counter and hug myself. "I am not going to do it, then. I'm not going to have an abortion. I'm going to keep the baby."

Olivia's squeal of glee shocks me a little bit. She lunges at me from across the kitchen, wrapping me in her arms and squeezing me tight. "Yes! I knew you were going to decide that."

I break away. "I will need help triangulating where Burn is going to be. Maybe in the next two or three days?"

"Wow, you are taking this very seriously. I appreciate your total commitment."

Olivia pulls out her phone and scrolls for a minute. "So, I found Burn on Instagram..."

"You what?"

"Just let me have this moment. I found him on Instagram, and according to his post from today, the whole family is gathering at the Morgan estate tonight for yet another charity ball. That's probably your best chance."

I blow out a shaky breath, and my heartbeat skyrockets. The very thought of having to tell Burn that he knocked me up is unnerving, if nothing else. "Okay. Okay. You're going to have to help me figure out what to wear to tell Burn that his one-night stand got me pregnant and I am keeping the baby."

Olivia beams at me, as though I just told her that she won the lottery. "I thought you'd never ask. Come on, come to my house. Let me dress you up. Then you can go in style."

I shake my head and roll my eyes, but I let her pull me out of the room.

Chapter Seventeen

DARE

T he Morgan estate is absolutely bursting at the seams with charitable donors and their hangers-on. It's the usual sort of crowd here: a packed house full of people in black tuxes and splashy, colorful ball gowns.

Honestly, it's what I've become used to. In the last few years, Remy has become increasingly charitable, especially when the charity involves him giving up the house for the night. He's a grumpy old motherfucker, but I have a sneaking suspicion that he's a deeply lonely old man.

I shut the door that separates the partygoers from the rest of the house. I can still hear the violin music and the murmur of voices, but as I turn and look at all my relatives, scattered here and there on the living room sofas and standing by the fireplace, I suck in a deep breath.

I hate these big events. In fact, when I take over the company, I am going to be glad to see them held at someone else's house for once. When Remy dies, this entire house is going to be a ghost town. And the balls and galas will follow him.

At the moment, no one even looks my way. Instead, my

brother, Daisy, and all my cousins are focused on the sight of my Uncle Felix going toe to toe with my father, both screaming at one another. Red-faced and clutching their fists, they have eyes for no one else.

"You guttersnipe!" My Uncle Felix howls. "You are an absolute piece of human garbage."

"That's nice coming from you. We all know what happened to your first and second wives. They both died under mysterious circumstances. Which I interpreted to mean that you paid someone to knock them off so you could avoid paying them alimony. So, you're actually a murderer!"

Felix golfs. "I'd like to see you present your evidence for that claim."

"If I had hard evidence? You would already be in jail," my father says.

"I'd be careful what you wish for. If I think I might go to jail anyway, what's another murder on my conscience? After two life sentences, why not add whoever I feel like adding?" He cracks all the knuckles on both his hands and glares at my father.

"We'll just have to see about that claim. When our dad gets here, I am contesting his will. I have my whole legal team already on it." He points at a rather standoffish group of men in suits that are bunched together in a corner, looking uncomfortable. They look as if they have been pulled from other businesses by a man with a vile temper. That man would be my uncle, so that all tracks.

My brother clears his throat, shooting me a look. "Look, I have no idea what exactly the nature of your deal with Remy was in the past. But he has made it perfectly clear that you and dad are to receive a token amount of money when he passes and not a penny more. He has repeatedly told me that the controlling interest in the company will only go to Dare or me."

My father grows red. His fists bunch up, and he looks at Burn as though he's about to launch an attack. It wouldn't be the first time that my father hit my brother or me. But it's been years since he was strong enough to hit one of us without repercussions.

I tense up, my hands gathering into fists. No matter what Burn does, I will still back him when the opposing party is my father. Burn and I have been twisted and damaged by our family legacy, but there is something to be said for the cruelty of my father and the way that Burn and I naturally became unspoken allies. A unit against my father, my Uncle Felix, and Remy. I'm not sure why exactly all the men in our family are out for their own interests or when my brother and I drifted apart, ending our childhood need for each other's support.

My dad casts a glance at me, and his lips curl up in a sneer. But before he can make any move toward either of his sons, the door bursts open and Remy barrels through it, looking as red and angry as I have ever seen him.

He looks around wildly, pointing a finger at everyone in the room. "How dare you all congregate here in my house and complain about how I choose to split up my assets that I earned after I'm dead?" He grits his teeth.

"Wait a second." The words are out of my mouth before I really think about them, but I just shake my head. "We are here for a gala. And then we were called into this room by dad, apparently. But we have nothing to do with any scheming on his part."

Remy levels me with a malevolent look. "Did I ask you for any more information? No. I'm here to shut this down. Tripp, you and your lawyers can get the fuck out of my house. And the rest of you?" He gestures toward the room. "You can go, too, double time. Everybody fucking leave."

"Just a second," my brother says. "I want to be clear about what you want us to do with your will."

I look at my watch, seething at how Remy talked to me. I got yelled at for literally no reason.

I glance at my watch, wondering if I could get out of here now and save the night. Maybe I can call Tristen and get him to go out for a drink. Somewhere that I can blow off some steam and pick up a girl or two.

Everyone in the room bursts into loud, cacophonous shouts at the same time. Rolling my eyes, I turn and leave the room. My footsteps are quick, as are my thoughts on the future as I head for the foyer.

When I'm approaching the foyer, I hear her voice. Talia says something, her voice agitated. I move closer, intrigued. In the next second, I hear Clive's voice.

"No one is here, Miss. I think you had better go home."

"I can hear them arguing!" Talia says.

I step into the foyer, and Talia looks right at me, going as white as a ghost for some reason. Clive looks between the two of us and arches a brow.

I jerk my head to the back of the house, indicating without words that he could leave. He turns without ceremony and heads out of the foyer, happy enough to leave me with the visibly upset Talia.

My brows arch and my lips thin as I stare at her. She's still dressed in her oversized winter coat, as if she's being swallowed alive and drowning in it.

She tosses her hair and puts her fiery copper hair in a messy bun, then raises her chin. "Are you Burn or are you Dare?" She says.

In an instant, I already know that I am going to lie. I'm not sure why she would be looking for Burn. After all, she claims to have no desire to see anyone in the family ever again. But the fact that she said his name first makes me curious about what she would say if she were talking to him. I purse my lips and tilt my head to one side. "I'm Burn. Why? Are you back for more?"

She swallows, and her gaze darts around the room, making her seem unsettled. "Is there a more private place where we can talk?"

I keep my face a blank slate, but inside I am full of questions.

What would Talia have to talk to Burn about?

I shrug, playing it cool. But I'm at a low simmer inside, almost ready to boil over with my need to find out.

"I can do that, sure," I say, keeping my tone light. "Why don't we head into the library? We should have plenty of privacy there."

Grabbing her by the arm, I steer her down the hall. We walk through the living room, my steps quickening so the family doesn't notice us as we pass. Then I walk her all the way down to the end of the house, near the kitchen. I open the library door and practically shove Talia inside, closing it after myself.

I look around at the bookshelves lining the walls and the overstuffed leather furniture. This room doesn't really have any windows, and it's lit by sconces along the walls, creating a warmer, more dimly lit environment.

Talia walks into the room, her eyes growing wide as she takes in the bookcases and the warm walnut wood that the bookshelves and the floor are made of. I take a few steps, stopping by a long couch and leaning against it. I cross my arms and look at Talia.

She looks taken aback, as if her thoughts have been quite derailed by the opulence and the books all around her.

I snap my fingers at her. She looks back at me with some surprise, as if she had forgotten about me for just a moment. "What do you want to talk about?" I simply ask.

Talia's face pales, and she smooths a hand over her long coat. "Well…"

She seems reluctant to tell me whatever it is that she came here to say. I try to figure out what my twin brother would do in this situation. He would probably act like an ass, no doubt.

I reach out a hand, beckoning her to come closer. Her mouth twists, and she gives me a hard look. I remind myself that I'm pretending to be my brother Burn, not my usual self. So I should be seductive rather than forceful.

I straighten and close the distance between us, grabbing her by the waist and pulling her close until the softness of her body is pressed against mine. I hear her breath catch, and she looks up at me with these wide, brilliant blue eyes.

I thread my hand into the hair at her nape and tug it back, so that she has no option but to look at me.

Bracing her back with my free hand, I slowly lean down to her lips, pressing my own against them. The taste of her lips is sweet, and the feel of her body is familiar. She offers no resistance to my embrace, so I lean her back and plunder her lips, using my tongue against her teeth until her mouth parts.

I kiss her harder, more deeply. Our tongues entwine, dancing like two figures dancing close together, undulating in a rhythm that is as old as time.

She smells good and has the sweet, light taste of mint. Her body is slight, and her weight is nothing against my own. Some animal instinct that I have is very excited by that, though I don't fully understand it.

She kisses me back, her lips moving so tentatively against mine. But then she seems to remember herself and pushes against my chest. When I don't give her space immediately, she protests.

"Burn!" She stops kissing me back and begins to struggle, her face scrunching up.

I growl at her, my lips leaving hers and my lips trailing down her neck, leaving little marks in my wake.

She grimaces, her face contorting. She drives her foot down hard on top of mine, causing a jolt of pain to radiate out from it. I freeze, uncertain how to deal with the pain. She takes advantage of my momentary lapse to wriggle out of my arms.

"I didn't come here for that, Burn."

I look at her, her chest heaving, her face flushed. She has this wary look in her eyes, like I am a known murderer, and she is just trying to stay alive.

I don't know why, but I like it when she looks at me that way.

Wiping at my mouth I smirk at her. "No? What did you come for then? Because if it is money, I have nothing left in my charity fund for you, little girl."

She looks at me and walks across the room and back, pacing, her hands shaping into fists. "You got me pregnant, Burn." She stops, pinning me in place with a hard gaze. "That's why I am here. I wanted you to know."

Letting my head rock back, I stare at her, trying to ascertain whether or not she is telling the truth. A grandfather clock in the corner begins to chime the hour as the silence stretches between us. I don't say anything. Or maybe it's that I can't. I am too busy thinking of what this might mean.

This changes everything. I tilt my head to one side and try to gauge whether she is serious. But it seems like she is.

"Is this a shakedown?" Sure, Talia seems too honest and too proud to do something like lie about being pregnant. But I don't really know her. Not well enough to guess.

She starts pacing again, wrapping her arms around herself. She shakes her head vehemently. "I wish it was. When I first found out that I was pregnant, I wasn't sure that I was going to keep it. But now, I think…" She trails off, turning away from me and walking slowly toward the other end of the room. "Now I think that I will keep it."

I run my tongue over my teeth. "How do you know? Have you been to see a doctor?"

She shakes her head. "No. But I have taken three different brands of pregnancy tests."

I stroke my chin, pondering. "And how do you know that it is mine?"

The question makes Talia turn around, her eyes crackling and snapping. She seems to be on the brink of screaming. "I think you know it's yours."

I shrug my shoulders. "Maybe. Maybe not. That isn't really the point."

Her face reddens. "My baby can only be yours. Do you understand what I'm saying? I've only ever slept with one person, once. And all roads lead to your door."

I snort. "You can't be serious. Are you telling me that you expect me to believe that you are a virgin?"

Talia crosses her arms, stalks up to me, and points a finger right in the center of my chest. "Was. I was a virgin. Now I'm carrying your child."

Her words ring out in the quiet of the library. I take a deep breath and look at her serious face. I'm going to have to come clean with her about my identity sooner or later. I might as well do it now.

I hold my hands up in a placating gesture. "All right, so let's say that you are pregnant and that it is Burn's child."

I see a note of puzzlement on her face before it is soon replaced with a look of understanding. "Are you fucking serious? You were lying about who you are again?"

"Lying is an awfully accusatory word."

Her nose flares, and she leans forward, giving my shoulder a hard push. "I can't believe you did that again, Dare! Who do you think you are?"

"Obviously that depends on what information I can get by acting as if I am my brother."

She makes a sound of disgust and starts to walk out of the library. But before she gets to the door, I grab her by the wrist and pull her back. She resists for only a moment before turning to look at me. "Let me go. I have to find Burn."

I raise my hand, attempting to calm her. "Just hear me out. Okay?"

She rips her wrist from my grip and crosses her arms, her expression humorless. "Hear you out about what? I'm not here to make any more deals with you, Dare. I'm here to inform your brother that I'm carrying his child."

Licking my lips, I motion toward the couch. "Sit down with me. In ten minutes, if I haven't said anything that's worth your time, I will pay you one thousand dollars."

Her brows wrinkle with confusion. "For what? I swear, you Morgans have too much damned money."

Grabbing her by the shoulders, I struggle to get her over to the couch and sit her down. I take a seat just inches away. She is looking at me with distrust. I don't blame her, honestly. I'm not usually the most trustworthy person.

"Okay." I lean in, adopting a very serious expression. "You know that my brother is already engaged."

Her lips curl. "Yes. I didn't know that at the time, though."

"You met Daisy. Remember?"

"I do." She gives me a look. "Where is this going?"

"If you go to my brother and tell him that you are carrying his child, he might offer you money to 'take care of it'. Or he might break up with Daisy in order to take you on as his fiancée."

She wrinkles her face up. "That's not... No. I have no interest in becoming engaged to Burn. Actually, I think that he's pretty despicable, now that the whole cheating scandal is out in the open."

"That doesn't really matter; my point is that Daisy is not the sort of person that you want rooting against your team. She is pretty nasty when something or someone gets in the way of her goal, and you and your baby would be in her way. She wants to marry my brother. She has worked for a long time, casing our family. You'd show up at the last minute and derail all her carefully laid plans."

Talia's brows furrow. "I don't want that. But there's nothing I can do about that. I have to tell Burn because he deserves to know."

I peer at her. "This kind of scandal could tear the whole family apart. It could cause a lot of problems."

"Again, what am I supposed to do? I'm just following the natural conclusion of events."

My heart thumps in my chest, and my mouth feels dry. I have a wild, reckless idea that is rattling around in my head.

Looking down into Talia's eyes, I grab her hand, taking it between both of mine. She looks at me, her eyebrows raising. But before she can say anything, I shake my head.

"You shouldn't tell Burn anything. You already know that he is a fucking liar. He cheated on Daisy and got you pregnant. Is that really the kind of person you want to spend your life with, or at least raise a child with?"

Her expression is skeptical. She exhales. "Maybe. I don't really know. As I've been saying all along, I don't know much about either of you other than the fact that you're both rich assholes."

"That's what I'm saying, though. I have a clean slate when it comes to cheating and jerking you around."

She puts her hands on her hips, leaning away from me and fixing me with a hard look. "You're just as deceptive as Burn."

"Yes, but that is all I've done, and that was out of desperation."

She opens her mouth and I silence her with a finger to her lips. Looking down at her, I say the words that seem so farfetched to me.

"What I'm trying to say is that you should marry me. Be my wife. Tell everybody that the child is mine."

Her eyes widen and her pupils contract. For several seconds, a shocked silence reigns between us. She blinks, and her throat works gently.

Finally, she pulls her hand from my grip and shakes it, as if trying to remove the traces of my touch. "Why would I do that?"

I grab her hand again, gripping it and looking at her intently. "My grandfather challenged us both to marry a woman and produce an heir. The first one of us that does it will win the company and billions of dollars."

"So?"

"So, Daisy will not look kindly upon losing out on being married to that kind of wealth. She doesn't let things go easily. When we were in college, her freshman-year room-mate didn't like Daisy's controlling ways. Daisy eventually wore her down and humiliated her enough that she dropped out of college and disappeared. Daisy does not let things go. I think she would actually have zero problem doing bodily harm to you and your baby if it suited her needs."

"What?" Her word comes out as a shout as much as a question. She breathes in and out slowly. Then she looks at me and shakes her head. "No. I'm sorry, Dare. It's not the worst idea. But it's easier if I try to go it alone. Less complicated, for sure."

"What do you mean go it alone? You're willing to be a single mother and deal with all the hassle that it entails rather than marry me?"

Her face softens, and she reaches out, putting her hand on my knee. It's intimate, and it makes me want to flick her hand off or say something sarcastic in response. But she gives me a tiny smile, and my bitter words are washed away.

I swallow and decide that this is not the time or the place for my sardonic sense of humor.

"You're presenting me with a great offer. There is no doubting that. But agreeing to that would be like agreeing to lie to everyone from here on out. I don't want a child who is born into a house of deception. I'm sure you can understand."

I give her a cold smile. I know exactly the words to say to make her agree. After all, she's only a human, and humans have a weakness for money. "I didn't even mention the best part of the deal."

She looks a little confused, scooting to the edge of the couch and looking as though she is about to get up. I put my hand on her knee this time, my fingers digging into her flesh as I give her the most intense look possible.

"I'm not sure what you mean," Talia says. She studies me, perhaps looking for flaws that she can pick apart.

"Agreeing to marry me comes with a cash reward. Being

my wife earns you five hundred thousand dollars that you can use any way that you see fit. Two hundred and fifty thousand dollars will be deposited into an account of your choosing as soon as we are officially married. And another two hundred fifty thousand when the baby arrives. Plus," I raise a brow. "I will pay for anything and everything that you and the baby need for the next eighteen years. Surely that will sway you to agree to my plan."

I sit back, a satisfied smirk on my lips. But Talia just looks confused.

"Do you really want the Morgan family business that badly? Eighteen years is a long time to tie yourself to another person just for a business deal."

I squeeze her knee and cock my head to the right. "There would be other benefits to being married. For instance, we could fuck like bunnies. I am game for it if you are."

She pries my hands from her body, getting up and walking away. "That sounds horrible," she says over her shoulder. "You make it sound like I would be in for a lifetime of tawdry sex just because I accepted a one-time cash infusion from you."

"And because you would theoretically be my wife. Don't forget that," I tease.

Talia turns, shooting me a glare. "No. How could I ever forget that?"

I sit back on the couch, putting my arms behind my back and stretching out. "The real question is, why should you have a cheater's baby when his identical twin brother is sitting right here, asking to raise the child?"

For just a fleeting second, I catch the conflicted look on her face. I hold my hands up, trying to stall her protests in their tracks. "You know what? You should think about it. You definitely shouldn't go tell my brother before you've had time to weigh all of your options. I'm only asking for a little time to let the genius of my plan soak into your system."

I rise from the couch, stepping closer and reaching out a hand. I take her hand and turn her palm upward, kissing the smooth skin. She looks at me again, that same look of conflict in her eyes. Then she pulls away, flushes, and makes up an excuse.

"I really have to go."

I grab her hand again, squeezing her flesh hard. "Tell me that you are not going to find Burn tonight. Tell me that you won't run to my brother and tell him about what I offered you."

She struggles, trying to pull her hand from my grip. "I am not going to talk to him tonight," she insists. "I'm going to think about it, like you told me to. Is that what you want to hear?"

I release her hand and give her a cool smile. "No. What I want to hear is that you will accept my proposal. But for right now? I'll take what I can get."

She steps back, ripping her hand from mine and I let her go. She opens the door and looks out into the hall. I suppose she is checking to see that my family has gone. I motion to her to get back from the door and then head outside, looking both ways. I fish my cell phone out of my pocket and send Clive a text. I hear movement in the service corridor just to the right of the library, and then Clive steps out. I swing open the door to the library and beckon to Talia.

"Come on. Clive can guide you off the property without anyone else knowing that you were ever here."

Her eyebrows go up, but she flushes and hurries through the doorway, only looking back at me for one moment before dashing through the servants' passage that Clive holds open.

Clive bows to me ever so briefly, and then I watch him pull the passageway door closed once again.

Pursing my lips, I pull out my cell phone. I feel like I have her in the palm of my hand. But corporate life has taught me to always have a backup plan. In case anything happens, I need to be absolutely sure that Talia will say yes to my offer.

I thumb through my contacts and then make a call. "Yeah, it's me. I need a huge favor."

Chapter Eighteen

TALIA

"Wait, so he just proposed to you? Completely out of the blue?"

I nod, walking beside Olivia. We are crossing Harwicke, heading for the Lucky Farms stables. It's mid-morning and sunny outside, for a New England winter day.

"Wow," Olivia says. "I mean... It's the most unromantic proposal I've ever heard. But then again, you get five hundred thousand dollars. So, factor that in, I guess."

I turn right, leaving the edge of Harwicke. We begin climbing the gentle slope toward the peak of the town.

The Morgan family estate sits at the top of everything, looking down on the town just as the family looks down on everyone that lives here. But the stables are settled at the bottom of the hill that eventually grows into a deep incline, becoming a bluff.

In the winter light, the dark landscape here looks especially harsh. Up this high, the sun throws odd shadows against the dark soil. We are on the edge of town now, with the sea to our right. Its dark waves wash up onto the shore and black rocks meet the harsh, pounding surf like a set of dark, stained giant's teeth. Once on the beach, the water's icy fingers reach out, trying to touch everything in its path.

Pulling my coat closer, I shiver and turn away. The stables are only a five-minute walk from here, and I need to get my head right before I get to the horses. They are very sensitive animals, and if I'm even a little mad or tense, whatever horse I am assigned will no doubt suffer for it.

"So?" Olivia asks. She slips her hands into her pockets as she scrunches up her face. Her hair is blowing all around her like a halo as the wind whips up.

I huddle in my coat and say, "You should have driven us. It's so cold right now. I wanted to walk, but it would've been a better idea to drive."

She snuffles and gives a halfhearted shrug. "I don't want to beat a dead horse, but I really must know. Are you going to tell Burn about the pregnancy? Or are you going to accept Dare's proposal?"

"Both sound equally terrible."

I squint out over the horizon. We soon come to a flat area, just a few minutes from where the stables are located. The ground here is made of rich, dark soil, which makes it perfect for horses to run around in.

"I know Dare's proposal is enticing. But I would be lying to everyone. You know? It seems like it would be hard to grow up in a house with two liars as parents."

"Yeah, I guess if you thought about it from your baby's perspective. I just thought..." She trails off, her lips thinning.

"Whatever you're thinking, I need you to say it out loud."

"Well, I thought that Dare offered you a way out. You say you want a family. And Dare is offering a way for you to have that. I know that he would probably be a less-than great husband, but you know that his money and resources would make sure that your child is set for life."

I nod slowly. "Yeah. That's definitely part of the reason why I'm struggling to make a decision. Just... Dare is undeniably very attractive, but looks fade. Then I'd be stuck with his personality, which is, to be honest, not great. I actually think I hate him."

"Yeah. I get that."

We come around a gentle curve in the road and the stables appear before us. There are a few small buildings, a barn, and a wide ring outside that is a fenced area where riders can trot and canter in circles.

I look at Olivia, who still looks distracted by our conversation.

"The question is, under what circumstances will you have this baby? Will the baby know who its real father is? Or will it think that its father is his or her uncle?" Her brow furrows. "Just saying that out loud is confusing."

I smile and link my arm with hers, tugging her toward the stables. "Let's forget about the baby and the proposal for just a little while. It's been forever since we volunteered here. We can try to enjoy our time while we're here, can't we?"

She sucks in a breath and gives her head a shake, smiling. "Yes, of course. Sorry. I just don't know how you are dealing with all this stuff."

"Pretty poorly. But hey, I am glad that you had the idea to come groom some horses. That will be really soothing."

"Just like when we were kids," she adds.

I nod and walk into the barn, thinking of how I used to love horses as a girl. I still love them now, but I was seriously horse crazy back then. Olivia and I both come from poor, working class families. All through our childhood, we would volunteer here on the weekends in exchange for a little riding time during the week.

It's been over a year since I've last been inside this barn, with its exposed beams, its hay-strewn floors, and its stalls built to house individual horses.

The old magic that I used to feel whenever I stepped in this building is still very much alive. I won't lie; I am excited just to be here. Each stall we pass is about fifty by fifty, and inside each one is a gorgeous horse munching on hay.

I stop at one horse in particular, a longtime favorite of mine. She is named Black Beauty, and she is an enormous black horse with not an ounce of fat anywhere on her beautifully muscular body. The smell of the stable and of horse dung is stronger in here. Although the stables have clearly been recently mucked out, my nose still twitches as I inhale the sickly-sweet odor of fermented horse feed, the smell of the dark soil that pervades every inch of the stables, and a hint of horse poop.

Olivia lets go of my arm and beams all around us. "I didn't know that this place could be such a mood lifter. But, honestly, the second I walk into the barn, I feel a million times better about everything."

"Same," I say.

I lean over a railing and greet Black Beauty, whispering that I missed her. I scratch her on the forelock, and she knickers in greeting.

"Well, if it isn't my two favorite girls!"

I turn from Black Beauty's pen and see that the owner of the stables is heading our way, dressed in knee-high leather boots, a pair of tan riding pants, and a spotless white dress shirt. She looks like what I imagine the inspiration for a Ralph Lauren photo spread would be. She is tall, her brown hair just beginning to gray at the temples, and she struts down the length of the barn towards us, looking every bit like a model.

"Gina!" Olivia calls. "I thought you said on the phone that you might not be here."

"What, and miss my two favorite volunteers?" Gina reaches us and gives us each a quick, hard hug. She isn't wearing any kind of weather appropriate jacket or anything. But come to think of it, I can't think of a single time when she expressed being the slightest bit chilly.

She beams at us and steps back, smoothing back a tendril of hair that has escaped from her ponytail. "Are you two going to ride today?" She asked.

Olivia looks at me with a frown and shoves her hands back in her pockets. I can tell that she doesn't want to ride, though I'm not exactly sure why. I shake my head in response to Olivia's question.

"If it's okay, Gina, I think that we will just groom today. We have a lot to talk about."

Gina arches a brow and looks at both of us suspiciously. "Is everything okay? Do you need me to do anything? You know I will do whatever I can."

Olivia reaches out and grabs my hand. "I think she just means that we have a lot of catching up to do. Right, Talia?"

My cheeks warm. "Yeah, totally. There is nothing to be alarmed about. Thank you for the offer, though."

Gina touches my shoulder and gives me a soft smile. "You got it. I have a private riding lesson coming up that I am going to go prepare for. But if you guys need anything, don't hesitate to ask. Thank you for grooming the horses. They always appreciated it, and so do I."

I can't not smile at Gina. "Of course. Anytime, really."

Gina is off then, stopping at one of the horse stalls and taking the Appaloosa out to the ring.

"Okay. Let's get to work."

Olivia looks around, her brow furrowing. "God, can you imagine if we didn't have to work here to earn our time in the riding ring? I don't know who Gina is giving a lesson to, but they are very lucky if they don't have to worry about how they will pay for their lesson."

I lean against the stall I'm in front of as I give Olivia a knowing look. "So that's what this is about? Did you bring me here to play groom at the stables because you want to show me that life would be easier if I were rich?"

Olivia walks around the stables, trying to pick a horse to groom. "I don't know what you're talking about."

"You are a terrible liar, Olivia."

I open Black Beauty's stall and let myself in, closing the gate after me. Olivia shrugs innocently, but she chooses the stall next to mine, a pretty palomino named Hurricane. "I don't know what I was thinking."

I pick up a long oval brush, its bristles sticking straight out. I then walk over to Black Beauty, letting her smell my hand. After a moment, she nibbles on my palm, and I start to brush her flank. The activity is rhythmic and soothing, not just to me but to Black Beauty as well.

Being at the stables doing an activity that we both wanted so badly to participate in as girls is obviously a gambit to get me to take Dare's deal.

Olivia turns from Hurricane with a frown. She points at me; her gaze is direct and intense.

"I want you to know that I'm not pressuring you to take this deal that Dare offered. I just wanted to remind you of the lifestyle we had as kids. And in doing so, I want to point out that there is an alternative."

I snort and keep brushing the horse's flank. "It's a life of relative poverty and drudgery, compared with a life of luxury and access. That's what you're saying?"

She walks around the palomino, disappearing behind its head. "I am not saying that those are the only two options. I am saying that they are among others. I know that you have always wanted a baby. And you have already said that you are going to have it. But the real question is, how are you going to pay for it? What if you have a kid who likes horses? Or flying planes? Or some other expensive hobby that you can't afford to pay for?"

My lips turn into a thin line. "I don't think that's entirely the point."

"Isn't it? That's only one tiny question when there are so many more. How are you going to feed the kid? How are you going to educate your baby when it's older? I just... I'm not advocating for Dare; really, I'm not. But I am saying that if you want to have this baby, you'll need to make some radical changes. You will probably need to sit down with your Aunt Minnie and have a tough conversation about money. Maybe think about moving out on your own at some point."

I shudder. "God, I can't picture my life living on my own."

Olivia pokes her head out from behind the horse, wrinkling her face. "I hate to say it, but Aunt Minnie is bad with money. Quite frankly, she is irresponsible with it. And if you keep living with her, you are going to run into this situation over and over again until she either stops giving away money she doesn't have or you don't live with her anymore. You know I love her dearly, but it's true."

I run my hand over Black Beauty's back, feeling a wave of uncertainty wash over me. I murmur, "And Dare is the solution?"

"He is *a* solution. Not the only one. Again, I want to

emphasize. You don't have to pick him. But you must have a plan. I am going to back you up, no matter what. But I need to know how to do that."

I take a deep breath as I walk around to Black Beauty's head, looking up into her dark eyes and running my fingers through her long, dark mane. "You're probably right. But let's talk about concrete pros and cons."

I hear the latch open and close and turn to see Olivia right behind me, her footsteps quiet as she approaches Black Beauty and pets her muzzle gently. "Okay. So, what are the pros that you could see from accepting Dare's proposal?"

I can't help but give a little laugh. "Well, we would get every physical thing that we've ever wanted. We would be fed, clothed, and have our pick of schools, all provided for by Dare. Plus, I wouldn't have to have this awkward conversation with Burn. I'm honestly dreading it."

Olivia takes the brush from my hand and runs it over Black Beauty's shoulder, humming a little to herself. She pauses. "And the cons?"

"God, where do I start? First, I would have to lie to everyone other than you about who knocked me up. That sounds tawdry, but it's how I feel. I would probably even have to lie to the baby. Plus, the baby would be raised as a Morgan."

"Is that a bad thing?" Olivia asked.

I pull my jacket around myself and look off into the distance. "The Morgan family isn't exactly what I would call close-knit. In fact, they are all at each other's throats the majority of the time. It's not really the dynamic that I want my kid to be raised around. Also, I personally find Dare repugnant. He'd have some say in how the child is raised. And the last thing I want for my child is for them to grow up to be a spoiled, rich child. Just... No."

"Okay. So, let's talk about what your plan would be if you decided to tell Burn and not to go with Dare's plan. Paint a picture for me."

I screw up my face, and Black Beauty nudges me with her nose, looking for attention or perhaps a treat. I bring my attention back to her and pet her neck again as I think about the question. "I'm not sure. I would tell Burn that I am pregnant. And then..."

I can't figure out what comes next. The idea of planning my life out is overwhelming for me. I have worked for years to get to where I am, though it may not seem like much to some people.

She stands on her tiptoes, looking at me over the horse's back. "Hey, you know that I am on your side, right?"

I blush and brush back a strand of my hair. "I know. Thanks for reminding me. I'm just out of sorts. And..." I purse my lips. "I'm trying to come to terms with the fact that I am growing a whole person inside my body. That part isn't quite real to me yet."

"Well, at least you know that you have a choice to make. When you have no choices, things are often more desperate and harder than they otherwise would be. At least Dare has a plan. That's more than anyone else has. Plus, whether you choose to tell Burn you're pregnant or accept Dare's proposal, you know that they are exactly your type."

I snort. "My type? How can I have a type? I've only ever had sex once."

She walks around the horse's head, her brows raised. "All the guys you had crushes on as a teenager and all the movie actors that you think are dreamy all look exactly like Burn and Dare. I'm sorry to say it, but you have a physical type that can't be denied."

"Olivia..." I protest.

She puts up a flat hand, palm out, stopping me from saying anymore. "If it wasn't true, we would not even be having this conversation. In fact, you wouldn't be pregnant."

I shoot her a glare and head out of the stall.

"Where are you going?" she asks.

"To watch Gina give her lesson," I announce as I sweep through the barn. Olivia follows me with a sulky look on her face.

Usually, we avoid watching the private lessons that Gina teaches. As long as I've known Olivia, her expression has grown sour each and every time that the topic has come up. Part of me thinks that she just resents the fact that neither of our families could ever afford anything so expensive.

Still, I head out to sit on the bench near the white picket fence that shapes the ring. Olivia plops down beside me, warily watching the figures move around the riding area.

Gina is standing next to a middle-school-aged girl, her kinky hair poking out from beneath her bright yellow T-shirt and lightweight Gucci jacket, which complements her glowing chestnut skin. The little girl grips the reins of her brown mare tightly, her face strained. Gina's voice rings out, her words muffled by her distance from where we sit. It's obvious that she gives the girl words of support and tips for more comfortable riding. The girl nudges her horse forward.

Olive leans in closer, her voice barely audible. "You see that little girl? That could be your daughter, Talia."

I look down, scraping some dirt with the toe of my boot. "I don't even know that I'm going to have a daughter. It could be a son."

"Okay, so your son could like horseback riding. What's your point?"

Olive slides over beside me, grabbing my hand and squeezing. I look up and into her intent gaze.

"Talia, you can provide more for your baby than you ever had in your own childhood if you choose to have Dare's child instead of just being a parent on your own. You know I only want the best for you. And that carries over to your baby, whom I will love and am very excited to meet. You two are my only concern."

I pull her into a tight hug, my eyes misting over. "I know. You're just looking out for me. I'm really glad that I have you as my best friend, Olivia."

We sit and chat for a while longer as we watch Gina's lesson progress. Then Olivia says she needs to head back to town to attend a meeting at work for her entire lab, and she can't be late to that.

I hug her goodbye at the curb outside the bookstore; she gives me a small wave and tells me that everything will be okay before she departs.

As I turn around and walk toward the bookstore, I see something out of place in the front window. At first, I think that it is an optical illusion of some sort. Aunt Minnie has gone overboard more than a few times when it comes to this front window.

But as I step closer, I spot Aunt Minnie on her hands and knees, picking up pieces of jagged glass from the floor. The display window has been completely smashed in on one side, leaving a gaping hole where someone grabbed every book that they could get their hands on.

My heart jumps into my throat. I rush inside, now that I can see the damage clearly. Not only has the front window been smashed, but the whole shop is in disarray, with reading chairs overturned, books and bookshelves on the floor, and all the piles of books kicked or pushed onto the floor.

"Aunt Minnie!" I shout. My hands fly up to my mouth. "Oh, my God! Are you okay?"

Rushing over to where she is still kneeling, I carefully help her to her feet. She has a broom and a dustpan in her hands, and she looks at me with a tearful expression. Her gray hair is wild and wiry, and her long, dark purple caftan is rumpled.

"I'm afraid they got away with everything in the cash register," she says. She wipes at her eyes. "Two men, wearing ski masks. They…"

"Wait, wait…" I say, shaking my head. "You saw them? Are you okay? What the hell happened?"

Minnie looks at me and then sets the broom and dustpan against the wall.

She rubs her hands over her face while shaking her head. "I don't know. They were big guys. And they said that they wanted the money that I owe for the store. I'm confused, because I don't think that my friend who loaned me the money has even called in my debts yet. I was under the impression that I had another month or two to come up with some of the money. But these guys knew about what I owed. When I couldn't give them anything, they started tearing the whole store apart and smashing the front window. They said that if I don't have anything for them when they come back in a week, they are going to break my bones."

Aunt Minnie looks at me, her face full of fear but trying to hold back her cascade of tears.

Her story fills me with so many emotions. The roar of blood pumping in my ears is so loud I can't hear her any longer. This is my absolute nightmare.

"Oh, Aunt Minnie!" Beckoning to her, I gather her in my arms and give her a tight hug. She begins to sob in my arms, apologizing profusely for having gotten herself into this mess. I let her cry for a couple of minutes, running my hand over her back and gently rocking her.

"It will be okay. Trust me, it'll all be okay."

"How can it be? She cries. Oh, Talia. I've really gotten myself into something that is too big for me to handle. What do I even do? Do I go to the police?"

I swallow, thinking of the money that Dare had offered me as part of his proposal. It's still insulting and unromantic. But now that it could save Minnie's life?

I'm starting to think that I should accept it and pay off her creditors. If I could save Minnie, her bookstore, and her home and give the leftover money to Hope House, that would be money well spent, as far as I'm concerned.

I rock Minnie back and forth, looking out the window toward the horizon.

I am done going over my options. I know what I need to do.

Chapter Nineteen

DARE

I grit my teeth and glare at my twin, my legs spread wide, and my fingers itching to do him harm. He leans against one corner of Remy's desk, glowering at me. Remy watches both of us from his broad desk, rocking back in his chair. My uncle Felix and my father are like a set of stone gargoyles, each perched in their corners of the office and watching our fight passively.

Burn slaps a hand down on the desk, drawing my attention.

"It's obvious I've already won. I think that because I am so much closer to being married and having a grandchild, I should be rewarded by being named the next CEO after Remy."

I roll my eyes and look at Remy, pleading my case. "He doesn't even have either of the qualifications that are necessary to win the race. He's having a hard time making Daisy move the wedding date up. That's why he is pulling this stunt."

Burn stands up, shooting me a glare, and then waving around the room. "I think we all agree on the facts. Simply put, Dare is getting nowhere with his desperate search to find a bride. He isn't going to win. So, I think that it is only fair to go ahead and name me the successor now."

He turns, directing his speech to Remy himself. "I pretty much have it in the bag. And despite what Dare says, I am persuading Daisy to move the wedding up."

I give a sharp, cold laugh. "I doubt that. I also doubt that she is ready to be a mother. When we were dating, she was not even sure that she would have a single child, much less an heir and a spare."

My brother frowns at me, crosses his arms, and taps his foot. "When you were engaged, she was a different person. She met me and decided to change. She says that with me by her side as a partner, she can do anything. Including having ten kids, if that's what I want."

"You know what? You fucking suck. And you're an asshole. But that doesn't even matter. Because I have a plan that is already in motion. And shortly, you'll all see just what it is. Trust me, it's great. At least, it is for me."

Burn's body tenses, his hands balling into fists. He narrows his eyes toward my face. I can tell that he's ready for violence.

Do I smirk at him? Or do I give him the same blank face that I have worked so hard to perfect?

"Fuck you!" Burn snarls. "I'll fucking destroy you."

"I don't see how, when I am going to win this competition and take over the family business."

Remy stands up with a suddenness that I wasn't expecting. He scowls at everyone in the room, then slowly turns to Burn. "Burn, I'm not going to declare you the de facto winner just yet. I can't be certain that you will give me a great-grandchild until you put that baby in my arms. And no, before you ask, adopting a child is not an option. It must be Morgan blood coursing through the veins of whatever child you bring in here."

My Uncle Felix stirs from the corner, rising from his chair and almost languidly walking over to the three of us. "No one is asking the important question. What if one or both are impotent?" He flashes a vicious smile. "I think you should include me in the race too. Let me do what your grandsons obviously can't do. I can lock down a wife this week and be trying to get her pregnant as soon as tonight."

Remy straightens his back, the movement appearing to be excruciating. He peers at my uncle, his lips curling. "Absolutely not. You had your chance, Felix. You blew it. And as for the twins being impotent? He swings his gaze around to us, making me straighten my spine with a single, cold look. "You'll see. You'll all see. These boys are my flesh and blood. They'll prove themselves virile."

"But Remy..." Burn tries to cut in.

Slicing his hand through the air decisively, Remy is done listening to us bicker. "That's enough. Now get moving. I have better things to do than to listen to you whine. And boys? I expect to hear big news from you very soon. Don't disappoint me."

Reflexively, the idea of what disappointing Remy looks like chills my veins.

"Dad, I was wondering if I could get a minute to talk to you about a new business venture." My father stands up, straightening the cuff of his wrinkled blue Oxford shirt.

"I don't think so. Fuck off now. I have actual business to do."

Remy waves his hand dismissively and turns his back on us.

I shake my head, because Remy was right. This was an immense waste of my time.

As I am leaving Remy's study, my phone buzzes in my pocket. I fish it out, scanning the text messages that I have received in the last thirty minutes with a bored, slightly annoyed eye. Then I see it.

A text from Talia Chance. Licking my lips, I open the message. It only says one word:

yes.

I stop in place, looking up thankfully and pumping my fist with a low hiss. "Yes."

Burn walks by me, purposefully slamming his shoulder into mine and sneering at me as he stalks past. But I hardly notice him.

Talia has just made my fucking day. No, she has made my whole life.

It's stupid that all my life choices have been reduced down to this little display of who wants Remy's love the most. But if Talia is convinced, I can move forward with my plan.

I head out of the estate, my mood shifting. I can't seem to stop grinning like an idiot. As I climb into my Porsche, I make a phone call by pressing one of the buttons on the dashboard.

"Call my lawyers," I command. A second later, one of my lawyers picks up his phone.

"Mr. Morgan," he says. "I didn't expect to hear from you before the deep sea drilling mineral rights were ready to be purchased. What can I help you with?"

"I need a prenuptial agreement," I say. I pull out of the driveway and head toward the town of Harwicke. "I'll text you the nitty-gritty details, but I need an ironclad contract. I am paying two hundred and fifty thousand now and two hundred and fifty thousand when she has our first baby. I want to be certain that there is a nondisclosure agreement built in about the money, too. She can't breathe a word about being paid or her child's paternity to anyone."

"Wow, okay. Most prenuptial agreements require both partners to wait a certain amount of time, say five years, before becoming fully vested. And then, of course, at ten or twenty years, there should be some wiggle room just in case you decide to divorce."

"No. We're not going to divorce. I want to make sure that she will never leave me. I want her to feel like she will be crushed if she decides to divorce."

My lawyer clears his throat. "I see. Well, we can talk about ways to do that."

"Great. When you have a contract for me to look at, email it to me."

"Okay," he says. But before he can speak again, I cut the call off.

I pay him a fuckton of money. I don't need to be nice on top of that.

I quickly dictate a text to my personal assistant, asking to meet him because I have a lot of news for him.

He replies with an address, and I gun the engine, heading into Harwicke.

I pull up outside Herbsaint, the bar that Tristen introduced me to. It's in a trendy part of town where there are tons of mixed-use buildings and warehouse lofts. I check the address and head into a building that sits across the street, five stories tall and newly refurbished.

The doorman greets me, asking me if I am Mr. Morgan. I tell him that I'm here to meet Rob, and he sends me up a newly installed stainless-steel elevator to the top floor. I step out, expecting construction or maybe an art gallery or something.

But the elevator opens into a huge, airy space with a kitchen on the left and a stylish and sleek living room to my right. Behind those rooms, there are rice paper walls dividing the rest of the spaces from my view.

Rob peeks his head out from behind the rice paper divider in the living room, his eyes full of excitement. "Isn't this place just everything?"

He gestures to the newly refinished walls, which are matte dark blue on the bottom and slick cream on the top. I look around, taking in the luxury finishes.

There are colorful chandeliers, each one a different shade of pale blue or light yellow. The metal finishes on every surface are chrome and bronze, and the marble floors gleam with gold accents. The living room has white couches that are lined with soft pillows. Overall, it looks like a lot of expense has gone into designing this apartment, if that's what it is.

"It's nice," I say. "What's it for?"

"Well, it's just been built out by a luxury design firm. You were saying that you wanted to rent or buy a place close to home that wasn't the estate or the hotel you live in." He looks all around him, gesturing to the whole apartment. "What do you think? It's very swanky."

I exhale, looking around. "What's it on the market for?"

"My realtor friend says that it's priced at five million. But since you can buy the property without any outside financing, I was thinking that you could offer four-point-four million for it."

Squinting at it I think for a second. "It could be nice to have a base of operations here instead of living out of the hotel. Plus, I have a new fiancée who would probably find the idea of having a home important."

Rob turns to me, running his thumb under his lapels. He has a look like he was just smacked in the face. "I'm sorry; I must have misheard you. Did you say you had a fiancée?"

"That's right, I am engaged."

Saying the words out loud feels odd. I don't think of myself as a romantic at heart, and yet there is some part of me that resists the title of fiancée. I know that I am not actually going to be swept up in a bunch of hokey, sappy feelings for Talia or anything. But a teeny, tiny sliver of my boyhood self struggles with my now-impending marriage.

Crushing that feeling to the ground and flinging it aside, I smile. "I'm getting married. That's exactly what is going to happen. As soon as possible."

He blinks at me. "But I thought that you were going to go through a matchmaker?"

I shake my head. "Nope. The woman I've chosen is perfect for me in every way," I bluff. "She is my ideal match."

I look around, my brow puckering. "I suppose that this place will do for us to live in as man and wife. We'll only need it until Remy picks me as the heir to the fortune. We'll eventually move to New York City. In fact, I plan to move the entire headquarters of Morgan Drilling to New York City." I smirk. "I've always hated this town, and now I can finally exact my revenge on it."

Rob begins to pace the floor, pulling out a phone and typing into it furiously. "When is the wedding?"

"Wedding? Oh. I don't know. It's not important. We'll probably just have one done by a justice of the peace one afternoon."

Rob looks up at me, stopping in his tracks. "That's it? That's how Dare Morgan gets married?"

I shrug my shoulders and walk over to the window, looking out at the view. From here, I can look down on the street corner and even see the rooftop patio that accompanies the bar across the street. I purse my lips.

"It's not important. I'm not marrying for love. I am marrying for money. And my bride-to-be feels the exact same way."

He follows me to the window, his gaze flicking out to take in the scene below. "Do you want to wait to have her see this place before you buy it?"

I snort. "Who cares what her opinion of where we live is? I don't care. You shouldn't care, either."

Rob stares at his phone, making more notes.

"I see," he murmurs.

I check my watch and sigh. "I must get going. But we should make an appointment to have a justice of the peace visit us wherever we are. Maybe we can do that next week." I pause. "Well, actually... Let's wait on that. First, I must have Talia checked out by a doctor. There are a lot of contracts that must be signed beforehand."

Rob arches a brow. "You're making your fiancée go to a doctor before you can get married?"

I wave him down. "I am marrying her because I knocked her up."

Rob puts his hand out, studying himself on the windowsill and looking gobsmacked. "You what?"

I grin and clap him on the shoulder. "That's right. There is already a new Morgan cooking in her oven."

He looks so shaken. The fact that I am lying only makes his response funnier to me, although honestly, it could just as easily have been me instead of Burn at the Raven's Head Club that night.

I could have taken pretty little Talia home. It's just a matter of logistics, really.

"Don't worry. I would've probably married her anyway," I lie. "She's great. Really."

She's anything but great. But I don't need my personal assistant to pick apart my choice of wife.

Rob puts his phone in his pocket and shakes his head. "I guess I am just having trouble taking it all in. That's a lot of news for one day."

Straightening the cuffs of my shirt, I jerk my head toward the elevator. "I must go. But get your real estate agent to call my lawyers and get the process of buying this place started. Hopefully, we won't be here for long. But you never know with Remy."

My good mood stays with me all the way back to the Morgan estate. I am still smirking as I walk in the door, hoping that I just happen to run into Burn but he's not here. Neither is Remy, it seems.

Damn, the one time I was looking forward to seeing the old bastard.

I must tell somebody, so I walk straight through the mansion, making a beeline for the kitchen. Magda is just putting blueberries on top of a lemon curd tart, her mouth pinched as she tries to decide if her dessert is done or not. When I burst through the double doors, she looks up at me in surprise, and then a warm smile spreads across her face.

"You're back!" She cries. She wipes her hands on her apron before walking over to me and giving me a quick, hard hug. She looks up at me, tucking her hair into a faded red handkerchief that she has wrapped around her head. I can feel her eyes on my face.

"You look happy today."

I grin at her. "Oh, was I smiling?"

She gives me a funny look and walks back to the counter-top, lifting the pie and bringing down a fancy glass lid. She carries the pie toward the refrigerator, and I move almost automatically to pull the refrigerator door open for her. She slides the pie in and then pats my cheek.

"Sit down. I'll make you some tea. Unless you are hungry?"

I walk over to take a seat at the counter and shake my head. "Tea is fine. I actually came here to tell you something."

Magda gets a white ceramic mug down from a cupboard, drops a teabag in from a box on the counter, and starts an electric kettle. With that done, she turns and leans against the counter, favoring me with a smile. "What is that my dear?"

I hold on to the moment before I speak, knowing that her reaction to my news is probably going to be the only truly favorable one I get. "Do you remember the young lady I brought to the manor before?"

She looks thoughtful for a moment. "The redheaded one?"

"Yes, her name is Talia."

She nods. "She seems very nice. You like her?"

I force a smile on my lips, neatly avoiding her question. "I actually asked Talia to marry me today. And she said yes."

I might be fudging the timeline just a little bit, but Magda's look of jubilant surprise is worth it. She rushes over, hugging me excitedly. I let myself enjoy it for a few moments, putting an arm around her and closing my eyes. I am not exactly starved for touch but it's not every day that I have Magda around. My life is not full of people that I feel like hugging.

The rest of my family is so cutthroat. And the women I usually sleep with are only interested in a few hours between the sheets, not in hugging.

When Magda steps back, she blots her eyes with her

apron. "I'm so happy. You found a good one with her; I can feel it."

I can feel the back of my neck heat slightly. "Thank you."

"What is her last name?"

I squint. "Talia Chance."

"And what does she do for a living?"

Magda fills my mug with water and places it before me. I drum my thumb against the cool stainless steel of the kitchen islands.

"I don't know. She works in a bookstore. It doesn't really matter. She will have to give up any job that she currently has when she marries me."

Magda studies me for a moment and then starts pulling out a pot and some potatoes for a future meal. "Does Talia know that?"

I scowl. "She is fine with it. Or rather, she will be."

Magda doesn't bother looking at me, but I can hear her disapproval in her voice as she begins sorting the potatoes. "Dare, you tend to decide important things without considering the feelings of others. So, does she really feel like she can just give up her work? Or is that something that you have decided for her?"

I dunk my teabag in my mug and take a sip. "She'll be fine with it. Trust me."

Magda straightens her back and wipes her hands on her apron, giving me a wary look. "I think you are taking the race to get married and have a baby too seriously. Perhaps you should slow down a little and think this through."

Setting my mug down, I push myself to my feet. Magda is the only person with whom I feel comfortable enough to be chastised by. But she is not helping the situation by asking questions like this.

I walk around the large kitchen island, touching Magda's

arm gently. "I know who I'm marrying. I know what I am doing. You have done a great job of looking out for me for so many years. But I need you to support me now. No more questions, no more poking the bear."

Magda smiles at me a little sadly and reaches up to pat my cheek. "Of course, my darling. I only want what is best for you."

Giving Magda a quick hug, I force a smile onto my lips.

My good mood has vanished now, turning sour under the light that she has shed on it. Perhaps my marriage is more delicate than it seems.

"I have to go," I say. "But I will bring Talia around to see you again. Okay?"

She smiles and starts rolling up her sleeves. "Of course. I'll be here." She turns away, walking over to turn on the tap.

I use my shoulder to push through the swinging door and emerge into the hallway, a sigh on my lips.

One thing has become clear to me. If my engagement couldn't stand up to Magda's gentle questioning, it will need a more solid foundation. I must make everyone believe that I am head over heels for Talia. That's the only way to make our short courtship seem like a romantic thing rather than the rushed hatchet job that it really is.

I'll have to know much more about her and be able to answer questions about her life. Plus, I'll have to be more comfortable touching her. And she will have to look like she is infatuated with me in return. We will both have to pretend not to hate each other to pull this ruse off. We will need to rehearse.

On my way to the front of the mansion, I run into Clive. He is on his knees in the foyer, his shirt sleeves rolled up, with a small silver mirror on a piece of newspaper on the floor. He is removing screws from the back of the mirror, his attention riveted.

I walk up to him, surprising him with a few words.

"What are you doing?" I ask.

His body jolts, clutching his chest, and he looks at me with great alarm.

"Oh! Mr. Morgan, I didn't see you coming." He exhales a shaky breath. "I'm just repairing this mirror so that it can be hung back on the wall."

He starts to stand up, but I wave him down. "No, no, don't get up. I am on my way out the door."

He arches a brow and puts down the screwdriver he is holding. "Is there anything I can help you with?"

I look down the long hallway, scanning it as I think about his question. "Actually, since you asked, could you call to have our estate on the coast of Maine ready for me to visit as soon as possible? I would love to take a date there for the weekend."

Clive bows his head. "Of course, sir."

"You know I hate it when you call me that. I'm not like Remy."

His lips lift at the corners in a rare smile. "No one ever said you were, sir."

I pause. "Could you also line up a team of hair and makeover experts to come to the coastal estate? I need my date to have a makeover. I need a new wardrobe for her, as well."

Clive sits back on his knees, pulling out a small notepad and a pen, and writing down a note with a flourish. "When will you need the team ready?"

"Probably tomorrow, around midday. I can let you know more in the next few hours."

"All right. Consider it done."

Pushing out my cheek with my tongue, I think of one final thing.

"Can you also have a doctor waiting for us at the airport? I need a female practitioner to give my date a physical exam. Just get a name for me and text it to my personal assistant. He'll take over from there and steer it to the finish line."

Putting his hands on his knees, he climbs to his feet and dusts off his hands. "I can do it for you right away."

I clap him on the shoulder, giving him a reassuring smile.

"That would be great. Now, if you don't mind, I have to go. I have a girl to hunt down."

Clive quirks a brow, but I just head out of the mansion, putting on a pair of sunglasses before sliding into my Porsche. Throwing it in gear, I rev the engine and then pull out of the driveway with a loud screech.

I have a fiancée to finesse and there is no time to waste.

Chapter Twenty

TALIA

Rushing into the back hallway of Tusk, I lean up against a wall and breathe out. I let my eyes close for just one second, conscious always of the buzz of the dinner guests, the chime of silverware against plates, and the scraping of chairs. It's only Thursday night, but the restaurant is jam packed, and I just need a moment, a few seconds, to rest my aching feet and quell my nausea.

The restaurant is full of all kinds of different food smells, often combining and conflicting. Just a moment ago, I inhaled a waft of seared steak as a customer cut into it. I stiffened and ran for the back room, where I am hiding out in the shadows now.

"The manager is looking for you," a blonde waitress calls down the hallway.

I suck in a breath and push off the wall, determined to see my shift through. I read online that the nausea should fade away after the first trimester. Pressing my hands against my abdomen, I try to keep that in mind as I hold my breath while I walk through the restaurant.

Danny, a restaurant manager that I don't really know, is

waiting impatiently at the hostess stand for me. He brushes a piece of fuzz off his dark lapel and checks his watch as I return.

"It's only seven p.m. You should be manning the host station or walking around the dining room, talking to guests, and clearing plates. I don't know how much clearer I can be."

I swallow and drop my gaze, stepping behind the hostess stand. "Of course. Sorry, I was just taking a bathroom break."

He frowns at me. "No more bathroom breaks for the rest of your shifts. Got it?"

Red as a beet, I gulp. "Of course. Should I make the rounds of the dining room, then?"

He opens his mouth to berate me, his expression already antagonistic. But stops when a short, balding man in an expensive-looking suit gets up from the bench he was waiting on and walks towards us. The customer looks between me and Danny, his expression aggrieved.

"I was supposed to be seated ten minutes ago," he complains. "My date is very hungry. How long are we supposed to wait?"

Pursing my lips, I turn toward the customer and give him a bright smile. "I'm so sorry that you have been waiting. It looks like your name is next on the list." I run my finger down the waitlist on the computer screen, remembering his name from when he first checked in at the hostess stand. "Tanner, party of two. Right?"

The man scowls at me and crosses his arms. "That's correct. I want to be taken to my seat now, if you don't mind."

I gesture out toward the dining room. "As you can see, the whole dining room is full right now. But a few tables are finishing up right now. Again, I apologize for the delay."

"Well, what am I going to get for waiting?" He demands.

Danny cuts me a look and intercedes, putting his hand in between the customer and me. "Mr. Tanner, if you would like a complementary cocktail, I would be more than happy to go grab them for you right now."

"That's not my name!" The customer says, his voice becoming louder. "That's my date's name. My name is Alex, and I want to sit down and eat right now. I see an empty table right there, too." He points to the chefs' table, a large twelve-person booth next to the host stand.

I jump in, trying to soothe him and explain to him at the same time that we have a special party booked for that table that will be here in ten minutes. The party has a reservation with a star next to it, indicating that the chef actually knows them. So, there is no way in hell that I can seat the complaining guest there.

"I'm sorry, sir. If you could just…"

The customer's face grows red, and he balls his fists up. "If you don't sit me at that table right now, I will rip you apart."

"Sir, she's just trying to…"

"I don't care what she is trying to do!" the customer screams.

My heart beats in my chest.

I don't understand why anyone would make this big of a scene or what he could possibly hope to gain from yelling at us. Danny moves forward, raising his hands in a conciliatory gesture. The man bats at Danny's hand, causing Danny to back away suddenly.

I look between the two men, trying to figure out the odds of a fight breaking out right here and now.

At that very moment, Dare decides to stroll in the front door of my restaurant. He is looking around and taking in the scene playing out before me.

As the customer starts yelling at Danny, Dare strolls over, arching a brow at me.

He looks down at me with a little smirk on his face. "You don't have to be here," he says coolly. "Do you want to leave with me?"

In the heat of the moment, I swear that I have never been so happy to see Dare. I nod tightly, my jaw tensing. My eyes mist up.

Dare holds his arm out to me with a cruel smile on his lips.

Taking his arm is the only natural solution here. So I do, stepping out from behind the hostess stand.

Danny's head whips around, taking note of Dare.

"What are you doing?" He thunders. "We're dealing with a situation here."

I swallow, my hand flying up to my throat. My other hand instinctively covers my belly—a new experience of just what being pregnant will entail.

But Dare doesn't wait for me to speak up. Instead, he snarls toward the two men, moving forward aggressively. They step back immediately, their eyes glued to Dare's exposed teeth. A vague look of horror splashes across Danny's face.

Without so much as another word, Dare guides me out of the front door. As we are leaving, Dare shouts back over his shoulder.

"She quits!"

"What?" Danny shouts. But soon his voice is muffled by the front door as it closes.

Dare quickly strides just a few feet in front of me and reaches to open the door of his Porsche. He looks at me, his eyes shining with a certain kind of mischief. He tilts his head to the side, indicating that I should get in. My pulse racing, I climb in the car, and Dare shuts the door firmly on me.

Dare climbs in the car and starts the engine; he looks at me with a smirk. "You know, you're leaving behind everything you ever knew. This town is a tiny pond. I am about to open your world and let you swim in the sea with all the big fucking sharks."

He revs the engine, a grin exploding over his face.

"What?" I ask, perplexed. "Where are we going?"

He loosens his tie, ripping it off and throwing it behind him. "To the airport."

"The airport? Where are we really going?"

He pulls off with a screech of tires, a mischievous look in his eyes once more. "Somewhere quiet where we can practice being engaged."

For some reason, his answer makes a flush creep up my neck. I buckle my seatbelt and bite my lip, looking out the window.

We arrive at the airport in record time thanks to Dare's driving, which takes us well over the speed limit almost the entire way. He drives me to a private tarmac, where a helicopter is waiting.

He turns off the car and then gives me a once-over, from my hair to my shabby dress and my booted feet. "Before I slide the engagement ring onto your finger, I need to know for sure that you're actually pregnant."

My cheeks feel hot. "How am I supposed to prove that to you?"

He jerks his head toward the small airplane hangar that we are parked next to. "There is a lady doctor inside that building, waiting for you. You just have to pee in a cup for now. Later, there will be blood tests. But all I need to know is that you are carrying a Morgan in your womb."

"I don't really feel comfortable showing anyone a test. But if it will make you feel more certain about it, then I guess I have no choice."

He gives me a chilling smile. "You really don't. I'll be waiting right here for you when you come out of the hangar."

Heading inside the hangar, I look around at the soaring ceilings and the small private plane that is parked in the middle of the large space.

"Are you Talia?"

I turn and see the doctor, a middle-aged woman with ebony skin and a short bob hairstyle. I nod, and she beckons me, leading me into a restroom. She offers me a cup, looking at me sympathetically. "I'm afraid I'll have to stay while you fill the cup."

"Really?" I ask. "Is that necessary? I obviously don't have anything with me. I can't mess with the results."

She gives me a sympathetic smile and clicks the lock on the door handle. "The sooner you do it, the sooner it will be over. Trust me, I am not getting any more joy out of this than you are."

I look at her, judging that she is telling the truth about that at least. "Do you mind turning around?"

She turns her back on me, and I go through the process of filling the little plastic cup she gave me, my face burning the entire time.

After I'm done and I've washed my hands, I hand the sample off to her. She has put on gloves, and she quickly and efficiently dunks a strip into the cup of my urine. Exactly one minute later, with me fidgeting all the while, she looks at me with a smile.

Pulling off her gloves, she announces, "Congratulations. You're pregnant."

She produces a small trash bag, into which she dumps the gloves, the test strip, and the urine.

"Thanks, I guess." I give her a little side eye as I let myself out of the restroom. She follows me, staying right behind me. When she sees Dare, she gives a thumbs-up signal.

I hadn't realized until that moment that Dare was nervous. As he gets the signal from the doctor, the easing of the tension across his face is obvious. He beckons to me, turning to the helicopter and points to the pilot, who is sitting inside. The rotators start churning, whipping up quite a wind. It's deafening from here, and I put my hands over my ears as I run up to Dare.

"We are not leaving in that, are we?"

He slings his arm over my shoulders, which causes me to tense up. He leans close, shouting in my ear. "Relax. This is your new life. Of all the things you have to get used to, this is one of the easiest."

"What if I don't want to go?" I ask, looking at the helicopter.

"Are you really going to say no to me now? Literally all your money hangs in the balance. If you don't do what I ask, I'll find another woman. I had options for my wife. You must realize that."

Glaring at him, I pull the edges of my coat closer together, a breeze whipped up by the helicopter running right through me. "That's an awful thing to say to the woman that you are supposed to be marrying."

He cocks a brow and grabs my arm. "Just be glad that I am picking you. You should feel lucky."

I'm not feeling lucky, I think. I clench my jaw and stare at the helicopter, my stomach already doing flips. But Dare doesn't wait and doesn't ask my opinion.

He just drags me toward the helicopter.

———————

I AM in my own pool of humiliation as we start to land, at last. My stomach has been upset since the lift-off point, but I was too busy replaying the scene in the hangar bathroom to even notice.

When we begin to descend, I turn to stare out the window. I've been so miserable this entire flight that I didn't even really notice that we were landing on a private helipad.

We never really left the shore, but I could tell we were going up north. The shore is rockier and the ocean is frothier here, the beach leading up to a dramatic cliff. Just beyond, there is a large white mansion sitting on the beach.

When the pilot sets the chopper down, Dare springs from the helicopter, ripping off his headphones. He doesn't even wait for me before turning and marching toward the house.

I clamber down from the helicopter, thanking the pilot, before I stop for a second. I put my hand to my mouth, fighting back the wave of sickness I feel.

If helicopters are the way that rich people get around, flitting from place to place, I don't want to be a part of it. Shuddering at the icy wind that rolls off the ocean, I hug my coat close and hurry to follow in Dare's footsteps.

As I finally catch up to him, he grins at me.

"So? It's nice being in the air for such a short time, huh?"

I screw up my face and look forward, noticing the edge of a building down below the edge of the cliff. I squint at it and try to keep my expression from being bitter.

"I think I hated it more than I have ever hated any trip in my life."

He snorts. Finally, seeming to notice me hurrying to keep up with his pace, he slows his steps.

"You didn't like the helicopter? Why didn't you tell me?"

"I was trying not to die or throw up."

"Well, you'll have to get used to it. I probably spend more time in the helicopter than I do on my private plane."

"That must be nice. I wouldn't know, because I've never flown anywhere. Not in a plane, not in a helicopter."

He stops in his tracks, confused. "Wait, what? Really?"

"Where would I even go? Harwicke is the only place I've ever known."

He gives a grunt of disgust. "We'll have to fix that." He starts walking again, leaving me to wonder how one would fix that exactly.

With the mansion looming large to our left, I point out the structure on the beach below. Winding steps that look precarious lead down from the cliff to the structure.

"What's that?"

"The boathouse," he replies. "We will go down there at some point, I imagine. I love to sail."

His comment startles me a little bit. I hadn't thought about what he might like to do. He exists in some parallel universe that I've constructed. Outside of anything positive, outside of liking, loving, or cherishing anything, to hear him say that he loves doing something like sailing... It's just an alien concept to me.

"Are you saying that you like to play with boats?" I ask.

He lets out a cold laugh. "If you want to put it that way, yes. I keep a sailboat and a yacht here."

"A yacht? You Morgans really have it all figured out, don't you?"

He stops again, his stare icy. "The Morgans aren't big fans

of boats. The boats are a holdover from the Mercers, my mom's family. It's the only thing I have left of her."

I blink, swallowing. Obviously, I've stepped on a touchy area. But before I can apologize or maybe make a joke to cut the tension, he whirls around and heads off toward the front door of the mansion.

Jesus, I have no idea why he is so sensitive about the whole thing. Maybe his mom causes a lot of drama or something. I have never met her, so I wouldn't know.

Dare is already fully inside the house before I even reach the front door. Stopping at the threshold, I look around. Everything that I can see is made of dark wood and has plain white painted walls. It is a little less fancy than the Morgan mansion in Harwicke.

Still, as I look to my right, there is a staircase made of that same wood, and there are several framed pictures on the wall of women and couples from older, possibly happier times.

An unknown gentleman comes up to me, his hair white, his suit dark, and his expression haughty. He carries a white linen towel over his arm as though he were about to serve me a meal. He casts his gaze over me and sniffs.

"Welcome to the Cliffs," he says. His voice is nasally, his words meaningless to me.

"Thank you." I say.

"Please, come this way."

I follow him through the hallway and into a wood-paneled room. Though large, the room seems vaguely claustrophobic, and I pinpoint the fact that there are no windows in here. There is, however, a fireplace with a crackling, snapping fire.

All around it are uncomfortable looking, overstuffed leather couches. There isn't so much as a table or a free-standing light fixture in here. The room is lit by sconces, which are doing a poor job of illuminating it.

Dare is already sprawled out on one of the couches, his coat messily cast aside. He looks at the butler and waves a hand, dismissing him. "We're fine. Leave us."

I stand in the doorway, shivering and looking around. The butler bows his head, and I move aside to let him pass.

Dare looks at me, the firelight playing tricks on his face. I swear I see a hint of hunger in those blue-green eyes of his. But it's gone in the blink of an eye, just as quickly as I saw it.

"For fucks sake," Dare announces. "Come in, sit down."

My teeth start to chatter. The fire may be nice to look at, but whoever designed the chimneys did a poor job at making sure that the fire would actually warm the occupants of the room.

I walk in and take a seat, pulling my coat close to my body. Dare looks at me for a moment and then stands up, going over to a pile of blankets on the end of the couches. He carries them back, unfolding them before slinging each layer on top of me.

"How did you grow up on the coast just like I did, and yet you have no innate weatherproofing?"

My teeth chatter. "I don't know," I manage.

He goes over to the door of the room and shuts it, then turns back and regards me.

"I'm going to need you to agree to a few things. And not just agree; I'm going to need you to sign a contract saying that you will do as I please."

I pull the blankets closer to me. They have a faint smell of must, like they have been lying on the couch for several years. Still, it's better than nothing.

Between my clenched teeth, I say, "Like what?"

He gives me a wicked look and starts to pace the room, like a tiger trapped in a cage. "I'm so glad you asked. The first point is that we will have an ironclad prenup. Essentially, it will be a guarantee for me that you can never leave without facing complete financial ruin."

"That doesn't seem fair." I spit out.

"It's not. It's not intended to be fair. It's intended to have dire consequences if you break the prenup."

Huddling under the blankets, I can't really think of how to come back to that. What do you say to a man as deranged as Dare?

"Well? What are the other things? I'm sure they're just as ridiculous."

Dare ticks off items on his fingers like he is making a grocery list or something. "For one thing, you'll have to try to forget all the standards that you have tried to live up to. Instead, you'll aim to meet my impossibly high standards. You'll have to fake it until you make it for at least a little while. But I have no doubt that you'll get there in the end."

I squint at him, licking my teeth. "Great. That sounds totally achievable and not at all intimidating."

He cocks his head and paces around the room, wrapped up in listing items and not really paying full attention to me.

"You also need to know that by marrying me, your child becomes mine. I am his father from that point on. No matter what, hell or high water."

Surprisingly, I don't have anything to add. That one actually seems rather sweet, in a fucked-up way.

"My fourth point is that you must keep the secret of the child's parentage and of our fake marriage safe from anyone ever knowing the truth. That means you can't tell your aunt, your friends, your doctor, or anyone else. If you see a therapist, I fully expect that you will lie about this one aspect of your life. No one can ever know. "

He turns, pinning me with his gaze. "I mean it."

I notice that my teeth are no longer chattering. I peel the

blankets away from my upper body and exhale dramatically. "That much we can both agree on. I don't want to tell anybody that I sold myself for my baby. So, the secret is just between us."

I glance away, my eyes narrowing on the horizon. If I were being completely honest with Dare, I would tell him that I've already spilled my guts to my best friend Olivia. But Olivia will never tell anyone. And I doubt that Dare is holding his own secrets close to his chest.

He resumes pacing, his back-and-forth movements nearly hypnotic by now. "Oh, I should think that you wouldn't want anyone to know," he agrees.

I feel a flush rising in my cheeks, but I refuse to be shamed by him. After all, I'm only doing what he wants me to do.

"Is there anything else that you want me to sign my name to?"

His lips lift at the corners, but he doesn't make eye contact with me. Instead, he just stalks back and forth, his circuit almost predetermined.

"Yes, I'm going to make a final point very explicit in the contract."

"Oh yeah?" I say, my eyes rolling. "What is that? A no-cheating rule?"

He stops dead, his head snapping toward me. The fiery look in his eyes makes me wish I hadn't said anything. "I didn't think I had to say that. But yes. There is no looking at other men, no flirting with other men, and no fucking around behind my back. I am the only man you'll ever look at. Do you understand, Talia?"

I gulp, feeling the blood draining from my face. His glare is so intense; his posture is primed and ready; his hands form loose fists. I'm so caught off guard by it that I just nod.

"I was kidding," I rush to explain. "Of course, I don't expect to sleep around. I don't expect to sleep with anyone."

His gaze doesn't falter for a second. Moving towards me, he kneels in front of me and grabs my hands.

"Swear it. Tell me right now."

My heart beats against my rib cage, a wildly fluttering bird yearning for freedom. My lips are dry, and I can't look away from my future husband. For just this second, no one else exists in the entire universe. He squeezes both my wrists in his hands, and he growls at me.

"Promise me! I want to hear it!"

"I… I promise. I swear."

"You swear what?" he says, giving me a shake. "Tell me."

I lick my lips; my blood is cold as ice and yet hot as fire all at once. "I'll never cheat on you."

"Not ever," he grits out, his voice low and rough. "Especially not with my brother."

My breath falters. "Of course not. The whole reason that I am marrying you is that I don't like your brother at all in any way."

"Good." He hisses. "Well, that brings me to the final point."

God, what could be so serious? He's looking at me now like he requires my consent to keep drawing breath or something. Like if I suddenly say no, he will stop living or something.

Dare's face is cruel, callous, and cold as he offers his final edict.

"Don't fall in love with me." He says it so seriously and with such perfect diction that I find his words confusing.

"What?" I ask, shaking my head as if to dislodge something from my ears. I must've misheard him.

"You can't fall in love with me under any circumstances.

It's a terrible idea. Love is messy. It's unpredictable. It's challenging. And I need the opposite of that from you. I'm looking for something as simple, easy, and predictable as the tides. That is what I am paying you for, Talia. You understand, don't you?"

The audacity of him telling me not to fall in love with him causes a bark of laughter to escape my lips. "You are insane. You know that, right?"

He growls and pulls my face closer to his. "I'm no fool. I've been led down the garden path before with a girl. And I'm not going to do it again. Do you hear me? Your kid..."

I can't help but spit back, "Our kid. Didn't you say that he would be your child, too, once I officially sign this contract?"

His lips thin, and he gives me an imperious look. "Whatever that's supposed to mean. I only meant that you should keep your mouth shut, darling girl."

A shudder runs through my body, radiating out from his grip on my arm to the very soles of my feet.

"I assure you that I am not going to just roll over one day and fall head over heels in love with you. Our situations coincided at the right time. But I still fundamentally hate your guts. I want my baby to have a great life. But I don't need some fairytale wedding or fantasy romance for that to happen. I can live without either of those things as long as my baby and I have a roof over our heads and food in our bellies."

Dare's lips curl. "Good. Because I have nothing to offer in that department. My ex-girlfriends have all accused me of being cold and unfeeling. Hell, when Daisy left, she said that she was getting a personality upgrade when she agreed to marry my brother. So, softness and kindness are not the qualities that you will find running rampant in my veins. I will be a strong father, and I will be richer than God. But don't ever expect me to love you. That's a bridge too far."

Don't ever expect me to love you.

His words sting just a tiny bit. Some little voice calls out somewhere deep inside, feeling like I deserve better. But that voice is small, stupid, and damaged. I don't need to listen to every gut impulse I have.

Lifting my chin, I glare at Dare. "Fine."

He gets so close that I can feel his breath as it leaves his mouth and fans over my lips. He stares at me, right through me, as if he can see into my soul, right down to the core of my shattered heart. My heart pounds, driving its rhythm against my chest.

"Fine," he says. "It's settled, then."

He releases me, pushing himself away, standing back up, and smoothing his hands down the front of his dark jacket as if I somehow rumpled it. He plows his hand through his short, dark hair and gives himself a shake.

I suck in a breath, wondering if every argument with Dare would be that intense.

"What else do we need to talk about now that you brought me here for the weekend?" The words escape me without me even thinking them through.

Dare looks at his watch, his eyes narrowing. He fishes his phone out of his pocket, his mouth pulling down at the corners.

"I need to work for a while."

Pushing the blankets off my body, I stand up. Dare cuts me a look, and I open my mouth. He holds up a hand, rolling his eyes, and shaking his head.

"Don't. You'd better get used to me saying that I must work. I'm going to be saying it well into my eighties, so you'll have to hear it for another fifty years if you sign my fucking contract. I know that you said yes because you needed safety and security, but you also signed up to deal with my working all the time."

I shake my head, my mouth pinching.

"It's true," he continues. "And besides that, I'll need a lot of time alone. Despite what it may seem like, I need plenty of down time to recharge myself fully."

I walk over to the fire, putting my hands out and feeling the warmth of it. "That sounds like what men tell their wives when they steal away for the weekend to see their mistress."

Dare turns away, walking to the door and yanking it open. "Maybe I am not the kind of man who takes a mistress. Maybe I have my yacht instead. She is always waiting for me with open arms. She doesn't need me to be anything but the man I already am."

I make a small sound of disgust. "You are a spoiled little boy. You know that? You just happen to be a billionaire, so you have yachts instead of toy ships. It's ridiculous."

Dare waves a hand up and down his body, issuing his ultimatum. "I am as you find me. The deal still fucking stands. You can take it or leave it, but decide which path you're on, and do it soon."

With that, he whirls, leaving the room. I'm left gawping at the open doorway, feeling the feeble warmth of the fireplace as it flickers against my skin.

Take him or leave him.

He is what he is. Even though I think he might actually be the fucking Devil.

Swallowing, I remind myself why I'm here. There is five hundred thousand dollars on the line. I yank the two halves of my coat closer, burrowing in it. To save Aunt Minnie, our bookstore, and Hope House, I can deal with the Devil.

Chapter Twenty-One

DARE

The sun has long since risen when I head outside, my jaw clenched, ready to pounce on anyone who so much as looks at me the wrong way. I know it's exactly the way that Remy usually behaves. His staff is all terrified of him whenever he gets into a mood because he lashes out and fires people left and right.

Not wanting to replicate that environment, I take a long walk outside.

When I reach the edge of the cliff, just beside the pathway that begins to slope down from here to the boathouse, I stare out into the ocean. It is still extremely windy outside, with the chilly air ripping at my clothes and tussling my hair.

The sea is especially wild right now, with the sun slanting behind me, indicating that it will soon be noon. I squint out into the horizon and think about why I am here.

Though I detest Talia and everything that she represents, she alone has the key to the Morgan empire growing inside her. Remembering that is hard, especially when I can't even talk to her without it turning into a fight and me storming out of the room. I must focus my anger.

If I want to lead the company and bring oil up from the depths of the coast here, I must think strategically rather than letting Talia turn my head. She seems to know just what buttons to push to arouse my rage.

Closing my eyes, I take a deep breath. Then I pull my cell phone from my pocket and text my assistant, Rob.

> I need the team of stylists right now. Make it happen.

I take a final breath in and slip the phone back into my breast pocket without waiting for a response.

I have a tangible goal. I need to marry this woman and claim my rightful place as heir to the family fortune. I can't let anything, or anyone get in my way.

I walk back to the house, and Talia is in the kitchen, eating a salad with sliced chicken breast and roasted chickpeas piled high on top of it. She is sitting at a long, wooden table with a metal mixing bowl and a fork, diligently eating forkfuls.

She glances at me, but I don't say a word. Instead, I open the refrigerator myself and frown as I pull out the various makings of a sandwich. I turn back around and find her watching me carry the ingredients to a counter with a hint of surprise in her eyes.

"What?" I ask.

She shrugs. "I never thought that I would see you constructing your own meal, that's all."

I pull two thick slices of bread out of a bag and put them down on the counter. "I would usually ask Alastair to do it, but he seems to be otherwise occupied somewhere."

"Is Alastair the butler?"

I nod. "He's been with our family for fifteen years. He is very competent at his job."

She stabs a piece of lettuce with her fork and nods slowly. "I think that's the first time that you have spoken highly of a servant in front of me."

I give a bark of laughter. "Are you kidding? The servants all around me are the only people who are good at their jobs. All the other corporate executives that flit around, hoping to lick Remy's boots, are basically useless."

Done with her lunch, she stands up and gives me a considering look. "It's interesting to know that you think that."

She picks up her bowl and carries it to the sink, leaving it there for a moment. She looks around, hesitating.

"Do you need help with something?" I asked dryly.

She huffs and crosses her arms. "I was just trying to decide if Alistair would prefer me to leave the salad there or if he would want me to put the leftovers in a Tupperware or something."

I give her a puzzled look. "What do you mean? Just throw the salad away if you are done eating it."

"What if I just want to save it for later? I don't want to waste food."

I roll my eyes. "It's just a little salad. Leave it on the counter. When you are hungry again, ask Alastair to make you another. Or something else. We're not exactly conserving our chickpeas here in the Morgan family."

She looks at me, dead serious. "I don't think that you realize how many people in the world would kill to have what you have. Just because you have plenty of food does not mean that you should throw it away. You should be more grateful than that."

Putting together my sandwich, I give her a long glance. "I think that I'm doing just fine."

Her mouth bunches, but she just shakes her head and

tosses her hair over her shoulders on her way out of the kitchen. I stop her before she leaves the room.

"Wait just a second."

Her back straightens, and she stops but doesn't turn around.

I press on. "I think we can both agree that your way of dressing does not fit into my world. A whole team of stylists is coming here to help you more fully commit to the new role you're going to have to take on."

Talia glances back at me, a ripple of distaste crossing her pretty face. "And what role is that?"

"You're supposed to be my flawless bride. Look at your competition. Take Daisy, for example."

A sour look pulls out her lips. "I'd rather not."

"You should consider her a good candidate for comparison, though. She might not be to your liking, but she is exactly what I need you to be. She's poised, elegant, and always dressed for the occasion, whatever it is. Her hair, nails, and skin are perfect. Her makeup is tasteful."

She gives a cold little laugh. "Maybe you should try to woo Daisy back, then."

Putting my sandwich down, I spread my hands on the counter and look Talia in the eye. "You're going to have to measure up—and not just to Daisy. But by the Morgan standard, that is impossibly high. You are the soon-to-be fiancée of a young, handsome billionaire. To be frank, you look like a street urchin right now."

I don't miss the flash of hurt that echoes in her eyes. She turns away, her hands tightening into fists. Her tone when she speaks is dripping with sarcasm.

"I'm sorry that I am so displeasing to you. It must be a terrible burden to have to remake such a bumpkin like me."

I cross my arms and try to keep my temper in check.

Talia turns her head, her gaze flitting over me as if weighing my value.

"Don't fight me on this. It's not a battle that you want to enter. We have unlimited resources. So, use them for once, and don't be a drama queen," I grit out.

She curls her lip and starts to leave the room once more. I watch her figure as she heads down the hallway, soon disappearing.

I know I was just telling her what needed to be said, but a small part of me wonders if I was too harsh. It is my goal to marry her, convince everyone that she is all that I have claimed she is, and ultimately to claim the prize. Morgan Drilling and the massive fortune that will be mine at the end of this long, winding road. So, what if there are a few bumps as I carry her up the hill?

Taking a deep breath, I pick up my sandwich again.

When I find her again an hour later, she is sitting in the large sunroom, staring vacantly into space while she sits on a white couch.

I glance out at the view of the ocean, the fading light throwing long shadows over the insulated double-walled glass of the sunrooms' exposed windows that make up three quarters of the room. I clear my throat and she seems only then to notice me, sitting up a little straighter on the couch.

"What, is the glam squad here already?"

I step into the room and sweep my gaze over the scene. "The glam squad will be here within the hour, I'm told."

She looks less than enthused. "Great. What do you need me for, then?"

I make a gesture with my palm. "Stand up. Let me have a look at you."

Spreading her hands on her chair, she lifts herself off the

couch and does a spin, turning herself around three hundred and sixty degrees. "Does this please you, my lord?"

The sarcasm in Talia's tone hits me like a stone wall. My lips twist as I give her an assessing gaze, my eyes traveling up and down her petite form. She's wearing her oversized coat, some sort of ill-fitting black skirt that hangs down well below her knees, and a pair of army boots. I purse my lips and shake my head.

"To be honest? Not really. All your clothes need to be burned."

The snotty smirk on her lips is wiped away, quickly replaced by a scowl.

"They are perfectly good clothes."

"For a commoner, maybe, but you're not a commoner anymore. That's what I'm trying to get through your skull. When you dress yourself, you must remember that you are representing me."

I wave to my body, plucking my lapel and straightening the cuff of my Oxford shirt.

"I take great pride in the way I dress. This suit?" I pinch the collar of my jacket between my fingers. "This is a bespoke wool suit from Italy. It's handmade and costs at least ten thousand dollars. This shirt? It's made of Egyptian cotton and silk, making it the nicest button-up that money can buy. The same goes for my shoes. They are custom-made to fit my feet, and I have one hundred pairs of them. Looking like you belong is almost as good as actually belonging."

Talia stands up and moves towards the window, masking her expression or perhaps just gazing outside while she mulls over my words.

"So what? What is it that you want me to do?"

All the sass and the fire that she previously had vanishes

in that moment. Her voice is quiet, her shoulders slightly rounded. She looks like a woman who's been defeated.

While I need her to comply with my wishes, I didn't want to crush her spirit entirely. Repressing a sigh, I move toward her, my arms crossing. I shift my gaze away from her body and begin making a list.

"The first thing that you need is poise. Women with their parents' money, women that have climbed the social ladder, and women who have married up—they all possess a strong sense of self. Rather, they walk around looking like they do, whether or not they have a sense of who they are." I wave my hand. "That's another discussion, I guess. But you need to act like you are the most important thing in the room. No, the most important thing in the world. You need to act self-possessed, and you need to demand, not ask, for everything. You must be an impressive choice for me, a billionaire. People must look at us together and think that we are a great match."

Talia crosses her arms and keeps looking out the window, walking a little further away. "As opposed to how we appear now?"

"If I saw us together now, would I be impressed? No, I would have questions. I see someone who is very careful about his appearance paired with someone who looks like an anonymous, mousy little nobody."

She raises her hands to her face, blotting at her eyes. She doesn't say anything, but I can see that my words have upset her. At some point, though, they would need to be said. She can't just expect to blend into my world of luxury and wealth without changing a single thing about herself. The thought is unreasonable.

She stands facing away from me, still looking out the window. Now I am certain that she is masking her emotions from me. But maybe that's a good thing. After all, I did tell her that she had to keep her feelings from reaching her face.

I leave the room for just a few moments, grabbing an electronic tablet and a pen. When I sweep back into the room, Talia looks at me, her face a smooth mask.

Looking at the tablet, I pull up the prenuptial agreement and offer it to her. "I've arranged to have my lawyers draw up our agreement. You'll need to sign on the dotted line before I can transfer any funds to you."

Looking at me with an anxious expression, she takes the tablet and pen from my hands and walks back to the window. She leans her head against the wall and begins reading.

"What is this?" She inquires, her voice low. I'm not sure whether she is talking to herself or not, but I clear my throat.

"It's just what we have already agreed on. What we talked about earlier. Plus, the contract lays out how much money you will receive in addition to the five hundred thousand. It says that you will get one hundred thousand dollars per year, deposited into an account of your choice. It also specifies a couple of points."

She looks up at me, and I can feel her weary gaze. "What kind of points?"

"You shouldn't ever tell anyone who fathered our kid. That includes doctors. Also, it stipulates that if you ever want to leave me, you forfeit everything I've ever given you, and you lose the kid in the bargain. Plus, you will need to maintain your looks and health for the foreseeable future."

Pushing out her cheek with the tip of her tongue, Talia looks down at the tablet as she scrolls through the pages. Without looking up, she says, "You know that I'm going to gain weight while I'm pregnant, right? Or do you not allow for that in your contract?"

Her words are so sharp, and her tone is downright acerbic.

For a split second, I am too surprised to respond. "Of course, it's not written in the contract because it's not necessary. I'm not going to require you to be any certain kind of way. I just want you to be healthy and presentable for as long as possible."

Her lips thin, and she looks up, piercing me with her blue gaze. "Healthy and presentable. How nice for you."

I roll my eyes, losing patience with her little tantrum. "As soon as you sign the contract, I will wire an initial payment into an account that I'll set up for you. I'll start with fifty thousand now, two hundred thousand when we actually tie the knot. The final two hundred and fifty thousand will come when you deliver the baby."

Pushing herself off the wall, she says, "Is that all? Does your document ask me to give you a piece of my soul in exchange for your dirty money?"

Talia moves as if she is going to brush right past me, out of the sunroom. But I grab her wrist and haul her to face me, fury rising within my chest. I look down into her eyes and lean close, not even trying to disguise the fact that I am abjectly threatening her now.

"You forget who you're talking to. I hold all the cards. If you want not only a better life for your baby but for your Aunt Minnie to be dug out of the financial pit that she is trapped in, you'll sign the contract."

Her eyes go wide, and her face pales a little. She whispers, "Don't you have doubts about this marriage? It's a big life-changing thing."

I release her wrist from my grip and tell her no. "I'm always certain of everything I do. I made this decision, and now we are both traveling down this path together. Sign the fucking contract already."

She stares at me for a few more seconds, tucking a fiery strand of her hair behind her ear. And then she releases a breath and bows her head, signing the contract.

Chapter Twenty-Two
TALIA

"Mademoiselle?" The butler asks gently.

I look up, cocking a brow. He steps more fully into the sunroom, which has become a de facto haven for me. It's warmer in here than anywhere else in the house and it's well-lit to boot.

The butler bows his head very slightly. "Your team is here. Shall I tell them to come in?"

Somewhat exasperated, I push out a half exhale. "Sure, why not? What have I got to lose?"

He bows again and then disappears.

As I watch, a whole team of stylists file into the room, descending like hawks searching for their prey. There are four women and two men, all dressed in stylish black clothes. The men are in impeccably tailored suits, the women in chic dresses and heels.

Something inside me wrenches as I watch them parade in, pushing a rolling rack of clothing and carrying the tools of their trades. One of the men carries six white shoeboxes, and everyone else has their hands full with manicure kits, a giant hairdryer, or a set of rollers for my hair. The man with the shoeboxes sets them down on one of the side couches and turns to me with an even smile. He extends his hand to me, bowing his blonde head. I can see that his nails are neatly manicured, and his suede loafers have been recently brushed.

"Hello, darling. My name is Stephen." He turns to the crew, pointing them out as he goes. "That is Jessica, Sam, Mary, Mathilde, and that gentleman over there is Percival. We're here to make you feel and look your absolute best. I promise, this will be completely painless, and you will feel radiant after we're done."

He sticks his hand out, raising his brows in inspection. My cheeks feel warm as I shake his hand, my gaze sliding from Stephen to the rest of the group. Suddenly, all the fiery passion that I had a few hours ago has vanished. When I introduce myself, I feel awkward and clumsy. "I'm Talia."

He shakes my hand and then looks at me with an assessing gaze. He gestures for me to turn around.

"Can we see you spin?"

Flushing even brighter, I do a quick turn.

To Stephen's credit, he doesn't so much as bat an eyelash. Neither do any of the rest of his team, either. They are all diligently working to set up their own individual stations. One for clothing, one for hair, and one for nails.

I notice that two of the women leave the room and return with their arms full of what looks to be quite heavy fabric. In no time flat, the women have set up a privacy curtain and hung an opaque white paisley cover around the box that they have created. It's about four by two, and just looking at it makes me nervous.

"Exactly what will I have done today that requires such modesty?"

"Oh, darling. Don't get caught up in that just yet. Let's just start with the basics."

Stephen escorts me to one of the couches, where Percival has spread a tarp over the whole seat. Percival smiles as he snaps open a large black rayon sheet with a neck hole cut out of it. Stephen introduces me, then hustles off to the rack of clothing, unpacking shoes and tucking them under corresponding outfits.

Percival cocks his head and says, "Do you mind if I take your hair down from its bun?"

I feel embarrassed, though I don't know why. I unwind my hair, and it cascades well past my shoulders.

I've never even had it cut by a professional before. Since I was little, Aunt Minnie has always cut our hair at the same time, over the kitchen sink. I never thought much about it until I got older. But even then, I figured that it didn't really matter because I always kept my hair put up in an untidy bun anyway.

Percival nods to himself, rubbing his hands together. He looks at my hair. "May I touch your scalp? I like to get a feel for the hair before I start cutting."

I swallow. "Sure, I guess."

He dives right in, and his hands work through my hair, from front to back. "God, I love your color. Who does it?"

I give him a curious look. "What do you mean?"

He bends his head closer, looking at the strands of my copper-colored hair. "Well, is this your natural hair color?"

"Yes," I say. "What else would it be?"

He smiles and runs his hands through my hair, combing out tangles with his fingers. "It's so beautiful. You're very lucky."

I feel my cheeks warm again, and I shrug. "Thanks, I guess."

He holds up a finger and, heading over to a full-length mirror, carries it back to me. I see myself in the reflection, my hair a ratty mass, my cheeks pink, and my skirt loose and ill-fitting.

"Can you take off your jacket?" He suggests. "Just set it right over there, if you don't mind."

Swallowing hard, I peel my coat off and discard it. As I walk back, holding my hands wide, I look in the mirror. I am wearing a thin black shirt tucked into the waist of my black skirt. It looks cheap, like an ancient artifact or something. Honestly, I've probably had the shirt since high school. I release a huge dramatic sigh, and Percival smiles patiently at me.

"Honey, I know. This is a lot. But we are just focused on your hair right now. So, let's talk about what kind of shape you would like. It has been suggested to me that you might like a shoulder-length cut. But I am also thinking that you would look very elegant with bangs. What do you think?"

Bangs? I stare at myself in the mirror, imagining the chunky bangs that I cut myself. I shake my head quickly, remembering all too well the disastrous self-inflicted bangs I had in middle school. "Nope, no way."

"All right. That's totally fine. What about length? Do you want it waist length or maybe shoulder length?"

I tilt my head to the side. Part of me very much wants to defy Dare by chopping off all my hair. But I keep that part of myself and tell that rebellious part of myself to be quiet. Now is not the time for that.

"Somewhere in between, I suppose."

He nods, his lower lip sticking out. "What about shape?"

I glance up at him, my eyes pleading with him.

"Don't make me ugly. Okay? Just make my hair look good."

He gives me a quiet smile and nods his head once. "I know just what to do. I'll take good care of you, I promise."

To my surprise, he does. I watch the hair fall away as he cuts, trims, and shapes my hair perfectly. At the end, when I look in the mirror, I am awestruck. I could easily be a totally different person. A chic, rich person's wife. Letting out all the breath in my lungs at once, a startled sound escapes my lips.

Percival looks worried for the first time. "Are you okay?"

I raise my hands to my face, putting them over my mouth. My eyes mist over, but I can't take my gaze off my hair. It's amazing what a good pair of scissors will do.

"It's incredible," I breathe out. "Oh my God. I didn't realize that... Thank you, Percival."

He beams at me. "Oh honey. It was my pleasure. Now let's get you waxed and wedding-ready."

"Waxed?"

I go through a full body wax and have my nails done at the same time. All the women bustle around me behind the curtain, attending to their jobs. I feel detached from my body, almost completely ignoring the pain, and floating around in my own head. One of the women puts a face mask on me while the other is busy waxing every single hair from my body.

Stephen then takes over, dressing me in a silky black thong and a black strapless push-up bra.

I stand near the rack of clothes as he pulls out long pink dresses and short pink rompers, smiling and talking to me. I barely listen, managing a forced smile.

"Talia?"

I glance up at Stephen, and he gives me a funny look. "You know what? I think you could use a little privacy." He leans his head to the side and calls to the rest of the glam squad. "Hey folks? Could you all take a break for a minute? Let's just give Miss Talia some room, okay?"

"Of course." Percival looks at each of the women. "Come on, ladies."

They head out of the room, their footsteps discreet.

Stephen pulls a silky off-white robe from the rolling rack, putting it around my shoulders. I thank him with numb lips and wrap the robe around myself, tying it. He touches my shoulder and looks into my eyes.

"Are you having a tough day?" he asks.

I'm a little surprised. It's the first time that anyone outside Aunt Minnie and Olivia has asked me that.

I swallow, trying not to burst into tears, and nod vigorously.

"Okay. That's okay. Let me make you a deal. You pick out three of these dresses and try them on. Let us accessorize you and slip on the matching shoes. And then, once you have seen them in the mirror?" He raises his hands, shaking his head. "I promise that I will leave you alone if you ask me to. I know that you have made a lot of changes today. But I swear, if you look in the mirror and you are not happy with yourself, I will personally do whatever is in my power to make it right."

Dashing away my tears, I nod. I give him a watery thanks, and he squeezes my shoulder.

"I know this is a big change. But I think that you know that it's needed. It had been a very long time since anybody had cut your hair or filed your fingernails. Other than that, you are just sort of refining your look. Okay? In reality, it's not really that much, I promise."

Sucking in a deep breath, I nod. "Of course. Sorry."

"Girl, don't apologize to me. Seriously, if you had any idea what your fiancé was paying the glam squad, you would not feel sorry for us at all."

That earns a laugh from me. "It's good to know that everyone is getting what they deserve."

Even me, I think.

"Can I call Percival back into the room to do some makeup while you change into the first look I've picked out for you?"

I nod, steeling myself. What will I look like in the mirror wearing new clothes? I can't even imagine it, if I am totally honest with myself.

Percival dashes on a little makeup. Rouge on my cheeks, color on my lips, a shimmery nude eyeshadow coupled with a black eyeliner.

I pluck the long pink dress from the rolling rack. "Can I try this on first?"

"You can try on anything you like." Stephen gives me a grin. "They'll all look stunning on you, I am sure."

The sleeves and the top layer of the dress are sheer. It's all a beautiful fuchsia color, coupled with a floral pattern that is vague and indistinct. Underneath is a tighter sheath. Thin straps meet a satin bustier and flow down to my feet. I wriggle into the dress and step into the shoes that Stephen places before me. Then he zips up my dress as Percival comes back with the body length mirror.

For a moment, I don't even recognize myself. I catch a glimpse of a gorgeous redhead in a killer dress. Chills run down my arms before I even realize that it is me.

I can't stop staring at myself. My hair is long, drawn back over my shoulder. My eyes look amazingly blue. My skin looks like flawless cream. And the dress… it shows off a little cleavage and manages to be quite clingy while also leaving enough to the imagination. The shoes he chose are pink high heels with a bright red sole. I can barely stand in them, but the effect overall is just stunning.

My hands fly to my lips, my eyes unable to stop raking up and down my own figure.

"Well?" Stephen asks. "What do you think?"

I look at him, my eyes filling with tears. I blot them away hastily, staved off by Stephen's own handkerchief. I laugh as I wipe away my tears, shaking my head.

"The dress is beautiful," I say. "Really beautiful."

"No. The woman is beautiful. The dress is just a garment until she puts it on."

"Excuse me, Stephen?" Stacy pops her head in, apologetic. "I'm sorry, but Mr. Morgan requests that Ms. Chance try on this dress." She looks at me with a polite smile. "He asked that you wear it tonight."

I look at the dress as she carries it over. It's a stretchy silver material that extends from a pair of tiny straps down to a lush swath of silver fabric and it ends abruptly.

"It's so short!" I exclaim.

Stephen leans closer to me, giving me a knowing smile. "That must be why your fiancé wants you to wear it."

I scowl.

Standing still, Stephen lets me out of the pink dress. I hold my hands up in the air while he slides the silver dress down onto my form.

The material barely covers my chest and flows down to stop at the middle of my thigh. I glance up into the mirror and frown.

I have only changed my dress, but in the mirror, a nubile young woman's legs, arms, and décolletage are on full display.

"Do I at least get to wear a shawl?" I grouse.

Stephen gives me a wink. "I have just the thing."

He pulls a caramel-colored shawl from the rack and drapes it over my shoulders.

I look more closely at the fox head that's now lying on my upper arm and scowl. "Is this real?"

"Definitely not. We aren't doing real fur anymore. But it looks real, doesn't it?"

I run my fingers down the length of the fabric, admiring the silky feel. "It's really nice."

"Good. I hope you're as happy with your transformation today as I am. Because honey, you look like a million bucks."

I flush, my first thought being that I am only worth half a million so far.

I tuck my hair behind my ear and smile softly. "Thank you. Thanks to the whole glam squad."

"It was our pleasure," Stephen says. "Call us anytime. I can have more rolling racks brought to you anywhere in the world. All you have to do is say the word."

Dare's world may not turn out to be so bad if it's populated by people like Stephen. I shake Stephen's hand and change my shoes, then look in the mirror a final time.

I look *completely* different. If my soon-to-be fiancé isn't impressed by this groomed, polished version of me, I don't know how else I can impress him. Pulling in my stomach and straightening my spine, I turn to the rolling rack once more. I begin sorting through the rack, making hasty decisions about which garments will blow Dare's mind.

Chapter Twenty-Three

DARE

I grunt and throw the stylus down next to my computer tablet. Looking at my watch, I find that three hours have passed. Not that I can really claim that I'm surprised or anything.

I drafted memos and read through a lot of the legalese about the specifics of paying for Morgan Drilling's deep sea mining rights.

It's familiar work, comfortable in its way. But now that I stand up and stretch, I have a strange feeling.

Usually, I embrace my work. I relish the fact that I'm the only one who can do what I do. But lately, I've had the sense that my other life, my quote-unquote "real life," is crowding in around the work life I've worked on creating for so long.

It's odd, that feeling. The guilt that I ought to read just one more brief and write another memo sticks around with me like a speck of glitter that you just can't manage to get off your skin three days after you visit the strip club.

And still, I am pulled toward the hallway. Curiosity is my main motivation. But if I were to be perfectly honest with myself, I would want to see the work I paid the glam squad to do.

I find Talia in the sunroom, sifting through the rack of clothing. She turns to me with a subtle smile on her face. My mouth opens, but I can't seem to make my brain form a single whole word. Instead, I stare at her, my expression one of perfect surprise.

I left behind a sad, worried creature with a tendency toward snapping at my hands. But now I am looking at a petite, slender goddess with red hair and flashing blue eyes.

Her toned legs look ridiculously long in the silver minidress I picked out. Her perky tits and tiny waist astound me. She pushes a hand through her hair, which falls below her shoulders in a timeless, effortless-looking hairstyle.

She notices me gawking at her and blushes, but she doesn't break eye contact. Instead, she turns to the right, posing like a model would at the very end of a runway.

"Holy shit," I exclaim. "I can't believe you look that good."

She tosses her hair and gives me a pained look. "Gee, Dare. Way to flatter a girl."

My neck heats, but I suck in a breath and refuse to be shamed. "That's not what I meant. What I meant..." I look her up and down again, more than a little caught off guard. "God *damn*. You are hot."

"I got a freaking haircut. Chill out."

I look her up and down. "You are definitely a completely different person from the mousy little girl that I sent stylists in to fix."

"I know what it is." Something in her face tightens and shifts. "I think I look more like Daisy and all of the wealthy women you've dated than I did before."

Pursing my lips, I shrug. "I don't know what the problem

is. I don't see anything wrong with you looking more like women of my echelon."

Talia snorts.

"I got a makeover to fool all the wealthy people in your orbit. But it seems like you just needed me to dress a certain way and wear my hair just so to think I'm worthy of you." Her nose wrinkles. "It's so shallow."

"It's shallow to want my fiancée to dress like she has two cents to rub together? Huh, I guess I am what you say I am then."

She rolls her eyes and wanders closer. From this distance, I can now see that she's wearing a thick coat of black eyeliner and a shimmery shade of eyeshadow that makes her eyes seem iridescent.

"I came to look for you, but you were working." She crosses her arms, cocking her head to the side as she approaches. "So? Do I pass the test? Am I acceptable to you now?"

Her words are certainly a dig at me. But I don't even care. I slowly nod my head, smoothing down the front of my suit jacket.

"I don't think I knew that that dress was so short. But it looks fantastic on you." I squint. "Why would you ever cover yourself up when you look like this?"

Her cheeks redden. But before she can say whatever catty thing comes to her, I hold up a hand. "Wait. Don't answer that. Let's just say that I feel much more comfortable presenting you to people as my wife-to-be. But more importantly, here's the question. Will the glam squad pick out a whole wardrobe for you?"

She rolls her eyes but nods. "Yeah. They've already started to fill the closets here, and they're ready to fill the closets back home too."

My gaze slips down to her breasts, which are accentuated by her tightly crossed arms. She notices my gaze and snaps her fingers, her voice sounding angry. "Hey. I'm up here."

I snort. "Am I not supposed to look? Because damn. If not, it's going to be a very hard time. And I do mean hard."

I flick my gaze to hers, smirking just a little. She flushes and pulls up the material at her cleavage, looking away. "Get over yourself."

"What, I'm not allowed to compliment you?"

She gives a tiny laugh. "No. That's not the deal. And I would know because you just made me sign it."

My eyes wander back to her tits and then to her hips.

"Listen, darling girl. My preference is that I usually date the heiresses and models that are looking for a man to spoil them in exchange for my quote, 'unusual' sexual needs."

Silently, she shakes her head. "No, no. I don't want to know. Let's just skip over that part. I am not the most experienced girl, but I know that I don't ever want to be one of those women. Just forget it."

I cock my brow. "You know, I sleep naked. And you are going to share my bed. What are you going to do when I undress myself?"

Her chin juts out, and she has that spark in her eyes, rebellious and resistant as ever. "You have to be kidding me. I'm sure you have plenty of bedrooms everywhere you go."

"Yeah, I do. But I expect you to fully commit to the fraud that we are a real couple. I won't force myself upon you, but if anyone goes sniffing around, they're going to find us sleeping in the same bed together every night. Once more, we are going to spend the rest of the weekend getting used to touching each other. We're going to rub each other and grope each other, because I want to prove to everyone in my family that you and I are in love with each other and obsessed with each other."

She gives a surprised laugh.

I glare at her. "Laugh all you like. But we are going to touch, kiss, and sleep in the same bed. Hell, we might even have sex... As long as you can keep your feelings for me from getting messy and entangled."

"That's crazy." She shakes her head and turns toward the doorway, moving past me.

I grab her, my hand moving as quick as lightning to grab her wrist. Hauling her around to face me, I grip her arm and pinch her chin between my fingers.

"Where are you going?" I grit out. "We are talking here."

"Having sex is what got me into this whole mess. I don't ever intend to confuse things between us by having sex with you. No thanks."

I look deep into her eyes, loving the passion and fire that I see. "Okay, let me ask you a question." I raise a brow. "Do you intend to be celibate for our entire relationship?"

She shrugs, trying to slip out of my grip. I refuse to move or let go.

"I don't know. But I do know one thing: having an affair is explicitly forbidden for both of us in our marriage contract. So, you had better figure something out or you are going to get really lonely."

I release her suddenly, and I glare at her. "What do you mean?"

She gives me a hearty smile. "If you had read the contract before you had me sign it, you would've seen that clause. It's written there in pretty cut-and-dry language. Infidelity is a no-no. It's one of the only reasons that I can pull out of our marriage without facing financial ruin."

I sneer. "You know what I hate? Your know-it-all attitude."

"Oh, go ahead. Avoid the question entirely. But let's not forget that I am carrying the child that will be the golden goose."

Damn. For a minute, I was so wrapped up in arguing with her that I forgot the whole reason we were here in the first place.

Talia is pregnant. I know it intellectually. But now this child, this unknown and unseen figment of my imagination, rises between us.

My gaze drops to her belly, which is currently flat as a pancake.

I have been so wrapped up in my goal to inherit the Morgan empire that I've never slowed down enough to think about the actual child. I still can't quite get a grasp on the reality of the situation. It seems far away, like a problem for future Dare to solve.

Talia lays her palms against her flat stomach while she's pursing her lips. "I haven't really spent that much time thinking about the baby," she admits. "But I know that it is at the center of this whole plot."

"I really haven't put that much thought into it. But I would marry anyone and hold anyone's child and claim it as my own if it meant that I got a leg up in this competition with my brother."

Apparently, that was the wrong thing to say, although I thought we were just admitting our feelings.

She glances at me, disapproval echoing in her eyes. And then she turns away and paces to the window. I expect some kind of snappy retort to be forthcoming. But Talia just stares out the window, three quarters of her face hidden from my view. The part of her face that I can see is smooth and without expression.

Checking the time on my watch, I see that there are still hours left in our day, so I decide to push on with my next objective.

Getting comfortable with Talia isn't going to be easy. I don't understand her on even the most basic level. And her obvious hatred of everything I stand for has been expressed aloud multiple times. But if I'm going to close this deal and win this inheritance race, I have to swallow and take my medicine.

"All right. Come on, turn around."

Talia looks at me, turning slowly around, her face puzzled. I gesture to her body, looking her up and down.

"Stand up straight," I say. "Like your parents raised you properly."

Her face turns as red as a beet. She glares at me, seeming humiliated.

"That's not funny," she hisses.

"What's not funny?"

She pushes out her tongue with her cheek; her hip jutting out, and she puts her arms across her chest. "The thing you just said about parents. That's not funny. Some of us were raised without our parents. That's literally why I am doing all of this. I must save my Aunt Minnie, her bungalow, and the children's shelter where my mother dropped me off when I was a little kid."

For a second, I am so taken aback by her words that I find myself speechless. "You didn't know your parents?"

"I didn't say that. My mom is still around, somewhere. But she never knew who my father was, and she found being a parent pretty stressful, from what I've heard. She had some kind of psychiatric emergency where she couldn't get ahold of her sister, my Aunt Minnie. So she dropped me off at Hope House. The people there called my Aunt Minnie, who rushed to pick me up. I haven't seen my mother since."

I screw my face up, unconsciously asking, "How did I not know this about you? This could be a real problem."

"You didn't know because you didn't ask. You didn't ask anything about me. Basically, all you know is that I slept with your brother once and that my womb is fertile."

Damn, she has got me there. I pause, my mind whirling. If Talia's mother shows up out of the blue, as a poor relative who wants something to do with those that suddenly get rich, it could be a problem. She could demand money, at the very least.

I turn to her, my expression careful. "Talia, about your mother..."

She arches a brow and turns away from me, walking along the wall of windows and reaching out to trace the windowsill. "I don't want to hear it unless it changes something between us; I don't really care about me not having a mom. It's not like I chose it for myself or anything."

I think about it for a long second. Does it actually change anything?

Talia is still pregnant with Burn's baby. Soon to be my baby, if everything else goes to plan. In practical terms, that's all that matters.

I suck in a deep breath and shake my head, entertaining her at last. "No, I don't think it makes a difference. This is the kind of thing that we need to know about each other, though. For instance, you should know that my mother is dead. You should know that my father is an alcoholic waste of space."

Talia reaches the end of the row of windows. She turns back, her other hand tracing the windowsill as she walks. "I didn't know about your mom either. I'm sorry."

I huff, uncomfortable at her vulnerability. "It was a long time ago." As if that really mattered. As if it makes my mother less dead or fills in the hole she left in my life many years ago.

"I'm just telling you so that if anybody asks, you already know. Now stand up straight. Put your shoulders back and hold your head up high."

Her mouth turns down, but she walks out into the middle of the floor and sucks in a deep breath, adopting a formal posture. I walk over to her, my hand touching her shoulder and pulling it back a little more. Then I touch underneath her chin, lifting her head.

"There. This should be your resting posture when you are trying to impress people. Basically, any time that you're around my family."

A flush creeps up from her chest to her neck. She looks at me but doesn't move. I give her a small smile and touch her shoulder again. She shivers and pulls away.

Before she can protest, I shake my head and look at her sternly. "If this is going to work, we're going to have to get very comfortable with each other. We are going to have to touch each other. We will have to kiss and do all the things that couples who are in love do. We don't have a choice if we want people to believe us."

Talia looks me in the eyes, her gaze inquisitive. "So... what are we supposed to do? Practice?"

My neck heats, but I press on. I nod and slide my hand from her shoulder to the nape of her neck. "That's exactly what we are supposed to do. That is what I brought you here for."

Her throat works as she swallows. I can smell the floral notes of her perfume. A tiny part of me wants to lean in close to her throat and get a better sniff. But I must restrain myself. Now is not the time or the place.

Instead, I wrap my arm around her waist and pull her close so she comes to me naturally, as partners do when they dance together.

Her hand touches my shoulder, smoothing the fabric that she finds there. I understand her feeling of trepidation. Her touch is so intimate. I look down into her big blue eyes, thinking for a moment that I need to escape this room and her gaze.

But no, I'm not going to do that. I'm going to man up, bear down, and get through this. It doesn't matter that she feels so slight in my arms. It doesn't matter that she smells good or that she is now dressed in a manner that would make my jaw drop under any other circumstances. It doesn't matter at all that I find her skin silky smooth to the touch or that I am hyperaware of the faintest stirrings of attraction that I feel.

My heart beats faster as I bring my hands low around her waist, cupping her ass and pulling it into rough contact with my body.

Her eyes widen, and her nostrils flare. "Dare!" she protests.

I smirk at her and shake my head. "It's better if we just dive in. We can take a ton of time to test the waters, or we can just submerge ourselves. Let's do it and be done with it."

Her lips tremble. "What do you mean, do it?"

I grunt and release her, rolling my eyes. This is proving harder than I anticipated. I don't feel the need to mention that my cock stirs when she says 'do it'. As if I'm a thirteen-year-old boy, and she's casually mentioning sex.

It has been a long time since I've gotten hard from just a girl talking to me.

She steps back and covers her chest with her arms. The

move is defensive, but it only draws attention to her cleavage. My gaze drops there, and she scowls at me.

"This is a terrible idea," she says. "You know that, right?"

"Yeah, well. If you hadn't already gotten horizontal with my brother, maybe this could go a different way. We could take our time and get to know each other before we started fucking like rabbits. But unfortunately, that wasn't meant to be. You just happened to sleep with my twin and got pregnant before we even met. So that forces a certain timeframe on us, doesn't it?"

She makes a soft sound of disgust and looks away, shaking her head.

I grab her by the hips, pulling her softly against my body and growling. "It does. So now you just have to deal with it. I'm about to kiss you, and you better get used to it. Don't forget, I have you and your child's entire future in my hand."

Talia looks up at me, her eyes wide. But she doesn't protest or push back against my body. Instead, she gulps and slips her arms around my neck, looking frightened but determined.

Her lips part as her tongue darts out to wet them. I can't help the animal instinct that takes over me at that point.

Pulling her against my waist, I bury my hands in her hair, my fingers pulling her head back. She exhales the tiniest gasp, and I realize that sound turns me on more than anything she's done to this point. I angle her head and plunge my mouth down against hers, mercilessly kissing her.

Her whole body shudders as I grip her waist, and I take that as a compliment. Her body tenses up as her hands push gently at my chest. Her response only throws kerosene onto my already-lit fire. It makes me hungry. I wrap my arm around her waist and lift her off her feet as I plunder her mouth, pressing my tongue against hers.

In this moment, I have complete control, dominating her small body so completely. I can feel fury of my own satisfaction running through my veins.

I know that I should stop myself, that I should bring myself in, but I can't. I am a feral beast, and Talia is my prey, locked into my deadly embrace.

My cock throbs and I thrust into her soft body, pulling back from her lips only long enough to let out a snarl.

God, Talia feels too good. I look down into her eyes and see terror written there, mixed with a note of pure desire. At least, that's what I like to imagine.

She pushes against me again, her brow descending as her small body fights mine.

I relax my grip and release her. My dick is so hard that it hurts.

"Jesus, Dare!" She quickly takes a step back, her eyes contemptuous. She wipes her mouth and straightens her dress.

At some point in our scuffle, her hair grew slightly disheveled. She moves to smooth it out, fanning it out across her shoulders.

My fingers clench; the feeling of the silky copper strands is imprinted on them.

"We can't do it like this," she says, looking shaken. "We can't get comfortable with each other, I mean. It won't work."

Wiping at my mouth, I drag in a stuttered breath. "Yes, we can."

"No!" Her eyes gleam as she stares at me. "I don't think so."

"Listen to me." I flick my fingers out, beckoning her closer. "You are the mouthiest, most stuck-up, most stubborn girl I've ever met. But for some reason, I find it arousing when you surrender to me. And I think you like it when I take control." I scan her face. "You want me to dominate you. Am I right, darling girl?"

"No," Talia says, her voice coming out in a breathy whisper. "I don't want you. I hate you."

"You might hate my personality. But you want me. You long for someone to show you how to be a good girl. Even now, as we stand here, your pussy is wet for me. I can tell."

Her breath leaves her in a scoff. She crosses her arms and rolls her eyes. The fragile moment between us passes, slipping away in that half a breath.

"I don't know what you want from me, Dare."

With that, she turns and flees the room, leaving me feeling more than a little foolish. Did I just imagine the flicker of attraction that flowed and sparked between us when I kissed her?

I think not. But Talia obviously feels differently about it.

I adjust my cock in my trousers and stare at the empty hallway she disappeared down, debating whether I should give her the night off and try again tomorrow.

I will not give up over one little misstep. Talia and I will emerge from this weekend seeming as if we have been lovers for ages. I've decided that it will happen…

Regardless of whether she likes it or not.

Chapter Twenty-Four

DARE

I find Talia in the darkened kitchen a little later. She looks up as I enter the room, and her brow puckers, but she doesn't say anything.

I beckon her with two fingers, demanding rather than asking. "Follow me."

I walk down the narrow, dark hallway into the sunroom. I don't wait for her. I take a seat on the first wicker couch I see, turning toward the door and crossing my legs.

When Talia appears at the door, she pauses. I look her up and down and jerk my head into the room. "Come here."

My tone leaves no room for argument.

She hesitates for several seconds, and I make myself wait, although I just want to jump up and grab her. But I need her to come to me this time. If she doesn't, I will have to rethink this whole fake relationship.

Running my tongue over my teeth, I give her a cool smile. "Talia, don't make me have to threaten your well-being. You wanted my money. You got it. So now you have to follow through on the deal. You must make people believe that you're in love with me. I brought you here for that specific reason: so that we have the chance to get acquainted before we spend the rest of our lives together. But if you don't want that, say so now. I can have my lawyers reverse the wire transfer, and you can go back to Harwicke."

She flinches as though I have threatened to hit her. Part of me feels bad, but I have to be determined, so that I win this little game between the two of us and I can inherit billions. She is merely a pawn in the Morgans' game of life-or-death chess.

There is no more time to deal with Talia gently.

"It's either yes or no, right now."

She takes a timid step into the sunroom, and I let out a silent sigh of relief. I hold out my hand, expectant.

Talia licks her lips and approaches me, running her hands down her new dress.

She takes the hand I've offered and sucks in a deep breath. Then she sits beside me on the couch, looking up at me as she hikes her knee up over mine. Sinking against my body, she makes herself comfortable. The whole time, Talia's gaze never leaves mine for a second.

"Like this?" Her voice is soft, almost seductive. I run my fingers along her arm, and she shivers.

"Just like that," I say, encouraging her. "I want you to be the best actress in a room full of phonies."

I see a flash of her pink tongue as she presses her lips together. She reaches out her trembling hand to touch my cheek, caressing it ever so gently. She rubs the tips of her fingers into the hair just behind my ear and then over the back of my head. I shudder, surprised at the touch.

It feels better than I expected for Talia to touch me of her own volition.

"Is this good?" she asks.

I nod, catching her hand and making eye contact with her as I bring her palm to my lips, then kiss her wrist.

Her skin is warm and smooth. Her breath catches in her throat at the movement of my lips on her skin. She doesn't resist, but I notice her racing heartbeat as I swipe my tongue over her pulse point.

I sweep a hand down her thigh, causing her to jump.

"Dare," she says. A warning, more than anything.

I am not really listening. I tuck a strand of her copper hair behind her ear and look her dead in the eyes. "This is the way that you need to look at me," I grit out.

She gazes back at me, her blue eyes staring right into my soul.

"Like this?" she asks.

I have to admit, hearing her ask me for my approval stirs something in me—something hungry and primal. Like something is lurking just below the surface.

I smirk and readjust myself, moving her leg just so my stiff cock presses against the inside of her knee. I know that she notices the contact because I hear her gulp for air.

I arch a brow. "What? I'm just a man. You can't expect me not to get turned on sometimes."

She shakes her head. "That isn't what this is about, Dare. We are trying to make it look good, not feel good."

"That's true." I tuck another strand of her hair back behind her ear and then move closer, my fingers entwining in her hair.

Turning her face up toward mine, I press my lips against hers. It's slower this time, more languid, less rushed. I brush my lips over hers once and then press them a second time, more forcefully and passionately.

She gradually responds to my kiss, opening her mouth just slightly and letting my tongue enter her mouth. Our tongues writhe together, wrestling slowly, making my cock stiffen.

At length, I pull back. The next step should be to pull her onto my lap and pull down her dress so that her tits are there before me. I've never seen them, but I imagine that they are small, perky, and perfect, and ripe for tasting.

I drop my fingers to the neckline of her dress, admiring the creamy abundance of her breasts, and she pulls back. Skittering off my lap, she arches a brow. "Dare, that was over the line."

"Over the line for who? It seemed like the only thing to do at that moment."

"You know I have put a boundary there. No hands below the dress. We can fake it without having to actually have sex."

"Are you giving me boundaries, darling girl?" I give her a cool laugh. "I don't believe in boundaries. Not between us. We are going to be married. We will not have secrets, and we won't have boundaries either."

She laughs, looking disbelieving. "You are so contradictory; I can hardly believe it. You have done nothing but tell me how I should act since I've been unfortunate enough to know you."

"Yeah, so?"

"So." She stands up and cocks her hip, pursing her lips. "Some people call those boundaries. And what's worse is that this whole thing? It's to fool your family. Where I come from, family is the only group of people that you can be your true self around."

"Well, you wouldn't know what it's like to have parents or grandparents. Maybe if you did, you would understand where I'm coming from."

She winces. "Jesus, Dare. You really don't pull any punches, do you?"

She turns, stalking out of the room. I watch her ass sway back and forth as she goes, strutting in her high heels.

I release a deep breath, leaning my head back and putting two fingers against the bridge of my nose. That was not how I thought that would play out.

My phone buzzes, so I fish it out of my pocket, looking at the screen. It's Tristen, a welcome reprieve from Talia's dramatics. I answer, still annoyed and agitated from my interaction with her.

"Hello?"

"Hey. Where are you? I've tried to call you all day."

"I finally got Talia to agree to be my fiancée. So, I took her to the coast, up to Maine. You know that little vacation house we have?"

He huffs a laugh. "Yeah, I know the mansion you mean. That's good news on the Talia front. I'm glad that our little stunt worked."

I pace at the window, looking out into the darkness. "Yeah. Thank you for hiring people to break into the bookstore for me and to show up at the restaurant that Talia works at to make a scene. I wasn't sure that it would work, but it obviously did the trick."

Tristen laughs. "It just so happened that I had a construction job going on with workers nearby. I just paid a couple of them to fuck up the bookstore. And the other part, finding people on TaskRabbit who were willing to play along with my plan… that was easy and cheap."

"Well, I will pay you via a bank draft on Monday. I really do appreciate you helping to coordinate the job. All Talia needed was a little push. I knew that she was already really worried about her Aunt Minnie. But thinking about hiring people to show up at her restaurant and cause a scene? That was something that I really couldn't have thought of on my own."

He chuckles. "Yeah, I'm not sure that I really approve of the way that you got Talia to agree to your proposal. But I am a creative bastard, if nothing else."

"Listen, it wasn't my greatest moment either. But I'll do whatever I need to do in order to win the company and inherit Remy's billions."

"Hey, I'm not here to judge. I'm just here to provide material support where I can. What are best friends for?"

"All right, I will see you soon. I am going to have this wedding within the month, so I will see you there if not sooner."

"That sounds like a good plan. I'll see you then."

I disconnect the call, a smirk rising to my lips. Sure, I might have pushed some invisible boundaries when I tricked my bride-to-be into saying yes to my proposal. But as they say, all is fair in love and war. In this case, it's fake love and an inheritance battle, but it's the same idea.

I go back to work for another hour, scanning pricing lists of the equipment that we would potentially need for drilling off the coast of Maine.

Around midnight, my head begins to throb dully. So, I tidy up my workspace and head upstairs to find a place to crash.

I make quite a bit of noise on the dark stairs, and when I emerge into the near pitch-black hallway, I open the first door that I find. It's a bedroom, but there is no one inside. I frown, pausing for a second.

I want to sleep, and I have never been great at sleeping with another person. But this weekend is all about getting comfortable with Talia. So I need to find her bedroom. It's not really what I want, but if we are going to convince everyone that our relationship is real, we need to at least be able to sleep in the same bed.

Besides, I can already envision how pissed Talia is going to be when I lumber into her room and start stripping.

I close the door with a smirk. It takes me a little bit of searching to find her in bed, dead asleep.

I open the bedroom door wide, noticing that she has chosen the room that is brilliantly illuminated by the glowing orb of the moon. It causes a bright square of moonlight to be thrown across the floor and odd shadows to leap up around it. The bed is quite large, and it is dressed in a dark blue comforter and white sheets. On either side of the bed, are two old bedside tables, made from the same pine wood as the walls and the floor. I creep forward, the floor creaking beneath my feet.

Talia is huddled beneath the comforter, her pillow clutched under her head, her mouth turned down. For a second, I think that she is frowning and might be awake. But when I take a couple more steps forward, she turns onto her back, her hand curling around her face, her copper hair spilling out across her pillow.

She's not awake—not even close.

I remove my jacket and toss it on a wooden-backed chair. My shoes and socks are next, tossed carelessly aside. I don't bother unbuttoning my Oxford shirt. I pull it over my head and discard it on the floor.

I begin to unbuckle my belt with my eyes fixed on Talia's sleeping form. As I unbutton my pants and pull them off, I'm already at half-mast just looking at her full lips.

Her tits and pussy are covered up with blankets. But though I can't see them, I can easily imagine them. I can feel her nipples under my hands, and my cock stirs as I imagine her creamy pussy just before I bury myself in it to the hilt.

No, that's not right. What I actually imagine is her looking me in the eyes and spreading her thighs while she touches her clit and moans. I imagine myself standing over her, stroking my cock as I guide her to orgasm using commands.

I smile and I start moving toward the bed. I rest one knee on top of the comforter, seeing how Talia will react. But she just shifts slightly, turning her head towards me without opening her eyes. My cock throbbing, I say her name.

"Talia." I lean in closer, inhaling a whiff of her flowery scent.

She begins to blink, gradually coming to consciousness. When she opens her eyes, it takes her about three seconds to realize that I am leaning down over the bed, fully nude. She jumps back, her eyes widening, her expression one of shock and a note of fear.

"Dare, what the hell are you doing?"

"What I should've done the first time I met you. I know that you have already slept with Burn, but you're my goddamn fiancée. And I'm attracted to you. There are sparks between us every time we touch. Why are we resisting so hard?"

She looks at me, her eyes never wavering from my face. "Dare, you are the one who said that I can't fall in love with you."

"Who is talking about falling in love? I'm talking about two people fulfilling each other's needs. It's as simple as that."

She shakes her head and starts to turn away, but I grab her hand and reach to cup her chin with my other hand, forcing her to look at me.

"Tell me that you don't lust after me." I scan her face.

"Tell me that you don't dream about me and wake up with wet panties."

Her throat works as she swallows. Her eyes peer through me, spearing me, making me feel insubstantial. "You wanted it clean and free of mess. To keep things transactional."

"And they can be. But there's no reason we can't fuck and keep the rest of our deal."

She shakes her head. "Dare, that's a terrible idea."

I see her gaze drop down to my cock, and I tense.

For a second, she licks her lips and then drags her eyes back up to my face. But I move like lightning, catching her lips with mine. She struggles against me, pushing me away. But I don't let her go that easily. I sink my hand into her hair and knot my fingers in it. I kiss her hard and with a burning passion, my whole body throbbing with need.

Talia shifts, rising slightly, and the blankets fall away from her body. I see that she is wearing a lacy pink teddy that the glam squad left for her. I want to rip that teddy from her body and expose her naked skin to my lips, my tongue, my teeth, and my cock.

She keeps struggling, her hand clawing at my chest, leaving a series of long, shallow scratches. I am only encouraged by that, though. Dragging her over to the edge of the bed, I kneel over her, my lips twitching.

"Are you going to be a good girl, darling?"

"Never," she hisses. In the next moment, she slaps me, her palm across my cheek. But I am not even fazed. I grab her hands and force her back onto the bed, snarling at her.

"You want me. I can see it in your eyes. And you're going to beg for me to fuck you by the end of the night."

Her expression contorts, and she shakes her head, her chin jutting out stubbornly. "I would never beg you. Not you, Dare."

My cock throbs. I take her lips, pressing mine against them almost violently, my tongue snaking against hers. She kisses me back, her tongue writhing with mine, but I am not looking for her compliance.

I like her fighting me, I like being the victor in our little games. It makes it all the sweeter when she eventually gives in.

"You need to make your peace with it. Once we sign the marriage certificate, that's it. We are together forever. Consider that for the next time that we share a bed. We might as well fuck and get it over with."

Talia raises her chin, throwing her hair back. She sweeps the sheet up to her chest, holding it there. I hate to be the one to tell her that I can clearly make out the outline of her hard nipples through the sheet.

She still wants me, whether she is able to admit it out loud or not.

"I'll marry you, Dare. I'll have your child. But I will never give up any of my virtues."

I can't help the full-throated laugh that leaves my chest. "What? What virtues? I'm pretty sure that I just showed you exactly who is in charge. Besides, it's not like you're a virgin anymore."

Her cheeks stain with blood. "I hate you."

"As we have discussed previously, you don't have to like me to fuck me. And you definitely don't have to love me to marry me. As long as you act like you're my one and only in front of other people, I couldn't care less what you think of me."

Her lips twist. "I'm still my own person, you know. I'll raise my child knowing that there are other people in the world, people who suffer hardships, people who can't afford million-dollar mansions or helicopters, or any of the other things that have been so important to your life."

"You know what you are? You are stubborn, and that's not a compliment. I still hate all the things that you stand for."

"That's perfect, because I will never be a Morgan at heart. We can tell everyone else a fairytale story, but we will both know that it's a lie."

I stand up, thundering at her. "It doesn't really matter because you will be a Morgan. And so will your child. So, you can just get used to lying to yourself now."

I stalk from the room, still buck naked and seething. What I yelled at her will definitely be true.

She will be a Morgan.

She'll give birth to a baby that will win me billions. One day, this will all seem like a distant memory, and I will reign over the world as Talia's husband and the head of Morgan Drilling Company.

Chapter Twenty-Five

DARE

Shutting out the blustery ocean breeze, the front door of my beach house slams with a heavy thud. I love everything about the coast, but the wind is brutal sometimes.

My footsteps echo through the house as I make my way down the hallway, dropping my phone and keys on the kitchen counter along the way.

I'd left early in the morning, venturing out in my yacht before Talia woke up.

I'm halfway up the stairs that lead up to my bedroom, eager for a much-needed nap, when I hear Talia's voice murmuring.

No, *moaning*.

"What the fuck?" I hiss. I slow as I approach, pressing my ear to the door.

Moans. Talia's moans are unmistakable from this distance.

"What the fuck?" I repeat under my breath.

Slowly, I turn the doorknob, cracking the door silently and peering inside.

The sight in front of me makes my heart skip a beat.

Talia. Fucking Talia.

Why is she fucking naked right now? It's the middle of the day and I expected her to be doing whatever it is that women do when men aren't paying attention to them. Maybe watching some TV or reading a book?

But this is something else entirely.

My cock instantly hardens at the sight of her spread out like a fucking playboy centerfold, her fingers buried deep in her pussy. Her thighs are spread wide open, showing me a clear view of her pussy. My mouth drops as she lifts her hips off the bed, rolling them around as she fucks first one, then two, then three fingers deep inside of her. When she pulls them out, they're glistening.

When she puts them in her mouth and moans, I almost come out of my skin.

What the actual fuck?

My hard cock has pulled all the anger out of my veins at the sight of her naked, but I quickly access it again, because despite how fucking sexy she might look right now, she's still touching herself without a thought in her head for me.

Who does she think she is? I've made my interest in Talia perfectly clear. There's no way I'm going to let her please herself without intervening.

I burst into the room, desire pulsing through my veins once more.

"What the fuck are you doing?" I demand.

She jumps up like she's been shot.

"Oh, my god!" She reaches for the comforter, but in her haste, it falls on the floor, leaving her completely exposed on my white silk sheets. "I can explain! I – I – um…."

"That's what I fucking thought," I snarl, closing the distance between us until she's forced to look up at me as I tower over her. She reaches for the sheet, but she's sitting on it, providing only a sliver of coverage over her perky tits, her nipples peeking out of the top, finally giving me a clear view of what I'd been only imagining up until now.

My cock throbs at the sight of her but I do my best to ignore it.

Her copper curls are tousled messily around her face, her eyes, wide with surprise at my sudden intrusion, twinge with a spark of fear that thrills me immensely – it's just too much.

Fuck.

"I'm sorry," she finally mutters, biting her bottom lip, sending me even more over the edge.

"Get up," I demand, my voice loud and booming.

"But I'm naked," she whines, pissing me off even more.

"I just saw your fingers buried deep in your pussy, Talia. I don't think your nakedness matters at this point."

The blush that creeps up her cheeks only serves to make my cock swell. Damn it all. Why am I so fucking turned on by her right now?

Her eyes dart down and when she sees my erection straining through my jeans, her entire demeanor changes. A cocky little smile spreads across her face as she looks up at me.

"Get out," she says, her voice low and steady now, the fear that had been there earlier quickly fading. "I'm trying to relieve some tension by myself, not trade barbs with you."

"Fuck off," I growl.

"You were watching me, weren't you? Before you came in?"

She arches a brow. Her eyes are all wide and innocent, like that's enough to fool me. I realize quickly what she's doing – trying to turn this around, like I've done something wrong, like she isn't the one who has somehow crossed a line.

"Yeah, I was fucking watching you, Talia," I say. I reach down, grabbing her hair and pulling her head back. She looks up at me daringly.

"Fuck off," she says, trying to push me away.

I shake my head, my gaze raking over her tits, her belly, the curve of her hips, now that the sheet has fallen away completely. "There isn't a single chance in hell."

I have a million questions. Mainly, who she was thinking about just now.

And absolutely no answers.

But suddenly, I don't give a fuck about the questions or the answers.

What I want is to see her fingers buried in her pussy again.

"Do it again, Talia," I say.

She cocks her head to the side, feigning confusion. "Do what, Dare?"

"Part your legs like a bitch in heat and rub your clit. I want to watch you. I want to be the one who *orders* you to come."

I lean down, peering into her eyes, searching them for any sign of resistance. My eyes dart down to her lips and she slides her tongue along the bottom one, tempting me, teasing me.

I know the game she's playing now, but two can play at that game, and she has no idea what she's getting into.

My lips slam against her mouth, my tongue forcing its way inside her mouth and tangling with hers as I kiss her deeply, possessively. She gasps as I reached out and pinch her nipple as I search her mouth, until she's moaning and arching her back, telling me everything I need to know.

I break the kiss and push her back onto the bed.

She falls back with a look of surprise on her face, her bright copper hair falling around her on the white silk pillow. Ignoring the fact that she looks like a fucking angel, I take a step back and stand at the end of the bed.

"I said, do it again, Talia," I growl once more. "I want to watch you fuck yourself. Like you were doing when I came in."

She starts to shake her head, but I lift a finger.

"I said, fucking do it, Talia. You're in my house. You wouldn't want me to change my mind about proposing to you, would you?"

She gasps, looking at me in disbelief.

"You wouldn't dare."

An icy laugh leaves me. I get close to her face, my lips almost touching hers. "I have made more important decisions for much pettier reasons. Try me, Talia. Look me in the eye and tell me what I won't do."

A shudder runs through her. "Dare…"

"Shut up and spread those thighs. Show me what I am spending so much money on, *darling girl*."

Talia's lips curl. Then she gives herself a little shake. To my utter pleasure, she sits up and slowly spreads her thighs, giving me the view I was demanding.

I see her glorious pink pussy, the tiny pucker of her ass, and miles of the creamiest skin imaginable. Everything, and I mean everything, is in my view. As I watch, Talia bites her lip and squirms as her pussy creams with excitement.

Fuck. Now that's something that might be worth more than half a million, right there.

"Good girl," I grunt. "Now touch yourself with your fingers."

She lifts her chin with pride, her eyes sparkling as she

reaches between her legs and begins fucking herself. My cock throbs painfully now and I reach down and squeeze it through my pants, aching for the relief that I know I'll receive eventually.

But first…I need this.

Talia puts on a show for me. Her nipples are rock hard the whole time, telling me she's enjoying it as much as I am. Her fingers work in and out of her pussy, her juices flowing over her hand endlessly as she moans and writhes under her own touch. I watch, taking note of the way she circles her clit a few times with her fingertips before pushing back inside of her depths. She throws her head back, closes her eyes and is really going for it now, but I'm not about to let her get off that easily.

"Talia!" I demand, her name booming out of me like a cannonball. She jumps, her eyes flying open and her gaze slamming into mine.

"What?"

"Look at me when you fucking come," I growl.

She lets out a long, sexy breath, shaking her head slowly, but just as I demanded, she holds my gaze and begins moving her fingers again.

"That's it," I urge. "Good girl. Come for me now."

Her hand flies through the air as she fucks herself harder and faster, until her entire body seizes up and a deep crimson blush washes over velvety skin, spreading up her neck and over her face. She cries out, fucking her fingers into herself with one hand as she frantically works her clit with the other until her thighs tremble and quake.

When her hands slow down, I know she's finished.

But I'm not.

"Get on your hands and knees," I demand again. I have no

idea if she'll do it, but we've come this far and she's not resisted. I may as well get as much out of this as I can.

I walk back to the side of the bed, unbuttoning my slacks as I go, smiling as she does just as I've told her to do. By the time I have my cock out at the edge of the bed, I don't even have to tell her what to do.

She looks up at me quickly and I simply nod, stroking my cock in front of her.

I nod, my hand wandering down to frame her breast. I tweak her nipple, causing a shudder of sensation to wrack her oversensitive body. Talia throws her head back, groaning.

I lumber to my feet. I gesture to her, my gaze like a burning brand over her naked body. "Come to me on your hands and knees, darling girl."

Talia rolls over and then pushes herself up, turning and moving toward me. I groan as I watch Talia crawling toward me.

Fuck. She's so damned perfect.

"Do you know how fucking hot you are right now?" I growl.

Talia stops when she reaches the edge of the bed, shaking her head slowly. My cock juts out proudly from my body. I step closer, brushing my lower thighs up against the silky sheets of the bed.

Talia reaches out to take my cock in her hand, looking up at me for guidance. Our gazes clash and I shiver.

The look in her eyes is everything I have been craving for years. And all it cost me is half a mil and my freedom.

"Fuck," I say, reaching out to rub my thumb roughly against her lower lip. "I think you're scared of me. And being the villain that I am, I am turned on by that. What a bad fucking man your fiancé is, darling girl."

I look down into Talia's big blue eyes for half a minute

more, my thumb rubbing roughly across the silken skin. She reaches timidly up to me but I shove her hand away, fisting my cock in my hand.

My gaze drops to her mouth. I tilt my head, giving myself a lazy stroke.

"Open your mouth, darling girl," I whisper. "Let me see that velvet tongue I've been dreaming about."

Talia licks her lips and opens her mouth. I run my free hand through the mass of her copper strands and then grip it, guiding my cock forward.

The last thing Talia sees before her face is buried against my skin is a drop of milky white semen leaking from the crown of my cock. I see her focus on it as I thrust closer to her face.

"Stick your tongue out," I coach. "Open your mouth, darling."

Talia sticks her tongue out and I prod it with the tip of my cock. It feels amazing, hot and tight, elastic and unfathomably deep. But as soon as Talia adjusts to my taste, I tug on her hair, lifting her throat. I nudge my cock into her mouth, inch by slow inch, hissing.

Fuck, that feels great.

Talia tries to put her hand up, to give herself a little control over how fast I move, but I knock it away.

"Don't," I grate out. "Just cover your teeth with your lips and try to relax."

Looking up at me, Talia covers her teeth and relaxes as much as she can. I renew my grip on her hair and glorify in the fact that she's fucking sucking my cock.

I am completely and utterly in control in this moment.

I keep pushing my cock inside her mouth, the tip almost brushing her throat. Lightning sizzles down my veins as I thrust, zipping around my whole body. Talia can't help but gag at the length of my cock, her whole body shuddering at once.

"Fuuuuck," I say, watching as Talia tries to control the reflex. It's so very appealing to know I have control of her very ability to breathe.

I flex my hips again, forcing my cock to touch the back of her throat. Talia gags again, throwing her hand up to shove herself backward with a gasp.

A loud sound bursts forth from my chest, a rumbling bass growl. She's only standing up for herself, but I'm not interested in her resistance right now.

I step back, pulling my cock out of her mouth with a pop. Talia looks up at me, sucking in breaths.

I stroke my cock, looking at down at her. "So much to do, so little time." I bite my lower lip and cocks my head. "I like watching you gag on my cock, darling girl. But I don't want you to be left out in the cold. I want you to come."

Tightening my grip on her hair, I push my cock even further inside her mouth, loving the feeling of her engulfing me completely. I moan, my release so close I can feel it building deep inside of me. The thought of coming in Talia's mouth is beyond exciting, but I want even more.

"Your mouth feels so fucking good. Fuck!" I say, fucking into her mouth over and over. "Touch yourself again, Talia. Fuck your pussy. I want to see you come with me."

She moans, the vibrations rocking through my cock as she reaches down and sinks her fingers into her pussy again, my cock twitching at the sight once more. I am so fucking close but I'm not about to come until she's coming too.

"Fuck yourself harder," I say, as I grab her head, guiding my cock deeper and deeper into her mouth.

"Good girl, good girl," I growl as her fingers disappear into her beautiful pussy. Her tongue is wet and smooth and hot as it works expertly around my cock. "Now, I want you to come. Come for me, darling girl."

She moans deeply, the vibrations once again sending me reeling and as I see her body tense up and shudder, I know she's coming and I let myself go, the pressure building up to a roaring thunder in my head until I explode in her sweet mouth, ribbons of hot white heat that she greedily sucks down, sending rivers of rolling pleasure ricocheting throughout my body.

Her tongue slowly swirls around my shaft, licking up all traces of my pleasure.

"Good girl," I sigh.

Talia wipes her mouth and darts a glance at me, her expression unreadable. She withdraws from me, curling up and pulling the blanket over her head. I look at her, feeling somewhat at a loss as to what I am supposed to say.

What does Talia want from me, exactly? I wonder as I lie down next to her.

Closing my eyes, I mull over the issue. And before I know it, I'm asleep.

Chapter Twenty-Six

The rest of the weekend passes in a blur. I grin and bear it as I spend my days pretending to fall all over my fiancé, touching his arm, kissing his lips, slipping my hand around his waist, and looking at him lovingly.

In the meantime, I try to call Olivia and update her on what is happening. But for some reason, all my calls go straight to voicemail. It's exceedingly frustrating.

By the time we call it a night, I slip upstairs and lock myself in the same bedroom. I don't want a repeat of last night, no matter how good he made me feel or how much just thinking about it makes my pussy dampen.

No matter how loudly I might have moaned.

Before I know it, we are on our way back to Harwicke. As we are closing in on the town, Dare looks over at me and reaches in his pocket. I'm expecting that maybe he is going to have me sign another document or something. But instead, he produces a small black velvet ring box.

Without a hint of ceremony, he puts it on the seat beside me and then looks away, leaving me to wonder what the box could possibly contain. There's no way that it holds a ring. Even Dare would know better than to just set the box down beside me.

I reach for the box and crack it open, lifting it. Inside is the largest emerald and diamond ring I have ever seen. It is a huge, absolutely gorgeous rectangular emerald set in the middle and several rectangular baguette-cut diamonds beside it. My mouth hangs open, and I try to estimate how much the ring is worth. Easily in the tens of millions of dollars.

I look at Dare, reaching out and nudging him with my elbow. He arches a brow and turns away from the window, casual as anything.

The fact that he would just hand me such a magnificent ring and expect me to know what to do with it is like acid sizzling in the pit of my stomach.

Dare flashes me a smirk. "It's a ring."

"And? What is it for?"

I feel beads of sweat break out on my brow every time I glance at the ring, so I reach down and close the lid to the box. He rolls his eyes. "It's an engagement ring. Do you really need me to spell it out for you?"

"Wow, could you be any less romantic when you just lean over and drop the ring on my lap?"

"I thought I was perfectly romantic when I wired you the money for our arrangement. If I didn't make it clear enough, this is not exactly going to be a normal marriage."

My feelings about the ring are complicated, and I try to sort them out as I stew in my own silence. I look out my window and see the town of Harwicke as we begin to approach. Slowly, I begin to make out the shape of the roofs.

I jump out of my skin as Dare grabs my hand and tries to put the ring on it. It's much too large and it slides on quite easily, the enormous emerald sliding to the side. I look at the platinum setting, and my lips twist. I don't know what I had imagined my engagement ring would look like, but this huge emerald is just not it. I can't tell if I dislike the ring because it is being forced on me or if I just genuinely don't like platinum or the way the diamonds catch in the sunlight, winking at me.

I try to pluck the ring off, but Dare grips my hand. He looks at me and pulls the ring off my finger, pursing his lips. "It doesn't fit. My assistant picked the damn thing out, so that tracks. I'll have it resized today and delivered to you before our engagement photos."

He had someone pick the damn ring out? Ugh. Of course he did.

I rip his fingers off my wrist and give him a sour look. "I need to go home first. I need to tell Aunt Minnie that I am engaged. She can't hear this from anyone else."

He flops a hand at me, rolling his eyes. "Tell her to meet us at the penthouse."

"What penthouse?"

He gives me a look. "I bought a penthouse for us. Keep up, Talia."

My brows furrow. "How was I supposed to know that you bought a penthouse for us? What if I hate it?"

He gives me a puzzled glance. "You won't. But even if you did, who cares? You only have to stay there when we are here in Harwicke. The rest of the time, we can stay at my Manhattan penthouse."

I want to argue with him, but the whole helicopter suddenly lurches, and my attention is diverted. I feel us descending, and I reach out my hands, clasping one on the door and the other on Dare's knee. Until the helicopter lands, I grip his knee, praying quietly, though I'm not sure to whom

I'm praying to. I've never been to church, much less been religious.

Once I climb out of the helicopter, feeling shaky, I text my Aunt Minnie the address of the penthouse that Dare gives me. It's a quick trip to the penthouse from the helicopter landing pad and I spend it trying to get over my motion sickness from being in the helicopter.

I look around as I climb out of the car. To my left is a trendy-looking restaurant. I squint and realize that it's Herbsaint, the same restaurant that Olivia took me to before. Looking around with some confusion, I notice that Herbsaint is in a huge warehouse loft building. Actually, now that I look around, all four corners of the intersection that I'm currently standing at have the same style of warehouse loft.

Dare grabs my arm and ushers me into the building across the street from that bar, but just before I step inside I hear Aunt Minnie's voice.

"Talia! Talia, wait!"

I whirl on my heel, looking around. I spot her pulling up in her ancient eggplant colored rusted Volvo, a true nineteen seventies artifact. She has the passenger-side window rolled down, and she pulls to a stop beside the building. I look at Dare, biting my lip.

He waves his hand dismissively and walks in the door. "I'll leave it to you. The doorman has your name."

As if I were just unimportant in the grand scheme of things. Jesus, Dare really knows how to make me feel small.

Rushing over to the car, I give Aunt Minnie a wave. Opening the door, I pluck several balled up pieces of paper off the front seat, gently tossing them behind the front seat. Then I crawl in and shut the door. She gives me several hard hugs, as if she sensed that what I needed most from her right now was some affection. I hug her for a solid minute and then release her with a sigh.

She looks at me quite seriously, tucking a strand of hair behind my ear. "Well, what happened? All you said on the phone was that you had to go out of town. I don't understand? Where did you go?"

Taking a huge breath. "Okay. I have to tell you something, Aunt Minnie. But I want you to promise me that you'll try not to freak out about it."

She straightens up, patting her wild, frizzy mane of gray hair. She looks more confused than anything.

"Well, I'll try. Where have you been? You're not in trouble, are you?"

"Nothing like that," I assure her.

"Is it Olivia? Did something happen to her?"

"No. Olivia has nothing to do with it." I purse my lips. "Actually, I've been calling her a lot, but I am not getting through. It just goes to voicemail."

"Isn't she at a biology conference this whole week?" Minnie asks.

"Oh. Yeah, of course. I am just caught up in my own drama." I grab her hand and give it a squeeze. "Okay. The truth is that I am engaged. I spent the weekend with my fiancé at his beach house in Maine."

Minnie looks completely and utterly shocked. "Who are you engaged to? Oh my God, is it Olivia?"

I shake my head and squeeze her hand. "No. Thank you, though, for being supportive of whomever I choose. But I'm afraid it's someone that you don't know. His name is Dare Morgan."

She looks like I hit her with a shovel. "Dare Morgan? As in Remy Morgan?"

I gulp and nod. "That's the one. He..." What I'm about to

say twists my stomach into knots. "He swept me off my feet. We've only known each other for a short time, but we decided to try to get married," I mumble. "Within the month, actually."

Minnie frowns. "My dear, I don't care who you marry. But are you sure that you want to marry someone so..." Her eyes narrow and I can see that she is trying to choose her words carefully. "Flashy, I guess? You could live in a shoe for all I care."

I grip her hand again and give her a tight smile. "I know it seems random. But he will provide for us in a way that we haven't been able to do for ourselves. And he..." I swallow. "He loves me. You'll see, we are very compatible."

Aunt Minnie looks at me with open skepticism. "Very compatible? I've never heard anyone who was in love with anyone else use that particular word. Is there something I don't know?"

Hesitating, I hold my breath for a long second. But then I nod slowly. "I am carrying his child."

Aunt Minnie stares at me, her hands clasping around her heart. "You are? I must say, Talia I had no idea that you were..." She blushes faintly. "That you... I had no idea about the pregnancy," she finishes at last. "You know, it's perfectly acceptable to have a baby without having a father or having to marry him."

"I think you know why I feel differently than you on that matter. I grew up without a father, and I felt like there was a huge chunk missing from my life for so many years. I want my baby to have all the things I didn't have."

Aunt Minnie wells up, blotting at her eyes. "I tried my best, Talia. Really, I did."

I grab her by the shoulders and pull her close, giving her another quick hug. "You did so well. I couldn't wish for a better person to grow up with. Honestly. But by agreeing to the marriage, I am not just taking care of my baby's future. I'm going to take care of you. And what about all the repairs that Hope House requires? They'll just be done without any more fuss. No more government red tape, no more town hall meetings. No more shady men paying off your debts."

A look of horror crosses her face. "Talia! You can't sacrifice your future for me!"

"I'm not. Really Aunt Minnie, I... I love him." I flinch. "I'm doing the best thing for everybody, including my unborn baby."

I pull back and look at her.

She is openly crying right now. "What about the bookstore? Are you still going to work there with me?"

"Once the baby comes, I think it will be difficult. But we will see what we can work out. You can afford to hire whoever you want to work there now. It'll be better than just hiring your niece, right?"

Minnie starts bawling.

She's really tearing my heart into pieces. I know marrying Dare is for the best. But at the moment, it doesn't really feel that way.

"Aunt Minnie." She looks up at me, wiping her cheeks. I give her a soft smile. "My mind is made up. There is no use in crying about it. Honestly, I am a lucky girl. Dare wants to marry me, and I am thankful for that. The only real question is whether you are going to support me or not."

Minnie looks mortified. "Of course. Of course I will. Anything that you really want, I want for you."

"Thanks. Do you really mean that?"

She nods, her expression grave. "Here."

She fishes beneath the edge of her dark gray caftan, lifting a necklace. She unclasps it and pulls a dainty gold ring off it, a simple diamond solitaire glinting in the middle. She looks up at me and offers the ring to me.

"You never met my mother. But she was a wonderful woman. And she left this ring for us. I think she expected that your mother or I would get married and find a use for this ring. But... That's not really how it went. But now I can pass it on to you."

I take the ring, blinking. "This was Grandma's?"

She closes my fist around the ring and nods. "It was. Now it's yours."

"Gosh, thanks." I give her another hug, feeling a little overwhelmed.

We peer out of the car and into the building. She looks at the doorman of the building, who is not even pretending that he is not watching our little drama play out. "Are you in that building?"

"I think so." I glance up at the huge building. It looks sort of vintage, like it was a factory at some point in the past.

Aunt Minnie pats her hair, still looking crestfallen. "Well, I hate to do this. But I actually have a shift at the Hope House that I am going to be late for if I don't run along right now."

"Of course. Thank you for coming by. I don't know the details about the wedding just yet, but I am sure that you will be the first to know. Well, maybe second. There's always Olivia to consider."

She gives me a sad smile and pats my hand. "Make sure that he treats you well. You hear? That's all that matters in the end."

I swallow and nod, opening the door. I'm ashamed to say that I wave goodbye and hurry across the street corner before she can say anything more.

She's absolutely right, and if I had any choice, I would know better than to choose Dare.

Chapter Twenty-Seven

TALIA

T aking the elevator to the penthouse, I swallow. I can't help but run my hands over my hair and the short black dress I chose from the rolling rack that the glam squad left behind. I don't know what to expect when I step through the doors, but the doors open and I move through them automatically, my eyes roving all around.

The entire loft is huge — absolutely monstrous. There are obscenely high ceilings with skylights, beautiful navy walls with twenty-foot floor-to-ceiling windows, and dark wood and tile flooring. Everything gleams; everything catches my eye.

To my right is a very stylish living room area that is separated from the rest of the house by thin rice paper walls. To my left, I see Dare leaning against the sparkling white countertop of a freestanding kitchen island that looks like a worn cement slab.

Dare is talking to a thin young man with slicked-back blonde hair and a dark wool sweater paired with black jeans. He is almost completely ignoring him in favor of the figures that sit at the granite end of that cement island, their hulking figures taking up all the space around them.

One is dressed in an elegant white silk top and dark pants. From here, I can see that she is clearly a female, although I didn't realize that women as tall and broad as her could also be rather refined and sophisticated. Her thick black hair is pinned up against her head, and she laughs at something that Dare says. Well, 'chuckles' is more like it.

Her counterpart is every bit as big as she is—massive like a tree trunk and tall as a skyscraper. He is dressed in black slacks, but he wears a slightly more casual black hoodie. Paired with his graying hair, it makes for a rather remarkable combination.

As I stand in the open living room, Dare looks over and spots me.

He raises his hand, hailing me. "Ah, the woman of the hour! Frick and Frack, meet Talia. Talia, meet Frick and Frack."

The two giants stand up, turning to greet me. I walk forward, my pulse pounding. I shake their hands, grimacing as Frick, the woman, grips my hand a little too hard.

"Hello. We are pleased to meet you." She smiles at me and her accent is thick, something vaguely Middle Eastern. It pairs well with her sandstone-colored skin, I think.

"Pleasure to meet you as well." I shake hands with Frack and wince again, as he is too strong for his own good.

Ending the encounter as soon as possible, I turn to the other young man. "And who is this?"

"That's Rob, my personal assistant," Dare says. "But don't pay him any attention right now. I really want you to meet your new security detail."

"Security detail?" I glance at Frick and Frack and then back to Dare. "Is that really necessary?"

He encourages me to step forward and then slides his arm around me. I freeze up at first, but he gives me a sharp look.

"Everybody that has money has security. It's really not optional for you."

Frick clears her throat and smiles evenly. "We will be with you all the time. There will be other guards with us, but we will be taking point."

I screw up my face. "If you think it's really needed…"

"It is, believe me. I'd rather have them following you around everywhere and nothing bad happen than be sorry after something bad does happen."

I give him a skeptical look but shrug. "Okay. I guess." I wave my hand to the whole penthouse. "Are you going to show me around?"

Dare smiles at Rob and then tells Frick and Frack they can wait downstairs in the security room on the fourth floor. Frack waves goodbye to me, Frick bows her head, and then they hustle to the elevator.

I take a deep breath and look at Dare while biting my tongue. He'll get an earful about it later, but for now, I'm focused on Rob.

"I'm sorry, Rob, was it?" I extend my hand, and he shakes it, his grip much less aggressive. "It's nice to meet you. Do you mind if I steal my fiancé for a minute?"

Rob blinks. "I swear, I thought that Dare had somehow tricked you into coming here. Hearing you say that is just surreal for me."

"Rob," Dare says with a glare. "Why don't you run along and make sure that the photographers get in here okay."

Rob nods his head and agrees. I'm left alone with Dare after his hasty retreat.

"Well? Shall I show you the place?"

I glance at the thin rice paper walls between this room and

the living room. "Sure. My only question is, those walls seem so thin. Will that not be a problem when the baby comes?"

"Oh, we won't be here that long. Maybe two months at the most. You'll probably barely be showing by then." He looks at me, his gaze tightening on my face. "You're about, what? Two months along?"

For some reason, the question hits me with a thud like a baseball bat to the chest. The wind is knocked out of me briefly, and I put my hands on my knees. Closing my eyes, I nod at him.

"What are you doing?" he asks sharply. "What is this?"

I suck in a deep breath and straighten. "Nothing. I just hadn't really thought about that quite yet. God, how can I already be two months into a pregnancy and barely have any idea?"

Dare picks at a piece of lint on his dark suit sleeve, shrugging a shoulder. "I don't know. This is the first one that I've ever been up close and personal with. I don't exactly have a lot of pregnant lady friends."

"Ha ha," I shoot back. "Well?" I slide my arm into his, feeling a hint of satisfaction at how well we fit together. "I don't know exactly what has come over me, but I am a little tired, to tell you the truth."

He smirks down at me and executes a mocking bow. "Allow me to show you the bedroom. Right this way, mademoiselle."

He shows me around the loft quickly, walking past the chic living room I have already seen, an office area, another all-white living room area that's quite cozy, and an empty space walled off on two sides.

The thin white paper walls seem just like a bare room. "What is this going to be?"

He shrugs. "Undecided. I thought maybe you would like

to pick out some furniture for whatever suits you. I've already filled a room with office equipment and a desk. So maybe this can be your private quarters."

I turn around and give him a surprised look. "You considered me before you thought about the layout of the apartment?"

Dare moves away, fidgeting. He is rarely uncomfortable, so I have a hard time pinning the emotion on him, but he certainly looks like he doesn't want to be having this conversation.

"Before you think about it too much, it's not like I did anything. When I was doing the planning, I left the room empty at Rob's suggestion. So you really have to think about him. He was key in picking out most of the furniture in this place and your engagement ring. I don't really like doing much of that stuff."

I nod and poke my cheek out with the tip of my tongue. "I'm getting a sense of that now."

He grabs my arm and hauls me on. "There are two more rooms. This one is the baby's room."

It is just beside the kitchen, although I notice that the walls are made of a sturdier material not unlike stucco. I step in and look around, gasping.

There is a gorgeous white crib sitting strategically in a sunbeam with a beautiful white mobile hanging over it. There's a changing table and a little white dresser, matching the theme of this room. Every surface is done in either stark white with tiny pink and green polka dots. There is even a toy bin in the corner, already stocked with toys. And my favorite part is the huge rocking chair with several little onesies hanging over an arm and a pink and white blanket folded neatly over the back. My eye catches on these little onesies, and I forget to breathe for several seconds.

"Oh my God." I turned to Dare, my eyes misting over. "Oh my God. I thought you said we weren't going to be here for very long?"

"We'll still have to have a place to stay when we are in town." He raises his hands and tries to calm me down. "It's missing a lot of things. I just asked Rob to get whatever you thought you would need. I am sure you will still want to shop for baby things before you... you know. Have the baby."

It takes me a minute to calm down, breathing big, deep breaths and blowing them out. "I never thought... I honestly hadn't even planned any of this out."

Dare waves a hand around the room. "You don't have to. You are not responsible for anything if you don't want to be. That's what's amazing about being rich. Well, that and the fact that we don't actually have to parent our own kids."

"What does that mean?"

"I was left with a nanny for most of my childhood and I turned out fine."

I turn a frown on him. "You did not turn out fine. You turned out like... Well, whatever *you* are. Besides, isn't the whole point of being rich that you can choose whether you want to spend time with your kids or not?"

He shrugs and starts to leave the room. "I guess when you put it that way, I can't argue." He heads to the other end of the loft. "Come on, there's one more thing that I want to show you."

With one last look over my shoulder, I leave the nursery and follow my soon-to-be husband. He leads me down the hall and then opens a door on his right, urging me to hurry. I rush through the door, and he smirks at me.

Here, the walls are again that thick stucco rather than the thin rice paper. There is a small doorway that leads into what looks like a bathroom and a huge four-poster bed right in the middle of the room. There are two wall cabinets that serve as closets, a pair of minimalistic white wooden bedside tables, and a pair of cozy armchairs sitting by a fireplace that vents all the way up to the roof. I open my mouth, looking around. It's like I just stepped into a home decor magazine. The linens on the bed are white and gray and expensive looking. Under my feet is a very curly, dark gray rug that feels luxurious.

"What do you think?"

I look around, nodding. "It looks pretty good. Is there a separate sleeping space for me?"

Dare stops and looks at me with a frown, his hands going to his hips. "I thought we talked about this. We are sleeping in the same bed from now on."

"No. You said that when other people were around, we would share the same room. But clearly, there is no one else here. Right?"

"Nice try. But I like having you where I can see you at all times. Anytime you're not with me, Frick and Frack will be on your tail. Besides, what if you get lonely at night and no one else is around? How would that benefit my interests if you had this all to yourself late at night?"

I huff at him. "Dare, be serious."

"I am serious. If you think that I am done fucking you, you are crazy."

"You are too much." I shake my head and turn around, walking back toward the front of the loft. Dare follows me, not saying a word. But I can feel his eyes on the small of my back, burning a hole right through me.

The rest of the day goes by pretty quickly. Dare forces me to pose for engagement photos, so I do, changing my outfit a few times at his request. I try to keep telling myself that even though he is going to essentially lie with these photos, it's all for a greater cause. The greater cause may be Hope House and Aunt Minnie, but whatever.

We were only fooling the Morgans, so I feel okay about it. Or at least that's what I tell myself.

I pose for the pictures, letting Dare move my body around and shout directions at the photographers. I feel awkward, but Dare keeps saying that the key is to stop obsessing over the fact that we are acting out a lie. I bite my tongue and submerge myself in the role, beaming at the camera and telling myself that I am the next Mrs. Morgan. I can't seem to turn my brain off, but at least I manage to keep my mouth shut.

After the photographers leave, I step out of the sky-high heels that the glam squad left for me and collapse on the white fuzzy couch in the living room. Dare smirks at me.

"Tired?"

"Yeah. I am really wiped even though we didn't do anything besides just let people take our pictures."

"Well, rest up. In two days, we announce our engagement to the family. So prepare yourself for that. Within a month, we will have a full-on wedding ceremony with everybody who is anybody gathering to toast us as a couple. Then, shortly after that, we can announce that the baby is on the way."

A feeling of overwhelm washes over me. I close my eyes, unable to hold back the sarcastic comments.

"Is that all? We're not going to scale Mount Everest or base jump or anything?"

If Dare realizes that I am not being sincere, he doesn't respond to the sentiment. "Just tell me that you are ready."

Sitting up, I splay my hand out on the couch and look at him, tilting my head. "I'm ready. It feels weird having to lie to anyone, much less a room full of your family. But I'm still prepared. I have made a decision, and now I'm going to commit to it, no matter what."

The smile on his face is icy cold. "That's good. You'll need that steel spine when we announce our engagement to my family."

Chapter Twenty-Eight

DARE

The next morning, I stroll into the kitchen, with two white-coated doctors following discreetly. Talia looks up from her breakfast, which appears to be a piece of dry toast. She looks at the doctors flanking me and swallows, wiping away the crumbs and depositing the rest of the toast in the kitchen sink.

"Talia, this is Dr. Smith and Dr. Nathan. These ladies are here to give you an exam."

"What kind of exam?" She asks, pulling at the hem of her tight white dress.

Dr. Nathan sets forward, smiling professionally. She is a very diligent OB/GYN that was recommended to me for her discretion.

She gives Talia a warm smile and extends a hand, ushering Talia toward the formerly empty room. "I'm a gynecologist and obstetrician. So is my colleague. We have brought in all the necessary items to give you your first ultrasound in the privacy of your own home."

Talia's eyebrows fly up. She glances at me nervously, but Dr. Nathan puts an arm around her, reassuring her. "Don't worry. We will provide you with not only discretion but also top-quality care. We are just going to take a peek inside and then draw some blood. Talk about what you're eating, what could help the baby. Just some basic things."

I follow the women to the door of the once-bare room. There is a pause, and Dr. Nathan turns around, looking me up and down.

"Talia, do you mind if Mr. Morgan is in the room?"

"I do, absolutely. He definitely can't be in the room for any of this."

I cock my head. "What? What about the birth? I need to be there. What will people think?"

Without hesitating, Dr. Nathan's palm stops at my chest as I stride toward the doorway. She gives me a polite smile. "Mr. Morgan, I think your fiancée would really appreciate some time to herself. We have months until she is due to give birth, so I suggest that you don't push things today. Is that okay?"

She asks me as if I can say no. But I realize that making a fuss right now will make me look like an asshole. I scrunch up my face and shrug. "How long will you need?"

"It depends. Approximately half an hour. If you want to come back to the doorway around then, we should have some sonogram pictures for you, if you want."

I make a face. "Yeah, all right. I will find somewhere else to be while you're doing the exam, I guess."

"Thank you." I look past her at Dr. Smith and Talia, who are currently talking quietly while Talia steps onto a scale. Dr. Nathan closes the door, and I clench my fists.

I want to be present for everything, mostly because the only way I can be absolutely sure that no one pulls the wool over my eyes is to see it myself. But seeing as how that is not an option, I turn away and head toward the kitchen. I feel a buzzing in my pocket, and I pull out my cell phone to see that Burn is calling me.

I'm not exactly sure when Burn last contacted me by phone, but I'm certainly curious. I pick up the phone.

"Burn."

"Dare. I am downstairs."

I glance toward the elevator, the phone is still pressed against my ear. "Downstairs where?"

"At your new loft apartment, apparently. The fucking doorman that you've installed at your building won't let me up even though we are twins. Something about how, if you wanted me to visit, you would have put me on a guest list or something."

I purse my lips. Glancing over my shoulder toward the back of the apartment, I weigh the pros and cons of having Burn in the apartment. It's too risky while Talia is just out of sight with the doctors attending to her. Something cold slides through my gut, and I clench my teeth.

"Dare? Are you going to be a normal human being and let me up?"

"No," I say finally. "I'll be down in a minute. Don't go anywhere."

I take the emergency stairs just beside the elevator, and I hit the ground floor in about a minute. Pushing out of the steel door, I see Dante, the doorman, standing beside my twin brother Burn. Dante raises an eyebrow, but I wave him off.

"He's fine. He probably won't be visiting again, will you, Burn?"

Burns lips thin but he gives me a cool smile. "We will see."

He pulls a white rectangle of paper from inside his suit's jacket pocket and smirks at me as he hands it over. It's heavier than I anticipated when I take the card stock from him, glancing at it. "Save the date," it proclaims. Burn and Daisy's wedding date is listed as two months from today at the bottom.

I look up at Burn, my eyes narrowing on his face. He lifts his chin, flicking his hair out of his face, and smiles.

"Well? Are you going to congratulate me?"

I purse my lips, reminding myself to control my expression. I give him a pleasant smile and a raucous clap on the shoulder.

"Congratulations."

He brushes off his shoulder and gives me a little glare. "Thanks, I guess."

If I am being completely honest, I am not even listening to the words coming out of his mouth at this moment. I'm trying to figure out if I can move my wedding date closer to my twin's as a kind of fuck you.

"I want the whole ceremony to be at the Manhattan Four Seasons. But Remy made a strong argument for having our wedding at the Morgan estate. Daisy says she doesn't care, so I had to give in to Remy's demands."

I look my brother up and down, trying to pretend to be unimpressed. "Is that it? Did you just drop by to taunt me with your save the date?"

Burn looks past me at the elevator, squinting. "No. In fact, I came to ask who you are holed up in here with. If it's some sleazy hooker, that's one thing. I can just go. But if it's someone else, I sure would like to know who."

I half a laugh. "Don't worry about her. It's none of your concern."

He arches his brow. "So it is someone, then? I'm assuming that it isn't just a prostitute. Or are you so desperate that you are trying to pull off a pretty woman?"

"You're an idiot. You know that right?"

I sneer. "We've got the same DNA, so if I'm an idiot, so are you."

"Then I am going to tell Remy that you are traipsing around with some hooker, telling her that you are going to marry her. If he finds out that you have paid for a wife..."

I cut Burn off. "Remy is a true capitalist. He would probably love me more for it if that were the case. But, and I cannot emphasize this enough, it is not. I have a girlfriend upstairs, and she has never been a prostitute in her life."

"Sure." His skeptical gaze rakes over me. "Keep telling yourself that."

"Yeah, yeah. You're just upset because I am making gains against you in this inheritance race."

"Ha. You wish. You'll win the inheritance race over my dead fucking body."

I lean closer, licking a canine tooth. "That can certainly be arranged, brother."

Burn growls at me, but I just look at my watch and shrug. "Well, this has been fun. But I have to get back upstairs and fuck my girlfriend, so…"

I stalk over to the elevator doors, pressing the button to call the elevator down. The doors open, and I give Burn a little wave. He flips me off and I hear his threat as I disappear inside the elevator.

"You'll never win. Just give up now. Morgan Drilling will be mine."

The doors sink shut, and I wait until the elevator starts to ascend before unleashing my fury by pounding my arm against the nearest wall five times. It doesn't hurt the elevator, but it definitely leaves all my nerves jangling. Who does Burn think he is?

Now I will be forced to make some serious moves.

Specifically, I need to marry Talia before I visit my family tomorrow to make the announcement.

I whip out my phone and start texting Rob. When I get back upstairs, I busy myself with arranging for a justice of the peace to come to the loft today. Then I look at the save-the-date card again and text Rob a picture of it, asking for him to make an almost exact copy of it with my name and Talia's name and to put the wedding date as two weeks from today. That should take the wind out of Burn's sails and cripple his announcement.

When I get done with that, Talia is finished with her appointment. She's standing in the living room with the two doctors, smiling at them. Something in me tightens and I move forward, wondering why their appointment was so brief. Is there something wrong with the baby?

"What happened?" I demand. "Is everything okay?"

The three women turn around, their expressions collectively positive.

"Everything is fine." Dr. Nathan smiles and puts her hands behind her back, clasping them as she talks to me. "We were able to get several sonogram pictures and have a good look at your baby. It looks healthy. About eight and a half weeks old, in my estimation."

I release the breath that I didn't even know I was holding in until just now. "Oh. Okay."

Talia smiles at me and offers me one of the square black-and-white photos that show her body against a grainy gray background, contrasting with the small, clear circle of her womb. The circle is a blob, with the larger blob being the one that I make out as the head. I squint and take the picture from her as she examines the first photo of the golden child. This baby is worth a giant fortune, and just seeing it makes my heartbeat speed up.

"What about the sex?" I ask, unable to take my eyes off the sonogram image.

My gaze slides to Talia, who is gazing at the picture and clasping her hands around her abdomen. "Did you find out already?"

She shakes her head. "Not yet. Dr. Nathan says that we have to wait a little while until the baby is eleven weeks old. "

My heart hammers. I struggle to keep a neutral expression because I am not sure what emotion will burst free if I allow myself to react.

"I want to know."

I hand the little photo back to Talia, who grasps it thankfully. She can't tear her eyes away from it. I can see that Talia is creating life right now as we stand here, and that's pretty impressive.

"Talia," I say, she looks up and I give her a serious look. "Do you want to know the sex?"

She nods, looking at Dr. Nathan. Dr. Nathan gives us both a long look.

"Good things come to those that wait." Dr. Nathan smiles at us and says, "Congratulations on your healthy baby, though."

Talia reaches out and grips my arm, beaming at the doctor. I'm not sure whether she is acting for the doctor's benefit or not, but I think that she's too overwhelmed to fake any emotions right now.

"Thanks," Talia says, sniffling. "You were very helpful."

Talia blots out her eyes again, and I feel a bit like a robot. Perhaps I should feel something, some stirring in my chest, but all life is a strange numbness.

I'm stiff as I address the medical professionals. "If that's all, doctors. You'll excuse us. We have a meeting with the justice of the peace that we should get ready for."

"You're getting married today?" Dr. Nathan asks. "Wow, it seems like all kinds of congratulations are in order."

Talia screws up her face and looks at me. "We are?"

"Thank you, doctors." I jerk my head toward the elevator and they are quick enough to leave. Once the doors shut behind them and I hear the elevator grind to life, I arch a brow.

"Burn stopped by to give me this." Fishing the save-the-date out of my pocket, I hand it to her. She takes it and frowns, but doesn't say whatever she is thinking.

"But what does that have to do with us?"

"I am in a race against the clock to beat my brother when it comes to starting a family. If he sets his wedding date for two months from now, I have to do everything in my power to beat that. So we will be married by the justice of the peace right now with a wedding ceremony to follow in the coming weeks."

She nods slowly, absorbing my information. "I see. Gosh, it's all just going by so quickly. I only accepted your proposal on Friday and yet here we are, getting married on Monday. It's a lot to take in."

"Yeah, well. If I have to, I will do nearly anything if it puts a crimp in Burn's style. I already texted Rob about how we need to go all out with the wedding ceremony in only two weeks' time. He is frantically getting all the arrangements made."

Talia is looking vaguely uncomfortable. "Is this a normal thing to do for people in your family? Not planning your own wedding but to have it planned for you?"

I shrug and check my watch. "Who knows? I'm not really interested in how other people go about planning a wedding.

If it's not obvious, I am as emotionally invested in this wedding as I am in who the upcoming contestants on The Bachelor will be. That is to say, I don't care at all."

"Not even for show?"

"Sure. But that can be arranged by Rob. Trust me, he will ensure that every last detail of our sham wedding is perfect. Now, if you are ready, I think we should be expecting the justice of the peace to walk through those doors at any moment."

Right as I say that, I hear the elevator humming to life, the car rising to our floor. Talia licks her lips and straightens her dress, her lips twisting.

"Should I change?" She looks down at her dress, her expression disapproving. "I'm not really in wedding attire."

"Why would you need to do that?" I ask. I start walking toward the elevator. "I'm having the justice sign a non-disclosure agreement. You're fine the way you are. We're just going to do this as quickly as possible. No muss, no fuss. We're just saying the right words so that the justice will fill out a form, more or less."

Her lips twist but she just shrugs. "Okay. Whatever you say."

"That's a good girl," I say with a smirk. "Now let's go greet the justice."

Chapter Twenty-Nine

DARE

The justice of the peace is a dark-skinned young man in a black shirt, black pants, and the little white collar that indicates he's a priest. He looks no older than Talia, but I honestly wouldn't care if he was the man in the fucking moon. He's just here to perform the mumbo-jumbo ritual aspect and marry us in the most official sense. He introduces himself as Reverend Terry and doesn't seem put off by my hurried attitude.

"Before I begin, I typically like to ask the two people that I am marrying a question. Is there anything that you want to say to the other person? Is there anything that the other person should know? This is the last chance for you to tell each other anything before I make you man and wife. So..." He waves a hand at me and Talia. I take Talia's arm, my lips thinning.

Talia looks up at me, her eyes curious. "Is there anything that you want to tell me before we tie the knot?"

I chuckle at that. "I think you know pretty much everything there is to know about me, Talia. I'm not a good man. But you already know that. Isn't that right?"

She flushes and looks away. "Let's not get into all of that right now."

"No, let's not. Is there anything that you need to tell me?"

Her gaze drops, and she hesitates for a moment then shakes her head. "I can't think of anything. Like you said, you already know what there is to know about me. At least, all the things I have tried to hide."

I give her a tight-lipped smile. "Let's get this show on the road then. The sooner we start, the sooner this all ends."

Reverend Terry looks at us, an expression of concern on his face. But I grip Talia's arm and smile at him, waiting him to proceed.

"All right." He pulls a piece of paper from his pocket, unfolding it. "Do you, Talia Chance take Dare Morgan to be your lawfully wedded husband?"

Talia swallows and nods, managing a small yes. She doesn't look at me; her eyes are fixed on some point in the distance. But I am not asking her to act right now. As long as I get her consent, I'm perfectly happy with it.

The Reverend clears his throat. "Okay. And do you..."

I cut him off. "Yes, I do."

As he looks between us, his brow furrows and descends. But like everybody else in my life, he has been paid for his discretion and willingness to perform the ceremony.

He sucks in a breath, looking at both of us. "By the power granted to me by the Lord above and the state of Vermont, I hereby marry you. You may kiss the bride."

I lean in close to Talia, briefly pressing my lips against hers. When I pull back, she grabs at my lapel and tries to prolong the kiss. But I pull back giving her a sharp look.

"Can we sign the marriage certificate now?" I direct my attention to the Reverend.

Talia flushes. The Reverend looks at both of us, gives his

head the tiniest shake, and then produces a copy. Then he hands me the original and bows his head. "There you go. Congratulations on your nuptials."

I arch a brow. "Thank you. Now if you don't mind, you can see yourself out."

His cheeks puff out and he gives me an annoyed look, flapping both sides of his blazer as he buttons them. Soon enough though, he goes down the stairs, the door swinging closed with a slam.

I turn to Talia, a smile playing on my lips. "Well? How does it feel to be Mrs. Morgan?"

Her cheeks flush and her eyes glitter a vibrant blue. She tosses her long red hair and gives me an impatient look as she crosses her arms.

"It feels exactly like it did three hours ago. You couldn't have rushed Reverend Terry anymore if you had tried."

"What, like our fake marriage is suddenly so important to you?" I make a dismissive sound and fan my fingers. "Don't pretend that it is more than it is."

Her tongue darts out to lick her canine tooth. "You are really something. Is there nothing that is sacred to you? Do you not think that you ought to take anything seriously?"

I snort. "Not really. I take my business seriously. There are times when I am sailing on my yacht and I lose my sense of humor because the stakes are life or death if you don't pay attention on the sea. But other than that, no. This wedding stuff is faker than a two-dollar bill, and I know that better than anyone. You should too."

She cocks her hip and shakes her head at me. "There is no winning with you. I should just get used to that."

"You took the words right out of my mouth," I say with a sly grin.

Her lips thin and she tosses her hair, turning toward the back of the loft and starting off in that direction.

"Where are you going?" I ask. But she doesn't answer. She just flounces off, disappearing from my sight.

Pushing my cheek out with my tongue, I follow her. I am dissatisfied that she decided not to keep arguing with me. For some reason, I've begun to enjoy our verbal sparring matches.

I catch up with her as she is entering our bedroom. As soon as she walks through the door, she pauses and takes off her high heels. There's something very intimate about the way that she picks up her heels and pads over to the closet with them. I stand in the doorway, crossing my arms as I watch her for a moment. She reaches back to her neck and unzips her dress, peeling back the fabric to expose her bare upper back. She wriggles halfway out of the dress, pulling the front of the dress down so that she is bare from the waist up except for a tiny black push-up bra.

My cock stirs to life. I must have made a sound because she whips her head around, her arms coming up to her chest. She glares at me, seeming violated by my intrusion.

"Do you mind? I'm trying to change."

"No, I don't mind." I step into the room, closing the door behind me.

She flushes and scowls as she pulls her dress back up to cover her front. "Dare, get out. I mean it."

I shake my head slowly, walking towards her with slow steps. I give her a rueful smile, drinking in the sight of her.

God, she is beautiful. I didn't think that she was anything to look at when I first laid eyes on her. But I can admit when I am wrong.

And damn, I was so wrong. She is gorgeous.

From where I stand, I can only see the miles of exposed

skin on her toned legs, her creamy thighs, and her lovely arms. I can't see her cleavage right now because she clutches her dress against it, but I know that her breasts are perfect and small, each one a mere handful for me. I know that her waist is impossibly small, flaring out to her hips, and that the crown jewel that is between her thighs is her glorious pink pussy.

"Get on the bed," I order her. "Now, before I decide not to ask nicely."

She gulps and looks like she has just swallowed a live frog. I start toward her and she scurries toward the bed, climbing on top of it and turning to look at me with wide, frightened eyes.

I smirk as I walk toward her.

Chapter Thirty

DARE

The sight of Talia perched completely naked on my bed, her beautiful tits rising and falling as she sucks in breaths, sends blood straight to my already-hardening cock.

Not every woman has this effect on me.

No, that's not true.

No woman has this effect on me. No woman but Talia.

She looks up at me with unsure eyes, her ruby lips swollen and tempting. Now that I've gotten a taste of Talia, I want all of her. No, fuck that. I need her. And I won't stop until I've had my fill, either.

I'm hoping like hell she won't scream bloody murder to stop me now, because I'm not sure letting her out of this room without sinking my hard cock into her hot pussy is something I'm truly capable of.

Stripping off my shirt and slacks, I jerk my head to the floor. "Clothes off, now. Don't fucking argue with me. I don't want to hear anything except the sound of your panties hitting the floor."

Talia's eyes widen. For a moment, I think she's going to protest. But I rip my shirt off and arch a brow at her.

"Do it, wife. It's time that we consummated the marriage. Fuck, I think I have wanted to be inside you since the moment I laid eyes on you."

She tosses her hair and looks at me quizzically. "You weren't saying that when you were forcing me to get a makeover at the beach house."

I snort. "Don't act like you don't want my cock inside you so badly that you don't even know what to do with yourself. Now strip."

To my surprise, she looks indecisive for only a few second before she tugs up the hem of her dress and flings it onto the floor. She's still wearing the black push up bra and matching thong and looking at her makes my cock throb with need.

"Fuck, darling girl. Take those panties and bra off before I rip them to shreds."

Talia hesitates again. I cross the floor in a few steps, a determined look on my face. She fumbles to rip her bra off and skim her panties down her legs just before I grab her ankles, pulling her legs towards me and positioning her exactly where I want her.

Her pussy shines in front of me like a promise.

My eyes rake up her body, drinking in the curves of her hips, the dip in her waist, the swell of those breasts that I can hardly keep my mouth off of, full and soft and perfectly round...

"You look like a fucking goddess, Talia," I say, as my eyes crash into hers, obliterating any doubts I may have had about sinking into her again when I see the look in her eyes.

She's soft.

Warm.

Open and welcoming.

As fucking hungry for this as I am, obviously.

And as she squirms beneath me, as I finally sink every single inch of my hard cock into her velvety pussy, she looks so fucking sexy I think I might lose it right then and there.

"Fuck, Talia!" I shout at her, almost angry at how fucking attracted to her I am. She's fucking irresistible and with a body that feels this good, that looks this good, I know I can easily become addicted to the way she feels wrapped around my cock.

For now, though, I just hold on for the ride.

My hands grip her hips tightly, pulling her pussy further down on my cock, needing to feel the depths of her as she spasms around me.

"Dare, your cock feels so good," she moans, her hands clawing at my shoulders as I slam into her with all my strength. Slowly, I pull out of her, tearing my eyes from her gaze and watching as her pussy grips my cock as I slide in and out of her.

Mesmerized, I push myself in, watching carefully, going as slowly as I can as I sink into her again and again. She envelops me in her heat, slick and writhing beneath me as if she can't get enough.

"Say it again," I demand, looking up at her again, her words turning me on just as much as the sight of her pussy wrapped around me.

She meets my gaze, lifting her chin once more and jutting her tits out towards me.

"I love the way your cock fills me up," she moans, the words barely scraping across her lips as I slam into her before she can get them all out. I throb hotly inside of her, relishing the slide in and out of her, slowing down as much as I can, but thrusting inside of her hard and fast. She spreads her thighs wider, wrapping them around my hips and pulling me deeper inside as I slam into her over and over, her tits swaying beneath me, her face flushing with pleasure.

I swell with pride knowing I put that there. When she groans in my ear, sultry and seductive and sexy, I know I'll never forget the way she's looking at me. The sounds she makes. The way she feels, wrapped around my body. It only makes me want to fuck her harder, longer, faster.

I grip her thighs and do just that, my hips flying through the air, my cock rocking into her with a steady rhythm the leaves her screaming my name.

"Dare, Dare, Dare, yessss!!!" She shouts, her cries echoing up through the room.

I know she's close to coming, and so am I, the pressure building up inside of me like a volcano waiting to explode all over her.

But it's way too soon for that...too easy, too predictable...

I pull out of her and the whimper that escapes from her lips is almost cute. She looks up at me, her eyes half-questioning, half-disappointment, but I ignore her completely. I'll wipe it all away soon enough.

"Get up," I demand. She looks up at me, hesitating, not moving. I grab her hips with a twinge of impatience, turning her over so that her ass is up in the air, leaving her open and vulnerable to me in the most delicious way. My hand lands on her ass, slowly admiring the soft flesh.

"You've got a great ass, Talia. I've always liked it," I whisper. The darkness of my bedroom, coupled with the unexpected intimacy and the vulnerability she's showing me with her ass up in the air like this turns me on like crazy.

Seeing Talia, my now wife, in this light, open and available and oh-so-fucking-willing to do as I command makes me high.

Reaching down, I grab a handful of her hair and sink my cock back into her again, then loudly smack her ass with my open palm.

"Oh!" She cries out, quickly looking over her shoulder at me. She squirms, her tits swinging below her. I hit her ass again and she grunts at the unannounced assault, but the way she pushes her ass back onto me so eagerly tells me she wants more of my cock, just as much as she wants my hand on her ass.

I smack her again and again as I continue fucking her, her stinging flesh turning the most beautiful bright pink. She's so wet, her pussy contracting violently as I sink into her over and over and over, effortlessly and smoothly, our bodies fitting together with surprising ease.

I lean down, my lips finding her neck as I pull her hair back, my cock deep inside of her as I gently bite down. She cries out, leaning back into me.

"You like that? You like my cock?" I whisper into her ear, pressing into her as deeply as I can.

"God, fuck yes! More, give me more," she says, arching her back and pushing her ass into me.

"You little slut. You can't get enough, can you?"

She looks over her shoulder at me, her eyes glistening with pure lust.

"Don't stop fucking me, Dare," she hisses. "Give it to me."

I shake my head at her wonton display, so uninhibited and unexpected...and so fucking welcome. She's the perfect little plaything and I am thoroughly enjoying her.

"Touch yourself again," I demand. "Play with your clit."

Without hesitation, she props herself up on one arm and reaches down, obeying me like the perfect little slut she is.

"That's it," I murmur, picking up the pace of my hips, my cock slamming into her over and over again. Her pussy clenches and grips my cock in waves of spasms that make my balls twitch, my cock ready to explode into her.

I slow down to keep from doing just that, enjoying myself way too much for it to be over.

The slower pace seems to suit her just fine, as she begins slowly rolling her hips in circles on my cock, her fingers still working her clit steadily. She's lost in her own pleasure, sliding up and down my cock like I'm not really attached to it at all at the moment.

I smirk, watching her slide up and down on me with abandon, igniting the extreme primal lust that I kept buried just below the surface. Talia's unlocking a part of me that I rarely access and for a few moments, I allow it.

"Talia goddammit," I roar, gripping her hips again and unable to take it slow any longer, I plow into her with as much strength as I can muster, my hips flying into her, harder and faster and deeper, my cock throbbing with hungry heat.

"Dare, fuck, my god!" She whimpers below me, holding onto the bed to brace herself as I search for the release I so desperately need now. Her pussy has a grip on me, it has taken hold of not just my cock, but my brain and I know in that moment that I'll never get enough of her.

She's so tight.

So fucking wet.

So fucking perfect.

And she's my fucking wife.

"Come here," I growl, rolling her over again until she's on her back, looking up at me with those big eyes, her thighs falling open and waiting for me to dive right back inside of her.

As soon as my cock slides back in, she wraps herself around me completely — her thighs around my hips, her arms around my chest, pulling me in as close as she can while I fuck into her. Her lips brush against my ear as her moans echo into my brain, the sensation of having her entire body completely wrapped around me just entirely too much to bear.

"Fuck me, Dare, fuck me. *Please*. Please don't stop," she begs, the words spilling from her throat. She's lost all inhibitions and it's the sexiest she's ever looked. "You feel so fucking good. Your cock is so hard inside me. I fucking love the way you are making me feel!"

Her words take me right to the edge. My lips crash into hers again, possessing her, the feeling of her submitting below me sending a surge of adrenaline rocketing through my veins, my heart racing with the darkest desire to consume her completely and make her mine.

In that moment, nothing matters outside of this room.

Talia's pussy belongs to me.

Talia's entire body belongs to me.

Talia, whether she knows it now or not, is mine. That engagement ring on her fucking finger has become her wedding ring, tying us both together for life.

My tongue tangles with hers, her body soft below me, taking every inch of me with ease, as if she'd been made to take everything my body has to give to her.

I tear my mouth from hers, slam my cock inside of her once more and glare down at her.

"You're fucking mine now, Talia, do you fucking understand that?"

She nods, her eyes wide.

"Fucking say it! Say it now!" I demand, a wildfire of desire consuming me completely.

"I'm yours, Dare. Fuck me like I'm yours. All yours."

Her words send me spiraling.

The thought of Talia, of her exquisite body, being all mine sends me crashing over the edge at last, the thought too much to contain within my flesh.

We shudder together with desire, with need, with savage and brutal lust, my cock exploding inside of her as wave after wave of my primal, intense, white hot heat pours into her, sending her into her own dance of lust, her fingernails tearing at the flesh on my back, my name dripping from her lips like a curse.

"Damn you, Dare! Damn you!"

Her head falls back on the bed, her eyes close as I capture her lips in mine again, my cock slowly sliding out of her soaked pussy. I smile down at her, drinking in her weakened state, immensely proud that I was the one to put her in that condition.

She's never looked more beautiful.

Breathing hard, I lie on my back and stare up at the ceiling. Talia rests next to me, eventually shifting her weight so that she rolls on her side and throws her leg across my thigh. I'm surprised she doesn't say anything or make herself vulnerable any other way. She curls on her side, almost just touching me but not quite.

Due to the difference in our heights, I can put my arms over my head and not intrude on her space more than she wants.

I feel Talia looking at me so I arch a brow. "What?"

"Nothing. Just... You know. That was the first time that we ever actually had sex. It's kind of like we were saving ourselves for marriage or something."

I rumble out a laugh. "Speak for yourself. I didn't save fuck all for marriage. I've tried everything."

She puts her elbow up underneath her head and gives me an inquisitive look. "Yeah? Everything?"

"Well. Not everything. But everything I want to try."

She nods slowly, taking a moment to absorb that tidbit. "Got it. So basically, that was nothing new for you."

She starts to roll away but I snake a hand out, fast as lightning and grip her upper arm. "Just wait a second. You don't have to do any of that."

"Any what?"

"All this huffing and puffing and pretense that girls always do. You don't have to pretend with me. Just like I don't have to pretend with you. That's what makes our fake relationship work. Mutual dishonesty."

She rolls her eyes but I draw my hand down her arm, grabbing her by the wrist and settling her hand onto my chest.

She's still a little huffy but I just ignore that. It's natural that her ego tells her to act that way, but I understand exactly what our relationship is. I give her money; she gives me a wife and a child. Transactional would be a fair way to describe it.

"We don't need the artifice. There is no reason for putting on a show here."

She arches a brow. "That sounds an awful lot like you're promising to be honest with me. Are you saying that?"

I shrug, clearing my throat. "Sure. As long as you are honest with me in exchange."

"About everything? Even money? Even if it doesn't flatter your ego?"

I laugh. "The truth rarely does. But yeah, I'm pretty much saying that."

She looks at me and then yawns. Her head drops down

onto my chest and she settles in like she has been doing it just like that for all of eternity.

I'm a little befuddled as to how to proceed, but I drape my arm around her loosely and stare up at the ceiling, contemplating my next move tomorrow. She falls asleep on my chest and soon the rhythmic sound of her deep breathing pulls me under.

Chapter Thirty-One

I n the passenger seat of the Porsche, I run a hand over my carefully curled mane of red hair. I glance at my husband.

My heart thuds. *My husband.*

God, he really is my husband now.

Dare holds the door open for me and takes my arm, giving me a little smirk as we walk up the few feet to the Morgan estate. I am just as nervous as I was the first time I saw the mansion with its time worn façade.

But I have been coached this time. I know better than to let my nervousness show.

Instead, I paste a smile on my lips and pull Dare an inch closer, cozying up to him as we approach the enormous front door of the Morgan estate. We are dressed to kill, Dare in his usual suit, me in a clingy white dress that is strapless and ends just below my knee. I think the flowers that decorate the low neckline are meant to suggests that one might get married in a dress just like this. However, I couldn't envision wearing such a dress on my wedding day. The clingy nylon fabric is almost see through.

It might be okay for some people's weddings, but it is a far cry from the fairy tale wedding I have somewhere deep down in my heart. I know that my marriage ceremony to Dare Morgan will not be nearly so casual as my dress implies.

I can't even sit down in this dress; then again, I don't imagine that I will be able to in the beautiful princess gown that Rob will put me in when I publicly vow to be part of the Morgan family.

As we walk through the doorway, my senses are on high alert. I'm surprised to find quite a few people at the Morgan estate when I step through the threshold. I lean close to Dare, whispering my observation.

"There are a lot of people here, all dressed in their Sunday best. It's funny, I don't think I recognize anyone, but I've lived and worked in Harwicke all my life. Where do you imagine these people hide out when they aren't at your family's mansion?"

His brow furrows and he puts his lips close to my ear.

"I think that Burn and Daisy have called all their family and friends to announce their wedding. I wasn't briefed before we came, but that seems like the obvious occasion."

I nod. "Makes sense."

"All right," Dare whispers. "Get ready to put on a show. My brother is heading this way."

Suddenly, I find that my mouth is dry as a bone. I scan the room, looking up all the lovely party guests in their finest cocktail attire. Out of the corner of my eye I see a waiter making the rounds with a stack of short glasses of amber liquid. Making eye contact with him, I raise my hand, summoning him with two fingers. He makes a beeline for me, and I take a glass off the tray before he even manages to tell us that it is whiskey.

I take a huge gulp just as Dare pulls on my hand, taking away the glass. "What the fuck are you doing?"

I look up at him and then realize that I am not supposed to be drinking. Beckoning for the glass, I spit the contents out. Dare frowns and shakes his head then puts the glass back on the tray. "Sorry. She is on antibiotics."

The waiter looks confused but Dare just leans forward, accepting a new glass and waving the waiter away again. Once the waiter moves on, I look at Dare. He gives me a cool smile.

"Take it easy. You look like a rabbit caught in a snare."

I glance around, whipping my hand at the people around me. "It's not an unfamiliar feeling. I'm trapped in a place where I don't know anyone. The rabbit and I are not in totally dissimilar circumstances."

Dare puts his arm around my waist and pulls me close. "I'm the only hunter you have to worry about right now, darling girl. I'll protect you from everyone else."

I part my lips to respond to him but I don't get the chance to say anything else.

Burn and Daisy strut over to us, looking pleased with themselves.

Burn's smile could not be more smarmy if he tried. "It's good of you to come to our little engagement party."

Dare gives him a smile that cuts like a knife. "It's the first time hearing of a gathering, actually. But that's all right, Burn."

"Dare, dear," Daisy says. Her voice is bright, but I can see that there is an edge to her words. "You haven't introduced us to your date yet."

Dare starts to open his mouth but I cut in first. "Actually, we have met. The last time I was here, you introduced yourselves."

Daisy cocks her head, her eyes narrowing on my face. "Are you sure?"

"I definitely remember you, Daisy. Dare has told me so much about you." I notice her flush, and I give her my big fake smile. "You know, if you want, my uncle is a neurologist. You should probably get yourself checked out if you are having trouble with your memory. It's only been two weeks, for god's sake!" I look to Dare. "Hasn't it, darling?"

Dare is looking at me like I have grown a new head. He blinks and then gives himself a tiny shake.

"She is right, Daisy. By the way, this is Talia. But I don't expect that you remember other people."

Burn laughs. "You make us sound like monsters. I assure you, Talia, we are not anything of the sort."

Just act like you belong, I tell myself. Smoothing a hand on my dress, I move closer to Dare. "Well, you will have to get used to me. Won't they, Dare?"

Dare's eyebrows go up and then he looks over at my ring finger. "Oh no! I forgot to give you your ring back. I had it resized."

Dare reaches into his pocket and produces the same black velvet ring box that I saw yesterday. I assume that he hasn't had the time to get it adjusted but he opens the box and plucks the ring out of the setting, sliding it onto my finger. To my surprise, it fits with ease.

I smile at him, leaning in for a kiss. He lays it on thick, smooching me several times and pulling my waist against his body. I pull back and give him a longing glance.

When I look at Burn and Daisy again, the sheer fury and envy in their eyes steals my breath away. I smooth my hand over my ribs, glancing nervously at Dare. Dare puts his arm around my shoulders and kisses my head as if he has done it a million times before. A shiver runs down my back but I just compress my lips into a thin line.

"Actually, we thought that we could add our note of celebration to today's festivities," Dare suggests.

"Don't you dare," Burn says, his voice low and threatening. "This is our engagement party."

Dare protests that, seeming to weigh the pros and cons, then shrugs. "I mean, we did get married yesterday. But hey, if you want us to keep it hush-hush for tonight, we will be glad to. Remy will still be here tomorrow."

Burn's eyes narrow on Dare's face. "I think that would be best. By the way, when I find out what cheap madam you bought her off, there will be hell to pay."

I look at Burn and Daisy, a note of puzzlement on my face. "A madam? I think you have me confused with someone else. Dare and I met at a party here. Outside, just a few weeks ago. I don't want to be too lovey-dovey, but I knew that I felt something for Dare the first time I laid eyes on him. Isn't that right, darling?"

Dare stares at me, murmuring, *you are perfectly right.*

The tender, loving way that he stares down at me makes me blush bright pink. But I swallow and raise my head, asking for a kiss. He knows just what I want, and he gives it to me in spades. His lips are hot, his tongue sinuous, the whole kiss is enough to set me on fire.

"This is our night," Daisy snaps. "You better respect that."

We pull apart and I kiss Dare's knuckles.

"No problem," Dare says. He doesn't look away from my face though.

Burn grabs Daisy by the hand and hauls her off, the two of them whispering like a couple of angry hens.

"Bravo," says a voice. I turn around and see a man that

looks familiar and one that I've never seen before. The one I've seen is Uncle Felix, I think. The one I haven't seen wears a three-piece suit and has sandy blonde hair. He is good looking. That is, if you aren't a such a sucker for the dark, tortured type as I am.

I find myself comparing him to Dare and finding the stranger lacking.

Dare jumps then, with a grin lighting up his face. "You came! Guys, this is Talia. Talia, this is Tristen and my Uncle Felix."

I fold my hands against my waist and nod at them, strangely unwilling to shake their hands. Tristen just smiles. Felix, the familiar looking one, is the same as Dare, only thirty years older and fifty pounds lighter. He has dark features and he is graying at the temples. Not graying, almost salt-and-pepper, except for a stripe down the back.

Felix doesn't say a word, just looks at me with an assessing gaze that chills my blood. Tristen is quick to greet me, though.

"So, you are Talia. I've heard a lot about you, but I wasn't entirely sure that you were real." He grins. "It's good to know that Dare hasn't completely lost his mind yet."

Dare gives him a sly grin. "Tristen and I went to high school and college together. We definitely got into our share of trouble."

Tristen gives me a conspiratorial wink. "Don't tell anybody. I prefer to leave them guessing."

"Felix, how are things?" Dare asks.

The older man looks at Dare, raising an eyebrow. "Things are fine. If you have time today, I would like to steal a few minutes to talk about the site where we are supposed to start the drilling."

Dare's brows furrow. "That's important. But I think

tonight is going to be more about personal intrigue, sadly. Talia and I just got married yesterday and I need to rub it in my brother's face. I already told him and Daisy and to say they were surprised is a delightful understatement."

Felix purses his lips. "I need two minutes. Just step over here and let me fill you in quickly."

Dare looks at me then shrugs. "We'll be right here. I'll be able to see you. Plus, Tristen can keep watch of you. He does a hell of a job washing my money so I am confident that he can guard you for two seconds and keep the jerks at bay."

I squint at him but don't say anything. Mostly, what comes to mind is that the biggest shark in the room seems to be his Uncle Felix. The guy gives me the worst feeling. But I nod and smile. The two men walk away, huddling and sharing secrets.

I give Tristen my brave smile and he rolls his eyes. "Men, am I right? Let me see the ring that Dare chose."

I hold out my hand to him and he steps closer to me, taking my hand and admiring the huge emerald on my finger. "It's nice. Actually, it's gorgeous."

"Dare didn't pick this out though, I think." His gaze flits up to me and he releases my hands. "Am I right?"

There is a sour taste in my mouth as I nod. "You are right. He didn't pick it out."

"Yeah, he has a habit of relying on his assistant to have good taste. Luckily, his assistant picks excellent furniture and clothing. Jewelry, too, by the looks of it."

My face burns but I nod. I have no idea who this person is or how much he might know about my life, so I am very careful with my next words.

"So, you've known Dare for a long time?"

Tristen glances at me, his gaze weighing his answer.

"You don't really want to know about that."

"But I do!" I protest.

Tristen steps closer, moving close to my ear. "I know how you two met. I know the whole story. You don't have to pretend with me."

Surprised, I step back. "I'm not sure what you mean."

He exhales a laugh. "I know the whole fake marriage gambit. And I also know that you're..." he mouths the word *pregnant* to me.

My cheeks stain with blood. I haven't met this guy and I don't know him from Adam but apparently, he knows all of my biggest secrets. When Dare and I leave this party, he's going to get an earful from me. Why would he not have mentioned Tristen before?

"I didn't know that Dare was so indiscreet," I finally manage.

"Oh, I didn't really mean it to come out like that. Dare is usually a black box. You tell him a secret and he never tells another living soul about it. But I just so happened to be around when the whole thing started up."

I cross my arms, trying not to let my agitation show. "That's nice," I say. "It's good that Dare has a friend, I mean."

Tristen looks at me, his expression growing tense. But before he can say anything, someone clinks a knife against a wine glass at the far end of the room. I turn away from Tristen, glad that I have an excuse to pay attention to anything else.

Dare takes my hand, squeezing it as he looks toward the other end of the room as it clears around Remy Morgan and the butler, who stands with a wine glass and a piece of cutlery.

Remy is wearing an off-putting light green cardigan over a white Oxford and rumpled khakis. He leans on his cane and when he gets the attention he called for, he waves Clive away.

"Hello," Remy grates out. "I'm so glad you could all be here tonight. My grandson Burn and his fiancée Daisy have set a date for their wedding. I never thought it would happen, honestly. But you know." He pauses and everyone laughs a little uncomfortably. He raises his hand and beckons to the back of the room. "Burn, Daisy, why don't you come up here?"

Burn and Daisy aren't the only ones moving. Dare clenches my hand and practically drags me to the front of the audience, elbowing his way past everyone else. Remy glances over at Dare and I, his brow knitting. But in the next second, Burn and Daisy step out into the circle that has been cleared to a room full of applause.

"There they are now," Remy says pointing at Burn and Daisy. "My grandson. The spitting image of my father, I always said."

Burn has the audacity to bow and wave to everyone, a smirk on his face.

Dare, raising his hand. "Actually, Remy... We have an announcement to make as well."

Burn and Daisy immediately turn their glares on us. If looks could kill, we would be pillars of ash by now.

Remy, pulling at his ear. "What's that, Dare?"

Dare starts moving forward, causing me to stumble. But he doesn't even seem to notice me at all. His gaze is fixed on Remy as he moves to the front of the room, trying to displayme to everyone present.

"Remy, I would like you to meet my wife,Talia. Darling, this is my beloved grandfather, Remy Morgan."

Remy's face could not be more surprised. He hobbles forward, leaning on his cane and extends his hand to me. I take it and he grips my forearm. I glance down at his fingers against the flesh of my arm. It looks like five stubby, spotty, bumpy red slugs are now trying to work their way under my skin.

I open my mouth thinking of all the things I could say to Remy. How he's a bastard. How his money and power have corrupted this town. How he has screwed my family over again and again.

Dare must have a sixth sense about this because he puts his hands on my waist and squeezes. I stand upright and look Remy in the eyes.

"Hello, Mr. Morgan," I say softly.

Remy looks me in the eyes and then releases my arm, stepping closer and cupping my cheek. "I see you married my grandson. I hope you're fertile."

My mouth drops open, but Remy turns away, hobbling on his cane once more.

"Everyone go back to the party," Remy shouts. The Morgans begin to talk amongst themselves.

He claps Dare on the shoulder.

"Good job," he growls. "Now get her pregnant."

He hobbles off toward Burn, who is still staring at me like he could strike me down at any moment.

Dare eases his grip, putting his hand around my waist and exhaling a huge breath. But before he can truly relax, a red-faced man wearing a rumpled suit and nasty expression steps in front of us.

Dare sighs deeply, his possessive grip on me growing even more tense.

Dare a throws up his hand, stopping the man before he can even say a word. "Look, Dad. Not tonight. Okay? Surely there is a bar somewhere that you should be plundering."

Dare's dad leers at me, wiping his mouth. His words

come out slurred and loud, the exact way you could only assume that he spoke. "I am Tripp, Dare's dad. I know that Remy acts like he's Dare's father, but I am. And I am here to tell you that it is not too late. You can still get an annulment. Because if I am sure of one thing, it's that this one... He's awful."

His breath is bad and I take a half step back to avoid him spitting on me as he talks.

"I know who you are," I tell Tripp, wrinkling my nose.

"Dad, stop. You're embarrassing yourself," Dare says.

He pushes me behind him, holding out a hand to ward Tripp off. But Tripp doesn't even seem to notice Dare. His eyes are locked on me.

"He'll let you down. He's never been anything but a disappointment. If his mother were here, God rest her soul, she would tell you the same."

Tripp's drunk words make me madder than I can ever remember being. I don't know that much about Dare's family, but I have seen his dad twice and both times he was drunk. Gives me a pretty good idea of just why Remy was the stand in father for Tripp's kids.

"Dad, fuck off. Don't talk to her. She doesn't want to be involved in our little family squabbles."

Tripp lashes out, whipping his hand at Dare. Then he tries to grab me. I catch a glimpse of pure malevolence on Dare's face.

"I'll fucking kill you if you try to touch her, Dad. I'm as serious as a grave."

Tripp lunges toward me again and manages to catch my dress where it flares out at the waist. He grabs a fistful of the dress and rips it, snarling.

Dare grabs his father and wrenches him back, raising his

fist. "I'll end you," he manages, his voice laden with threats. "You will fucking die, old man."

"Stop it!" My voice leaves me in a shriek. I clutch at Dare, stopping him from hitting his father. I turn to Tripp, my face growing red. "Stop it right now. Leave Dare alone, you big bully. Go bother someone else."

Tripp and Dare both turn and look at me.

I realize that my words were loud enough to draw the attention of the surrounding people. My face goes an even deeper shade of red, but I lift my head, giving Tripp a haughty stare. He sneers at me and then clambers to his feet, lurching off toward the other side of the room.

"Fucking tyrant," Dare spits, his eyes still fixed on his father's retreating figure. "If he ever lays a finger on you, I'll kill him. Hell, I'll kill anybody who touches you. And I'll do it *gleefully.*"

I put my hands on my hips, my lips twisting. "I have to say, Dare. I don't much care for your father. I hope that you don't take offense to me talking to him like that."

Dare whips his head around, his eyes fastening on me. To my surprise, he grabs me by the waist and hauls me close, his lips descending until they reach mine. He kisses me hard, his lips demanding, his breath coming out of his nose in a snort. It's like kissing a dragon, or so I imagine.

I give myself over to Dare, pressing my mouth against his lips. He kisses me back, his hands digging into my waist, and I feel my pulse speed up. But then he slowly ends the kiss.

"I take that as an agreement that I should always talk to your dad like he's a menace?"

Dare smooths back my hair, tucking a strand behind my ear. His gaze is direct and intense. "I'm going to reward you later, darling girl. Just remember that."

We circulate for a little while longer, making sure that we

are never far apart. I make sure to pretend to enjoy Dare's possessive hold on me.

Well, maybe I don't have to pretend *that* hard.

Dare, for his part, makes sure that he kisses me every few minutes. All in all, quite a spectacle for anyone that hasn't met me yet.

And the best part is that I think it's working. If I have to be honest about it, I don't even hate his kisses as much as I could. There is a low tickle at the center of my stomach, thinking about what Dare promises me.

What will he reward me with in bed, I wonder? The question makes me shiver.

At one point, Dare steps away but keeps me in his eye line. I meet a lot of Dare's female cousins and eventually I grow tired of my plastered-on smile and the continual shaking hands.

I excuse myself to go to the restroom and slip out the first exterior door that I see, which happens to lead to the gardens. Releasing a sigh, I lean against the outside of the mansion and look at the hedge maze.

It brings a smile to my lips before I remember that my marriage, such as it is, remains a hoax.

My phone buzzes in my purse. I blink and fish it out.

I haven't heard it go off in days. At first, I think that maybe it's just Olivia checking up on me. But instead of seeing texts from her, there are a series of texts, all from a number I don't recognize.

Gulping, I shiver against the cold night air and read the text messages.

Dare is a liar.

He is not to be trusted.

Want proof?

There is a picture of Dare and Tristen from the side, their heads bowed as Tristen whispers something and Dare smiles wickedly back at him.

You didn't just agree to marry him out of the blue... you were pushed. Dare had people damage your aunt's store and leave threats. He also had people come into the restaurant you worked at and pretend to be impossible to please customers.

A video appears on my screen.

There is a short clip, shot in the dark. A squat balding man in tears rubs his hands over his eyes and looks directly at the camera with a pleading expression. "I'm sorry. I was paid to break some windows at some broad's bookstore. I broke the front window and went inside to mess some stuff up and then left the message that I was told to leave. I really didn't mean..."

The video cuts off abruptly but I am completely shocked. I lean over, trying to catch my breath.

This man is clearly talking about Aunt Minnie's bookstore. My fingers shake as I play the clip again, trying to gain any additional clues. But the video is too brief for that, and I am ready to close my phone when a final text comes through.

Get out while you still can.

I blink rapidly, unable to process what I have just read. Could this be true? Could Dare have really paid someone to intimidate me into thinking that circumstances were more dire than they really were? Would Dare do something like that?

The answer comes to me without even having to really think about it. Yes, of course he would. Dare is the first person to say that he is a cutthroat businessman first and only out for himself.

No muss, no fuss, no romance.

Acid fills the pit of my stomach and I close my eyes, tears leaking free and running down my face.

What have I done? Here I was, trotting around this party, performing like a trained pony for Dare. And he fucking let me. I can't even blame him, because that is the nature of the devil.

The devil is silver tongued, incredibly sexually attractive, and will steal the breath right out of your lungs.

God, I feel so stupid. Dare is the fucking devil. I should have known from the second I laid eyes on him, but I let him woo me with money and the lure of a fairytale life for my unborn child.

I don't know who would have sent the evidence to me, but I do know that if I don't leave now, I might never get away from Dare Morgan completely.

Shoving my phone into my purse, I turn toward the front of the mansion and begin to run.

About Vivian Wood

Vivian likes to write about troubled, deeply flawed alpha males and the fiery, kick-ass women who bring them to their knees.

Vivian's lasting motto in romance is a quote from a favorite song: "Soulmates never die."

Be sure to join her email list to keep up with all the awesome giveaways, author videos, ARC opportunities, and more!

VIVIAN'S WORKS

MARRIED AT MIDNIGHT SERIES
FORBIDDEN BILLIONAIRE ROMANCE
DEAL WITH THE DEVIL
WED TO THE DEVIL
VOW TO THE HE DEVIL

Ruined Castle Series
Forbidden Billionaire Romance
The Scottish Billionaire
The Beast
The Nanny
The Caress

Broken Slipper Series
Forbidden Billionaire Romance
The Patron
The Dancer
The Embrace
Possessive

Ravaged Dream Series – Coming 2023
Forbidden Billionaire Romance
Grumpy Billionaire Boss
Sweetly Forbidden Intern
Dirty Workplace Secret

Dirty Royals
Forbidden Royal Romance
The Royal Rebel
The Wicked Prince
His Forbidden Princess
Royal Fake Fiancé

Lyon Dynasty World
Dark Billionaire Romance
King's Capture
Queen's Sacrifice

Sinfully Rich Series

Steamy Billionaire Romance
SINFUL FLING
SINFUL ENEMY
SINFUL BOSS
SINFUL CHANCE
SINFULLY RICH

HIS AND HERS SERIES
HIS BEST FRIEND'S LITTLE SISTER
CLAIMING HER INNOCENCE
HIS TO KEEP
HIS VIRGIN

THE ADDICTION DUET
ADDICTION
OBSESSION

OTHER BOOKS
WILD HEARTS

For more information....
vivian-wood.com
info@vivian-wood.com

Made in the USA
Monee, IL
28 February 2023

28530754R00213